cauldron

cauldron

jack mcDevitt

ace books, new york

THE BERKLEY PUBLISHING GROUP
Published by the Penguin Group
Penguin Group (USA) Inc.
375 Hudson Street, New York, New York 10014, USA
Penguin Group (Canada), 90 Eglinton Avenue East, Suite 700, Toronto, Ontario M4P 2Y3, Canada
(a division of Pearson Penguin Canada Inc.)
Penguin Books Ltd., 80 Strand, London WC2R 0RL, England
Penguin Group Ireland, 25 St. Stephen's Green, Dublin 2, Ireland (a division of Penguin Books Ltd.)
Penguin Group (Australia), 250 Camberwell Road, Camberwell, Victoria 3124, Australia
(a division of Pearson Australia Group Pty. Ltd.)
Penguin Books India Pvt. Ltd., 11 Community Centre, Panchsheel Park, New Delhi—110 017, India
Penguin Group (NZ), 67 Apollo Drive, Rosedale, North Shore 0632, New Zealand
(a division of Pearson New Zealand Ltd.)
Penguin Books (South Africa) (Pty.) Ltd., 24 Sturdee Avenue, Rosebank, Johannesburg 2196,
South Africa

Penguin Books Ltd., Registered Offices: 80 Strand, London WC2R 0RL, England

This is an original publication of The Berkley Publishing Group.

First edition: November 2007

Library of Congress Cataloging-in-Publication Data

McDevitt, Jack.
 Cauldron / Jack McDevitt.—1st ed.
  p. cm.
 ISBN 978-0-441-01525-2
 I. Title.

 PS3563.C3556C38   2007
 813'.54—dc22

                          2007024279

PRINTED IN THE UNITED STATES OF AMERICA

10 9 8 7 6 5 4 3 2 1

Acknowledgments

I'm indebted for advice and technical assistance to David DeGraff of Alfred University; Michael Shara of the American Museum of Natural History; and Michael Fossel, author of *Cells, Aging, and Human Disease*. Walter Cuirle and Travis Taylor helped out at the galactic core. Thanks also to Ralph Vicinanza, for his continuing support. To Maureen McDevitt, for her comments on an early version of the manuscript. And to my editor, Ginjer Buchanan. Star chart by Curtis Square-Briggs.

Dedication

For Jamie Bishop

Out of the night they come,
Raining fire and rock,
Raking the cities of man*,
Living storms,
Shaped in the Devil's Cauldron.

—<u>Sigma Hotel Book</u>
(Translated by Phyl)

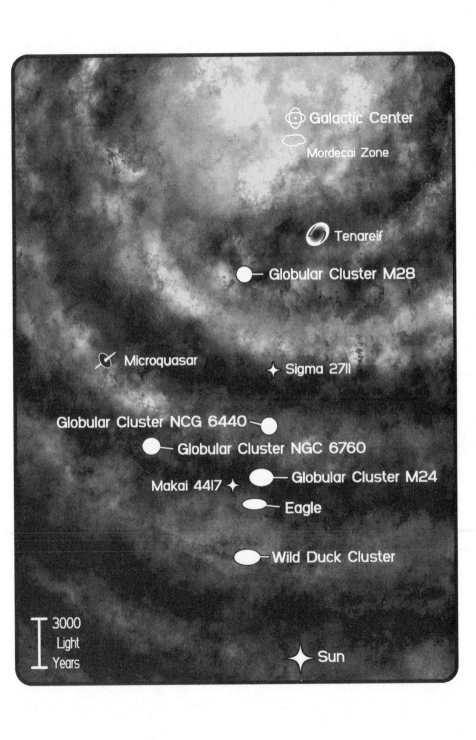

prologue

Cherry Hill, New Jersey.
December 16, 2185.

THE CALL CAME, as such things always seemed to, in the middle of the night. *"Jason?"* Lucy's voice on the other end. Tense. Excited. But she was trying to sound professional. Unemotional.

Jason Hutchins's first thought was that Lucy's mother had suffered another breakdown. The woman was apparently given to nervous collapses, and the family always called Lucy. Teresa, also awakened by the call, raised an arm in protest, then pulled a pillow over her head. "Yes, Lucy? What's the problem?"

"We have a hit!"

That brought him fully alert.

It had happened before. Periodically they got a signal that had set off alarms. Usually it vanished within minutes and was never heard again. Occasionally, it was a human transmission bouncing around. Never during the two and a half centuries of the search had they gotten a legitimate strike. A demonstrably artificial transmission that could be confirmed. Not once. And he knew as he rolled out of bed, as he grumbled to Teresa that no there wasn't a problem, that he'd be back in an hour or so, he knew that this would be no different.

It was at times like this, when he conceded that SETI was essentially a religious exercise, that it took a leap of faith to sit down each day in front of the screens and pretend something might actually happen, that he wondered why he hadn't looked for a career that would provide at least the opportunity for an occasional breakthrough. Whole generations of true believers had manned the radio telescopes, some in orbit, some on the back side of the moon, a few on mountaintops, waiting for the transmission that never came. They joked about it. Waiting for Godot. I know when it happens, I'll be at lunch.

"I do it for the money," he told people when they asked.

A LOT HAD changed since the early days of the project. The technology, of course, had improved exponentially. There were starships now. It was possible to go out and actually *look* at the worlds orbiting Alpha Centauri and 36 Ophiuchi and other reasonably nearby stars. We knew now that life existed elsewhere, even that intelligent life had flourished in a few places. But only one extant technological world was known, and that was a savage place, its nation-states constantly at war, too busy exhausting their natural resources and killing on a massive scale to advance beyond an early-twentieth-century level.

So yes, there *were* other places. Or at least there *was* one other place. And we knew there had been others. But they were in ruins, lost in time, and the evidence suggested that once you entered an industrial phase, you began a countdown and survived only a few more centuries.

But maybe not. Maybe somewhere out there, there was the kind of place you read about in novels. A place that had stabilized its environment, that had conquered its own worst instincts, and gone on to create a true civilization.

He wore a resigned smile as he left the house. It was a clear, moonless night. The skies were brighter, less polluted, than they had been when he was young. They were beginning to win that battle, at least. And, if there were still occasional armed arguments between local warlords, they'd gotten through the era of big wars and rampant terrorism.

With starflight, the future looked promising. He wondered what his daughter, Prissy, who'd still be young at the dawn of the new century, would live to see. Maybe one day she'd shake the mandible of a genuine alien. Or visit a black hole. At the moment, anything seemed possible.

He climbed into the flyer. *"Where to, Jason?"* it asked.

LUCY WAS SO excited when he walked in she could barely contain herself. "It's still coming, Jason," she said.

"What are we listening to tonight?" He'd been gone several days, at a conference, and had lost track of the schedule.

"Sigma 2711," she said. It was an old class-G located out beyond NCG6440, roughly halfway to the galactic core. Fourteen thousand light-years. If it turned out to be legitimate, it wasn't going to be somebody with whom they could hold a conversation.

Lucy was a postdoc, from Princeton. She was energetic, driven, maybe a little too enthusiastic. Marcel Cormley, her mentor, didn't approve of her assignment to the Drake Center. She was too talented to waste her time on what he perceived as a crank operation. He hadn't said that to Hutchins's face, of course, but he'd made no secret to his colleagues about his feelings. Hutchins wasn't entirely sure he was wrong. Moreover, he suspected Lucy had come to the Center primarily because Cormley had opposed it. However that might be, she had thrown herself into the work, and he could ask no more than that. In fact, enthusiasm was probably a drawback in a field that, generation after generation, showed no results. Still, she was getting experience in astronomical fundamentals.

"Does it still look good, Tommy?" he asked the AI.

Tommy, who was named for Thomas Petrocelli, the designer of the first officially designated AI, took a moment to consider. *"This one might be a genuine hit,"* he said.

"Let me see it." Jason sat down in front of a monitor.

"It repeats every seventeen minutes and eleven seconds," said Lucy. Light bars flickered across the screen. "The sequence is simple." Four. Then two clusters of four. Then four clusters. Then four clusters of eight. And eight of eight.

"It keeps doubling," he said.

"Up to 256. Then it runs backward."

"Okay. What else is there?"

"You get about two minutes of the pattern. Then it goes away, and we get this." A long, apparently arbitrary, sequence began. He watched it for several minutes before turning aside. "Tommy," he said, "are we making any progress?"

"It has markers. But ask me later."

Lucy stood off to one side, her gaze tracking between him and the AI's speaker. She looked as if she were praying. Yes, Lord, let it be so. She was blond, a bit on the heavy side, although she never seemed to lack for boyfriends. They were always picking her up and dropping her off.

Jason pushed back in his chair. He wasn't going to allow himself to believe it was actually happening. Not after all this time. It couldn't just drop in his lap like this. It had to be a system bug. Or a hoax.

Lucy, apparently finished with her entreaties to the spiritual world, returned to her chair, pressed her hands together, and stared at the screen. "I wonder what they're saying."

Jason looked around for coffee. Lucy used only soft drinks, so there was none available.

She read his mind, had the grace to look guilty, but said nothing. Had the evening been quiet, she'd have offered to make it.

He sat down in front of one of the displays and brought up Sigma 2711. It was seven billion years old, give or take a few hundred million. Maybe a quarter more massive than the sun. At fourteen thousand light-years, it was far beyond the range of the superluminals. But there was evidence of a planetary system, though nothing had been sighted directly.

If the transmission got a confirmation, he could probably arrange to have the Van Entel take a look. The giant telescope would have no problem picking up planets at Sigma, if they existed.

"What do you think, Jason?" she asked.

The first streaks of gray were appearing in the east. "It's possible," he said. "Tommy, get me somebody at Kitt Peak."

Lucy broke into a huge smile, the kind that says Do with me as you will, my life is complete. "And they told me," she said, "nothing ever happens over here."

"Kitt Peak," said a woman's voice. She seemed oddly cheerful, considering the hour.

"This is Jason Hutchins," he said. "At Drake. We need confirmation on a signal."

"You got a hot one, Jason?" He recognized Ginny Madison on the other end. They'd been together at Moonbase once, long ago.

"Hi, Ginny. Yes. We have a possible. I'd be grateful if you'd check it for us."

"Give me the numbers."

"I HAVE A *partial translation,"* said Tommy.

"On-screen."

"Much of the text is an instructional segment, providing clues how to penetrate the message."

"Okay."

"Here are the opening lines."

GREETINGS TO OUR (unknown) ACROSS THE (unknown). THE INHABITANTS OF SIGMA 2711 SEND THIS TRANSMISSION IN THE HOPE THAT COMMUNION(?) WITH ANOTHER (unknown) WILL OCCUR. KNOW THAT WE WISH YOU (unknown). THIS IS OUR FIRST ATTEMPT TO COMMUNICATE BEYOND OUR REALM. WE WILL LISTEN ON THIS FREQUENCY. RESPOND IF YOU ARE ABLE. OR BLINK YOUR LIGHTS(?).

"I took the liberty of substituting the name of their star. And, of course, I did some interpolation."

"Thank you, Tommy."

"Considering their desire to strike up a conversation, it's unlikely they expected their message to be received so far away. This was probably aimed at a nearby system."

"Yeah. I expect so."

"Jason," said Lucy, "what do you make of the last line?"

" 'Blink your lights'?"

"Yes."

"Metaphorical. If you can't answer, wave." He stared at the screen. "The frequency: I assume it's 1662."

"On the button." The first hydroxyl line. It was where they'd always expected it would happen. The ideal frequency.

GINNY WAS BACK within the hour. *"Looks legitimate,"* she said. *"As far as we can tell. We've got confirmations through Lowell and Packer. We also ran it through ComData. They say it's not ours, and we can't find a bounce."* Another broad smile. *"I think you've got one, Jason. Congratulations."*

WORD GOT AROUND quickly. People began calling minutes after Ginny had confirmed. Has it really happened? Congratulations. What have you got? We hear you've been able to read some of it? These were the same people who'd passed him politely in the astronomical corridors, tolerating him, the guy whose imagination had run past his common sense, who'd wasted what might have been a promising career hunting for the LGMs that even the starships couldn't find.

But he was well beyond starship country now.

Within a few hours Tommy had more of the text. It included a physical description of the senders. They had four limbs and stood upright, but they were leaner than humans. Their heads were insectile, with large oval eyes. Bat ears rose off the skull, and they had antennas. No sign of an olfactory system. No indication of an expression, or even if the face was capable of one. "Are the features flexible?" he asked Tommy. It was an odd question, but he couldn't resist.

"Information not provided, Jason."

"How big are they?"

"No way to know. We share no measurement system."

That brought Lucy into the conversation. "You're saying they could be an inch tall?"

"It's possible."

Jason propped his head on his hands and stared at the image. "Judging from the relative size of the eyes, it looks as if they live in a darker environment than we do."

"Not necessarily," said Tommy. *"The smaller a creature is, the larger its eyes should be relative to body size. They have to be big enough to gather a minimum amount of light."*

There was more. Details of the home world: broad seas, vast vegetative entanglements, which eventually got translated as *jungles*.

And shining cities. They seemed to be either along coastlines or bordering rivers.

"*There are large sections of the transmission I still cannot read,*" said Tommy. "*Some aspects of the arrangement suggest they may be sound patterns. Speeches, perhaps.*"

"Or music," said Lucy.

"*It is possible.*"

"Translate *that*," she continued, "and you could have a hell of a concert."

Descriptions of architecture. Jason got the impression the aliens were big on architecture.

Accounts of cropped fields, purpose unknown, possibly intended as vegetative art.

"They're poetic," said Lucy.

"You think? Simply because they like to design buildings and grow flowers?"

"That, too."

"What else?"

"Mostly, that they're putting a bottle out into the dark."

JASON CALLED HOME to tell Teresa the news. She congratulated him and carried on about what a wonderful night it was, but the enthusiasm had a false note. She didn't really grasp the significance of the event. She was happy because *he* was happy. Well, it was okay. He hadn't married her for her brains. She was a charmer, and she tried to be a good wife, so he really couldn't ask more than that.

Just before dawn, the transmission stopped. It was over.

By then all sorts of people had begun showing up. His own staff of off-duty watchstanders. The people who had for years not noticed that the Drake Center even existed: Barkley and Lansing from Yale, Evans from Holloway, Peterson and Chokai from Lowell, DiPietro from LaSalle. By midmorning the press had arrived, followed by a gaggle of politicians. Everybody became part of the celebration.

Jason broke out the champagne that had, metaphorically, been on ice for two and a half centuries and ordered more sent over from the Quality Liquor Store in the Plaza Mall. He held an impromptu press conference. One of the media types pinned the name Sigmas on the creatures, and that became their official designation.

After she'd gotten Prissy off to school, Teresa showed up, too, along with her cousin Alice. She was clearly delighted by the attention her husband was getting, and she sat for hours enjoying the warm glow of reflected celebrity. It was, in many ways, the happiest moment of his life.

YEARS LATER, WHEN he looked back on that day, after the Sigmas had faded into history, it wasn't the call in the night that stood out in his memory, nor Tommy's comment, *"This one might be a genuine hit,"* nor even the message itself: *"Greetings to our (unknown) across the (unknown)."* It wasn't even Ginny's confirmation. *"We can't find a bounce."* It was Prissy, when she got home from school, where she'd already heard the news. It was odd: Nine years old, and she understood what her mother had missed.

"Daddy, are you going to send a message back?" she'd asked. He was home by then, exhausted, but planning to change clothes and re-turn to the Center.

"No," he said. "They're too far away, love."

"Even to just talk to them? They sent *us* a message. Why can't we send one back?"

"Do you know about the pharaohs?" he asked.

"In Egypt?" Her dark eyes clouded with puzzlement. What did pharaohs have to do with anything? She was a beautiful child. Armed with her mother's looks. But she had *his* brain. She'd be a heart-breaker one day.

"Yes. Do you know how long ago that was? King Tut and all that?"

She thought about it. "A long time," she said.

"Thousands of years."

"Yes. Why can't we talk to the Sigmas?"

"Because they're not there anymore," he said. "They're dead a long time ago. They were dead long before there were pharaohs."

She looked baffled. "The people who sent the message died before there were pharaohs?"

"Yes. I don't think there's much question about that. But they weren't really people."

"I don't understand. If they died that long ago, how could they send us a message?"

"It took a long time for the message to get here."

Her dark eyes got very round. "I think it's sad that we can't say hello back to them."

"I do, too, sweetheart," he said. He looked at her and thought how she had touched ultimate truth. "They're starting to build very fast ships. Maybe one day you'll be able to go look."

PART ONE

prometheus

chapter 1

Thursday, January 11, 2255.

FRANÇOIS ST. JOHN did not like the omega. It lay beneath him, dark and misty and gray. And ominous, like an approaching thunderstorm in summer. It was a vast cloudscape, illuminated by internal lightning. It seemed to go on forever.

They'd measured it, estimated its mass, taken its temperature, gleaned samples from deeper inside than anyone had been able to penetrate before, and they were ready to start for home.

The omega, despite appearances, was by no means adrift. It was racing through the night at a velocity far exceeding anything possible for an ordinary dust cloud, running behind the hedgehog, its trigger, closing on it at a rate of about thirteen kilometers per day. In approximately three thousand years it would overtake the object and hit it with a lightning strike. When it did, the trigger would explode, igniting the cloud, and the cloud would erupt in an enormous fireball.

The omegas were the great enigma of the age. Purpose unknown. Once thought to be natural objects, but no more. Not since the discovery of the hedgehogs twenty years earlier. Nobody knew what they were or why they existed. There wasn't even a decent theory, so far as François was aware. The lightning was drawn by the right angles incorporated into the design of the hedgehogs. The problem was that anything with a right angle, if it got in the path of the cloud, had better look out.

He was surprised by the voice behind him. "Almost done, François. Another hour or so, and we can be on our way."

It was Benjamin Langston. The team leader. He was more than a hundred years old, but he still played tennis on weekends. There had been a time when people at that age routinely contemplated retirement. "You got anything new, Ben?"

Ben ducked his head to get through the hatch onto the bridge. It was an exaggerated gesture, designed to show off. He enjoyed being the tallest guy on the ship. Or the most put-upon. Or the guy whose equipment was least reliable. Whenever anyone had a story about women, or alcohol, or close calls, Ben always went one better. But he knew how to speak plain English, which set him apart from most of the physicists François had been hauling around these last few years.

"Not really," he said. "We'll know more when we get home. When we can do some analysis." He had red hair and a crooked smile. He'd probably injured his jaw at some point.

"I have to admit, Ben," François said, "that I'll be happy to be away from the thing. I don't like going anywhere near it." The *Jenkins* was supposed to be safe for working around an omega. The Prometheus Foundation, its owner, had rebuilt her several years ago, taking away the outer shell and replacing it with a rounded hull. No right angles anywhere. Nothing to stir the monster. But he'd seen the holos, had watched the massive lightning bolts reach out and strike target objects left in its path. The thing *was* scary.

He looked down at the cloudscape. It *felt* as if there were something solid immediately beneath the gray mist, as if they were gliding over a planetary surface. But people who'd done work around omegas said that was always the impression. One of the uncanny features of the omega was its ability to hang together. You would have expected it to dissipate, to blur at the edges. But the clouds weren't like that. Ben had commented that they had nearly the cohesion of a solid object.

In fact, Ben admired the damned things. "It's beautiful, isn't it?" he said. He sounded awed.

That wasn't the way François would have described it. But he pretended to agree. "Yes," he said. "Beautiful." Dead ahead, and deep within the cloud, a red glow appeared, expanded, brightened, and finally faded. It lasted only a few moments, then it was gone, and they saw nothing except their own navigation lights, captured and blurred in the mist.

It happened all the time, silent flowerings of ruby light.

They talked about incidentals, about the long ride home, which would take approximately three weeks, and how good it would be to get out of their cramped quarters. Ben admitted that he missed his classes. He was one of those very occasional academic types who seemed to enjoy the give-and-take of a seminar. His colleagues usually talked about it as if it were a menial task imposed by an unthinking university interested only in making money.

"*François.*" The AI's voice.

"Yes, Bill, what have you got?"

"*Cloud's changing course.*"

"What?" That wasn't possible.

"*I've been watching it for several minutes. There's no question. It's moving to port, and below the plane.*"

It couldn't happen. The clouds stayed relentlessly in pursuit of their triggers unless they were distracted by something else. The lines of a city, perhaps. But there were certainly no cities anywhere nearby. And no gravity fields to distract it.

"It's picked up a geometric pattern here somewhere," said Ben. He peered at the images on the monitors. "Has to be." But there was nothing in any direction save empty space. For light-years. "François, ask Bill to do a sweep of the area."

François nodded. "Bill?"

"*We need to get out in front of it.*"

Ben made a face. "We'll lose contact with the probe if we do that."

François wasn't sure what kind of data the probe was collecting. The only thing that had mattered to him was that it was the last one. He looked at Ben. "What do you want to do?"

"Are we sure the cloud's really changing course?"

"*Yes.*"

"Then let's find out why."

"Okay," François said. He gave instructions to the AI, and the sound of the engines began to intensify. He switched on the allcom.

"Leah, Eagle, Tolya, strap down. We're going to be executing a maneuver in a minute."

Leah was *Mrs.* Langston. Like Ben, she was a specialist in various aspects of the clouds, physical structure, nanotech systems, propulsion. The objective of the mission was to learn something about their makers, who they were, what their capabilities were, why they sent the damned things out into the Orion Arm. Into the entire galaxy for all anyone knew.

Eagle's real name was Jack Hopewell. He was a Native American, the mission's astrophysicist, the department chairman at the World Sciences Institute. He claimed to be a full-blooded Cherokee, but he always smiled when he said it, as if he didn't really mean it. François thought there might be a German back there somewhere, and maybe an Irishman.

Tolya was Anatoly Vasiliev, a nanotech specialist from the University of Moscow. She was on the verge of retirement, had never seen an omega, and had pulled every string she could find to get assigned to this mission.

Leah responded with that very precise Oxford voice: *"François, what's going on?"*

He explained, while—one by one—the three indicator lamps brightened. Everybody was belted down. Ben slipped into his seat, and the harness closed around him. "All right, guys," François said, "I'll let you know when we're done. This is going to take a few minutes." He switched back to the AI. "When you're ready, Bill."

The *Jenkins* was, of course, moving in the same direction as the cloud, pacing it. François extracted the yoke from the control panel and pushed it gently forward. The engines grew louder, and the cloudscape began to move aft. Swirls of mist accelerated, swept beneath the glow of the ship's lights, and blurred. Bill announced he'd lost contact with the probe.

It took a while, but eventually the horizon approached.

"The omega is still turning," said Bill.

More electricity flashed through the depths. To François, the cloud seemed *alive.* It was a notion that had respectability in some quarters. No one had really been able to demonstrate the validity of the proposition one way or the other. And François would readily have admitted he had no evidence to support his impression. But the thing *felt* alive. That was why he didn't entirely trust the assurances of the engineers who told him the *Jenkins*, because of its rounded edges, was safe. Who could really predict what one of these monsters might do?

They soared out past the rim, the leading edge of the cloud. "See anything yet, Bill?" he asked.

"Negative. But the turn is slowing. It's settling in on a vector." Bill adjusted course and continued to accelerate.

François looked out at the stars. There was no nearby sun. No nearby planet. Nowhere it could be going. "You figure that thing can see farther than we can, Ben?"

Ben sighed. "Don't know. We still don't know much. But it has potentially a much larger reception area than we do. So yes, it probably *can* see farther. Maybe not optically, but in some sense."

The cloud was dwindling behind them, becoming part of the night, a dark presence blocking off the stars, illuminated only by periodic lightning. It could have been a distant storm.

"Still nothing?" asked François.

"Not yet," said Bill. *"Whatever it is, it's dead ahead. The omega has begun to decelerate."*

He eased back on the yoke and opened the allcom: "Going to cruise, folks. If you need to get anything done, this would be a good time, but don't go too far from your couch."

Minutes later Leah's head pushed through the hatch. "Nothing yet?"

"Not a thing," said Ben.

Leah was in her nineties. She was tall and graceful, with dark brown hair and matching eyes. A good partner for Ben, given to trading quips with him, and easily, as far as François could see, his intellectual equal. "Okay," she said, starting back. "Let us know if you see something."

François had known Leah for thirty years, had hauled her to various destinations during his Academy days, before she'd married Ben. Before she'd *known* him, as a matter of fact. He'd made a play for her once, in those halcyon times, shortly after his first marriage had gone south. But she hadn't been interested. He suspected she'd thought she wouldn't be able to hold on to him.

A half hour slipped past while Bill sought the reason for the omega's course change. François began to wonder if the AI had misread the omega. Ben had fallen silent, was going over some notes, and François was sitting with his head thrown back, half-asleep, when Bill stirred. You could tell Bill was about to deliver an announcement of some significance, because it was inevitably preceded by an electronic warble, the AI's equivalent of clearing his throat. *"François, object ahead. Range 3.4 million kilometers."*

Ben immediately looked up. Studied the display. "What is it?" he asked.

"It appears to be a ship."

"A ship?"

"Yes. An artificial construct of some kind. It is not under power."

Ben turned to look out the viewport. "François, who else is out here?"

"Nobody. Not supposed to be anybody."

What the hell? "Bill, what kind of ship?"

"I don't know. We're too far away."

IT LOOKED LIKE a collection of cubes, or boxes, of varying sizes connected by tubes. Some of the tubes ran straight from one box to another, others angled off in various directions. None curved. It was all right angles, a target made for an omega.

The thing resembled a child's toy, a puzzle to be manipulated until all the cubes lined up one way or another. Despite Bill's assessment, it was most definitely *not* a ship. *"I was in error,"* said Bill. *"I see no visible means of propulsion. Furthermore, if there were a method not apparent to us, I doubt the thing would hold together under acceleration."*

"A space station of some kind?" asked Ben.

"Possibly a habitat," said François. "I really don't know what to make of it."

"What's it doing out here?"

François gave them a ride. With the cloud coming up in the rear, he wanted to get to the object as quickly as he could. So he accelerated, then threw on the brakes. He burned fuel heedlessly. Ben grinned down at him. "That's good, François. You're learning."

"Bill," he said, "how much time do we have?"

"The omega is still decelerating. If it continues to slow at its present rate, after we arrive, we will have approximately twenty-three minutes before the cloud comes within strike distance."

Ben stared at the object and looked pained. "François, it's *alien.*"

"I know."

"It's priceless."

"I know that, too, Ben."

"Can we save it? Push it aside?"

"How big is it, Bill?"

"I am not able to estimate its mass. But the largest of the segments is eleven times the diameter of the ship. It dwarfs us."

"Couldn't we accelerate it?" said Ben. "It's big, I know, but it's adrift."

François counted nine boxes. "It wouldn't matter. We have no way to control its flight. The thing would just roll off to the side when we started pushing. All that would happen is that the goddam omega would adjust course."

Eagle and Tolya had crowded into the hatchway. Leah was behind them. "We have to do something," Tolya said. "We can't just let this happen."

"Damn right," said Eagle.

François raised his hands. "We don't have much choice. For what it's worth, we're recording everything."

"That's not worth *much,*" Leah said.

"There's nothing else we *can* do." He pulled at one ear. "Bill."

"Yes, François."

"Is the thing hollow?"

"It appears to be."

Leah broke in. "When we get there, we'll have a few minutes. We need to find a way in."

François squeezed his eyes shut. "No," he said. "Absolutely not. That's the last thing we want to do."

"Look, François." She was trying to sound reasonable. "We can probably find a hatch or port or something. We can get in, take a quick look around, and clear out." She was already opening the storage locker and grabbing for air tanks and an e-suit.

"No," said Ben. "Absolutely not."

Tolya looked frantic. "I'll go, too." All the women on the flight were deranged. "What do you want to do," she demanded, "just give up?"

François wanted to remind her she was only a student. Not here to give directions to anybody. But Ben took care of it with an icy look. "Forget it," he said. "Nobody's going anywhere. Twenty minutes won't be enough time."

"He's right," said François.

Ben was a bit too daunting for her, so Tolya turned on François. "What the hell do *you* know about it? What are we going to do? Just stand by and watch the idiot cloud blow that thing up? Spend the rest of our lives wondering what it might have been?"

IT WAS TUMBLING. Slowly.

"*I wonder how old it is?*" Leah checked Ben's air tanks. "*You're all set.*"

They were in the airlock, carrying lasers and tool belts, ready to go. Eagle and Tolya had wanted to go along, too, but fortunately there were only three e-suits on board, and nobody got to use the captain's. It was a violation of regulations.

"You guys go over," said François, "cut your way in, take a quick look, and get back here."

"*Don't worry,*" said Ben.

"Look, Ben, so you know: There really isn't time to do this, and I'm not going to put the ship at risk. When it gets close, I'm clearing out. Whether you two are back or not."

"*Understood,*" said Ben.

"*Goddam it.*" Leah shook her head. "*You worry too much, François.*"

He saw no advantage to the design of the object. The cubes seemed to be connected in a totally random fashion. *Purely aesthetic,* he thought. *Somebody's idea of art.*

He looked at the rear view. The black patch was growing, systematically blocking out stars.

"*Hatch locations,*" said Bill, marking four sites on the display. François picked one that allowed easy access from the *Jenkins* and maneuvered alongside. It was located on one of the smaller cubes, on the outer rim of the cluster. It was less than average size, but it was larger than the *Jenkins*. He eased in as closely as he could, lined up the hatch with the ship's air lock, and instructed Bill to hold the position. "Okay," he told Ben.

His navigation lights played off the surface of the object. It was battered. Corroded. It had been there a long time.

Ben opened the outer hatch. *"It's pretty worn,"* he said.

"You've got seventeen minutes to be back here," François said. "Okay? Seventeen minutes and we take off. Whether you're on board or not."

"Don't worry," said Leah. *"Just keep the door open."*

Right.

An imager picked them up as they left the ship. Followed them across the few meters of open space to the hatch. Whoever'd used it had been about the same size as humans. Which meant Ben would have a hard time squeezing through.

"Incredible," said Leah. She was examining the hull, which was pocked and scored. *"Cosmic rays. It is* ancient."

"How old do you think?" asked Ben.

Bill sighed. *"Use the scanner, Ben. Get me the hull's composition, and I might be able to give you an answer."*

Ben wasn't sure which of the devices he carried with him was the scanner. He hadn't used one before, but Leah knew. She activated hers and ran it across the damage.

"Good," said Bill. *"Give me a minute."*

Ben made an effort to open the hatch. There was a press panel, but it didn't react. Leah put her scanner back in her belt and produced a laser. She activated it and started cutting. *"This is a disaster,"* she said. *"What were the odds of finding something like this? And then to have it sitting right in front of that goddam avalanche back there?"*

Ben drew his own laser out of his harness, but François cautioned him not to use it. Two relatively inexperienced people cutting away was a sure formula for disaster. So he stayed back. Leah needed only minutes to cut through. She pushed a wedge of metal into space, put the instrument away, and stepped inside the ship.

"Turn on the recorder," François told her.

Each wore an imager on the right breast pocket. The auxiliary monitor came to life, and François was looking down a dark corridor, illuminated by their headlamps. Shadows everywhere. The bulkhead looked rough and washed-out. Whatever materials had originally lined it had disintegrated. The overhead was so low that even Leah couldn't stand up straight.

Something was moving slowly down the bulkhead. Ben saw it, and the picture jumped.

"What is it?" asked François.

Dust. A hand, Leah's, scooped some of it up, held the light against it.

"*Scan it,*" said Bill. Leah complied. The AI's electronics murmured softly. "*Organics,*" he said.

"*You're saying this was one of the crew?*"

"Probably," said François. "Or maybe they kept plants on board."

"*I wonder what happened here?*" said Ben.

After a long silence, Bill said, "*I've got the results on the cosmic ray damage. It's hard to believe, but I've double-checked the numbers. The object appears to be 1.2 billion years old.*"

Ben made a noise as if he were in pain. "*That can't be right,*" he said.

"*I've made no error.*"

"*Son of a bitch. François, we've got to save this thing.*"

"If you can think of a way, I'll be happy to make it happen."

Leah broke in: "*There's something on the wall here. Engraving of some kind. Feel this, Ben.*"

He put his fingertips against the bulkhead. Then he produced a knife and scraped away some dust.

"*Careful,*" she said.

François couldn't make out anything.

"*There* is *something here. It's filled in.*"

Leah moved to her right. "*More here.*" She ran her fingers down the bulkhead, top to bottom. "*Not symbols,*" she said. "*More like a curving line.*"

"Nine minutes," said François.

"*For God's sake, François. Give us a break.*"

"What do you want me to do, Ben?" He was having trouble keeping the anger out of his voice. Did they think he wouldn't have saved the thing if he could? Did they think he didn't care?

He listened while they tried to get a better look at the bulkhead.

The object was tumbling slowly as it moved, and the dust had been crawling around inside it all this time. It would have long since wedded itself to any apertures, openings, lines, anything on the bulkheads. "It's hopeless," François said.

It wasn't going well. He heard mostly invective, aimed at the dust, occasionally at the omega. "*Can't be sure of anything,*" Leah said. She looked around. A few pieces of metal were bolted into the connecting bulkhead.

"*Might have been cabinets,*" said Ben, "*or shelves, or an instrument panel of some sort.*"

"Better start back," said François.

"*We can't just give up.*" Ben sounded desperate. He literally stabbed the bulkhead. "*We may never find anything again as old as this is.*"

"Before the dinosaurs," said François.

Leah was breathing hard. "*Before multicellular life.*" The comment was punctuated by gasps. "*Think about that for a minute. Before the first plant appeared on Earth, something was sitting here, in this room. We can't just leave it.*"

François was getting a creepy feeling. The black patch behind the *Jenkins* kept growing.

THEY GAVE UP. Ben had found a plate fixed to the bulkhead. He'd been trying to break it loose and he finally took a swipe at it with a wrench. It broke away and disappeared into the darkness. "*Maybe the name of the place they came from,*" he said.

Leah touched the spot where the plate had been. "*Or maybe the Men's Room.*"

They went through an opening into a connecting tube. Toward a cube several times the size of the one they were leaving. "No," said François. "Your time's up. Come back."

"*It'll just take a minute, François,*" said Leah. "*We're just going to take a quick look. Then we'll come right back.*"

He wondered whether the tubes had originally been transparent. They looked different from the interior, a different shade of gray, and were smeared rather than flaking.

He took a deep breath. "Bill, I don't much like the way this is going.
"Nor do I, François."

He counted off another minute. "Ben," he said, finally, "that's
enough. Come back."

"We're on our way." They'd entered the new cube, which consisted
of another chamber and several doorways.

He wondered if, in some oddball way, they felt secure inside the
object. Maybe if they were on the bridge, where they could see the
omega closing in, they'd hustle a bit more. Behind him, Eagle and
Tolya stood watching, saying nothing, hanging on to each other.
François couldn't resist: "Doesn't look like such a hot idea now, guys,
does it?"

"Nyet," said Tolya.

He turned back to the AI: "Bill, put everything we have into a
package and transmit to Union. Everything on the cloud, and on *this*
damned thing. Whatever it is."

"It will take a minute or two."

"All right. Just do it."

The omega brightened. A series of lightning bolts.

"Nothing here," said Ben. He swept his light around the interior.
Some objects were anchored to the deck. It was impossible to determine what they had been. Chairs, maybe. Or consoles. Or, for all they
knew, altars. And boxes on either side of an exit. Cabinets, maybe.
Leah cut one open, flashed her light inside. *"Ben,"* she said, *"look at this."*

She struggled to remove something. *"Maybe a gauge of some sort?"*
She brushed it carefully, and held it up for inspection. François saw
corroded metal. And symbols. And maybe a place that had supported
wiring.

"François," said the AI, *"the cloud is close. Our departure is becoming
problematic."*

"That's it, guys. Time's up. Come on. Let's go."

"There's something over here," said Leah.

François never found out what it was. Lightning flared behind
him.

Ben got the message. *"On our way,"* he said. They started to move.
Finally. But Ben tripped over something, and bounced along the passageway. *"Son of a bitch."*

Bill responded with an electrical display, the sort of thing he did to show disapproval.

"You okay?" said Leah.

"Yeah." He pushed her away. *"Keep going."* And he was up and running, pushing her before him.

It's hard to run in grip shoes and zero gravity. Especially when you're not used to either. They hurried back down the connecting tube. François urged them on. Maybe it was his voice, maybe it was inevitable, but, whatever the cause, Ben and Leah had become suddenly fearful. Panicky.

"The data package has been dispatched, François."

"Good," he said. "Bill, be ready to go as soon as they're on board."

"We can proceed on your direction."

"Ben, when you guys get into the lock, shut the outer hatch and grab hold of something. We're not going to wait around."

"Okay, François. It'll only be a minute."

Bill rattled his electronics again. He was not happy. *"Electrical activity in the cloud is increasing. It might be prudent to leave now."*

François considered it. The idiots had put him and the ship in danger.

Moments later they left the object and clambered into the air lock.

"Go, Bill," he said. "Get us the hell out of here."

ARCHIVE

A team of astronomers announced today that the omegas appear to have originated in the Mordecai Zone, a series of dust clouds approximately 280 billion kilometers long, located near the galactic core. They are unable to explain how the process works, or why it should be happening. "In all probability, we will not know until we can send a mission to investigate," Edward Harper, a spokesman for the team, said during a press conference. When asked when that might be, he admitted he had no idea, that it is well beyond the capabilities of present technology, and may remain so for a long time.

—*Science Journal*, March, 2229

LIBRARY ENTRY

1115 hours, GMT. *Jenkins* reports loss of main engines. Damage apparently incurred during hurried acceleration. Details not clear at this time. Rescue mission scheduled to leave tomorrow morning.

—Union Operations log entry, Saturday, February 3

chapter 2

MATT DARWIN FILED the last of the documents, accepted the congratulations of his senior partner, Emma Stern, sat back in his chair, and considered how good he was. A natural talent for moving real estate. Who would have thought? That morning, he'd completed the sale of the Hofstatter property, a professional office building in Alexandria. Its owners had come to him after months of trying to move the place, and he'd done it in a week, even gotten two prospective buyers bidding against each other.

His commission, on that single sale, almost matched his annual take-home pay back in his Academy days. "Must make you wonder why you didn't get started earlier," Emma said.

She was tall and graceful, with two personalities, cordial, funny, and lighthearted for the customers, skeptical and strictly business for her employees. She could be vindictive, but she approved of Matt, recognized his talent, and was somewhat taken by his charm. He'd told her once she'd have made a good Academy pilot, had meant it, and had won her heart forever.

"How about we close down early and celebrate?" he said. "Dinner's on me."

She wasn't young, but she could still light up the place. "Love to,

Matt. But we have tickets for *Born Again* tonight." She let him see she regretted declining the invitation. "How about we do it tomorrow, okay? And *I'll* buy."

Kirby, the AI, announced that Prendergast had arrived for his appointment with her. They were trying to decide on a place to locate his pharmaceutical distribution operation. He was being forced to relocate because of rising waters. Can't go on building dikes forever, he'd been saying. Find me a new place. Preferably on top of a hill.

So she turned a radiant isn't-life-grand smile on him and left. Matt had nothing pressing and decided he'd take the rest of the day off.

Stern & Hopkins Realty Company (Hopkins had moved on before Matt joined the firm) was located on the third floor of the Estevan Building, across the park from the Potomac Senior Center. A few years ago, he'd received an award over there for shepherding a damaged ship and its passengers back home. It had been the Academy of Science and Technology then.

He watched as the front door of the old administration building opened. That was where they'd given him his big night, called him onstage in the auditorium, and presented him with the plaque that now hung in his den at home. An attendant came out onto the walkway, pushing someone in a wheelchair. Despite all the medical advances, the vastly increased longevity, the general good health of the population, knees still eventually gave way. And bodies still went through the long process of breaking down.

He got his jacket out of the closet and pulled it around his shoulders. "Kirby?"

"*Yes, Matt?*" The AI spoke with a Southern accent. Emma was from South Carolina.

"I'm going to head out for the day."

"*I'll tell her.*"

When he got home, he'd call Reyna. Maybe *she'd* like to do dinner this evening.

THERE HAD BEEN a time when the land now bordering the Potomac Senior Center was a golf course. The golf course was long gone, converted into a park, but the area was still called the Fairway. Matt lived in a modest duplex on the edge of the Fairway. It was about a mile and a half from the office, a pleasant stroll on a nice day. He passed young mothers with their toddlers and infants, older people spread out among the benches, a couple of five-year-olds trying to get a kite into the air. Sailboats drifted down the Potomac, and a steady stream of traffic passed overhead.

A sudden gust lifted a woman's hat and sent it flying. The woman hesitated between pursuit and a child. Matt would have given chase, but the wind was taking it toward the horizon, and within seconds the hat had vanished into a cluster of trees fifty yards away.

He passed a chess game between two elderly men. *That's how I'm going to end up,* he thought, *splayed across a bench looking for ways to spend my time. Thinking how I'd never made my life count for anything.*

In Emma's presence, he always pretended he couldn't be more satisfied with his job. He was, she said with mock significance, one of the great salesmen of their time. She meant it, more or less, but it wasn't exactly the kind of life he'd envisioned. She'd been concerned about his background when he'd first shown up at Stern & Hopkins. Isn't this going to seem dull after piloting starships? You really going to be satisfied hanging around here when you might have been spending your time at Alva Koratti? (She always made up the name of a star, and pretended she couldn't quite get it right. So she had him cruising through Alpha Carlassa, and Beta Chesko, and Far Nineveh.) We don't want to take you, Matt, she'd said, then lose you and have to train someone else.

He'd assured her he was there to stay. He pretended he loved representing people who were buying and selling real estate. He made jokes about how much better the money was (that, at least, was true), and how he liked working regular hours. "I must have been crazy in the old days," he'd told her. "I'd never go back."

She'd smiled at him. A skeptic's smile. Emma was no dummy, and she saw right through his routine. But she liked him enough to hire him anyhow.

He'd left his chosen profession because there was no longer a market for star pilots. The Interstellar Age was over. He'd stayed with the Academy until they shut down, then he'd gone to work for Kosmik, hauling freight and passengers to the outstations. A year later, Kosmik began cutting back, and he'd caught a job piloting tours for Orion.

When things turned dark for Orion, he was the junior guy and consequently first to go. He'd gotten a job managing a databank operation, mining, sorting, and analysis done here. He'd hated it, moved on, sold insurance, managed a desk in a medical office, even done a stint as a security guard in an entertainment mall. Eventually, he'd taken a girlfriend's advice and tried real estate.

So here he was, on a fast track to nowhere, piling up more money than he'd ever dreamed of.

The last hundred yards was uphill. His neighbor, Hobbie Cordero, was just getting home. Hobbie was a medical researcher of some sort, always going on about genetic this and splenetic that. He was passionate about what he did. Matt envied him.

They talked for a few minutes. Hobbie was short and dumpy, a guy who ate too much and never exercised and just didn't worry about it. He was involved in a project that would help fend off strokes, and he was capable of telling Matt about it while wolfing down hot dogs.

Sometimes, the conversation with Hobbie was the highlight of his day.

So Matt drifted through the afternoons of his life, rooting for the Washington Sentinels, and getting excited about selling estates along the Potomac and villas in DC.

REYNA WAS USED to his moods. And she knew what caused them. "Quit," she advised.

They'd skipped dinner, gone for a walk along the river, and ended at Cleary's, a coffeehouse that had prospered during Academy days and was now just hanging on. "Quit and do what?" he asked.

"You'll find something."

He liked Reyna. She was tall and lean, with blue eyes and dark hair, and he loved the way she laughed. There was no real passion between them, though, and he didn't understand why. It made him wonder if he'd ever find a woman he could really relate to.

She was good company. They'd been dating on and off for a year. They'd slept together a couple of times. But he didn't push that side of the relationship because he wasn't going to offer to make things permanent. She was the woman he spent time with when no one special was available. She knew that, and he suspected she felt much the same way. "Like what?" he asked.

"How about a federal job? I understand they're looking for tour guides in DC."

"That would be exciting."

She smiled at him. *Everything's going to be all right. You're putting too much pressure on yourself.* "Have you thought about teaching?"

"Me?"

"Sure. Why not?" She stirred her coffee, took a sip, rested her cheek on her fist. Her eyes locked on him. She was showing a little perspiration from their walk.

"What would I teach?"

"Astronomy."

"I was a history major, Reyna."

"They won't care. *Star pilot.* You've been out there. They'd love you."

The coffee *was* good. He had a Brazilian blend, sweetened with tapioca. "I don't think so. I can't imagine myself in a classroom."

"I could ask around," she said. "See what's available." She looked away, out the window at the river. "There's another possibility."

"What's that?"

"I've a friend who works in a law office in Wheaton. They're looking to hire an analyst. Apparently, you don't need a legal background. They'll teach you everything you need. They just want somebody who's reasonably smart."

He couldn't see himself working with contracts and entitlements. Of course, until these last few years, he couldn't have imagined himself spending his days in an office of any kind. Maybe what he needed in his life was a good woman. Somebody who could make him feel as if he were moving forward. Going somewhere.

Maybe two good women.

"What are you smiling at?" she asked.

HE'D JUST GOTTEN in the door at home when Basil, his AI, informed him there was a news report of interest. "*I didn't want to disturb you while you were out.*"

"What's going on?" he asked.

"François was in an accident. They're sending out a rescue mission."

"François St. John?" That seemed unlikely. François was a model of caution and good sense. *"What are they saying? Is he okay?"*

"Presumably. There are no reports of injuries. But apparently the ship is adrift."

"What happened?"

"An omega. They got in its way."

François was the guy who wouldn't quit. When everything was shutting down, he'd found a way to stay with the interstellars. Most recently he'd been working for the Prometheus Foundation. Probably for expenses and lunch money. "We have details?"

"They're running an interview with Dr. Golombeck now."

"Put it on. Let's see what happened."

Golombeck's image appeared. He was seated at a table, looking forlorn, saying something about a derelict ship. He was a thin, gray man. Gray mustache, gray clothes, gray skin. He didn't look as if he had ever been out in the sun. He was, of course, the director of the Prometheus Foundation.

François and Matt had never really been friends. They'd not seen enough of each other for that. But they'd met periodically in the Academy ops center and at the outstations. They'd had a few drinks together on occasion, including that last memorable night at Union when the Academy announced it was closing down. There had been four or five of them present when the news came. Matt had returned less than an hour earlier from a flight to Serenity. François and one of the others had been scheduled for outbound missions, which had been delayed two or three days without explanation, and finally canceled. A couple of the others had been going through refresher training.

The talk, of course, had centered on the conviction that it wasn't really happening. A shutdown had been rumored for years, but the common wisdom was that the threats were always designed to shake more funding out of Congress. There was some hope at the table that it was true this time, too.

But if not, what would they do?

They'd talked about getting piloting jobs with Kosmik and Orion and the other starflight corporations. But the field was drying up, and everybody knew it. One female pilot had talked about going home to Montana. "Maybe work on the ranch," she'd said. After all this time, he could still remember the way she'd tilted her head, the way her blond hair was cut, the pain in her eyes. Couldn't remember her name, but he remembered the pain.

Work on the ranch.

And François. He'd been solid, quiet, competent. The kind of guy you wanted playing the action hero. He was a born skeptic, thought nothing corrupted people quicker than giving them promotions. What was he going to do now? He'd shaken his head. Stay in the backcountry, he'd said. Ride the ships. Matt seemed to recall that he'd added he would never stoop to selling real estate for a living. But that was a false memory. Had to be.

"They were trying to salvage what they could out of the derelict," Golombeck was saying.

The interviewer was Cathie Coleman, of *The London Times*. She sat across the table, nodding as he spoke. Her dark skin glistened in lights that did not exist in Matt's living room. He described how the Langstons had boarded the derelict, had cut their way into it. How they had cut things a bit too close. How the derelict was by far the oldest ever discovered.

"And you say this object was a billion years old?"

"That's what they're telling us, Cathie."

"Who was flying around out there a billion years ago?"

"That's a question we might not be able to answer now."

"Were they able to salvage anything?" she asked.

"A few relics, we know that, but we don't know what specifically. Apparently almost everything was lost."

Matt halted the interview. "How far away are they?" he asked the AI.

"Two hundred sixty-four light-years."

Almost a month travel time. Well, they clearly had adequate life support, so there was really nothing to worry about. Other than losing a billion-year-old artifact. What would *that* have been worth?

"The rescue ship is leaving from here?"

"Yes, that's correct."

"*Dr. Golombeck.*" Cathie took a deep breath. Big question coming. "*Are you going to be able to salvage the* Jenkins?"

"*We don't know the extent of the damage yet. They were hit by lightning. We'll send a team of engineers out as soon as we can assess what's needed. We'll do everything we can to bring the* Jenkins *home.*"

There'd been a time, during the peak of the interstellar period, when someone would have been close by, when help would have arrived within a few days, at most. That was only twenty years ago. Hard to believe. The era was already being described as the Golden Age.

IN THE MORNING, Golombeck was back. He'd been a bit optimistic, he admitted. The Foundation would have to write the *Jenkins* off. "*Beyond repair,*" he said.

The interviewer, Wilson deChancie of Chronicle News, nodded. "*Professor,*" he said, "*there aren't many people left doing serious exploration. And Prometheus is now down to one ship.*"

"*That's correct, yes.*"

"*Will the Foundation survive?*"

"*Yes,*" he said. "*We'll survive. There's no question about that.*"

"*I'm sure our viewers will be happy to hear that.*"

"*Yes. We do not intend to give up and walk away from the table, Wilson. And by the way, I should mention we'll be conducting a fund-raiser. That'll be at the Benjamin Hotel, next Wednesday, at noon.*"

"*The proceeds to be used to buy another ship?*"

"*That's our hope, yes. The problem, of course, is that no one manufactures superluminals anymore. The few operational vehicles that remain are extremely expensive.*"

"*I'm sure they are.*"

Golombeck turned and looked directly at Matt. "*The public's invited, of course. And again, that's Wednesday, at twelve. There'll be a luncheon, and your viewers can secure reservations by calling us directly.*"

The code appeared at his knees.

DeChancie nodded solemnly. Expressed his hope that the event would be successful.

Elsewhere, experts argued that the derelict could not possibly have been a billion years old, as reported.

On another show, one guest asked the others on the panel whether anyone could name anything the Prometheus Foundation had discovered during its five-year lifetime. *"Anything anybody really cares about?"*

The panelists looked at one another and smiled.

IN THE MORNING, Matt sent Prometheus a donation. He wasn't sure what impelled him to do that. He never had before, had never even considered it. But he felt better when it was done. They responded within the hour with a recorded message, an attractive young woman standing in front of a Foundation banner, blue and white with a ringed star in the center. She thanked him for his generosity, reminded him it was deductible, and invited him to attend the Wednesday luncheon at the Benjamin Hotel in Silver Spring. The guest speaker, she said, would be Priscilla Hutchins, a former star pilot and the author of *Mission*.

Her name induced a moment of pride. When, years from now, his grandkids asked him what he'd done for a living, he knew he wasn't going to bring up real estate.

He had a leisurely breakfast, bacon and eggs, and headed for work. It was a cool morning, with rain clouds coming in from the west. But he could beat the storm. Or maybe not. The possibility of getting drenched added a bit of spice to the morning. It wouldn't matter. He had extra clothes at the office.

He strolled past the Senior Center, ignoring the rising wind. The place was well maintained, with clusters of oaks and maples scattered in strategic places and more benches now than there'd been in earlier times. The morning's stream of flyers were already passing overhead, most making for DC. Across the Potomac, the Washington Monument seemed poised to free itself from the gravity well.

On impulse, he detoured into the grounds, following the long, winding walkway that used to be filled with joggers and physical fitness nuts. It was concrete until you got past the main buildings, where it converted to gravel, entered a cluster of trees, and circled the Morning Pool. At the far end of the pool, the trees opened out onto a stone wall. If he'd walked to the end of the wall, he would have been able to see his office.

Despite the fact it was located along the eastern perimeter of the old Academy grounds, this was the South Wall, on which were engraved the likenesses of the fifty-three persons who had given their lives during the Academy's near half-century existence. Fourteen pilots and crew (the latter from the days when ships needed more than a pilot), and thirty-nine researchers. There was Tanya Marubi, killed in the Academy's first year when she tried to rescue a paleontologist who'd blundered into a walking plant of some sort on Kovar III. The plaque stipulated that the paleontologist had escaped almost unharmed, and that Marubi had taken the plant down with her.

And George Hackett, who'd died during the Beta Pac mission, which had discovered the existence of the omega clouds. And Jane Collins and Terry Drafts, who'd found the first hedgehog and revealed its purpose when they inadvertently triggered it. And Preacher Brawley, who had run into a booby trap in a system that was referred to on his plaque simply as *Point B*.

EMMA WAS WAITING for him when he got to the office. She was watching the latest *Jenkins* reports. "Anything like that ever happen to you, Matt?" she asked. "You ever get stranded somewhere?"

"No." He made immediately for the coffee. "My career was pretty routine. Just back and forth."

She studied him. "Did you know the pilot?" she asked.

"I've met him."

"Well, I'm glad he came out of it okay."

"Me, too."

They were in his office. The wind was rattling the windows, and rain had begun to fall. "You must be glad to be here," she said. "Real estate's not the most glamorous way to make a living, but it's safe."

"Yes."

"Did you ever know anybody out there who . . . ?" Her voice trailed off.

"One," he said. "I trained under Preacher Brawley."

"Who?"

Brawley had been the best there was. But he'd lost his life when he got ambushed by an automated device that there'd been no way to anticipate. Matt had set out to be like his mentor. And gradually came to realize nobody could be like the Preacher.

She nodded and smiled and after a minute glanced at the clock. Time to get to work. "Do you have anything pressing at the moment, Matt?"

"No. What did you want me to do?"

"Take over the Hawkins business. I think it's a little too complicated for Anjie."

Too complicated for Anjie. "Why don't I just give her a hand?"

LIBRARY ENTRY

THE JERRY TYLER SHOW
Guest: Melinda Alan, Astrophysics Director, AMNH

JERRY: Melinda, we were talking back in the lounge before we came on and you said the omega incident was the worst scientific setback in history. Do I have that right?

MELINDA: Absolutely, Jerry. I can't think of anything that remotely compares with it.

JERRY: Okay. Do you want to explain why?

MELINDA: Sure. Previous to this, we've known that there was intelligence in the galaxy going back over a million years—

JERRY: Let's take a moment here to explain to our audience. You're saying we've known all along that, a million years ago, there were intelligent aliens.

MELINDA: That's right.

JERRY: How did we know that?

MELINDA: The omega clouds. They come from the galactic core. They travel pretty fast, but they still need more than a million years to get here.

JERRY: What exactly are they? The omegas?

MELINDA: We have no idea, Jerry.

JERRY: But there's no question in your mind they're mechanical objects? Launched by somebody?

MELINDA: That seems to be a safe assumption.

JERRY: So whoever's out there could be a lot older than a million years.

MELINDA: That's so, yes.

JERRY: Okay. Now talk about the loss of the artifact.

MELINDA: One point two billion years, Jerry. That ship, station, whatever it was, was so old the mind has trouble grasping it. We'll probably not see anything like it again. It was older than the dinosaurs. In fact, that vehicle dates from a time before any multicellular life had developed on Earth. Think about it: There was nothing on the planet you would have been able to see. Who knows what the artifact might have revealed had we been able to retrieve it?

JERRY: It's okay. Take a second to catch your breath.

MELINDA: (*Wipes her eyes.*) I'm sorry. I don't think I've ever done anything like this on camera before.

chapter 3

PRISCILLA HUTCHINS LOOKED out across the tables and saw a lot of empty places. Maybe her act had gotten old. But the diminishing crowds had been a long-term trend, and the Foundation's other speakers were running into the same problem. The loss of the *Jenkins* wasn't helping. She saw Rudy Golombeck slip in through the side door, take a quick look around, shake his head, and leave as quickly as he'd come. "I'll take questions now," she said.

"Hutch." Ed Jesperson, up front. A medical researcher. "My understanding is that we know where the omega clouds come from. Is that right?"

"Ed, actually we've known for a long time. More or less. We've been able to backtrack them. And yes, the point of origin seems to be in a cluster of dust clouds near the galactic core. We can't get a good look at the area. So we don't know precisely what's happening."

Spike Numatsu was next. Spike was the last survivor of a band of physicists from Georgetown who'd organized campaigns on behalf of the Foundation for years. "Is there any possibility of sending a mission there to find out? I know it would take a long time, but it seems as if there should be a way to do it."

There was a lot of nodding. "We can't stretch the technology that far," she said. "A flight to the galactic core would take seven years. One way." She paused. "We've thought about an automated flight. But we don't have the funds. And we're not sure it could be made to work anyhow. Basically, we need a better drive unit." More hands went up. "Margo."

Margo Desperanza, Margo Dee to her friends, hosted parties and galas and a wide range of benefits for Prometheus. It struck Hutch that there were few new faces that day. Mostly, only the true believers were left. Margo Dee didn't know it yet, but Rudy was going to ask her that afternoon to serve on the board of directors. "Hutch, do you see any possibility of a breakthrough? Whatever happened to the Locarno Drive?"

What, indeed? "There's always a possibility, Margo. Unfortunately, the Locarno didn't test out." It had been the brain child of Henry Barber, developed in Switzerland, an interstellar propulsion system that was to be a vast improvement over the Hazeltine. But it had gone through a string of failures. Then, last year, Barber had died. "I'm sure, eventually, we'll get a better system than the one we have."

"You hope," said Jenny Chang in a whisper from her spot immediately to Hutch's left.

Eventually, the big question showed up. It came from a young blond man near the back of the dining room: "If we did develop the capability to go there, to find out who was sending the omega clouds, wouldn't it be dangerous? Wouldn't we be telling them we're here? What happens if they follow us home?" It was a question that had been gaining considerable credibility among American voters, and, for that matter, worldwide. Politicians around the globe had seized on the issue to scare the general public and get themselves elected on promises to restrict interstellar travel.

"The clouds were produced millions of years ago," Hutch said. "Whoever manufactured them is a long time dead."

The crowd divided on that one; some supportive, many skeptical. The blond man wasn't finished: "Can you guarantee that? That they're dead?"

"You know I can't," she said.

Someone wanted to know whether she believed the theory that an omega had destroyed Sodom and Gomorrah.

Someone else asked whether the clouds were connected with the moonriders.

The moonriders, known in various ages as foo fighters, flying saucers, UFOs, and beamrunners, had, until modern times, been perceived as myth. But the Origins incident of two decades earlier had removed all doubt. More recently, a flight of the objects had been seen, scanned, recorded by a team of physicists. "We don't know that either," she said. "But it feels like a different level of technology. If I had to put a bet down, I'd say they're separate phenomena."

Did she know François St. John, the pilot of the *Jenkins*? Or the Langstons? Or Eagle or Tolya?

"I know them all," she said. "We'll be glad to see them safely back."

When it was over, she thanked her audience for their donations and for being receptive. They applauded. She stayed behind to answer more questions, signed a few copies of her book (actually written by Amy Taylor, a senator's daughter who'd grown up to achieve a lifelong ambition to qualify as a star pilot only to find no positions available), and wandered out into the lobby. She was pulling her jacket around her shoulders when an extraordinarily good-looking young man asked if he might have a moment of her time.

"Of course," she said. He was probably the tallest person in the room, with dark skin, dark eyes, leading-man features. The kind of guy who made her wish she was twenty again. "What can I do for you?"

He hesitated. "Ms. Hutchins, my name is Jon Silvestri." He said it as if he expected her to recognize it. "I have something the Foundation might be interested in."

They were standing in the lobby. Another man, a guy she thought she'd seen somewhere before, hovered off to one side, obviously also interested in speaking with her. "I don't work for the Foundation, Mr. Silvestri. I'm just a fund-raiser. Why don't you stop by the offices later today or tomorrow? They'd have someone available to talk to you."

She started to move away, but he stayed in front of her. "I'm *Dr.* Silvestri," he said.

"Okay."

"They asked you about the Locarno."

"And—?"

He moved closer to her and lowered his voice. "The Locarno is legitimate, Ms. Hutchins. Henry hadn't quite finished it before he died. There was still testing to be done. A few problems to be worked out. But the theory behind it is perfectly valid. It *will* work."

Hutch was starting to feel uncomfortable. There was something a bit too intense about this guy. "I'm sure, whatever you need, they'll be able to take care of it for you at the Foundation offices, Doctor. You know where they're located?"

He must have realized he was coming on a bit strong. He stopped, cleared his throat, straightened himself. And smiled. There was a tightness to it. And maybe a hint of anger. "Ms. Hutchins, I used to work with Henry Barber. I helped him develop the system."

Barber had been working for years, trying to develop a drive that could seriously move vehicles around the galaxy, something with more giddyup than the plodding Hazeltine. "*Riding around the galaxy with a Hazeltine,*" he'd once famously said, "*is like trying to cross the Pacific in a rowboat with one oar.*"

The other man was checking his watch. He was maybe forty, though with rejuvenation techniques these days it was hard to tell. He could have been eighty. She knew him from somewhere. "Dr. Silvestri," she said, thinking she shouldn't get involved in this, "how much work remains to be done? To get the Locarno operational?"

"Why don't we sit down for a minute?" He steered her to a couple of plastic chairs facing each other across a low table. "The work is effectively done. It's simply a matter of running the tests." A note of uncertainty had crept into his voice.

"You hope."

"Yes." He focused somewhere else, then came back to her. "I hope. But I see no reason why it should not function as expected. Henry did the brute work. It remained only to make a few adjustments. Solve a few minor problems."

"He died last spring," she said. "In Switzerland, as I recall. If you've an operational system, where's it been all this time?"

"I've been working on it."

"*You* have."

"Yes. You seem skeptical."

He looked so *young*. He was only a few years older than Charlie. Her son. "Barber hadn't been able to make it work," she said. She looked back to where the other man had been standing. He was gone.

"Henry was close. He simply didn't have all the details right. What we have now is essentially his. But some things needed to be tweaked."

She started to get up. Just tell him to drop by the office. Maggie can deal with him.

"I'm serious," he said. "It *will* work."

"You sound uncertain, Dr. Silvestri."

"It hasn't been tested yet. I need sponsorship."

"I understand."

"I came here today because I wanted to make it available to the Prometheus Foundation. I don't want to turn it over to one of the corporations."

"Why not? You'd get serious money that way. We wouldn't have anything to give you."

"I don't need money. I don't want it to become a moneymaking operation. There aren't many people left doing deep-space exploration. I'd like you to have it. But I'll need your help to run the tests."

It didn't feel like a con. That happened occasionally. People tried to get the Foundation to back various schemes. They'd ask for a grant, hoping to take the money and run. The organization had had a couple of bad experiences. But this guy either meant what he said, or he was very good. Still, the possibility that he had a workable drive seemed remote. "You know, Dr. Silvestri, the Foundation hears claims like this every day." That wasn't quite true, but it was close enough. "Tell me, with something like this, why don't you get government funding?"

He sighed. "The government. If they fund it, they own it. But okay, if Prometheus isn't interested, I'll find somebody else."

"No. Wait. Hold on a second. I guess there's nothing much to lose. How sure are you? Really?"

"Without running a test, I can't be positive."

An honest answer. "That wasn't my question."

"You want me to put a number on it?"

"I want you to tell me, if the Foundation were to back this thing, what would our chances of success be?"

He thought it over. "I'm not objective," he said.

"No way you could be."

"Eighty-twenty."

"Pro?"

"Yes."

"What kind of improvement could we expect over the Hazeltine?"

"Canopus in about ten days."

My God. With present technology, Canopus was three months away. "You'll need a ship."

"Yes."

"The truth, Dr. Silvestri, is that you're here at the worst possible time. We just lost the *Jenkins*."

"I know."

"You probably also know I'm not authorized to speak for the Foundation."

"I'm not sure about your formal position, Ms. Hutchins. But I suspect you have influence."

"Give me a number," she said. "I'll be in touch."

THE FOUNDATION ROUTINELY set up a green room at its fund-raisers. Guests were invited to drop by, bring friends, and meet the people behind Prometheus. When Hutch walked in, Rudy was cloistered in a corner with a group of Rangers. That was the designation given to contributors who met a given minimum standard. It seemed a trifle juvenile to Hutch, but Rudy claimed it made people feel good and brought in additional money.

She picked up a scotch and soda and commenced mingling. She was never entirely comfortable during such events. She enjoyed playing to an audience, had discovered she could hold listeners spellbound, yet had never really learned the art of simple one-on-one socializing. She found it hard to insert herself into a group already engaged in conversation, even though they invariably recognized her and made room for her. The Foundation events were particularly difficult because she always felt that she was essentially begging for money.

When she found an opportunity, she drifted off to a side room and asked the house AI to provide whatever it had on Jon Silvestri. "A physicist," she explained. "Associated with Henry Barber."

One of the walls converted to a screen, and a list of topics appeared. *Silvestri and Barber. Published work by Jon Silvestri. Silvestri and Propulsion Systems.*

He'd appeared in several of the major science journals. Had been on the faculty at the University of Ottawa for two years before being invited by Barber to join his team in Switzerland. Born in Winnipeg. Twenty-six years old. Named to last year's "rising stars" selections by the *International Physics Journal.*

There were lots of pictures: Silvestri on the Ottawa faculty softball team. Silvestri performing with a small band in Locarno. (He played a trumpet.) She listened to a couple of their selections and was impressed.

It wasn't great music, but it wasn't the clunky sort of stuff you expected from amateurs.

There was no mention of specific awards, but she suspected he might have been overshadowed, working with Henry Barber.

Satisfied he was legitimate, she returned to the green room.

WHEN THE RECEPTION was over, Rudy took her aside and thanked her. "I thought contributions would be down," he said. "But I suspect they find you irresistible."

She returned a smile. "What would you expect?"

Rudy was short, energetic, excitable. Everything, for him, had a passionate dimension. He lived and died with the Washington Sentinels. He loved some VR stars, loathed others. He enjoyed country music, especially the legendary Brad Wilkins, who sang about lost trains and lost love, and who had died under mysterious circumstances, probably a suicide, two years earlier. He knew what he liked at the dinner table and would never try anything new. Most of all, he thought humanity's future depended on its ability to establish itself off-world. The failure of the Academy, he maintained, marked the beginning of a decadent age. "If we don't get it back up and running," he was fond of saying, "we don't deserve to survive."

He had started as a seminarian in New England, had gone through several career changes, and had eventually become an astrophysicist. He was the only astrophysicist Hutch had met who routinely used terms like *destiny* and *spiritually fulfilling*. Rudy was the ultimate true believer.

On this night, however, he was not in a good mood. "They think space is dead, some of them," he said. "Pete Wescott says that unless we can find a way to make money out of it, he'll have a hard time justifying further support. What the hell—? Nobody ever told him this was going to be easy."

"I have a question for you," Hutch said.

"Sure." He drew himself up, as if expecting bad news. He'd had a bit too much of the wine. Rudy had a low tolerance for alcohol. She'd suggested once or twice that he not drink at these events, but he inevitably waved it away. Silly. Never had a problem.

One of the Rangers tried to corral him for a picture. "I'll be right along, George," he said, and then turned back to Hutch. "What've you got?"

"Do you know Jon Silvestri?"

He made a face while he thought about it. "One of Barber's people."

"He was here today."

"Really? Why?"

She pointed to a chair. "Sit for a minute."

Rudy complied. He looked worn out. "What does he want from us?"

"Oh, Rudy." She sat beside him. "He might have something to *give* us."

He looked around at the few people left in the green room. "Was he back here?"

"No."

"So what did he want to *give* us?"

"He says he's been working on Barber's FTL drive."

"The Locarno."

"Yes."

"It was a failure."

"He says that's not so."

Rudy's eyes closed and a pained smile appeared. "Lord," he said, "would that it were true."

"Maybe it is."

"I doubt it. So what's he want with us?"

"It looks as if he's going to ask for a ship. To run some tests." She recounted their conversation.

When she'd finished, he sat staring at the wall. At last his eyes came back to her. "What do you think? Does he know what he's talking about?"

"I have no idea, Rudy."

"The Locarno. Think what a break that would be." His eyes brightened. "If he *does* want a test vehicle, we'd have to use the *Preston*." With the loss of the *Jenkins*, it was all they had left. He scratched a spot over his right eyebrow. "Did he seem to think he could really make it work?"

"He says *probably*." Two hotel bots came in and began collecting leftover food. The Ranger who'd been standing at the doorway, waiting to talk with Rudy, wandered off.

"Well," he said, "let's find out."

SCIENCE DESK

SCIENCE HAS ENDED, SAYS JULIANO
"Issues That Remain Are Not Open to Scientific Inquiry"

Connected Story—see editorial:

WHY IS THERE SOMETHING AND NOT NOTHING?

WORLD COUNCIL WILL CLOSE SERENITY
Last Interstellar Base Outlives Usefulness
Will Shut Down at End of Year

BRING EVERYTHING HOME, SAYS MARGULIES
"Deep Space Never Made a Dollar"

SPACE FLIGHT AMBITIONS A DELUSION?
"Time to Grow Up," Says President
"Coming Home Marks Beginning of Maturity"

MAMMOTHS DOING WELL IN INDIA, AMERICA

WHALE BEACHINGS A MYSTERY
Scientists Test the Water

COMET OLDER THAN SOLAR SYSTEM
9 Billion Years and Counting

PHYSICISTS, THEOLOGIANS DISCUSS END OF DAYS
Fourteenth Annual Vatican Symposium
Lights Out in a Few Trillion Years
Does Anybody Care?

SCIENTISTS ANNOUNCE IMMORTAL CHIMP
Will Not Age, Researchers Say
Treatment to Be Available for Humans by End of Decade
But Where Will We Put Everybody?

SOUTH AMERICAN REFORESTATION
PROGRAM NEARS COMPLETION

COLLAPSE OF ICE SHEETS MAY BE IMMINENT
Race Is Close Between Stabilization Effort and Ongoing Melting

PUERTO RICAN AMAZON PARROT SPECIES FOUND
Believed Extinct in 21st Century
Bird Alive and Well in Lesser Antilles

THIS YEAR'S HURRICANE SEASON EXPECTED
TO FOLLOW TREND
Number, Intensity of Storms Should Decrease
Chief Forecaster Hopeful Worst Is Over

SCAM ARTISTS CLAIM TECHNOLOGY TO
HARNESS VOLCANIC POWER
Investors Bilked
Police: "They Got Away Clean"
Tidal Wave Technology Next?
Victims Mostly Elderly

STUDIES SUGGEST MARRIAGE, BUT NO CHILDREN,
KEY TO LONGEVITY

BLACK HOLES MAY DISSIPATE MORE QUICKLY
THAN PREVIOUSLY THOUGHT

ARK ON ARARAT MAY NOT BE NOAH'S
Replica Probably Built in Ancient Times
Intended to Commemorate Biblical Event?

ARE LITTLE PEOPLE SMARTER?
Studies Suggest Correlation Between IQ and Size
Smaller May Be Better

chapter 4

MATT WASN'T ENTIRELY sure why he'd wanted to speak with Priscilla Hutchins. He didn't really know her. He'd just been starting his career when she'd left the Academy. Maybe it was no more than the craving to say hello, I used to pilot superluminals, too. I understand what you're talking about.

"There's almost always someone, after one of these events," she had told her audience, "who asks how I got my start. 'I have a nephew who talks about piloting starships,' he'll say, in a tone that suggests the kid has other problems as well. 'Never been much into travel out there myself. The Earth's big enough for me.' And you know, I feel sorry for him. The train's long since left the station, and he's still standing on the platform.

"I honestly can't imagine what my life would have been without the opportunity to sit on the bridge of a superluminal, to cruise past Vega IV. To see Saturn's rings from the surface of Iapetus. To stand on the beach at Morikai, on a warm summer afternoon, with the wind blowing behind me and a silver sun high overhead and to know that I'm the only living thing on that entire world.

"And I know what you're thinking. This is a woman who's spent a lot of time alone. In strange places. You have to expect she'd be a bit deranged on the subject." That drew laughter from the audience. "But let's talk about why the interstellar effort matters.

"Once you've been out there, and seen what it's like, how many worlds there are, how gorgeous some of these places are, how majestic, you can never settle for staying in Virginia." She talked about good times on the flight lines, described what we'd been learning about our environment and about ourselves, and even brought in Destiny and DNA. "If some of the current politicians had been around a few thousand years ago," she'd said, "we never would have gotten out of Africa. Boats cost too much.

"To close everything down now, to say we've had enough, let's just park on the front porch, which is what we're doing, is a betrayal of everything that matters." She'd looked out over her audience. "What would we think of a child who had no curiosity? Who was given a sealed box and showed no interest in its contents? In the end, we have to decide who we are."

When she'd finished, somebody asked whether she thought it was true that the human race, to ensure its long-term survival, needed to get off-world. Establish colonies. Immunize itself against catastrophe.

"That's probably so," she'd replied. "It makes sense. But that's not the real reason to go. If we stay here, where it's warm and comfortable, we'll die a kind of spiritual death. And I guess maybe it wouldn't matter because we'd probably not be worth saving."

He wasn't sure what he'd have said to her had he gotten the chance. Maybe just that he thought she was right, and that he wished her well. But a guy in a light blue suit had cornered her in the lobby. He'd waited a few minutes while they talked, begun to feel either impatient or conspicuous, and finally decided to hell with it.

They were having a reception in the green room, but he decided he'd invested enough time, took a last look at Hutchins, who seemed to be trying to break off the conversation, and wondered briefly whether he shouldn't help out. She'd probably welcome being rescued. In the end, though, he simply left.

IT WAS AN afternoon filled with paperwork, clearing up the administrative details on the sale of a town house on Massachusetts Avenue, going over a right-of-way agreement, making sure the licenses were in order. When he'd finished, he needed to make some adjustments to the inventory. Then talk with the company lawyer, who was looking into a property dispute, one of those domestic things where one party wanted to divest the property and the other was trying to hang on to it.

It was an easy way to make a living. He was making more money than he ever thought possible. And, God knows, his social life was better than it had been during his Academy days. Nothing like regular hours to put women in your life.

The secret of success for any good real estate agent lay in his ability to connect with the clients. Which meant having a naturally friendly disposition toward strangers and, often, people who tried your patience; and the ability to project it. Sounded simple enough, but Emma insisted they were qualities she rarely encountered. Most people, she said, are out for themselves, and any reasonably observant buyer will pick that up right away in a real estate agent. "If they decide you're faking it, they may still buy the property if they like it enough. But you won't sell them anything that has only marginal appeal."

Matt had only to be himself. Take customers around to look at properties. Wait for them to say yes. File the documents. Collect his commission. He remembered a friend from high school who used to say he wanted one of those jobs where you slept in a bed in a store window. The idea had actually seemed appealing at the time. No responsibility. No way to go wrong. And you'd get a regular paycheck. It was more or less what he had now. The paycheck, of course, wasn't regular, but the flow of money was substantial and presented no problem. Why then did the thought of going back to Stern & Hopkins in the morning, and every morning until he retired, fill him with horror?

THE SECOND WEDNESDAY of the month was a night routinely devoted to the Arlington Businessmen's Association dinner. The event was held at the Liberty Club, and it was required attendance for anyone in the community who expected to be taken seriously as an entrepreneur, CEO, or whatever. Emma had encouraged his attendance, and he had for four years been trying to persuade himself that it was an enjoyable way to spend an evening.

He arrived toward the end of happy hour, paid up, collected a rum topper, stopped for some small talk with George Edward and his psychologist wife Annie, bought a few tickets in the raffle being conducted for this month's worthy cause, and finally wandered into the dining area.

He sat down with the same group he usually sat with, another real estate agent and his wife, the director of a medical test lab and her father, a retired construction contractor, and the owner of a landscaping business, who was accompanied by a son. Emma usually joined them with her husband, but she'd told him she wouldn't make it that night.

They talked about nothing he'd be able to remember ten minutes later. The food came, chicken on a bed of rice, tomatoes and celery. Somehow the chefs at the Liberty always managed to flatten whatever flavor the meal might normally have had. But the bread was good.

The guest speaker was from a local investment house. His topic was Building Your Portfolio. He was a small, nervous-looking guy who squeaked a lot. He overdramatized everything, made it all sound like the outbreak of a world war, and went on at length citing price-earnings ratios, how the problems in Africa were going to affect the markets, why corporate bonds were not a particularly good investment at the moment. The woman on Matt's right, the real estate agent's wife, looked at him and rolled her eyes. Matt agreed. After Hutchins's passionate pitch for the stars, this was pretty slow going.

When it was over, he mingled. Abraham Hogarth, *Dr.* Hogarth to anyone not belonging to his circle, invited Matt to meet his daughter. Hogarth ran an operation that monitored consumer trends and advised retailers how to market their products. Matt had never believed Hogarth really possessed a doctorate. He seemed a bit too impressed by the title, the kind of person who would very much have liked people to refer to him as Excellency.

The daughter was attractive, and Hogarth suggested Matt might come some evening for dinner. You and I share a lot of interests, he said. (Matt had no idea what those might be.) We'd love to have you over, wouldn't we, Bessie?

Bessie looked embarrassed, and Matt felt sorry for her. She didn't need help with men, but with her father pushing her as if she were damaged goods, the poor woman was at a distinct disadvantage. Some of the resentment showed in the way she responded to Matt.

Somebody else wanted to know whether he'd be playing tennis over the weekend. Matt did play most Saturdays. Other than walking between the office and home, it was the only exercise he got. Yes, he said, he expected he would.

The evening ended, more or less with a whimper, and he was on his way out the door when Julie Claggett spotted him. Julie was an English teacher at Thomas MacElroy High in Alexandria. Her father, a charter member of the Liberty Club, owned the Longview Hotel. "Matt," she said, "have a minute?" Julie was a nicely tucked blonde, congenial, energetic, the kind of woman who always got her way. Like any good high school teacher, she was pure showbiz. She could have drifted through life, hanging around the pool. But instead she used her considerable talents trying to demonstrate to reluctant kids that reading was fun.

"I was wondering if I could persuade you to come over and talk to a couple of my classes?"

His appearances at MacElroy High were becoming an annual event. "Maybe this time about real estate?" he asked, innocently.

Her smile was a killer. "Seriously." She liked him to go in and explain to her students what Quraqua looked like from orbit, and how it felt to ride alongside a comet. "Do the routine about how space is made out of rubber, and why my kids weigh more in the basement than they do on the roof."

"Okay."

"And why they get older more quickly waiting for the bus than they do riding it." She grinned. "It works, Matt," she said. "Every time you come in and talk about this stuff, there's a surge of kids at the library."

She had the material down, and could easily have done the routine herself. But Matt had the credentials. He'd been *out there*.

"Sure," he said. "When did you want me to come over?"

HE GOT A call from Ari Claggett in the morning. *"Matt,"* he said, *"I wanted to thank you for agreeing to help Julie at the school. She tells me her students really enjoy listening to you."*

He was surprised. Julie's father had never before said anything about his efforts. "You're welcome, Ari," he said. "I enjoy doing it."

Claggett was a big man, tall, overweight, with a voice that implied he knew exactly what he was talking about. *"They don't get enough of it,"* he said. *"Kids spend too much time listening to people like me just push information at them. Julie says you show them a lot of passion."*

"I just go in there and say what I think," said Matt. "Most of her students have the impression the world ends at the space station."

"I wasn't really talking about outer space," he said. *"I was thinking about books. Julie says most of her students—not all, but most—have never discovered why they matter."* He appeared to be at home, seated in a leather divan, lush white drapes pulled behind him. Matt could see something else was on his mind. *"Sometimes I wonder where we're going to be by the end of the century."*

Claggett's interest in education was no secret. He'd pushed local politicians to get more money for the schools, and had long campaigned to get parents involved. You live or die with the parents, Julie had quoted him as saying. If you don't have them on your side, you're helpless. "We'll be okay," said Matt. "The kids just need somebody to turn them on. Maybe Orion could arrange free tours for some of them." Ari sat on Orion's board of directors.

He allowed himself to look as if he thought it was a good suggestion. *"Why don't you and Julie make the request? Come up with a scheme and put it in writing? We couldn't send the whole school, but we could consider giving some awards to a few of the kids."* He nodded. Why not? *"It shouldn't be a hard sell. It would be pretty good PR for Orion."*

"Yes, it would."

"Which suggests something else." Ah. Finally, we were getting to the

reason for the call. *"Listen, Matt, I have a proposal for you. If you're interested."*

"Okay."

"We're putting together an advertising program. Orion is. We want to have a few well-known former star pilots do spots. You know, stand on the bridge and say how much fun it is to take one of the tours. How educational it can be. The money's not a whole lot, but it wouldn't take much of your time. And I thought it was something you might enjoy doing."

He hesitated, not certain why. Yes, he'd be glad to do it. "Sure," he said.

Ari plunged ahead: *"We're going to get maybe five or six guys to do this for us. You're our first choice. It's my way of saying thanks for what you've been doing for Julie."*

Funny how it became Ari doing a favor for *him*. "I'm not much of an actor."

"Don't need an actor," he said. *"We're looking for people who believe the message."*

HE HAD DINNER with Reyna that night. The conversation eventually got around to the loss of the *Jenkins*. To the narrow escape of the people on board. "You know," she said, "I know you don't want to hear this, but it makes me glad you're not still out there. Say what you want about real estate: At least it's safe."

NEWSDESK

POLAR BEARS RELEASED FROM CAPTIVITY
Latest Effort to Replenish Species

REPORTS OF RELIGIOUS EXECUTIONS IN MIDDLE EAST
Death Penalty Still in Place for Muslims Who Go Astray
Christian Missionary Reported Among Victims
World Council Demands Access

LONGEVITY A GLOBAL PROBLEM
Are People Living Too Long?
"Bosses Linger, Politicians Stay Forever," Says Melvin

HAPPINESS GENE UNCOVERED
"A Little Tweaking Will Go a Long Way"
Some Want It Banned
Yuvenkov: "Relentlessly Happy People Will Become Slaves"

MINNESOTA TEACHER FIRED FOR PRAYING TO ZEUS
Religion in Public Schools?
Or Violation of a Basic Freedom?

GREENWATCH SAYS CLIMATE HAS STABILIZED
Conditions Worsening at Decreasing Rate
"Light at End of Tunnel," Says Bokely

NUMBER OF MEAT-EATERS DECLINES ELEVENTH CONSECUTIVE YEAR
Health, Ethical Considerations, High Prices Are Factors

MCGRAW CONVICTED ON ROBOTICS CHARGE
Violation of Prohibited Technology Act
Sentencing Set for Next Week
Court May Seek to Set Example

DAMAGED STARSHIP SAW BILLION-YEAR-OLD ARTIFACT

chapter 5

RUDY INSISTED HUTCH be present when Jon Silvestri came in to make his case. "Why?" she asked. "I'm not a physicist. I can't pass judgment on what he says."

In the background, the volume turned low, Brad Wilkins was singing about the Savannah Express, rolling through the night.

Rudy's fingers drummed the edge of his desk, the way they did when he was being forced to waste time explaining the obvious. "He came to you. I think it'll be more comfortable all around if you're here."

He also brought in Paul Parmentier, a physicist who specialized in Hazeltine technology and spatial structure. Paul was a little guy with a big mustache and a reputation for driving his colleagues crazy. He closely resembled Banjo Hawk, a walk-on comic who was enormously popular with high school dropouts. Oddly enough, it was the big mustache that made it work. Hutch never understood why Parmentier would want to cultivate the similarities. It was as if he longed to be one of the guys. It was a curious attitude for an accomplished physicist.

Paul's feelings lay close to the surface. He never forgot a slight, and any criticism of an idea he supported was deemed personal. Nevertheless, Rudy insisted there was no doubting his mastery of the field. You want to talk about transdimensional drives, he was your guy. Paul got there early and started by telling them before Silvestri had arrived that he didn't think a more effective system than the Hazeltine was possible. But he was willing to keep an open mind.

Paul had been a consultant for the Foundation since its beginning, not because of any philosophical leaning toward exploratory starflight, but simply because of his connection with Rudy. They were old friends. Hutch suspected Rudy was the only one he had. They constituted one of those unusual pairings in which both men had courted the same young woman, both had married her, both had been cast aside by her, and through it all they had maintained the friendship. How they'd managed that, Hutch couldn't imagine. The former wife had been a good catch, quite attractive, and herself a biologist of no mean accomplishment. The last time Hutch had seen her, she'd insisted she would never marry another physicist. Maybe not marry again at all.

Paul was about forty, with red hair and expressive eyes. You always knew what he was thinking.

Within five minutes of his arrival, he was explaining why it was impossible to move across the galaxy any more quickly than the Hazeltine drive would allow. Hutch caught something about manifold derivatives and net inconsistencies, but could make no sense of it. She suspected Rudy was lost, too, but he nodded in all the right places, asked a few questions and, if he was as puzzled as she, did a decent job hiding the fact.

Twenty minutes later, right on time, Jon Silvestri arrived. He stood in the office doorway, almost as tall as the door itself, hesitating, not sure which of the occupants to address. Rudy escorted him into the office, and he smiled at Hutch. "I appreciate your seeing me," he said. "And I wanted to say first that I was glad you were able to save the people on the *Jenkins*." Rudy thanked him, and Hutch took them through the introductions.

Silvestri was nervous. He was young, and he probably knew both Rudy and Paul by reputation. Moreover, the two older men were suspicious of him, especially Parmentier, and there was no way he could not be aware of the fact. Their suspicions were driven, of course, by his extraordinary claims. There might also have been a problem with the way he dressed. He wore a dark gray business suit, the sort you might get at Christiansen's. It was out of the mainstream for a profession that took pride in rumpled clothes. If you're paying attention to your wardrobe, Rudy believed, your mind isn't sufficiently occupied.

Within minutes they were talking about bending space and juggling local parameters and manipulating tensor beams. Silvestri inserted a chip into Rudy's AI. They closed the curtains to darken the room, and the AI, at Silvestri's direction, provided a series of images, representations of quantum forces, logarithmic spirals, hyperboloids, and God knew what else. He asked the AI to hold this image or that while he made his points. They might have been salient. Or not. Hutch couldn't tell from the reactions she was seeing. Paul got behind Rudy's desk, found a pad, and took to writing things down. He asked a lot of questions.

"Ah, yes," Silvestri would say. "I probably wasn't very clear on that. Let me try it another way."

And so it went, through the morning. The critical thing was that Paul didn't cut the meeting short. Rudy continually looked from one to the other, trying to follow the arcane dialogue. Eventually, Hutch got up and slipped out, apparently with only Rudy noticing. She wandered around the offices, talked to the help, stretched her legs, hit the washroom, and went back. They were still going strong.

Silvestri was explaining that he didn't know precisely how effective the drive would be, which seemed to translate into how much ground it would cover. "Can't be sure until we run a test."

He went into a description of where "Henry" had gone wrong. (Hutch had trouble adjusting to referring to one of the century's certified geniuses in so familiar a manner.) He laid too much reliance on asymmetrical vertices, Silvestri said. Not enough on something else that escaped her.

He finished with a flourish and a broad smile, implying that it was all so simple, how could we have missed it first time around? He glanced over at Hutch. Paul traded looks with Rudy, pursed his lips, let his head drift back until he was studying the ceiling. "Okay, Jon," he said. "Thank you."

Silvestri retrieved his chip. "You're welcome."

Paul sat back. "It would help if you'd leave that for us."

"Okay. Sure." He put the chip on the edge of Rudy's battered desk. "You understand, no copies are to be made. And none of it is for publication."

"Of course. Give us a few days to look it over, and we'll get back to you."

Silvestri had obviously been hoping for more. Those dark eyes clouded. He looked down at Paul. The decision-maker. "Be aware," he said, "I could have gone elsewhere. Orion would love to have something like this. Tours to black holes. To places where stars are being born. They'd give a lot."

Rudy's mouth tightened. "So why didn't you take it to them?"

Silvestri looked directly at Rudy. "I know how they'd use it," he said. "I'd prefer you have it."

WHEN HE WAS gone, the room went quiet. Paul stared at the notepad he'd been using. Rudy's eyes swiveled from Paul to Hutch to the door and back to Paul. Hutch shifted her weight, and her chair squealed. "What do you think, gentlemen?" she asked. "Any of that make sense to you?" She was, of course, really talking to Paul.

Paul stared straight ahead, past her, past Rudy. "I don't know," he said. "It's too much to digest at one time."

"You must have a sense of it, though," insisted Rudy. "Does he sound as if he knows what he's talking about?"

Paul was nodding and shaking his head no at the same time. "Yeah," he said. "Maybe." He picked up the chip, turned it over, examined it, put it in his pocket. "My gut reaction is that it can't be done. Nobody seriously believes it's possible to outrun the Hazeltine. And by the way, that could be the real reason he didn't go to Orion or Kosmik. They aren't going to spend money on a boondoggle."

"Then you think—what?"

"Give me some time. We'll keep an open mind. There's nothing to lose, and Henry Barber thought the project was sufficiently worthwhile to spend his last years on it. And he must have trusted Silvestri. So I'll take everything home and get back to you as soon as I can."

"Paul," Hutch said, "when Barber was running his tests, the drive system kept blowing up. They lost, as I recall, three ships."

"I know."

"Do you think it might happen again?"

"*Might?* Sure. *Will* it? I don't know."

THE ACADEMY OF Science and Technology had not collapsed in the usual sense. The government hadn't wanted to be accused of neglecting an organization with so many accomplishments. So, less than two years after Hutch left, they had reorganized the Academy, centralized it, according to the term then in vogue. It meant it had been subsumed into the federal structure, designated semiautonomous, and eventually taken over wholesale by the Department of Technological Development.

Since leaving the Academy, Hutch had lived a quiet life. She'd stayed home and reared her two kids, mostly. She'd also set up as a guest speaker, and had discovered there was no end of audiences who were willing to pay to hear her talk about her Academy years. She drew lessons for them in leadership and management, explaining why it was important to encourage subordinates to speak freely, why decision-makers should sit down with people who disagreed with them. She talked about what happens when managers intimidate people. She gave examples, sometimes naming names, of life-and-death decisions that had gone wrong even though information to make a rational call had been readily available. "If things blow up," she was fond of saying, "and if the boss survives, he'll inevitably claim that some underling dropped the ball. Didn't tell me. Harry should have spoken up. Said something. But the truth is that when your people don't tell you what you need to know, it's a failure of leadership."

She had seen much of it in her lifetime, at the Academy, in government, and in the private industries with which she'd had to deal during her years as director of operations. There was a tendency everywhere to believe that if you could perform a job, you could supervise others performing that same job. It was a view that led to mismanagement, inefficiency, failure, and sometimes carnage.

Life at home was quiet. Tor was gone, the victim of undiagnosed heart disease. Maureen and Charlie were both away at school. Maureen would graduate next year with a degree in history. She planned to teach, and had shown no interest in following the career arcs of either of her parents. Charlie, on the other hand, seemed to have his father's artistic aptitude. Very few people, however, made a living moving paint around on a canvas. But however that turned out, it seemed clear there'd be no more star-pilots in the family.

Hutch never said anything, never pressed her kids about it. Careers were their call, not hers. And, of course, star pilots barely existed anymore. Another ten years, and she suspected nobody would be leaving the solar system.

Still, it hurt that her passion for the interstellar deeps had not passed down into the family.

THE PROVIDED WISDOM was that when you had an AI, you never came home to an empty house. He (or she) was always there to greet you when you walked in the door. Even if he'd been instructed to say nothing, as some were, you still felt his presence. But, of course, it wasn't the same. AI or not, her home still had echoes.

She missed the kids. When they'd left for school, much of the family's energy had gone with them. Now, as the flyer angled down out of the traffic stream and settled onto the pad, she looked at the house, dark despite the lights that came on to greet her, and it seemed abandoned.

After the chindi business, she'd retired from piloting to marry Tor and had taken an administrative job with the Academy. That had lasted about a year. She'd been unable to cope with riding back and forth to work every day. (They'd lived in Alexandria then.) And she'd felt horribly bored preparing personnel reports and staff studies. Tor had encouraged her to quit, and finally she had.

But it had been more than that. She'd wanted to go back to the interstellars. They'd talked it over, and Tor reluctantly had given his blessing. She could still recall his going up to Union that first day when she was heading out to Beta Pac with a team of assorted specialists who were going to try to discover whether anyone on that unhappy world remembered the days when they, too, had moved among the stars. (They found nobody. There were a few inscriptions, a few legends, that seemed to hark back to the Monument-Makers, but their descendants had no memory of who they had once been. And it struck Hutch as the ultimate irony that the race that had left monuments all over the Orion Arm because they wanted to be remembered by whatever other species might eventually show up had been forgotten by their own.)

Tor had gone with her to Union, had helped carry her bags, had gone on board the *Phyllis Preston* with her. It was then brand-new. Eventually, after years of service, it would be transferred to the Prometheus Foundation. At the time, she'd almost been in tears when she took her seat on the bridge, said hello to the AI, and began running down her preflight check-off list. It had been one of the most emotional moments in her life. There was a time she'd thought that a sad commentary, but that was years ago. She was wiser now. She loved the superluminals and the vast deeps between the stars and she was simply never going to get past that.

Tor had stayed while her passengers, one by one, filed in. They'd introduced one another, and he'd lingered until it was time to start. She still remembered him as he went out through the hatch, and moments later appeared at one of the station viewports. He'd waved, and she'd waved back, and the *Preston* had come to life. The countdown had hit zero, and she eased the yoke forward. She'd taken it out herself, rather than let the AI do it. She'd waited too long not to milk the situation for every ounce of pleasure. But she'd watched Tor, with his right hand raised, sliding past the viewport until he was gone. Outside the launch bay, she'd accelerated, poured the juice to the main engines, but she kept seeing Tor drifting away. Less than a year later she'd been back full-time at the Academy.

She had no regrets.

Not really. Had she stayed in space, her marriage could not have survived. She'd have missed all those years with her husband. Maureen and Charlie would not exist. And she'd have gone down with the Academy, as so many others had.

Tor, of course, was gone now. Yet something else was missing in her life.

She'd have liked to take the *Preston* out again.

When she was a teen, her father had schooled her on the importance of setting priorities. "I could have had a decent career cataloging star clouds and speculating on the properties of black holes," he'd once told her. It would have brought prestige, recognition, better money.

Instead, he'd spent his time at the Drake Center listening for that first intelligent murmur from the stars. While his colleagues learned not to take him seriously. Even after it had actually happened, after the historic signal had come in and the first link with an advanced civilization had been established, he was written off as a kind of by-stander to an event that was a matter of pure luck.

Anyone could have done it. All that was necessary was a little per-sistence.

He'd told her that everything else paled beside first contact. In the end, who would really care what the temperature range was inside the Korialus Cloud?

Like Tor, he'd been taken from her too soon. Her dad had died young of a heart ailment no one knew he had. Disquieting similarity there, too. But he'd lived long enough to know his life had mattered. As had her husband.

It occurred to her that, if the Locarno Drive actually worked, if it gave them a decent range, they could send somebody out to Sigma 2711. Maybe find out who had sent that long-ago signal. To her dad.

ARCHIVE

THE DOWNSIDE OF INTERSTELLAR TRAVEL

A general sense of well-being set in around the world when we were able to destroy that oncoming omega cloud a few years back. In the wake of that happy event, though, we've had time to consider the level of technology that produced the object, and the malice, or indifference, of its makers. It's hard to say which is worse. Which more threatening. But never mind what the intent might be. We know what the effect has been.

Shortly afterward, we concluded, or most of us did, that the moonriders were really out there, and not simply computer mal-functions or delusions. And they, too, seemed to have a hostile streak.

The world beyond the solar system is largely unknown

country. A dangerous place. The discovery of a billion-year-old starship in the *Jenkins* incident should warn us that there are presences, beyond the solar system, that are enormously far ahead of us. And, as much as we would like to believe that the passage of time necessarily tempers the natural hostilities we bring with us out of the jungle, or out of whatever passes for a jungle in remote places, it does not appear to be the case. If our recent encounter with the moonriders proves anything, it is that they are no friends of ours. Are they a danger to us? We'd be prudent to assume so. However much those with a more liberal view would like to reassure us, we cannot rely on the goodwill of extraterrestrials.

Earth has been a safe haven for thousands of years. It is a very small place in a very big galaxy. We now have every reason to suspect our security lies principally in the fact that we are effectively unknown. We should keep it that way. We should withdraw our starships, and keep our heads down. In a universe that may house hostile creatures with technologies millions of years beyond ours, it is the surest road to survival.

—Martin Kobieleski, "The Long Night,"
in *Weapons of War*, edited by Bryan DosCirros, 2255

chapter 6

FOR RUDY, THE Locarno Drive presented the moment of truth. The loss of the *Jenkins* had severely damaged the Foundation's reputation. Despite the response to Hutch's luncheon appearance, support had dropped off significantly.

The first call had come from Lyle Cormier, the organization's most generous single supporter. He was in his office, dressed in one of his trademark black-and-white ensembles. *"Probably best to give it up, Rudy,"* he'd said. *"The world is moving on. There are historical forces at work here, and there's just no point trying to fight them."* Cormier always talked that way. He hadn't said outright that he would cut his support, but it was implicit.

There'd been a flood of others. During the first few days, longtime contributors had gotten in touch, had called or come by, and the message had always been the same: Rudy, you know I've always been a hundred percent behind you and the Foundation. But times are changing. No point beating a dead horse. It's just money down a rathole. No matter what we do, does anyone expect we're really going back out to the stars? When was the last time a new superluminal rolled off the production line?

That was another expression he heard all the time. Going back to the stars. As if we'd ever really been out there. The deepest penetration had been the Trifid, three thousand light-years away. An eleven-month flight. They had never really gotten clear of the immediate neighborhood.

Environmental problems had proved to be every bit as intractable as originally predicted. The solutions were expensive. No real value was forthcoming from the interstellar effort. So it was inevitable that it would come to be perceived as a boondoggle. *Boondoggle* became the title of the book by Gregory MacAllister that had so effectively summed up the arguments against the superluminals. It was a worthwhile effort, he'd said. Acquiring knowledge is always worthwhile. But we need to leave it to another generation. First we have to get the planetary house in order.

MacAllister was right, to a point. But there was a good chance that, when this generation died off, people would forget how it had been done. *Give it up now*, Rudy thought, *and we may be giving it up forever.*

They needed a jump start. And the Locarno might provide that. *If it worked.*

After his conversation with Silvestri, he waited anxiously for Paul's reaction. When he heard nothing over the course of a week, he initiated the call himself. *"Working on it,"* Paul said. *"Best not to rush. These things take time."*

RUDY HAD NO family. He'd been married three times, but his wives had all left, citing different reasons. He was inattentive. He was cold. He came on too strong. He was inexpressibly dull. That had been Eve, the last one. He had argued that he didn't think *dull* was reasonable grounds for divorce, but this was an enlightened era in which one needed only cite a reason to the soon-to-be ex-spouse. The law required no more than intent by either party.

"I'm sorry, Rudy," she'd said. *"You're nice and everything, but all you ever want to talk about is the North Star. For God's sake, you really need to get a life."*

Rudy *had* a life. He loved what he did, and his days were lived on the knife-edge of passion. On more than one occasion Hutch had told him that he was a fanatic. But she'd meant it as a compliment. Why were there no available women around like her? (Technically, of course, she had been available since the death of her husband, but he sensed she did not see him as a prospect.) However all that might be, there was no evading the reality that the Foundation was down to the *Phyllis Preston*.

One ship to explore the universe.

And Jonathan Silvestri wanted to take her, tear out her Hazeltine drive and replace it with something from Switzerland that might, or might not, take them deeper into the Orion Arm. And if it didn't work, he'd have to put the Hazeltine back, assuming there was a ship to put it back into. How much would all that cost?

He was paging through the financial report. There was enough to buy one more ship. It wouldn't be a new one, of course. There were no new ones anymore. Grosvenor, Hudson Bay, and the other one-time major manufacturers were turning out interplanetary ships, oceangoing vessels, farm tractors, and aircraft. And, in the case of Hudson Bay, entertainment centers and robot dishwashers.

He scanned the listings for available vehicles. Kosmik was offering three from its onetime fleet. Orion had a couple up for sale. No guarantees on any of them. *Caveat Emptor.*

The Foundation had taken good care of the *Preston*. The rational thing to do, if Paul approved the Locarno effort, would be to pick up one of these bargain-basement jobs and use *that* for the test. It would strain Foundation resources, but it was a better idea than risking the only ship they had.

He called the operations center at the space station. A technician blinked on. *"Union Ops,"* he said in a bored voice.

Rudy identified himself. Then: "We have some new equipment to check out. We may want to set up a test flight within the next few weeks. Control it from the station. How much of a problem would it be to do that?"

"You mean no pilot?" asked the tech.

What else could he mean? "That's right."

"Sir, all you'd have to do is turn it over to the ship's AI. Just tell it what you want done, and it'll run the test for you."

AIs were not really independent intelligences. They were software packages that mimicked intelligent entities. At least, that was the common wisdom. But nobody could prove it was indeed the case. Rudy was obsessed with the notion that AIs were alive. Chip, in his office; Amanda, at home and in his flyer; and the assorted voices that made life easier in restaurants, hotels, wherever. Maybe they were sentient, and maybe they weren't. Whatever the truth, they put on a good show. And Rudy was taking no chances. He intended to remove the AI from whatever ship was used, in case the drive blew up during the test.

It was no coincidence that the ship was named for the celebrated twenty-first-century humanitarian. But he couldn't give his real reason to the technician without getting laughed at. "The nature of the test requires the AI be disconnected," he said.

The technician shrugged. *"There'll be a charge. But we can do it that way if you really want to."*

"How much advance notice would you need?"

He made a sucking sound. *"When are you going to do this?"*

"Not sure yet we will. If it happens, it'll probably be within the next few months or so."

"Hold on." He consulted another screen. Talked with someone Rudy couldn't see. Nodded okay. *"Depending on how busy we are, I'd say a few days would do it. A week, maybe, if you want to get a berth at a specific time."*

HE SPENT THE next three days reassuring Prometheus subscribers that the end had not come, that the Foundation was not going under, that it was true this was a dark time, but that was all the more reason to rally round the flag. He actually said that. Yes, it was the oldest of clichés. But it worked. Some callers said okay, Rudy could count on them. Somebody even thanked God for people like Rudy, who didn't give up as soon as things began to go south.

Toward the end of the second week, Hutch called. "I don't know," he told her. "He hasn't said anything yet."

"Have you called him?" She was a beautiful woman, he thought. Dark, penetrating eyes, an intense energy, and a sense of what mattered. She was at home, wearing a white blouse and a gold necklace. Behind her was a wall of books.

"Of course. He knows I'm anxious to hear."

"Okay. Let me know when you have something."

Silvestri called less than an hour later. "I'm still waiting to hear," Rudy said. "Just be patient a bit longer."

"*Rudy, this is using up a lot of time.*" He was behind a desk or table, his hands folded, his chin propped on them. "*I wish we could move things along.*"

"It's a good sign," Rudy said. "He's taking a long look. That usually means he's impressed." Actually, Rudy was making it up as he went along.

Silvestri's expression hardened. He saw right through Rudy's happy talk. "*It* will *work.*"

"Nobody hopes for it more than we do," he said. "But you must understand, it means a considerable investment on our part. We have to be sure what we're doing."

PAUL CALLED THE next morning. "*It might be okay.*"

"Marvelous." Rudy would have gone into ecstasy, but Paul wasn't smiling.

"*Of course, you understand there's no way to be absolutely certain,*" he said, "*until we run the test flight.*"

"I understand that."

"*I'm trying to think how to say this.*"

"Just say it."

"*I think it'll work.*"

"You want to put a number on it, Paul?"

"*I can't. Not with any certainty. But I'm optimistic.*"

"Okay, then. We'll do it."

"*You should be aware, though, that if it doesn't perform as expected, there could be a catastrophic result.*"

"Destruction of the vehicle?"

"*Yes.*"

"Okay."

"*Still, if it succeeds, it will be one hell of a payoff.*" Paul lounged in a leather chair, wrapped in an oversized gold sweater. He allowed himself a smile. *"Look, Rudy, I'd like to see you try it. Because I'd like to be around to see it work. And maybe that's clouding my judgment. But it's worth backing."*

THOMAS MACELROY HIGH School was the home of the Explorers. It was named for the commander of the first ship to travel beyond the solar system.

When Matt arrived, he paused, as he always did, to look at the lander standing outside the main entrance. It was an AKV Spartan model, the kind routinely used on the old Academy ships, manufactured in 2229 by Starworks. It had at one time been aboard the *Bill Jenkins* when that ship found the nascent civilization at Lookout in 2234. The lander had descended on 117 worlds, four of which, including Lookout, had supported biosystems. Its history was inscribed on a bronze plaque mounted beside the hatch. The hatch itself remained closed and locked to protect the interior from the weather and the vagaries of the students. And, probably, old star pilots who'd get in and not want to leave.

He'd had one of these aboard the *Resnick*.

ACADEMY OF SCIENCE AND TECHNOLOGY was emblazoned in black letters on the hull, along with the familiar logo, Socrates' scroll circled by a star. The after section carried the school's name, with the seventeenth-century four-master that served as their motif, along with their sports designation EXPLORERS in script. A sudden gust of wind pulled at the trees, and he drew his jacket around him. A car eased into one of the parking places. An older woman got out and marched into the school building. A parent, he thought. And judging by her expression, the kid was in trouble.

Some things never change.

He followed her inside, signed in at the office, and collected a teenage escort who took him to the library. Julie was there, talking to a small group of students. She saw him, smiled brightly, and came over. "Good to see you, Matt," she said. "You'll have two eleventh-grade classes to start. They'll be here in a few minutes."

"Okay."

"Can I get you something?"

They had fresh-squeezed orange juice. While he sampled it, bells rang, the room emptied, the hallways became active, and a fresh batch of kids began pouring into the library. Some of them looked curiously in his direction, but for the most part they were preoccupied with each other. Julie gave them a couple of minutes, asked if he was ready to go, strode to the lectern, and called them to order.

They settled in, and she introduced him. Matt Darwin. "He's a retired star pilot."

Not really retired. Unemployed. That sounded better.

Matt never used lecterns. They got between him and his audience. He'd been seated on a tabletop, and he stood upright as the audience's attention swung his way. "Mr. Darwin flew Academy missions. You know what the Academy was, right?" A few hands went up. Julie looked at a tall, dark-eyed girl in back.

"They used to do exploration missions," the girl said.

In front, a male student rolled his eyes.

"Very good, Sylvia." Julie looked down at the male. "Mr. Darwin, Harry, has been farther from Alexandria than anyone here could imagine."

She took a seat along the side where she could watch Matt and her students.

Matt thanked her and looked around at the audience. "You have a lander out on the lawn in front of the school," he said. "I'd like to tell you a little about it."

ARCHIVE

The people who argue that we confront a vast unknown, that it has already shown itself to be dangerous, and that therefore we should hide under our beds, do not speak for me. Nor do they speak for the Prometheus Foundation.

That's not to say there's no risk involved in exploration. We don't know what's out there, and we don't know what we might blunder into. But there's a risk in just sitting home, as well. For one thing, if there are predators loose, we'll be better off if *we* find *them*, rather than the other way around.

Moreover, if we decide to wait things out, our technological progress will slow. What's more important is that we'll lose any claim to greatness. We'll become an embarrassment to our grandkids. Eventually, a generation with some courage will show up, and they'll hold us in contempt.

—Priscilla Hutchins, addressing State Librarians
Association at Athens, Georgia, April 11, 2254

chapter 7

RUDY AND HUTCH looked at four interstellars and settled on a Grosvenor 352, the *Happy Times*, which the Foundation bought from Orbital at auction. The ship was forty-two years old, had hauled freight and passengers out to Serenity and the other stations, and on one occasion had been immortalized by Whitmore Covington in his *Quantum Dialogues*, conversations on the state of the human race supposedly conducted on the ship during a flight to Nok, whose idiotic inhabitants continued to kill one another over dwindling resources with early-twentieth-century weapons.

Despite its claim to fame, the cost was minimal because the ship's Hazeltine engines were inoperable. That was, of course, irrelevant to Rudy. So he saved substantial money, and in addition picked up a vehicle whose historic value, if the Locarno Drive went nowhere, would allow it to be resold later. "Of course," his occasional companion Ellen Simons told him, "if the Locarno's a flameout, the Foundation's going to have to shut down anyhow."

Mouths of babes. Ellen was a pessimist, and was always ready to explain why something wouldn't work. It was the reason she and Rudy would never get serious. But about this, she was right. The Foundation was on its last legs. Poking around the vast unknown with one Hazeltine ship wasn't going to get anyone excited. They needed the Locarno.

PAYING FOR THE *Happy Times*, as well as financing the installation of the new drive, drained the Foundation's resources. Silvestri virtually moved onto the station to assist the work of a team of technicians. That part of the operation didn't go well. The technicians didn't really need him, and they quickly took offense at his presence. "We've got the basic unit," one of them complained to Rudy. "All we have to do is tie it in to the ship's systems. We just don't need him looking over everybody's shoulder all the time."

So Rudy arranged a series of public presentations for Silvestri. He'd be doing guest appearances at colleges and universities and talking to Rotary groups and press associations and whomever else Rudy could round up. When he presented the package, Silvestri smiled. *"They've been complaining to you, haven't they?"*

"Yes," he said. "Come on home. We can use the PR."

In fact, Rudy would have kept the project quiet had he been able. He'd have preferred to present the world with a successful test rather than hang himself out there to look silly if the Locarno fizzled. But with so many people involved, word would inevitably leak out, so he called a press conference and announced what they were trying to do. It became a big story for about two days. But other events, a grisly murder in a Chicago teknopark, followed by a fresh bribery scandal involving several congressmen, pushed it aside. Meanwhile, several physicists gave interviews. All admitted they saw no reason to suppose a better drive was impossible. Nonetheless, they were uniform in predicting failure. Eliot Greeley, the renowned cosmologist from the University of London, remarked that, "Hell, *anything* is possible, unless it's specifically prohibited. But that doesn't mean you can *do* it."

When he called Hutch, pretending to be upbeat, she caught his mood and pointed out that the experts had been saying much the same thing about FTL travel in general until Ginny Hazeltine had proven them all wrong.

As a counterbalance, Paul became increasingly enthusiastic with each passing day. "I think we're going to make it happen, Rudy," he said. "Keep the faith."

Ah, yes. And so he did. When the Foundation's contributors got in touch to urge Rudy on, he told them he was confident, but they should keep in mind it was a gamble. It may not work. Whether it does or not, we'll still need your support.

The most stinging rebuke came from Joe Hollingsworth, who had been one of the Foundation's founders. Hollingsworth arrived in his office one morning to excoriate him for wasting resources on a crank project. He was one of those intimidating figures who commands everyone's attention when he enters a room. He didn't stand out physically in any way. He was not quite six feet tall, part African, part Massachusetts Yankee, part Mexican. Dressed impeccably. But you knew he was there, and you always got the feeling he'd just come from advising the president. "Rudy," he'd said, "you're throwing money away and, more significantly, you're demolishing the Foundation's reputation. When the *Happy Times* goes out there and blows up, which is what's going to happen, nobody will ever take us seriously again."

"It won't blow up," Rudy had said.

"Doesn't matter. Anything short of an all-out success is going to make us look foolish. Why didn't you talk to us before you started all this?"

Why indeed? "Because I knew you'd veto it," he'd replied in a burst of indignant candor. "Because there are always people on the board who think we can't get the job done and somebody else should take the risk. Joe, I wanted *us* to be the ones to do it. Because it would ultimately give us the inside track on using the system."

"Good." Hollingsworth sounded as if he was talking to a child. "For an ego trip, you risk everything. If it fails, as it will, it will be the end of the Foundation. Worse, it'll be the end of the interstellar effort in our lifetime. Well done, Rudy."

There were others. A substantial fraction of their contributors were unhappy. They demanded to know how much the project was costing and were warning him that if the experiment didn't work, they would be withdrawing their support.

So sending Silvestri on a public relations tour was not a bad idea.

Moreover, he surprised Rudy with his ability to charm his audiences. The references to quantum fluxes and spatial entanglement were gone. Instead, he told them what the Locarno would mean. Easy access to places that had been weeks and months away. The establishment of colonies would become practical, should we choose to go that route. Travel that had once been limited to people with large bank accounts would become available to everybody. "People will be able to vacation in the Pleiades the way we do on the Moon. It will be like replacing fifteenth-century sailing ships with jets."

Nevertheless, it seemed too good to be true. Rudy told himself he'd feel better about it if he could understand it. None of it was Rudy's specialty. He was an astrophysicist by trade. He understood the dynamics by which stars formed and died. But nuclear processes and stellar collapse and the rest of it all seemed fairly straightforward in contrast with this multidimensional talk. Had he been around in the last century when Ginny Hazeltine was claiming she was going to be able to get to Alpha Centauri in a few hours, he'd have been one of the skeptics.

ON FEBRUARY 19, a Monday, word came that the *Itaki* had found the *Jenkins*. On the twentieth, Rudy received a message from François, informing him they'd all been taken aboard the rescue ship and were on their way home. Everybody, he said, was in good spirits. *"Sorry we lost your ship."*

The *Itaki* arrived at Serenity on March 1. *"I thought they were closing the place down,"* François reported. *"But they're telling us it'll take years."*

The following day he sent another transmission: *"Rudy, I know the Foundation is down to one ship now, and you have no need for two pilots. So I'm taking a job out here. Going to run shuttles around the station while they decommission the place. Ben and the others will be returning on the* Itaki. *I'll miss working for you. I've enjoyed it, and I'll look forward to seeing you when I get back. In a couple of years."* He smiled and signed off.

THREE DAYS LATER, the *Phyllis Preston* returned from a mission. Rudy was there, of course, when she docked. He took Jon along.

The *Preston* had been poking around in the Hyades, 150 light-years out. The cluster was thought to be about 625 million years old. It was, like all clusters, changing over time as heavier stars sank toward the center and stars on the periphery were propelled outward after near collisions.

Like most of the relatively small bubble of space into which humans had ventured, it was basically unknown country.

The system consisted of slightly more than two hundred stars, or slightly fewer, depending on how you structured your count. The *Preston*, conducting a general survey, had been away almost six months. It had visited about a quarter of the systems. They had found one living world, on which the biological forms were still single-celled. Early reports indicated they would need another two billion years before multiple-cell forms appeared.

There was a gas giant that *might* be harboring life in its atmosphere. The mission wasn't equipped to test for that. Which meant a second flight would be needed to make the determination. Everyone knew, of course, there would be no second flight.

You could tell how desperate the exploration effort had become by the ages of the researchers. You rarely saw young people on the flights anymore. With only a couple of privately supported organizations running missions, there was simply no space available. The research teams were inevitably department heads or award winners. No more postdocs, the way it had been in the old days.

Rudy missed the old days. He'd been out three times, for a total of about eight months. He'd twice been to local systems, and once to M44, the Beehive, where he'd awakened one morning to a magnificent view of the eclipsing binary, TX Cancri.

He remembered sitting in the operations room on that flight with Audrey Cleaver, from the University of Paris. Audrey had commented that the day would come when they would give almost anything to be able to come back and repeat that experience. At the time, he'd thought Audrey was talking as much about being young as she was about watching the binary.

But it was true. And not in the sense that he'd like to go back to that particular system, as that he wished he could return to that milieu, to live again in a world where everybody was going out to the stars, where the taxpayers happily supported the initiative, and even the politicians were excited. Where people *cared*.

RUDY AND JON greeted each of the *Preston* researchers as they came out of the tube, asked them how the flight had been, had the instruments performed okay, had it been worthwhile. They all seemed satisfied with the results of the mission but were tired and glad to be home. And of course, like every returning mission, they had one regret that nobody ever admitted to: no sign of a living civilization.

The last person off was Armand (Cap) Shinyu, its pilot. Rudy introduced Jon, and Cap's eyes went wide. "You're the guy with the Locarno," he said.

"Yes." Jon flashed a covert grin at Rudy. It's nice to be recognized.

"Well, good luck," said Cap. He expressed his regrets over the loss of the *Jenkins* (which he'd already done by hyperlink, but this was the first time he and Rudy had actually been together since the accident). "Thank God nobody was hurt," he said.

"François couldn't get them to leave the derelict."

"Is that what happened?" Cap was an average-sized guy with huge shoulders, a beefy face, and thick white hair. And an extraordinary baritone. He *sounded* like a seven-footer. He'd once been a teacher of Eastern literature.

"That's what happened."

Cap shook his head. "For smart people," he said, "some of them can be pretty dumb."

"Yeah. Can we buy you dinner?"

They wandered down to the Quarter Moon. It was quiet, mostly empty, an off-hour. "I've been hearing from my wife," Cap said.

"How's Carrie doing?"

"She's okay. But the business with the *Jenkins* shook her up a little."

"I guess I don't blame her."

A bot arrived to take their orders. Cap studied the menu, decided he wasn't very hungry, and settled for a salad. "Rudy," he said, "she's never been happy with this job."

Rudy ordered a bottle of German wine. "I know." He was surprised she'd put up with it at all. The Foundation didn't pay that much, and her husband was away six and seven months at a time. He'd offered to arrange things so she could go along. But they had kids, and there was no way to manage it.

"She'd just like a normal life. Now she's wondering how dangerous it is."

"You're not going to leave us, are you, Cap?"

Two of his passengers were seated on the other side of the dining area. They looked over, saw Cap, and waved. He waved back. "She refused even to come up to meet me. She's never done that before."

"I'm sorry. I wish there were something we could do."

"I do, too, Rudy." He turned his attention to Jon: "Is it going to work?"

Jon's eyebrows rose slightly. "Oh, yes," he said.

"How fast is it?"

"We aren't sure yet. Have to conduct some tests first."

"Well," he said, "it would be a godsend to have something that would move a bit faster than what we have now."

Rudy held his gaze. "Cap, this is a bad time to ask, but after we finish the testing, and we're sure it'll do what we want it to, would you be open to piloting the first mission?"

"Rudy," he said, "I don't think so. If I were to do something like that, Carrie would file for separation. I think I've reached a point where I should pull the plug."

"We just lost François," said Jon.

"I'm sorry to hear it. What happened?"

Rudy sighed. "He decided we didn't have a future. So he got another job."

"Piloting?"

"Shuttling."

"That's a comedown."

"Money's probably a good bit better," said Rudy.

"Yeah. I guess." The wine arrived. They uncorked the bottle, poured three glasses, and drank to the Foundation. To each other. And to the Locarno.

* * *

RUDY TOOK ADVANTAGE of the opportunity to inspect the *Happy Times*. The engineers were not entirely pleased to see him, and especially not Jon, but they brought them on board, and their supervisor explained that they were conducting the first set of calibration tests for the QDU. The Quantum Disruption Unit. Rudy had no idea what it was or what it would do. Neither, he suspected, did the supervisor.

"It's what will give us access," said Jon. He explained its function, which had something to do with spatial manipulation. While they talked, results were coming in. Jon parked in front of one of the displays, followed the operation, looked up periodically to give Rudy an encouraging nod, and, after a half hour or so, broke into a wide smile. "It's going to work, Rudy," he said.

JON SILVESTRI'S NOTEBOOK

... Happiest day of my life ...

—Sunday, April 29

PART TWO

locarno

chapter 8

HAD HE BEEN able, Rudy would have kept the media away from the test run. But there was no way to do that. Interest was high, and journalists crowded into the launch area and spilled out into the passageway. The networks, always hungry for news and ready to expand any sort of event into a major story, had begun broadcasting live two hours before Rudy arrived on the scene.

Also present were a few politicians who had championed the cause, and who had been actively trying for years to get the government to support an interstellar program. And, of course, Rudy had saved room for the Foundation's five board members. Hutch and a few other supporters were also on hand.

The first question had come when reporters had spotted him in the main concourse. "Dr. Golombeck, why did you remove Doris?" Doris was the test vehicle's AI. He'd known that issue would surface. The action had already turned him into a cartoon figure, depicted rescuing toasters and reading lamps from trash collectors.

He was tempted to point out that several religious groups had raised the possibility that AIs had souls. But hardheaded scientific types were supposed to be tougher than that. Reasonable. The *Voice of Truth* had commented that the next thing anybody knew, "These weak-kneed do-gooders would be representing us in the greater galaxy, and giving whatever might be out there the impression we're ripe for plucking." So he simply explained that they'd made test modifications on Doris, that they did not want to have to repeat the process, and that she was not necessary to run the test. So he'd pulled her clear. Just in case. It didn't satisfy everyone, but it would do.

THE *HAPPY TIMES* waited serenely in its bay.

When they were a few minutes from launch time, Rudy asked for quiet, thanked everyone for their support, called Jon to his side, and introduced him as "the man everybody here already knows." He gazed contentedly out across his audience. He loved moments like this. Whatever concerns about failure he'd entertained had drifted away. What the hell. If you tried to climb Everest, there was no disgrace in not making the top. "Ladies and gentlemen," he continued, "we'll be operating the *Happy Times* from here. Since Dr. Silvestri's drive has never been tested, there'll be no one on board the ship when it goes into transit.

"It will launch from Bay 4"—he checked his watch, tapped his earpiece for effect—"in approximately eleven minutes. Forty-two minutes later, after the system has charged, we'll trigger the Locarno, and the *Happy Times* will enter a set of dimensions we haven't previously penetrated." His smile grew larger. "We think." Jon, still beside him, grinned and said he hoped so. It got a round of laughter.

"If all goes well, it will reappear 3.7 billion miles from here before you can count to six. A standard vehicle, using the Hazeltine, would complete the jump in just under a minute."

Somebody wanted to know how far 3.7 billion miles was? Saturn? Uranus?

"Think Pluto," he said.

"Rudy." George Eifen, of *Science News*, stood near the door. He'd grown a beard since the last time Rudy had seen him. "Is that really correct? Six seconds?"

Rudy smiled contentedly. "George, we've been doing one minute to Pluto for the better part of a century. Nobody notices because nobody ever goes to Pluto. We make these runs out to Rigel or wherever, and it takes a few hours, or a few days, so the rate of passage is lost. People don't see what Ginny Hazeltine accomplished. Well, with the Locarno, we hope to do even better."

He smiled again, but he tried to appear uncertain. Hopeful. Don't want to look smug. Make sure the thing works first. "When it arrives, it'll send a radio signal back here. It's now"—he checked the time— "almost noon." Greenwich Mean Time, of course. "If all goes well, it'll be on the edge of the solar system at about 12:45. The radio signal will need six hours to get back here." He glanced around the room. "By seven or so this evening, we'll know whether it's been a success."

A small man off to one side waved a hand. "There's no chance it would *hit* Pluto, is there?"

Rudy chuckled. "Pluto isn't there at the moment," he said. "So there's no danger of a collision. In any case, there's a matter detector on board. It would prevent the *Happy Times* from trying to materialize in the same space as a solid object."

They directed a few questions at Jon. How did he feel? How confident was he? In an era when the urge to travel in deep space seemed to have gone away, did he foresee a practical use for this kind of drive?

Jon explained that he didn't believe the current malaise was permanent. When he finished, Rudy pointed at the clock. They were down to four minutes. "Dr. Silvestri," he said, "will launch for us."

Jon took his seat at the controls. Someone handed him a cup of coffee, and the room quieted. Rudy moved back out of the way. The displays activated, and they had views of the Bay 4 launch doors from several angles. Orbiting telescopes had also been included in the mix. If everything went as planned, they'd have visual coverage until the moment the *Happy Times* made its jump. That part had been easier to arrange than he'd expected. The Locarno experiment commanded a fair amount of interest.

The station director wandered in, saw Rudy, came over, and shook his hand. "Good luck," she said.

Across the room, Hutch caught his eyes. Here we go.

The media people were speaking into their microphones, watching the countdown, trying to convey the tension of the moment. A few technicians stood out in the passageway. Margo Dee, who looked gorgeous, gave him a thumbs-up. Big moment for the Foundation.

Two minutes.

The room fell silent, save for a few whispers.

Once Jon hit the button, everything would be automatic.

Rudy couldn't remember the last time he'd tried prayer. His parents had been staunch Presbyterians, but it had never really taken with him. Nevertheless, he found himself speaking to Someone, delivering one of those if-you-are-there pleas. If he'd ever wanted anything in his life to succeed, this was it.

Fifty seconds.

The *Happy Times* was considerably larger than the *Preston*, and much bulkier. Designed to accommodate lots of cargo. It wasn't the vehicle he would have chosen for something like this. Its main engines were outsize, the hull still carried the faded logo of Orbital Transport (which they hadn't gotten around to removing), and external latches provided additional hauling capability.

He'd have liked something a bit more photogenic.

The final moments went to zero. Jon leaned forward and pushed the button.

NOTHING HAPPENED.

The *Happy Times* stayed firmly attached to its dock. Rudy glanced over at Hutch. She smiled. Be patient.

He turned back to the ship. Still nothing.

The launch doors began to open, and the umbilicals floated away. The ship edged away from the dock. Its maneuvering thrusters activated, and it started to turn on its axis. Big lumbering thing that it was, it moved with surprising grace. He watched with a sense of pride.

The picture on the displays changed. They were looking down on Union from God knew where. The ship moved deliberately out through the launch doors. Its tubes lit up, and it began to accelerate. A few people applauded. Premature. Way too early.

It dwindled quickly to a star. Then it was gone.

"Okay, folks," said Rudy. "Nothing more will happen for the next forty minutes or so. Break time."

Journalists closed in on him and on Jon. Mostly they wanted him to speculate, to talk about the implications of a ship that could travel to Pluto in six seconds. He tried to explain that wasn't really what happened, that the device folded space, that the ship passed through the folds. But, of course, nobody could visualize that, so the reporters made faces and asked whether he couldn't explain it in plain English, and he had to say he couldn't because the words don't exist, and anyhow he couldn't really visualize it himself. Nobody could.

"If it works, will we be going to the Cauldron?"

It was the popular term for the Mordecai Zone, the cloud cluster RVP66119.

Thought to be the source of the omegas.

If there had ever been a question whether the lethal clouds were a natural phenomenon, it had surely been answered, at least in Rudy's mind, when the courses of hundreds of the objects had been traced back to that single narrow place near the galactic core. The Cauldron. The Devil's Cookpot. The site from which countless omegas were dispatched to attack civilizations wherever found.

Well, that wasn't exactly right. They attacked geometric structures, artificial designs that incorporated right angles. But the effect was the same. There were some who thought civilizations were not deliberately targeted. That they just happened to get in the way. Hutch was among those who subscribed to that notion. But if indeed it was sheer indifference, that somehow suggested even a deeper level of evil at work.

The Cauldron was symbolic of an ultimate malice, a demonic manufacturing plant, a factory that poured forth unimaginable destruction down the ages. And across the light-years. Those who maintained it was a conscious diabolical force, and they were many, seemed even to Rudy to have at least half of the truth.

The project had been led by Edmund Mordecai, and the area had been named for him. The Mordecai Zone. But most people knew it only as the Cauldron.

We knew precisely where it was, fifty-seven light-years out from the core, a pinpoint in orbit around the massive black hole at the center of the galaxy. But it was shrouded by vast clouds of dust and hydrogen, so no one had ever seen it.

Rudy had known the question was coming. "We're taking this one step at a time," he said. "Let's confirm that the system works first.

Then we can talk about mission profiles." He liked the sound of that. Mission profiles.

Hutch was surrounded, too. She'd been out of the business a long time now, a former pilot herself during the glory days, but they hadn't forgotten her.

"Rudy." Jani Kloefmann from *Norway at Night*. "Tell us about the AI. Are you really worried about hurting the hardware?"

"Just a precaution," he said. "In case the test goes wrong, it would be one less thing we'd lose."

"AIs aren't expensive," Jani said.

"This one is. She's had special training." The question was inevitable, and he'd come prepared. He opened a briefcase and removed a black box. "We asked Doris what *she* wanted, and she said she'd prefer to stay here and talk with the people from the media." He raised his voice a notch. "Say hello, Doris."

"*Good morning, Jani.*" She had a cool, professional voice. "*And be assured, I'm quite happy to stay here and keep my feet on the ground.*"

" 'Your feet?' " said Jani.

"*Sorry about that, Jani. But people tend to get the point when I use metaphors.*"

Rudy wasn't worried about the *Voice of Truth* and its allies. He was enough of a politician to know that virtually the entire planet agreed that AIs were *people*.

A HALF DOZEN telescopes, four in orbit and two mounted on the station, had picked up the big cargo ship and were tracking it. Rudy wandered through the room, talking with reporters, shaking hands with the politicians, thanking the board members for their support. Through it all, it was impossible not to watch the clock.

He was surprised at how effectively Jon handled the media. He moved easily among them, telling jokes on himself, obviously enjoying being the center of attention. There was none of the exaggeration or self-importance or condescension that was so common with inexperienced people thrust into the spotlight.

He relaxed, and watched the *Happy Times*, barely visible now, a dull star off to one side of the moon. The minutes slipped easily away.

A countdown clock ticked off the time remaining as the Locarno charged. Then, precisely on schedule, the ready lamp lit up. All systems were go.

Moments later, the star blinked out, the ship vanished from the screens. Rudy walked over and shook Jon's hand.

If you watched a vessel making its jump with the Hazeltine system, you saw it gradually turn transparent and fade from view. The process took only a few seconds, but the transition was visible. It had not been like that on this occasion. The *Happy Times* had simply disappeared from sight.

Rudy inhaled twice, held his left wrist out so he could see his watch, and counted off six seconds. Then he allowed himself to look hopeful. "Ladies and gentlemen," he said, "if everything has gone as intended, the test vehicle has just jumped back into normal space, but it is out in Pluto's neighborhood. It should now be starting a transmission to us. *That* transmission doesn't have the benefit of Jon's drive, so it will need about six hours to get here. It should arrive this evening at approximately 7:04. That could go a few minutes either way. There's some imprecision in our ability to gauge exactly how far a jump will take a Locarno-equipped vessel. In any case, we'll be back here tonight listening to the radio. I hope you'll all join us."

And, on cue, Doris delivered her line: *"Ladies and gentlemen, thank you for coming. Refreshments will be served in the dining area."*

SOME OF THE politicians and Foundation people retired to a meeting room that Rudy had arranged. Others, who wanted something more substantial than finger sandwiches and oatmeal cookies, fanned out among bars and restaurants to wait out the interval. Jon appeared confident. "It'll be okay," he told Rudy. "We're through the most dangerous part of the process. The one I was worried about."

"Which one was that?"

"Entry. It's where the math was most uncertain."

"I see."

"If we were going to have a problem, that's where it would have occurred."

"You're sure it didn't?"

"I'm sure." They were sitting in armchairs with a potted palm between them. "It would have exploded."

"At the moment of transition?"

"Yes, indeed," he said. "Right there in River City. For everybody to
see." He was drinking something. Looked like brandy. "Have no fear,
Rudy. It's over. We're in business."

Hutch, who wasn't personally invested quite the way Rudy was,
had taken a wait-and-see attitude. She had a vague sense of how far
Pluto was, at least much more so than anyone else present, and her
instincts warned her that nobody could get out there in six seconds.
Of course, her instincts also told her that getting there inside a
minute was just as absurd. It was odd that she'd never thought of it
in those terms. All those years, she'd sat down on the bridge, activated the system, and they'd drifted through an interdimensional
haze for a few days, or a few weeks, and she would arrive in another
star system.

She stopped to think how far Alpha Centauri was. A mere four
light-years down the road. It didn't sound far. Yet, had we been limited
to the velocity of the first moon flights, a mission to that dull neighbor
would have required more than fifty thousand years. One way.

When asked in Rudy's presence about her reaction to the experiment, she said she was confident. Everything was going to be fine. It
might have been the moment that brought her doubts to the fore-
front. "I'm never going to get used to this," she told one reporter. "An
armload of dimensions, space-bending drives. Sometimes I think I'd
rather have been around when they flew the first planes."

"I don't know," Rudy said. "They weren't big about women in
cockpits in those days."

AT ABOUT FIVE o'clock, GMT, when they were starting to talk about a
late meal, Paul showed up. "My treat," he said. Nobody gave him an
argument.

They knew they'd get no peace in one of Union's restaurants, so
they gathered in Rudy's room and had pizza sent up. The dinner was
a quiet one, everybody watching the clock, lots of talk about how
good the food was, people looking out the window and making philo-

sophical remarks about the planet below. They were over one of the oceans, but Rudy had no idea which one.

He hated having to wait for the results. Had it been a Hazeltine flight, they could have used its associated FTL comm system, the hyperlink, and everyone would have known the result within a few minutes. The Locarno had not yet been adapted for a hyperlink. There was no point spending the time and effort until they knew whether the transport system worked. Consequently, they had to wait it out. And radio signals, which crawled along at the speed of light, took forever.

That should be the next project, he decided. If everything turned out all right today. Rudy had already asked Jon whether it could be done. "It'll be expensive," he said. "And it'll take time. But yes. I can't see any reason why not."

They watched some of the reports, watched their own interviews, laughed at the things they'd said. "The entire galaxy will be within reach," Rudy had told New York Online.

"Right." Paul shook his head. "If you don't mind three-year missions."

"That's still pretty decent," said Hutch. "The other side of the galaxy and back. In a few years."

One of the board members, Charles McGonigle, who also headed the Arlington National Bank, chuckled and looked around. "Any volunteers?"

"I'd go," said Rudy, turning serious.

Paul looked pensive. "Not me."

Rudy was surprised. "Really?" he said. "You wouldn't go on a flight to the other side of the galaxy?"

"Are you serious? That's the problem with the Locarno. It puts all this stuff within range. But what's really going to be there that we haven't already seen? If we've learned anything at all these last few decades, it's that the galaxy looks pretty much the same everywhere. Dust clouds, empty worlds, a few ruins. The stars are all the same. What's the big deal?"

Rudy took a moment to chew down a piece of pizza. "It's someplace we've never been before, Paul. The other side of the forest."

*   *   *

AT A QUARTER to seven they trooped back down to the control center. Jon was escorted by reporters, who never seemed to tire of asking the same questions. Margo Dee took him aside to wish him luck. "Let's hope," she said, "this is a day we'll always remember."

By seven the room had settled down, they were up live on the networks, and Jon was back at the panel. The clock activated with three minutes to go. When the signal arrived, it would come in the form of a voice message, the words *Greetings from Pluto*. Jon had argued for a simple series of beeps, especially with the world watching. "It has a little more class." But Rudy was part showman, had to be, or the Foundation would never have survived. So *Greetings from Pluto* it became. They were using the voice of a well-known character actor, Victor Caldwell. Caldwell, a major force in promoting the Foundation, had died the year before. But his baritone was known around the world.

Hutch stood in a corner calmly drinking coffee. She could be a cold number when she wanted to.

The room went dead silent as the last seconds drained off. Rudy told himself to relax. The counter hit zero, and everybody strained forward. He could hear himself breathing.

Somebody coughed.

Somewhere a door closed. Distant voices.

Jon pushed back in his chair.

Plus one minute.

Rudy shoved his fists into his pockets. Come on, Victor. Where are you?

Reporters began to look at one another. Jani Kloefmann leaned in his direction. "When do we reach a point where it becomes a problem?" she asked, keeping her voice low.

"Don't know, Jani," he said. "We're in unknown territory here."

Two minutes.

WHEN SIX MINUTES had passed, Jon stood up and faced the cameras. His face told it all. "No way it could have taken this long," he said. "Something's wrong."

It was as if the air went out of the room. Everything deflated.

There was another barrage of questions, a few laughs, and lots of people talking on commlinks.

Rudy took time to commiserate with Jon, who managed to maintain a brave demeanor. "I don't understand it," he said. "The numbers were right. It should have worked. It *had* to work."

They waited a half hour. People came over to shake their hands, tell them they were sorry. Then the crowd drifted away. Rudy decided he'd waited long enough. He corralled Jon and Hutch, was unable to find Paul, and went up to the main concourse. While they walked, Jon speculated that maybe there'd been a problem with the *Happy Times.* "Maybe the main engines were defective," he said. "Maybe they screwed up the wiring. That's all it would have taken. With no AI on board, nobody would have known."

They ended in the Orbital Bar & Grill, where they could watch the sun rise. It was soaring into the sky as the station rushed toward the horizon. Not like on the ground, where movement wasn't quite visible.

Jon couldn't stop talking about where things might have gone wrong. He mentioned several possibilities, other than the ship. "There *are* areas," he confessed, "where the theory becomes elastic. Where the parameters are not entirely clear. Where you have to test. Find out." They needed to learn from this, he continued. Make some corrections. He thought all it might take would be an adjustment in fueling correspondences.

And, of course, another ship.

Rudy wondered why he hadn't brought these details up before.

"WE NEED TO find a tech," Jon said. "One of the people who helped with the launch."

"Why?" asked Hutch.

But he was already signaling for his bill and pushing himself away from the table.

Rudy and Hutch followed him back to the operations section, where they prowled the passageways until they found a technician who seemed to have time on her hands. Jon identified himself. "I was part of the *Happy Times* experiment earlier today," he added.

She nodded. "I'm sorry about the way it turned out, Dr. Silvestri."

"I'd like to look at the last few seconds again. The ship's transit. Can you arrange that?"

She gave him a sympathetic smile and took them into a room with several cubicles, all empty. "Pick one," she said.

He sat down in front of a display, and she brought up the *Happy Times*, adjusted the clock, and froze the picture. Twelve fifty-eight P.M. One minute to jump. "Thanks," he said.

"Sure." She explained the controls. "This starts it again. This freeezes it. And this slows it down or speeds it up. Okay?"

"Fine."

"When you're finished, just leave it. I'll be back in a few minutes."

He started it forward, and played it in real time. The ship filled the screen, moving quietly against the field of stars. The clock counted down, and it vanished.

He backed it up and ran it again. At a slower pace.

Watched as it blinked out.

Something was there.

He ran it again, still more slowly this time, and slower still as it approached the critical moment.

The ship began to fade out of the three-dimensional universe. The transition started in the *Happy Times*'s after section, where the Locarno Drive was installed, and moved forward.

Something else was happening: The ship was bending, folding up, as if it were cardboard, as if an invisible hand had taken hold of it, had begun squeezing it. Or maybe pulling it apart. Metal bent in extraordinary ways, and in those last moments, as it faded to oblivion it no longer resembled a ship. Rather it might have been a clay model that had simultaneously exploded and crumpled.

He threw his head back in the chair. "It didn't survive entry."

"No," Rudy said. "I guess not."

LIBRARY ENTRY

The failure of the Locarno Drive is a major setback for us all. The talking heads are telling us we're better off, that it could only lead to another interstellar age, and thereby drain funds needed elsewhere. And it may be true that there are places too dangerous to go. New York Online has cited the classic Murray Leinster story "First Contact," in which a human starship encounters an alien vessel, and neither ship feels it can safely leave the rendezvous point without risking the possibility that the other will follow it home. And thereby betray the location of the home world to God knows what.

That is the argument we are now hearing from those who think we should not venture into deep space. The stakes are too high, the risk too great. What chance would we have against technologies wielded by a million-year-old civilization? And these fears have been underscored by the recent discovery, and subsequent loss, of an alien vessel said to be more than a billion years old.

But one has to ask whether we wouldn't still be sitting in the middle of the forest if we were a species that first and foremost played it safe.

Eventually we will move out into the galaxy. We will, or our children will. If we can perfect a drive to enable more extensive exploration, then we should do it. And I'd go a step farther. One of the objections most often raised to the development of an enhanced transport system is the fear that somebody will make for the galactic core, stir up whatever force exists in the Mordecai Zone, and bring them down on our heads. This is haunted house logic. If somebody is still there, still orchestrating the omegas that drift through the galaxy blowing things up, maybe it's time we explained things to them.

A new propulsion technology might put us in a position to stop the production of omegas. That will not matter much to any but our most distant descendants. The omegas are, apparently, already in the pipeline for well over a million years to come. But if we can shut the operation down, we should do it. We owe that much to ourselves, and to any other reasoning creatures in the path of the damned things.

—Mark Ingals, *The Washington Post*, June 5, 2255

chapter 9

HUTCH HAD TAKEN care to see that she and Rudy sat together on the shuttle flight back to Reagan. However things went, she wanted to be with him. Either to celebrate the moment. Or to limit the damage. Jon was staggering a bit, but he was young, and seemed strong enough to rebound. In fact, he was already talking about where he thought the problem lay. Rudy was another matter.

As the vehicle fell away from the station and began its descent, she saw that, beneath the brave front he'd put on for the media, the guy was stricken. "Rudy," she told him, "we knew all along the odds were against us." She almost said *long shot*. In fact, she was the only one of the inner circle who'd believed that.

He was staring listlessly out the window. "I know."

Rudy was an optimist, the kind of guy who thought you could do anything if you put your mind to it. The immediate problem was less that the test had failed than that they'd lost the *Happy Times*. "Listen," she said, "why don't you take the day off tomorrow? Come over to the house? I'll make dinner."

Rudy managed a smile. "Do I look that desperate?"

"Hey," she said. "I'm a decent cook."

He squeezed her hand. "I know. I mean, that's not what I meant."

Whatever. "You need to get away from it for a bit. You and Jon both. We'll make a party out of it."

He still avoided looking at her. "You know that business up there today all but destroyed the Foundation."

She knew. "What's our situation?"

"It leaves us with payments to make on a ship we no longer have."

"It wasn't insured?"

"Insurance was out of sight. Everybody knew what we were trying to do." The eyes finally found her. "It's a pity. Imagine what a working drive would have meant."

"We'll need to find new donors."

"In this atmosphere . . ." His voice trailed off.

"They'll be there," she said. "This isn't the first time the Foundation's been a little short."

"A *little*?" He laughed. It was a harsh, ugly sound, not at all characteristic of the Rudy she knew.

"There *is* one possibility," she said.

They punched in drink orders, and she thought he hadn't heard her. "What's that?" he asked finally.

"If Jon can figure out what went wrong, we still have the *Preston*."

"What? Let him lose our *other* ship?" He squeezed his forehead. "No, Hutch. We aren't going to do that."

She was quiet, for a time. "Look," she said at last, "it's a gamble, sure, but it could pay off."

"No. I'm not giving him another ship to play with."

"IT'S THERE," JON insisted. They were standing on the roof of the terminal, watching Hutch climb into her taxi. She waved as it lifted off, and her eyes brushed his. He caught a faint smile. She knew he'd been waiting for a chance to speak to Rudy alone, and she knew why. "We just have to make some adjustments. Run the tests until we get it right."

But Rudy looked beaten. His eyes were bleary, and he had adopted a manner that was simultaneously apologetic and resentful. "I don't think you understand the position the Foundation is now in, Jon," he said. "We invested a lot in the Locarno. We were counting on your getting it right."

That hurt. "Some of these things," he said quietly, "don't lend themselves to exact calculations. We have to try them. See what works."

"That isn't what you've been saying."

"Sure it is. You just haven't been listening."

Rudy's eyes were closed. He was trying not to sound bitter. "I know, Jon," he said finally. "It's not your fault. Not anyone's fault, really. You're human, and humans screw things up. It happens. It's as much my doing as anybody's."

"Rudy, I didn't screw things up."

"Okay, Jon. You didn't. Let's let things go at that."

"You don't want to try again?"

"What? Risk losing the *Preston*? No, I don't think so." He jammed his fists into his pockets. "No. Not a chance."

The air was heavy. "It *will* work, Rudy."

He grunted. "Everything I've read, everybody I've talked to, they all say it can't be done. They can't all be wrong." His cab drifted in and opened up. Rudy tossed his bag in back and climbed in.

"Paul thought it would work."

"Paul was wrong."

Jon held the door so Rudy couldn't close it. "There was a time," he said, "when everybody agreed that heavier-than-air flight would never work. And another time that we'd never get to the Moon. Sometimes you just have to *do* it."

Rudy gave the driver his address. "I'm sorry, Jon. I really am. But let's just let it go, okay?"

JON ROUTINELY TRAVELED with his commlink turned off. He didn't like being subject to calls when he was out of his apartment or away from the lab. That was his own time. Consequently, when he walked into his apartment after returning from Union, his AI informed him the circuit had been busy. *"You have 114 calls,"* it said.

"From whom, Herman?"

"Four from family, eleven from friends, colleagues, and acquaintances, fifty-two from persons identifying themselves as the media, eleven from assorted well-wishers, thirty-four I can only identify as cranks, and two from charities seeking donations."

He sank into a chair and sighed. "Nothing corporate?"

"No, sir."

"Delete the media."

"Done."

"What kind of cranks?"

"Some threatening your life because they think you are going to arouse whatever's producing the omega clouds. Or similar concerns. I referred them for analysis. So far none looks dangerous, but you will wish to show some caution. Just in case."

"What else?"

"Thirteen claiming they already have an ultra star drive. Seven claim to have devised it themselves, but say they can get no one to listen. Five say it was a gift from extraterrestrials."

"That's twelve."

"One says he found a design in a vault inside a pyramid."

"Valley of the Kings?"

"He didn't specify."

He'd hoped Orion or Lukacs or somebody would have tried to get in touch to offer him testing facilities. *Don't these nitwits understand how valuable a decent drive would be?* He mixed a bourbon and soda and responded to the personal calls. His mother. His uncle Aaron. Two cousins. Everybody offered sympathy. Assured him they knew that the Locarno would work next time. Ditto with his friends.

"Let's see the well-wishers, Herman."

A list scrolled onto the screen. He scanned the names. Nothing rang a bell. He sampled a few of the messages. Hang in there, Jon, they said. Man was designed for something greater than the Earth. (You could always tell the crazy ones. They talked about 'Man' rather than 'people.' They couldn't go two sentences without citing 'destiny.')

The world was full of lunatics. Herman had trouble sorting them out. If they didn't rave and threaten, the AI didn't see them for what they were. And Jon was reluctant to provide a list of key words and phrases. Sometimes perfectly sane people also said those things. His father was fond of saying that *his* destiny was to be overwhelmed by unintelligible kids. Dad wasn't big on physics, and Jon's sister was a lawyer.

"Get rid of them," he said finally.

ARCHIVE

NOMAD GENE FOUND

Scientists announced yesterday that the restlessness gene has been discovered. It is believed to be responsible for the inability of so many people to derive a sense of satisfaction from their lives, no matter how successful they have been. In addition, it may make it impossible to settle down into a quiet life. Persons believed to have possessed this gene include Francis Bacon, Charles XII, Winston Churchill, and Edna Cummings.

—*Chicago Tribune*, August 6, 2021

SPECIALISTS WARN AGAINST NOMAD MANIPULATION

Prospective parents looking for a quiet home life with submissive kids may want to think twice about neutralizing the so-called nomad gene, the French Psychiatric Society warned today. Manipulation is difficult to reverse, and researchers have discovered that a strikingly high percentage of those who have achieved success in a wide variety of fields, have an abnormally active nomadic impulse. The conclusion: If you want creative and successful children, resign yourself to jousting with rebels.

—*Le Monde* (Paris), August 9, 2021

chapter 10

MATT DARWIN WAS also disappointed by the failure. "I'm not surprised you'd feel that way," said Reyna. "But I really can't see what difference it makes."

He shrugged. How could he explain it if she did not understand already? She was practical and down-to-earth. Thought real estate mattered. She was a political junkie, and she was intrigued by technology that could be put to practical use. But a star drive that made the entire Milky Way accessible? What was there on the other side of the galaxy that anybody really cared about?

They sat at the Riverside Club, with its lush, moody view of the Potomac, surrounded by well-heeled types who thought exactly as she did. If it didn't produce a practical benefit, it wasn't worth doing. But he'd been looking forward to the Locarno Drive, to being able to watch the first real deep-space missions go out.

There were a hundred commentators already, speculating about the fatal flaw. Some were citing Jacobsen, the towering genius of the first half of the twenty-third century, who'd predicted the Hazeltine would prove to be the last word. *"Lucky to have that,"* he'd been fond of saying. *"We used to think it would take centuries to get to Alpha Centauri. Be grateful. The structure of the universe simply won't allow an alternate drive. It can't be done."*

He'd died trying to prove himself wrong. But there'd been numerous claims for a new system over the past two decades. Government had funded some, private industry others. Nothing had worked. Nothing came close. By the time news began leaking out of Barber's camp, that he was closing in on a workable system, nobody believed it.

"I'd just like to know what's out there," Matt told her.

She looked out at the river. A cabin cruiser, its lights casting a glow on the water, was moving slowly past, leaving laughter and music in its wake. "Dust and hydrogen, Matt. And empty space. We'll never do better than where we are right now." Her eyes were gorgeous, and they promised all kinds of rewards if he just got himself together.

"This place has too many lights," he said.

She glanced around them, thinking he was talking about something else.

HE SLEPT AT her place that night. Usually, he avoided bedroom encounters with Reyna. One-night stands with people he barely knew were better. Reyna was attractive enough, beautiful really, and usually willing. But she was a friend as well as an occasional date, and he could not jettison the feeling he was taking advantage of her. She was an adult, knew what she was doing, knew there was no future for them. So it should have been okay. But somehow it wasn't. She was good company, a guarantee against spending weekends alone, but eventually he *was* going to walk. Or she would. So he tried to keep everything at arm's length. It wasn't easy to do if they were tangled up in a bedsheet.

That night, when the signal hadn't come back, and the networks had shown the pictures of the shattered *Happy Times*, he'd known the Locarno was dead. Jon Silvestri and the rest of the Foundation crowd had tried to put the best face on things, saying they'd take a look at the situation in the morning, that maybe they could find the problem. But he knew they wouldn't, and it weighed on him, as if he were personally involved. Defeat was in their voices, in their eyes. "They're not going to try again," he told Reyna.

"How do you know, Matt?"

They'd looked beaten. Maybe they had figured out why the Locarno hadn't worked; maybe they'd known all along it wasn't going anywhere. It might have been nothing more from the start than a gamble. A toss of the dice. And they'd lost.

He'd been in no mood to go back to his lonely apartment. So when she'd invited him up, he'd gone, and they sat on her sofa drinking dark wine and watching the aftermath, watching the commentators tell each other it was just as well. "The Interstellar Age," said one of the guest experts, "is over. It's time we accepted that."

Later, while Reyna lay asleep beside him, his mind wandered. Where had the Golden Age gone? Twenty-five years ago, when he was just coming to adolescence, people had predicted that everyone who wanted to move off-world would, by the middle of the century, be able to do so. There was talk of establishing colonies at Quraqua and Masterman's and Didion III. But there'd been complications, objections to killing off the local biology, long-range health issues, the question of who would pay for a massive transfer of people and supporting equipment. The world was crowded, but moving people elsewhere would never be an answer. People reproduced far more quickly than they could be moved around in ships.

One day, maybe, a human presence would extend through the Orion Arm. Maybe people would even fill the galaxy. But it wasn't going to happen anytime soon.

He listened to the sounds of passing traffic. Somewhere in the building, there were voices. An argument.

"It's the Gorley's, Matt."

"I thought you were asleep."

Her legs touched his. But she held him at a distance. "They're always fighting."

"Sounds ugly."

"He's told me not to get married."

"Really?"

"Ever."

The argument was getting louder.

"You don't have to say anything, Matt." She pressed her lips close to his ear. "I know this isn't going anywhere. But I want you to know it has been a special time for me."

"I'm sorry, Reyna," he said.

"I know. You wish you loved me." She looked glorious in the light from the streetlamps filtering through the windows. "It's just as well. Nobody gets hurt this way."

They didn't stop what they were doing. She didn't get up and walk off. Didn't go into a sulk. But the passion had gone out of the evening, and everything was mechanical after that. She told him it was okay, she understood. He waited for her to say she had to move on. But she didn't. She simply clung to him.

He'd never understand women.

MATT SPENT THE morning showing clients around. They were look-ing at commercial properties, land that could be rezoned for malls and bars if the right buttons were pushed. He took one of them to lunch and did more escort work in the afternoon. When he finally got back to the office, everyone had left except Emma and the finan-cial tech.

She poked her head in, asked how things had gone, and expressed herself satisfied with the results. In fact it had been a good day. No sales had been confirmed, but two big ones were on the cusp. And one they'd thought would back out was hanging in. But he still had a cloud over his head and wasn't sure whether it was Reyna or the *Happy Times* debacle. Moreover, he couldn't understand why the *Happy Times* problem really mattered to him.

He kept telling himself it had been a good day. But he felt no sense of exhilaration. In fact, he rarely did. He was capable of feeling *good*. But *exhilarated*? That was a thing of the past. That was a woman who took his breath away. Or maybe gliding through a system of moons and rings and spectral lighting. Over the years, after a successful day, he'd gone out with Emma and the others to celebrate. They'd headed out for Christy's and toasted each other the way the researchers had when they discovered living cells on a remote world. But he'd just never felt very much.

"Headed home," she said. "We have tickets tonight for *Group Sex.*" The show, of course. It was a live musical at the Carpathian. "By the way, you been near the news today? They've apparently given up on the new star drive."

"Why?" he asked. "Did they say?"

"I guess because everybody says it won't work." She said good night and, minutes later, was gone. Matt put on the news, directed the AI to find the Locarno stories, and poured himself a coffee.

SILVESTRI INSISTS LOCARNO IS VALID, said the *Capital Express.*

The *Post* headlined: LOCARNO CRASHES.

The *London Times* said: STAR DRIVE FIASCO.

Commentary was similar: DEEP-SPACE SYSTEM SHOULD BE DUMPED. WHERE DO WE GO FROM HERE?

He found an interview with a Prometheus spokesman. The guy was small and washed-out and tired-looking. But he claimed the Foundation hadn't made up its mind yet. "*We're still looking at our options.*"

Would the Foundation risk its remaining ship in another test? "*Anything's possible.*"

The spokesman could say what he wanted, but it was easy enough to read the signals. Unless someone intervened, the Locarno was dead.

Two people, one of each sex, discussed the drive itself on *The Agenda.* They were both identified as physicists, and they claimed to have gone over the theory. Both found it defective. It looks good on the surface, the woman said, but it doesn't take into account the Magruder Effect. She was unable to explain the Magruder Effect in terms lucid enough for Matt. Her colleague agreed, adding that Silvestri had also not allowed sufficient flexibility for the required level of interdimensional connectivity. "*You'd be able to get a vehicle out to Pluto,*" he said, "*but you wouldn't recognize it once it arrived.*"

"*How do you mean?*" asked the interviewer.

"*It would be bent out of shape by hypertronic forces. That's what happened to the* Happy Times."

"Jenny." Matt was speaking to the AI. "Get me what you can on Jonathan Silvestri. On his scientific reputation."

"*One moment,*" she said. Then: "*Where would you like to start?*"

*   *   *

THE ONLY WORKING physicist Matt knew was Troy Sully, to whom he'd sold a villa outside Alexandria two years earlier. Sully worked for Prescott Industries, which manufactured a wide range of electronic equipment. He'd come to the NAU from northern France, expecting to remain only a year, but had instead found his soul mate—his expression, not Matt's—and elected to stay.

"*There's no way to know, Matt,*" Troy told him over the circuit. "*Let me advise you first it's not my field.*"

"Okay."

"*You get into some of this highly theoretical stuff, and you have to do as Silvestri says: Run the tests. Until you do that, you just don't know.*"

"But if almost every physicist on the planet says it can't happen, which appears to be the case, doesn't that carry some weight?"

"*Sure.*" Troy was a big, rangy guy. He looked more like a cowboy than a researcher. Except for the French accent. "*But you have to keep in mind that what people say for the record isn't necessarily what they really think. When physicists are asked to comment, officially, they tend to be very conservative. Nothing new will work. That is the safe position. One does not wish to be branded an unskeptical dreamer. If it should turn out that this Silvestri's notions were in fact to prove correct, you would hear every physicist within range of a microphone explaining that he* thought *there was a chance it would happen because of so-and-so. You understand?*"

"I assume if you were to bet—"

"*I'd say the odds against it are substantial. But the truth is, with something like this, there's no way to know until you try it.*"

JON HAD DINNER at Brinkley's Restaurant across the park and came back to another flurry of messages. "*There's one that might be of interest,*" Herman said. "*Do you know a Mr. Matthew Darwin?*"

"I don't think so."

"*He wants to know if you need a new test vehicle.*"

Jon was planning on spending the evening watching *Not on Your Life*, a Broadway comedy. He needed something to laugh at. "What have you got on Darwin, Herman? Who is he?"

"A real estate agent, sir."

He snickered. "You sure? Have we got the right guy?"

"That's him."

"A real estate agent."

"There's something else of interest." There was a sly pause. *"He used to pilot superluminals, mostly for the Academy."*

"Really? You think he knows where we can lay our hands on a starship?"

"I don't know, sir. It might be worth your time to ask him."

"Did he indicate whether he was representing someone?"

"No, Jon."

"All right, let's get him on the circuit and hear what he has to say for himself."

MATT DARWIN WAS seated by a window. He looked too young to be a guy who'd been piloting for years, then built another career in real estate. It was hard to tell a person's age this side of about eighty if he took care of himself and got the treatment. These days, of course, everybody got the treatment. Darwin could have been in his twenties.

He looked efficient rather than thoughtful. A bit harried rather than at ease. He had black hair, brown eyes, and there was something in his manner that suggested he had no doubts about himself. *"I appreciate your calling, Dr. Silvestri,"* he said. *"I'm sure this has been a hectic time for you."*

Jon was in no mood for idle chitchat. "What can I do for you, Mr. Darwin?"

"I might be able to do something for you, Doctor. I've been watching the reports about the Locarno. I'm sorry things went wrong yesterday."

"Thank you."

"It sounds as if the Foundation won't try again. Is that true?"

"It looks unlikely."

"Okay. Clear something up for me, if you will. This propulsion method, the Locarno: Its power source, I take it, is different from the Hazeltine."

"I'm sorry, Darwin. I'm really worn-out. This has been a long few days."

"Doctor, I can imagine how difficult it must be to come by another starship

to test your system. *If you'd be kind enough to answer my question, I might be able to make a suggestion."*

He was tempted simply to say good night, but something in Darwin's manner implied it might be a good idea to continue. "The Hazeltine is powered by the main engines," he said. "You know that, I'm sure. The Locarno carries its own power pack. It has to, because the power flow has to be carefully modulated. You need a rhythm. Trying to control the power flow from a starship's engines simply isn't practical."

"So you really don't need a set of engines?"

"Only to charge the power pack."

"Can't that be done in advance?"

"Sure. But it goes flat with each jump."

"All right. But you don't need a starship's *engines, right?"*

From the mouths of real estate dealers. "No," he said. "Actually, we don't."

"Okay." Darwin allowed himself a smile. *"Why did you use a starship in your test? Why didn't you try a shuttle? Or a lander? Something a little cheaper?"*

Jon had no answer. Using a different kind of vehicle had never occurred to him. Jumps were always made by starships. Not by landers. But he saw no reason they couldn't have done it that way. "You're right," he said. "That probably would have been a better idea."

"Okay," said Darwin. *"So all you need for the next test is a lander."*

Or for that matter, a taxicab. Well, maybe not. They'd need something that could navigate a little bit. "Thank you, Mr. Darwin. You may be on to something." Even a lander, though, would not come cheap.

"I might be able to supply one, Doctor."

"A lander? You could do that? Really?"

"Maybe. Are you interested?"

"How much would you want for it?"

Darwin's face clouded with disapproval. *"You have an ultimate drive, and you can't spring for a lander?"*

Jon laughed. "Probably not at the moment."

"Let me look into it. I'll get back to you."

*   *   *

"MATT," SAID JULIE, "that's goofy." They were sitting in Cleary's, over lunch, while a soft rain pattered against the windows. "They won't do it."

"How do you know?"

"Look, it's a great idea. But they're a school board. They aren't usually tuned to great ideas."

"What can we lose by asking them?"

"Oh," she said, "by all means, ask them. I'm not suggesting you shouldn't. But I'd hate to see this guy blow up our lander. And the board is going to feel the same way."

"Maybe I can give them a reason to take the chance."

"I hope you can. But I can tell you they won't be happy." She was eating roast beef on rye, with a side of potato salad. She took another bite and chewed it down. "Six thousand physicists can't be wrong," she said. "That'll be their position."

"Julie, you know most of the people on the school board."

"Yes, but I don't have any influence over them. They don't take teachers very seriously."

"You don't think there's a chance they'd go along?"

She lifted her iced tea and jiggled the cubes. "What you'd have to do is persuade them they'd get something out of it. They're politicians, Matt. Maybe you could tell them what it would mean to their careers if they took a chance with the lander, and it worked. Next step—"

"The governor's house. Beautiful. I like that."

She grinned and took another bite out of the sandwich. "I'll be there to watch the show."

"Julie," he said, "how long has the school system had the lander?"

"Six years. No, wait, I think it's more like five. It was my second year here when they got it."

"All right," he said. "Thanks. You have any idea what kind of shape it's in?"

"Not very good, I wouldn't think. I mean, there's no maintenance program. It's just been sitting on the lawn, getting rained on." Her eyes sparkled, and he read the message: You'd just love to get back out there, wouldn't you?

"Can you arrange to open it up for me? Let me take a look at it?"

NEWSDESK

PENGUINS MAKING COMEBACK
Off Endangered Species List After Half Century

CAN MACHINES HAVE SOULS?
AI at St. Luke's Requests Baptism
Congregation Splits Down the Middle

INTELLIGENCE A LEARNED TRAIT?
New Study: Anybody Can Be a Genius

WINFIELD TELESCOPE TO BECOME OPERATIONAL TOMORROW
Expected to Provide First Glimpses of Extragalactic Planets

KENNEDY SPACE CENTER TO BE NATIONAL MONUMENT
Eight-Year Reclamation Effort Planned
Shuttles, Capsules, Rockets to Be on Display

TURMOIL CONTINUES IN MIDDLE EAST
World Council to Promote Liberal Education
Mullahs Denounce Plan

EARTHQUAKE KILLS SEVEN IN JAPAN

ANTIGRAV BELTS TO HIT MARKET FOR CHRISTMAS
Several States Push for Ban
Drunks at 2000 Feet?

HUMANS RETAIN BRIDGE TITLE
AIs Own Chess, But Weak at Nonverbals
Roman AutoMates Last in Berlin Tournament

HANLEY WINS NATIONAL BOOK AWARD FOR *LIGHTS OUT*

BABES AT MOONBASE ENDS 29-YEAR RUN
Succeeds The Twilight Diaries *As Longest-Running Broadway Show*

TORNADOES HAMMER DAKOTAS
Seven Dead in Grand Forks

chapter 11

THE HEAD OF the school board was Myra Castle, a staff assistant at a pharmaceutical company. Myra had political ambitions, was perpetually annoyed, and had, he suspected, never held any kind of authority position until she was elected to oversee the county educational system. If Julie could be believed, she was a petty tyrant. Myra had once introduced Matt to her husband as "the space guy" who went over to MacElroy occasionally to talk to the kids. When he called and asked if he could meet her for lunch, red flags must have gone up. "*Why?*" she asked.

"I have an idea for the school system. Something you might be interested in using."

She was a small, pinched woman. One of the few, apparently, on whom the rejuv treatments had minimal effect. She was only in her fifties, but was visibly aging. "*What's the idea, Mr. Darwin?*"

"I'd rather talk to you in person. If you can find the time. I know you're busy."

"*Yes, I am, as a matter of fact. It would help if I knew at least generally what this is about.*"

So much for Matt's charm. "I wanted to talk to you about the lander."

She had dark skin, narrow features, and wore a perpetual frown. She struck Matt as one of those occasional school board types who was in the business because she was still angry at her own teachers from years before and saw it as an opportunity to get even. The frown deepened. *"The lander?"* She had no idea what he was talking about.

"The one out front of MacElroy."

"Oh."

"I think there's a way the school system could get some serious benefit from it."

She brightened a bit. *"I can't imagine what we might do with it that we aren't doing already, Mr. Darwin. We allow the children to go into it periodically, and we even open it up sometimes to the parents. What more is there?"*

"Could you manage Delmar's tomorrow? My treat?"

DELMAR'S WAS A pricey restaurant off the Greens in Crystal City. It got crowded around lunchtime, and they didn't do reservations, so Matt got there early and had already commandeered a table when Myra walked in. He waved to her, and she nodded in his direction, flashed a peremptory smile, stopped to speak to a group of women seated by the window, and came over. "Hello, Mr. Darwin," she said. "It's good to see you."

She seemed more at ease in person than she had over the circuit. They exchanged niceties for a few minutes, ordered their drinks and entrées, and Matt said some favorable things about the school system, and how well it was doing. Some of the credit for that belonged to the board.

It was transparent enough, but she appeared to buy it. She tried her drink, a cordial, and explained how being on the board wasn't the picnic everybody seemed to think it was. She went on in that vein until her food came, a chef's salad and a turkey sandwich. Matt had a plate of fried chicken. She tried the salad and bit into the sandwich. "If you'd care to explain what this is about, Mr. Darwin, I'd be interested in knowing what you want to do with my lander."

He told her. Jon Silvestri was probably on the verge of one of the major discoveries in history. Nobody knew for sure. If it worked, it would, finally, open up the stars. But Silvestri needed a test vehicle.

The lander, if it was still in reasonable working condition, would be perfect for that purpose. "It would cost the school system nothing," he explained. "The only thing put at risk would be the vehicle itself. At worst, you could replace it with a cannon or something. Even if the effort failed, the school board would get credit for assisting scientific progress. But if it works, and there's a decent chance that it will, anyone associated with it is going to look pretty good. Global coverage. Think about that. Worldwide and the Black Cat."

She pushed her tongue against the side of her mouth. "This is the same guy who ran the experiment the other day, right?"

"Yes, it is. But he's been making some adjustments—"

"Didn't they lose the test vehicle?"

"He thinks he's corrected the problem."

"I see." She took another bite from the salad and let her eyes drift away. "He's fixed everything."

"Yes, he has."

"Then why has he—are *you*—coming to us? Surely if he's got this star drive put together, there'd be a lot of people out there who'd be interested. And willing to let him have a lander."

"If a corporation gets involved," Matt said, "things get complicated. They want guarantees. Control."

"I see." She studied the sandwich as if it were prey. "And the lander is all he needs? Not a *ship*?"

"No. The lander would be sufficient."

"Why didn't they use a lander the first time? Seems as if it would have been less expensive."

Matt grinned. "It never occurred to them."

"And these are the people you want us to trust?"

His grin widened. "They're physicists, Myra. They don't think the way the rest of us do."

"I see."

Time to press the attack. "Look, the reality is that it's an unforgiving world. You have one failure, and everybody counts you out. I've looked into Jon Silvestri's background. The guy who developed the system. He's good. It's probably going to work. And we can be part of it. I mean, what have we got to lose? The lander's not a big deal to the school system."

She was nodding, probably without realizing it. "Matt—It *is* okay if I call you *Matt*?"

"Sure."

"Matt, first of all, the lander has been out there for years. What makes you think it would still fly?"

"I've looked at it. It would need some work, but it should be okay."

"And I take it you want to use the lander to run the next test."

"Yes."

Tongue in cheek again. "What's your connection with this?"

That was a good question. Maybe it was just that he wanted to see it happen. Maybe. "I'm not sure," he told her. "We could use a breakthrough like that. And it seemed to me to be a golden opportunity for the county. To help out and get some good PR."

"That's it? You're not being paid?"

"No, ma'am. After the test is over, if all goes well, you get the lander back, it will have achieved historic value, the school board gets noticed around the world, and the lady who made it happen gives interviews on the Black Cat."

"I'm sure." She was trying to look unimpressed. As if she had conversations like this every day. "Can you guarantee we'd get it back in the same condition it's in now? Can you guarantee we'll get it back at all?"

"Myra, I wish I could."

She finished the turkey. Cleaned up the last of the salad. A waitress showed up. Would they like some dessert?

The people at the next table were beginning to get a little loud. They were going on about politics.

"Matt," she said, "why don't they just buy one?"

"I suspect they would if they had the money. That's what makes it an opportunity for us."

"The lander at the school isn't new. But it already has historic value. If you were to take it and lose it, or damage it, it would be a severe embarrassment."

"I think people would understand. I think you'd get credit for trying."

She fell silent. Withdrew within herself. Then: "We'd want them to sign a waiver of liability. If something happens, we can't be held in any way responsible."

"I'm sure there wouldn't be a problem."

"Okay. Matt, I won't *give* it to you. But I will offer a trade."

"A trade."

"Yes. I'll be running for the state senate next year. I'd like your support."

"Why would anybody care what I thought?"

"Former star pilot. That carries some weight."

"Okay," he said. It would be simple enough. Painful, but easy. He was sure he could find something nice to say about her without bending the truth too far. "Of course," he said. "Whatever I can do to help."

"Good. It'll mean some speaking engagements. And I'll want you to appear with me occasionally at other public events."

"Of course. Easily done."

"I'm sure." She finished her drink. "Also—"

"There's more?"

"MacElroy needs a decent science lab. Update subscriptions aren't all that expensive, but the equipment is. And the AI should be replaced. The school system is broke. We're always broke." She smiled. "It's a good cause."

"Wait a minute. You want me to do something to update the science program?"

"Yes. Why are you looking at me like that?"

"I just—"

"Maybe I'm not who you think I am, Mr. Darwin."

"How much?" he said.

She thought about it. "We've been looking at the Eastman High Complex. In Arlington."

"How much?"

"One-fifty should cover it. If it doesn't, we'll make up the rest."

"Myra, you're talking a lot of money."

"I'm sure it's far less than a lander would cost. But if you can't manage it—"

"No. Let me see what I can do."

"Excellent. Get it done, and we'll name the lab for you." She glanced at the time and got to her feet. "That was excellent. Have to go, Matt." She thanked him for the lunch, for the company, and swept away.

"YOU HAVE THE lander, Matt?" asked Silvestri.

"Not yet, Jon. I'm working on it."

"It would be nice. If you get it, where will it be coming from?" He looked as if he'd just returned from a workout. Shorts, drenched T-shirt, towel around his neck.

"Let me worry about that. I have one question for you, and I need an honest answer."

"Sure." A woman appeared in the background. Young, slim, red-headed, good-looking. Also in a sweat suit.

"Will it work this time?"

"Matt, I can't promise anything. But yes, there's a good chance. I've figured out where it went wrong."

Matt wondered if he'd allowed himself to get carried away. "How much will it cost to install the Locarno? In the lander?"

"It won't be cheap. But I think I can talk Rudy into underwriting it."

"Rudy Golombeck?"

"Yes."

"What if he says no?"

"Then I'll just cut a deal with one of the corporates. I don't want to do that, but I will if I have to." The woman had ducked out of sight. Silvestri glanced after her, and Matt wondered if he was more interested in getting to her than he was in the drive. *"Anything else?"* he asked.

"I guess that's all."

"Good. Talk to you later. Let me know how it goes."

Silvestri broke the link, and Matt stared at the space where the physicist had been.

He called Crandall Dickinson, who coordinated speakers at the Liberty Club. "Crandall," he said, "who's the next scheduled speaker?"

Dickinson was in his office. Matt could hear a basketball game, the volume turned down. The display was obviously off to one side. Dickinson kept glancing at it while they talked. *"Next speaker?"* He passed the question to the AI, glanced at the game, looked down at the response. *"Harley Willington. Why?"*

Harley was a local banker. They brought him in every couple of years, and he talked about the national debt and global fiscal trends. It was never practical stuff that anybody could use. Harley had a degree in economics from Harvard and liked to show it off. "Could we move him to another time, do you think? If I came up with a celebrity speaker?"

There was a roar and Crandall sucked air between clenched teeth. The other side had scored a big one. He stared at it for a few seconds, then turned back to Matt. *"I don't know, Matt. That always creates a problem. You have any idea what kind of message a last-minute cancellation sends?"*

"Crandall, I know. And I wouldn't ask, but it's important."

"Why? Who's the celebrity?"

"Priscilla Hutchins."

"Who?"

"The star pilot. The woman connected with rescuing the Goompahs."

He shook his head. *"Who the hell are the Goompahs?"*

"Okay, look. She's a good speaker. If you plugged her in, she'd give you a serious performance."

"Matt, I don't mind adding her to the speaker list. But why don't we let her wait her turn? We could put her on"—he turned aside, checked something, came back—*"in September. That be okay?"*

"Crandall, this is important. We need it to happen this month."

The guy was really suffering. *"Who is she again?"*

"Priscilla Hutchins."

He wrote it down. *"You owe me,"* he said.

"One more thing."

"There's more?"

"I just wanted you not to cancel Harley until I get back to you."

That brought eye-rolling and a loud sigh. *"You haven't set it up with her yet, right?"*

"I'm working on it now."

"What's the big hurry, Matt?"

"It's important. I'll explain it to you when I have a minute."

The other team apparently scored again. Crandall looked again to the side, groaned, and disconnected. Matt's AI congratulated him. *"I thought you were very good,"* he said. *"I didn't think he was going to go for it."*

"Everything's politics. I've done him a few favors. Now, see if you can connect me with Priscilla Hutchins."

"Ah, yes. Good luck."

HUTCHINS WAS OFF somewhere, out of touch, and he needed two days to locate her. In the meantime, Crandall called and insisted on a decision. Matt told him to cancel the banker.

"What happens if we don't get What's-her-name?"

"We'll get her. Don't worry." If not, he'd dig up a history teacher over at the school to come in and talk about the five worst presidents, or some such thing. It would still be a considerable improvement.

WHEN HE FINALLY caught up with Hutchins and explained what he was trying to do, she didn't take it well. *"Let me get this straight,"* she said. *"You've committed me to do a fund-raiser to equip a high school lab so they'll let you have a lander that's been sitting out on the grass for the last few years. Do I have that right, Mr. Darwin?"*

"Yes, ma'am. As far as it goes."

"And you've talked to Dr. Silvestri about using the lander to run the next Locarno test?"

"Yes."

"And he thinks that's a good idea?"

"Yes, ma'am."

"Tell me again who you are."

Matt explained. Former star pilot. A number of years with the Academy. Worked for you briefly when you were director of operations. Want to see the Locarno program work.

"Why me?"

He thought, *Because we're kindred souls.* But he said, "I've seen you speak. And I thought you'd be willing to help."

Hutchins was an attractive woman. She'd been around a long time, but you had to look hard to see it. Black hair, dark eyes, fine cheekbones. She might have been thirty. But her manner suggested she was not someone to be jollied along. *"Mr. Darwin, don't you think it might have been a good idea to check with me first?"* She was at home, seated on a sofa behind a coffee table. Behind her, a painting of an old-style starship dominated the wall.

"I wasn't sure I could get you plugged in. I didn't want to have you accept, then have to go back to you and explain that the club wouldn't make the change."

"*What makes you think the Locarno will perform any better* this *time?*"

"I've spoken with Jon." The use of the first name was too familiar, and he regretted using it but couldn't get it back.

"*As have I. What's your background in physics?*"

"Limited," he said.

"*So you base your conviction on what? Silvestri's sincerity? His optimism?*"

"Ms. Hutchins, I've talked to a physicist who says it's possible."

"*That's a step forward. I suppose we could have a power failure at any moment, too.*"

He was beginning to get annoyed. "I was hoping to find you a bit more open-minded."

"*Open-minded to what? An outside chance that maybe, just maybe, Silvestri has it right? You want me to invest an evening to go down there and try to persuade people to kick in money on an outside chance?*"

"If you do it, the high school will get a new science lab. Isn't that worth an evening of your time?"

"*Don't even try it, Matthew. I won't be hustled into this thing. If I participate, I become part of the project. It blows up again, and my reputation takes a beating.*"

"You're already part of the project, *Priscilla*. You were standing with the others in the control room on Union, weren't you, when they lost the *Happy Times?*"

She smiled at him, but there was something menacing in that look. "*There's a difference between participating in a failed experiment and participating in the same failure a second time.*"

"I'm sorry to have bothered you, Priscilla. I'll try to get somebody else."

"*I'm waiting to be persuaded. Why should I do this?*"

"Because," he said, "it might work. Do you really need another reason?"

Somewhere, down the street, he heard kids laughing and shouting.

"*When and where?*" she asked.

ARCHIVE

This AKV Spartan model, from the William Jenkins, *is awarded to the Thomas MacElroy High School by Armis Reclamation, in recognition of the accomplishments of staff and student body, and of their many contributions to the community. Presented this date, June 3, 2250. Fly High, Explorers.*

–Engraved on the marker at the lander site,
Thomas MacElroy High School, Alexandria, Virginia

chapter 12

ONE THING COULD be said about Priscilla Hutchins: She didn't do anything halfway. She let Matt know that when she came for the fundraiser, she'd be bringing guests. Eight of them. Could he arrange to seat them up front? They would be, she said, part of the show.

With no idea who was coming, or what she was planning, Matt and the Liberty Club accommodated her. So on the second Wednesday of June she arrived with a small contingent, consisting of six men and two women. Matt recognized two of them, the British actress and singer, Alyx Ballinger; and the gadfly editor, Gregory MacAllister.

Hutch shook his hand, introduced him to everyone—several of the names rang bells—and told him she was looking forward to the evening.

They had a choice of roast beef or chicken dumpling, with broccoli and mashed potatoes. It was a detail that, for whatever reason, he would always remember.

They had drawn a substantial crowd, bigger than they'd had in a long time. When the dinner was finished, the club president went to the lectern. There was some business to take care of, a treasurer's report and announcements about one thing and another. Then she paused and looked down at Hutch's table. "As you're aware," she said, "we made a late change in our guest speaker for the evening. We have with us tonight the former director of operations for the Academy of Science and Technology, a woman who has been about as far from home as it's possible to go. Please welcome to the Liberty Club, Priscilla Hutchins."

Hutchins rose to polite applause, exchanged a brief word and a hand clasp with the president, and took her place at the lectern. She nodded to someone in the audience, thanked the club for inviting her, and paused. "It's a pleasure to be here tonight," she said in a clear, casual voice. She had no notes. "Ladies and gentlemen, we all know the interstellar program has gone into eclipse. That hasn't happened because of a conscious decision by anyone. It's simply the result of a reallocation of resources. Which is to say, we don't consider it important anymore. We know, however, that eventually we'll be going back. The question before us now is whether *we* will do it, or whether we plan to leave it to our grandkids."

She looked around the room. Her gaze touched Matt, lingered, and moved on. "Matt Darwin tells me you're community leaders. Businesspeople, lawyers, planners, teachers, doctors. I see my old friend Ed Palmer over there." Palmer was the Alexandria chief of police. Darwin was surprised she knew him. "And Jane Coppel." Jane ran an electronics business in Arlington. She greeted a few other people. Then: "I know, as long as organizations like the Liberty Club exist, the future's in good hands."

That brought applause, and from that point she had them.

"You may have noticed I brought some friends. I'd like you to meet them. Kellie, would you stand, please?"

An African-American woman in a striking silver gown rose. "The lander from the *Bill Jenkins* is on display at the high school. The *Jenkins* is a famous ship. It led the rescue effort at Lookout when an omega cloud arrived and threatened to engulf the nascent civilization there. Kellie Collier"—she nodded toward the woman in the gown—"was its captain."

It was as far as she got. The audience rose as one and applauded. She let them go, then collected another round of applause: "An entire civilization lives today because of her courage and ingenuity."

During those years, everybody'd loved the Goompahs, pretechnological creatures who had gotten their name from their resemblance to popular children's characters. Most speakers at this point would have asked the audience to hold their applause. But Hutchins was too canny for that. She wanted everybody revved up.

Eventually the noise subsided, and Kellie started to sit down, but Hutch asked her to stay on her feet. "Her partner at Lookout," said Hutchins, "was Digby Dunn. Digger to his friends. It was Digger who discovered that Goompahs believed in devils, and that the devils looked a lot like us." The place rocked with laughter, then, as Digger stood, broke into more cheering.

"The gentleman on Digger's right is Jon Silvestri. Jon has been working on an interstellar drive that, we hope, will give us access to the entire galaxy."

Silvestri was reluctant to stand. Digger pulled on him, and the crowd laughed and gave him an enthusiastic hand. They were on a roll and would have cheered anyone at that point.

"Eric Samuels," said Hutchins. "Eric was a major part of the rescue at the Origins Project." Eric stood, waved, smiled. He was moderately overweight, and he looked not at all heroic. More like somebody who'd want to stay out of harm's way.

"The gentleman to Eric's left is Gregory MacAllister. Mac was one of the people who got stranded on Maleiva III a week before it got sucked into a gas giant." MacAllister, a global celebrity on his own, rose to a fresh wave of enthusiasm. "Mac was there because he's never stopped being a good reporter. There were moments, though, when I suspect he wished he'd stayed on the *Evening Star*. I should point out by the way, that the *Evening Star* was stripped a few years back and set in orbit around Procyon. There *is* no *Evening Star* anymore. Nor any ship remotely like it.

"Across from Mac is Randall Nightingale, who was also with us on Maleiva III. I owe Randall a special debt. If it weren't for him, I would not have survived the experience. Ask him about it, and I'm sure he'll tell you anybody would have done what he did. All I'm going to say is that he knows how to hold on to his women."

That brought some wisecracks, and Nightingale waved and grinned. "Somebody that gorgeous," he said, "only an idiot would let go."

"Alyx Ballinger," continued Hutch, "came all the way from London to be with us tonight. She is one of the first people ever to set foot in an alien starship. She'll be appearing in the fall in *Virgin Territory*, which, I understand, will have a run on Broadway before opening at home. Am I right, Alyx?"

Alyx flashed the smile that had won the hearts of two generations of guys. "That's right, Hutch. Opening night is September 17."

"Finally," Hutch said, "the first guy to understand what the omega clouds were, and to engage with them: Frank Carson."

All eight were on their feet now, and the audience was having a good time. People who'd been outside in the lobby and in an adjoining meeting room crowded in to see what was going on. Eventually the place quieted, and Hutch made her pitch for donations. When she'd finished, volunteers moved out among the diners and took pledges while she thanked them for their help, explained how the money was going to be used, and warned them it was a gamble. "But everything worthwhile involves a gamble," she said. "Careers are a gamble. Marriage is a gamble. Think about that first guy to try a parachute. If we wait for certainty, life would be terribly dull."

She thanked the audience, invited them to stay for the party to follow, and turned it back to the president.

MATT HAD A hard time getting near her afterward. When finally he got to her side, he thanked her and told her she should have been a politician. "The way you orchestrated that thing in there," he said, "you'd have gone to the Senate. Easily."

Her eyes narrowed. "Matt, I didn't say anything in there I didn't mean."

"I know that. That's not what I was trying to say."

"Good," she said. "You probably need a drink."

"Bringing your friends was a stroke of genius."

"Thanks. It was Eric's idea." She glanced over at Samuels, who was waving his arms as he described the attack at the Origins Project. "He's a PR guy. He worked for the Academy at the time. Now he helps politicians get elected."

"Oh."

She shrugged.

People had clustered around each of the guests, and he found himself wandering from one group to another. Digger Dunn was entertaining Julie and a few others with a description of unearthing what had appeared to be a television broadcasting station on Quraqua. "We actually had the tapes, but we couldn't lift anything off them."

"How old were they?" asked the superintendent of the Arlington school district.

"Thirteen hundred terrestrial years. Give or take. When I think what might have been on them." He laughed. "An alien sitcom, maybe. Or the late news."

"Maybe a late-night comic," said Julie.

"Listen." Digger became suddenly serious. "We'd have *loved* to know whether their sense of humor matches ours. Whether they even had a sense of humor."

"Is there any reason," Matt asked, "to think they might not?"

"The Noks don't have one," he said. "Other than laughing at creatures in distress." He grinned. "You'd love the Noks."

"It probably explains," said a communications technician, "why they're always fighting with each other."

Alyx Ballinger was talking about *Glitter and Gold*, which she'd produced. Somebody changed the subject by asking her how it had felt to go on board the chindi. "Spooky," she said. "But *good* spooky. I loved every minute of it."

Adrian Sax, the teenage son of a restaurant entrepreneur, asked what was the most alien thing she'd seen.

"The Retreat," she replied.

"I've been there," said Adrian. "It didn't seem all that alien to me. Oversize rooms, maybe. The proportions are a little strange. But otherwise—"

She nodded. "Well, yes. You're right. But it's overlooking the Potomac now. It used to be on a crag on one of the moons circling the Twins. Two big gas giants orbiting each other. In close. You've seen them, right? Three systems of rings. A gazillion moons. You go out and sit in that living room *there*, and you'd feel differently.

"*Remote* doesn't quite do it, you know what I mean? They were a hundred light-years from *anywhere*. People walk around talking about what it means to be alien, and they start describing the physical appearance of the Monument-Makers or how the Goompahs stayed in one part of their world and never spread out. You know what *alien* means to me? Living in a place like the Retreat and not going crazy."

Somebody asked Randall Nightingale about the sea lights on Maleiva III. "According to what I read," he said, "you guys were doing mathematical stuff with something out in the ocean that kept blinking back. Was it a boat?"

"I don't think so," Nightingale said. "It was night, but we still could see pretty well. Neither of us saw anything that looked like a boat." He was referring to MacAllister, who'd been with him that evening.

"So what were you looking at? A squid that could count?"

Nightingale sighed. He was discouraged, not by the question, Matt thought, but by not having an answer. Matt wondered whether people asked him all the time about the lights in the sea.

"We're not ever going to know," he said. "Something more valuable than we'd been aware of was lost when Maleiva III went down."

Matt talked with Frank Carson about that first encounter with the omega clouds. "Hutch figured out it was trying to destroy the lander," Carson said. "That it didn't have anything to do with us personally."

"So what did you do?"

"We landed, got out of it, and ran for the woods." His face shone as he thought about it. "She's also the one who put things together about the omegas," he said. "She's always more or less given me credit for it, but she was the one who discovered the math patterns." He hadn't been young at the time, and a half century had passed. His hair was white now, and he'd gained a little weight, and added some lines around his eyes. But he seemed to grow younger as he thought about those earlier years. "It was a good time to be alive," he said.

WHEN THE EVENING finally ended, and the guests had gone, and the first tallies came in, the Liberty Club was pleased to discover they'd exceeded their objective by a considerable amount. Matt was now in a position to trade a laboratory for the *Jenkins* lander.

"What's wrong, Matt?" asked one of the volunteers. "We couldn't have done much better."

"Just tired," he said. *Just a real estate agent.*

MACALLISTER'S DIARY

Hutch is as persuasive as ever. Pity she can't see reason. The last thing we need is starships. The problems are along the coastlines and in the agricultural areas. Until we get the greenhouse situation under control, this other stuff is a waste of resources. I was embarrassed being there tonight. Still, there was no way I could say no when she asked me to come. And she knew that. Sometimes I think the woman has no morals.

—Wednesday, June 9

chapter 13

MATT BROUGHT IN technicians to inspect the MacElroy High School lander and get it ready for flight. They spent several days working on it, seated an AI and a new antigrav unit, replaced the attitude thrusters, installed a pair of what Jon called Locarno scramblers on the hull, and upgraded life support. When they'd finished, Myra arranged a brief Saturday ceremony. It rained, and they had to move the proceedings indoors. A lot of kids came anyhow. Some media arrived, and that was what Myra cared about. She took advantage of the occasion to comment formally on the proposed state sales tax, which she opposed. She hoped to ride that opposition to the senate. When she'd finished, she summoned Matt to the lectern and formally handed over the keycard. "Bring it back to us, Matt," she said. And everyone laughed and applauded.

The vehicle was scheduled to be delivered to Vosco Labs to be fitted with the Locarno Drive unit. Vosco was in North Carolina, and would have provided a pilot, but Matt couldn't resist delivering it himself. In preparation for the event, he'd renewed his license. He strode out under stormy skies with Jon Silvestri trailing behind. "Got to get my luggage," Silvestri said, peeling off and heading for the parking lot. The attendees came out and gathered under a canopy.

Matt unlocked the vehicle and opened the hatch. He turned, waved to the spectators, and climbed inside. It was like coming home. He slid into the pilot's seat, pushed it back a notch, and started the engine. He did it manually rather than instructing the AI to take care of it. He ran through the checklist. Fuel. Antigravs. Thrusters. Navigation. Everything seemed in order.

Silvestri came back, carrying a bag, and got in. Matt closed her up and locked down the harnesses. "All set?"

"You sure you can fly this thing, Matt?"

He answered by easing her off the ground. The people under the canopy waved, and he cut in the engine and swung around in a long arc toward the south. He didn't have to do that. The lander could have turned on a dime. But he did it anyhow.

HE FELT FIFTEEN years younger as they soared over southern Virginia. "You okay?" Silvestri asked.

"Sure. Why?"

"You look funny."

"Second childhood, Jon."

THEY DELIVERED IT and returned home the next morning. Hutch asked how the test was to be conducted.

"Same as last time," said Jon. "We'll send it out and have it tell us when it gets there."

"Okay," Hutch said. "But if it works—"

"Yes?" said Jon.

"If it works, you'll need a way to retrieve it. The school's going to want it back, right? How are you going to handle that?"

"We'll bring it back the same way it went out," he said. "That's why we have the Locarno."

They were at Cleary's, in the back, with Matt. A piano tinkled show tunes from the previous decade. "Can I make a suggestion?" she said.

"Sure."

"When it comes back, it'll be too far out to return to Union on its own. Unless you're willing to wait a few years. Somebody will have to go get it."

"There'll be plenty of volunteers," said Matt.

"I know. But I suggest you invite Rudy to do it. He'll have the *Preston* available. And I think he'd like to be part of this."

"Hutch, I thought he wanted to keep his distance from us."

"Not really. He was just acting out of frustration. He doesn't want to see the Foundation go under. It's because he's a believer, Matt."

"Okay, I'll ask him."

"Good. He'll be grateful for the opportunity."

VOSCO, WORKING UNDER Silvestri's direction, needed three weeks to complete the job. Silvestri looked irritated when he called Matt to say they were ready to go. *"The techs are all retros,"* he added. *"They swear by the great god Hazeltine. They kept telling me I'd kill myself."*

Matt was in his office, after having spent a futile day showing medical buildings to people who, he now realized, had never been serious. "Maybe you can go back and say hello after we ride the lander to glory."

"Yeah. Let them read about it."

"So we can pick it up tomorrow?"

"They want another day or two to complete certification. Say the end of the week to be safe."

"Okay, Jon. I'll set up a launch date. You have any preferences?"

"Sooner the better."

"All right. Meantime, we'll leave it where it is until we're ready to take it up to the station. We can do that, right?"

"Yes. That's no problem. There'll be a charge."

"That's fine. We can cover it." He called Union Ops, got the watch supervisor, and explained what he wanted.

"Okay," the supervisor said. *"I hope it goes better this time."*

"Thanks."

"I assume you're speaking for the Foundation?"

"It's not involved anymore."

"All right." He was studying a monitor. *"Things are slow. We can do the launch tomorrow if you want."*

"We won't be ready that quickly. We'll need three or four days. Make it four."

"*How about Monday? Around 0900 hours?*"

"Okay. That's good. Can I arrange to have one of the scopes track the lander until it makes its jump? Like we did last time?"

"*There'll be a nominal charge.*"

"Do it."

THE CONTRAST BETWEEN the launch of the *Happy Times* two months earlier and the send-off given to the MacElroy High School lander could hardly have been more stark. The observation area had a decent crowd, but the tension was different. You might have said expectations were low. There was a comedy hour aspect to the proceedings.

Matt invited Hutchins, and she showed up with Rudy, but there were no other VIPs on the scene, no politicians, only one or two scientific observers. There were a few people from the Liberty Club and a delegation from the high school.

The media was represented, but they were primarily there for the sideshow aspects of the event. They were interviewing the kids and their teacher-escorts, and each other. Also on the scene were a few members of the fringe press. These were the guys who specialized in hauntings, scandal, prophecies, and celebrity marriages and breakups. One of them wanted to know whether they'd removed the AI, as Rudy Golombeck had for the earlier attempt. "After all," he said, with a nod to his colleagues, "we wouldn't want to hurt anybody."

They all had a good laugh at Rudy's expense. Pulling the AI had never occurred to Matt. It was after all just talking hardware. But he did feel a bit uncomfortable, now that he thought of it. Well, it was too late.

The questions, this time, were a bit off center. "Even if the lander makes it out to Pluto, do you anticipate the jump would have any negative medical effects on a pilot?"

"If it doesn't work this time, do you plan to try again?"

"Did you know that some people who traveled with the Hazeltine system had a history of bad dreams on their return? Do you think that might happen with this new system?"

"Dr. Somebody had suggested the possibility that the Locarno, after it crumpled the *Happy Times*, took it into another reality. Did Dr. Silvestri want to comment on that possibility?"

When Matt replied that the questions were becoming strange, one reporter, from *Scope*, laughed and said sure they were, but all they wanted was an entertaining answer. *We know nobody takes this stuff seriously.*

"We'll use the same general plan as last time," Jon explained to the crowd. "This time the AI will be running things. It'll take the vehicle out about forty minutes and make the jump. It'll travel 3.7 billion miles, to the orbit of Pluto. And, if all goes well, it'll send a radio signal back."

He sat down in front of one of the viewports. Matt wished him luck.

"It'll be okay," Jon said. "I corrected the problem. This one's going to Pluto."

They got the call from Union Ops at 8:23 A.M. *"Okay, Matt,"* said the watch officer, *"we're ready to go."*

Jon sat back, nothing to worry about, and folded his arms. On-screen, the restraining lines let go and began to withdraw. Attitude thrusters fired. The vehicle moved away from the dock and redirected itself toward the exit. Launch doors opened. The MacElroy High School lander eased out of the station. When it was well away, its engine ignited, and the lander began to accelerate.

Jon took a deep breath. Somebody said, "Here we go."

The onboard AI had been named in honor of Henry Barber. *"All systems in good order,"* Henry said. *"Estimate thirty-seven minutes to transit."*

Matt got fresh coffee for them both. Hutch came over and gave him a calming smile. However things go, it won't be the end of the world. Rudy huddled a few minutes with Jon. A news team from Worldwide moved in and set up.

The display gave them a crisp picture of the lander, as well as the rim of the Moon.

Matt drank his coffee, talked with reporters, talked with people who'd just wandered in to watch, talked with Rudy. Rudy congratulated him for coming up with the idea to use the lander. "Wish we'd thought of it earlier," he said.

Exactly on time, Henry informed them the ship was about to make its jump. *"I will be in touch with you this afternoon,"* he said. *"At seventeen minutes after three. Give or take a few minutes."*

Then it wasn't there anymore. The last thing Matt saw was the MacElroy fourmaster emblazoned on its hull.

Jon pulled the recordings up, and they studied the images during the seconds before transit. The lander remained clear and bright as the time ran down to tenths of a second. They went through it methodically, moment to moment. The lander looked okay. No twisting or collapsing this time. No indication of any problem.

They looked at one another, and Jon ran it again. Slower. Hundredths of a second. And again it simply winked off. Between 76/100's and 77/100's of a second. No bending. No crumpling.

Jon rested his chin on his folded hands. "I think we've got it this time, Matt."

THEY FOUND HUTCHINS seated in the Quarter Moon, talking with a reporter. She introduced him, George Somebody from the *Savannah Morning News*. "I know you needed a vehicle," George was saying, "but whichever one of you folks came up with the idea of using the one at the high school was pure genius. And it's a great way to get students interested in science."

"Here's the guy," said Hutchins, nodding at Matt. "He's been contributing his time to the school off and on for years."

Matt tried not to look too pleased. George asked a few questions, mostly about how the school became involved. "Creative teachers," he said. "And Myra Castle."

"Who?"

"A school board member who cares." He had a hard time delivering that one with a straight face, but he did his best.

"Okay," said George. "Good."

"Something else," said Jon. "We got some kids interested in what we've been doing these last few weeks. If some of them go on to careers in the sciences, maybe that will have been enough."

George turned off his recorder. He looked at Jon and smiled. "You don't really mean that, but I like the sentiment." He thanked them, saw someone else, and hurried away.

Matt turned back to Jon. "That will have been enough? Are you serious?"

"Am I serious?" said Jon. "Listen, Matthew, I want to hear that signal come in at three o'clock. It's all I really care about."

Matt sighed and looked at the overhead. "Whatever happened to simple honesty?"

"It's all PR," said Hutchins. "If we ever produced a person who was unrelentingly honest, everybody would want him dead."

At the far end of the dining room, a bank of clocks showed the time in Tokyo, Paris, Berlin, London, New York, and Rome. Union was officially on GMT, but visitors were free to maintain whatever time zone they wanted. All services operated on a twenty-four-hour schedule. Restaurants could always provide breakfast or dinner or a nightcap.

The Locarno experiment was running on Washington time, where it was just after noon.

They collected more reporters and some MacElroy students, but Jon and Hutchins were both good at dealing with them, so Matt relaxed and enjoyed the show. Hutchins pointed out to several of the kids that "Jon's device" might one day take them to the far side of the galaxy.

One of the kids wondered if we'd ever be able to go to Andromeda.

"Who knows?" she said. "Maybe."

Everyone they met wanted to know whether the Locarno would work this time.

Jon inevitably shrugged his shoulders. "We'll have to wait and see."

THE ORIGINAL PLAN had been to retreat to Matt's room after lunch, but things went so well in the restaurant that, with the encouragement of management, they stayed. People began coming in from the concourse to shake their hands and wish them well. Rudy wandered in and bought a round of drinks.

Janet Allegri called Hutchins to wish her luck. The name struck a chord with Matt, but he couldn't place her until Hutchins explained.

She was part of the original mission that had uncovered the omegas. She'd written a best-selling account of those events.

Strangers asked for autographs, took pictures, introduced their kids.

Matt knew he should have been enjoying himself. But he'd have preferred the good times *after* he was assured of success. This was premature. "Better to do it now," said Hutch, in a moment of cold honesty. "Might not be able to later."

When it got close to three, they broke away and, trailing kids and reporters, went down to the lower deck and made for the observation area. This time there was no plan for an actor's voice announcing good news from Pluto, or whatever the message was to have been. When the transmission arrived, a white auxiliary lamp mounted on the panel would switch on. That would be it.

A small crowd waited. And if the tension had been missing earlier, it was present now. People shook their hands and made way as they entered. One of the kids, seated in Jon's chair, hurriedly evacuated. Others made room for Matt and Hutchins.

The room became quiet, except for whispered comments. *They sure the radio beam has enough energy to get here?*

I don't think I realized Pluto was that far.

Matt's eyes drifted shut. He was tired. Not sleepy. Too rattled to be sleepy, but he had no energy left. He wanted it to be over.

It was 3:03. Fourteen minutes to go. Matt thought how it would be to return the lander to the school after a successful test. He'd circle the school a couple of times and, while a cheering crowd watched, set it down in its accustomed place. Get out and shake everyone's hand.

He held the picture in his head, replaying it, and finally opened his eyes. It was 3:04.

The launch bay was nearly empty. Only two ships were visible. While he stared through the viewport, not even aware he was doing so, somebody took his picture. One of the MacElroy science teachers. "Hope you don't mind," she said. And whispered good luck. A few people hurried through the doors, fearful they were late.

He looked around to see Hutchins watching him. She smiled as their eyes connected. Mouthed the words *Almost there.*

Jon was holding on to his coffee cup, not drinking any of it, just hanging on while his gaze wandered around the room. It swept across Matt, not pausing, not reacting. Whatever facade he'd been using, it was gone now. Only one thing mattered.

Somebody put a hand on his shoulder and squeezed. Julie. She hadn't been there earlier. "Hi, Matt," she said. "Big day, huh?"

There was a fudge factor. No way to be sure precisely how far the lander might have traveled. The signal could be as much as a minute early. Or a minute late. Probably no more than that.

Could be anytime now.

Everybody was watching the signal lamp.

He became aware of a barely audible heartbeat in the deck and bulkheads, rhythms set off by the systems that supplied power to the station.

One of the kids giggled.

A chair scraped.

Jon seemed not to be breathing.

A girl whispered, "Stop."

Then it was 3:17.

Matt looked at the lamp. It was one of several status lights set in a vertical row. Six of them altogether. The one he was watching was four from the top.

Then it was plus thirteen seconds.

Fourteen.

Fifty-two.

He closed his eyes. When he opened them, about a minute later, the lamp was still unlit.

TABLOID ROUNDUP

PSYCHIC SAYS INFERNAL FORCES BLOCKED STAR DRIVE TEST

Josh Coburn, the celebrated psychic from Havertown, PA., said today that dark forces are at work to ensure that humans do not succeed in making long-range penetration into the greater galaxy.

OMEGA CLOUDS MAY BE A HOAX

EDEN FOUND

Former Paradise Now Desert in West Saud
Bones May Have Been Adam's
Scientists to Try DNA Analysis

GHOST OF AI HAUNTS MISSISSIPPI TOWNHOUSE

END OF DAYS NEAR

"All Signs Point to November," Says Harry Colmer

HEAVEN LOCATED

Astronomers Reveal Shocking Photos
Giant Star Cloud on Other Side of Galaxy

JESUS' FACE SEEN ON EPSILON AURIGAE MOON

WOMAN HAS CHILD BY NOK

First Human-Alien Hybrid
Experts Said It Couldn't Happen
Named Kor After Father

HURRICANE MELINDA SENT BY GOD?

Billy Pat Thomas Says Evidence Points to Divine Anger
Church-Going Back Up in Mississippi

ATLANTIS FOUND

VAMPIRE LOOSE IN ALBANY?

Six Victims Drained of Blood
Bite Marks on Throat
Police Baffled

PSYCHIC TREES ON QURAQUA

Branch Patterns Reveal Future, Experts Say

SHOCKING TRUTH BEHIND MURDER OF PREACHER'S WIFE

chapter 14

MATT HAD RESERVED his room at Union, expecting, hoping, to party through the night. Instead he canceled out, said good-bye to Hutchins and Jon, and caught the earliest available shuttle back to Reagan. Some of the students were on board. They wished him better luck next time.

Reyna called him en route. "*Sorry,*" she said.

He looked out the window. The skies over eastern North America and the western Atlantic were clear. "I guess we lost the school's lander," he told her.

"*I guess. But they knew there was a chance that would happen.*"

"I know. Maybe next time we should just send a missile."

"*Is that practical?*"

"I don't know. Probably not."

She didn't say anything for a minute. Then: "*You okay?*"

"Oh, yeah. I'm fine."

"*What will you do now?*"

"Back to my desk at Stern and Hopkins."

"*No, I mean, are you going to give up on the drive?*"

Two kids across the aisle were laughing hysterically at something. "It's not really my call. But unless somebody is willing to donate another lander, yeah, I'd say *my* part in this drill is finished."

Another pause. *"What time are you getting in?"*

"A bit after eight."

"Can I treat for a drink tonight? Meet you at World's End?"

"I appreciate it, Reyna, but it's been a horribly long day. Let's do it tomorrow, okay?"

MATT RARELY ATE at home. He didn't like eating alone, so he usually went to Cleary's or one of the other local restaurants. But not tonight. He picked up a roast beef sandwich at Reagan and took it with him in the taxi. It was a fifteen-minute flight below threatening clouds. As the vehicle descended onto his ramp, rain began to fall. He paid, went inside, said hello to the AI, kicked off his shoes, and turned on the news. There was nothing on the Locarno. Religious warfare was heating up in Africa and the Middle East, and a squabble was developing between the NAU and Bolivia over trade agreements.

He switched to *Loose Change*, one of the season's dumber comedies, but it played just about at the level he needed. He poured a cup of coffee and nibbled his way through the sandwich. Not much appetite.

Jon had been hiding his feelings when they'd said good-bye. He'd thanked Matt and pretended not to be discouraged. There'll be somebody out there, he'd said, who'll be willing to take a chance.

And the truth was, he had less reason to be discouraged than Matt did. Jon could go back to tinkering with the theory. The corporations *would* come forward, and he'd get to try again. But Matt was done. He could expect to spend the rest of his life in northern Virginia, moving town houses, and wondering how things had come to this.

Well, he told himself, at least you have your health.

He could not sleep, so he stayed up, and was watching *Last Train to Bougainville*, a more or less incomprehensible mystery, when the AI's voice broke in: *"I'm sorry to disturb you, sir. But you've a call."* The room was dark except for the blue ring of light emanating from the clock. It was a few minutes short of midnight. *"It's from Union. From Dr. Silvestri."*

No. He was done with it. Didn't want to talk about it anymore. "Just tell him to go away, Basil."

"Are you sure, sir?"

He tried to straighten himself. One of the cushions fell on the floor. "Yes. No. Okay, put him through. Audio only."

"*Yes, sir.*"

"Hello, Jon." Matt rolled over onto his back. His eyes were closed. "What's going on?"

"*Matt.*"

"Yeah."

"*We've got it. It came in.*"

"What came in?" A new pledge of support? An offer of another lander?

"*The transmission.*"

That brought him awake. "The one we were waiting for?

"*You know any others?*"

"What happened? Why the delay? Did the equipment break down?"

"*It must have. We don't know.*"

"*When?* When did you hear it?" He was already annoyed that Jon had been so slow to let him know.

"*A few minutes ago.*"

"You're kidding."

He flicked on the visual. Jon was sitting in an alcove off one of the concourses. He looked tired, relieved, and puzzled. "*Do I look as if I'm kidding?*" he said.

"Good. Great. So the Locarno worked, right? It's out where it's supposed to be?"

"*Matt. We don't know that either.*"

"When *will* we know?"

"*It'll take a while. The only thing I can figure is that the onboard system didn't trigger the radio when it was supposed to.*"

"Yeah," said Matt. "That sounds like what happened."

"*There's another possibility.*"

"What's that?"

"*You remember we talked about uncertainties in the theory? It's why we had the fudge factor in the timing. We weren't sure precisely how far it would go.*"

"Sure."

"*It might have gone a lot farther than we thought.*"

"You mean it might have traveled longer than the six seconds it was supposed to?"

"Maybe. Or it might have stayed with the original program. And covered a lot more ground than we expected it to."

HUTCHINS HAD SPENT the evening with friends and gotten in at about eleven. Her AI commiserated with her, and the house that night felt emptier than usual.

She'd never really put much confidence in the Locarno. It had been a shot in the dark. She'd spent her career with the Hazeltine, and it was hard to accept the idea that there might be a more efficient system. Getting old, she told herself. She'd become resistant to change. But still, going to Pluto in a few seconds was just too much. Nevertheless, she was glad to see someone trying. Even if she doubted the motivation. Jon seemed less interested in providing impetus to the interstellar effort than he did in garnishing his own reputation. She'd heard his claims about doing it all for Henry Barber, and maybe there was some truth to them. But she wondered whether, in his eyes, Henry Barber's significance didn't lie in the fact that he'd provided an opportunity for Jon to make a splash.

Well, however that might be, Jon was a decent enough guy, and maybe even a world-class physicist. There was no way she could judge that. Unless he managed to put something out on the edge of the solar system in about the same time that it took her to get to the kitchen.

She had too much adrenaline flowing to try to sleep, so she grabbed a snack and sat down with a murder mystery. George provided the appropriate musical score, and she was thoroughly caught up in it when Jon called with the news.

JON SILVESTRI'S NOTEBOOK

Thank God.

—Friday, July 13, 11:52 P.M., EDT

chapter 15

IT WAS THE supreme moment of Jon's life. Even the news that Henry Barber found him acceptable, thought he could help the Locarno research effort, paled into insignificance. But there was, of course, no time to celebrate.

Why was the radio signal almost eight hours late? "The lander's pretty old," the watch officer told him, in a tone that suggested it was a sufficient explanation.

"All right," Jon said. "Can I send it a message now?"

The watch officer pushed a press pad and a light went on. "Go ahead, sir."

Where are you, Henry? Jon folded his arms and took a deep breath. "Henry," he said. "Come home. Signal when you get here."

The chief of the watch had been standing off to one side. He was a thin guy with sharp eyes and a pointed brown beard. He'd betrayed no previous reaction, but now he came over and looked down at Jon. He didn't know what to think. "Did it work?" he asked.

"Maybe," said Jon. "We'll see."

Only one of the five stations in the ops center was manned. It had obviously been designed in a more optimistic time.

He called Rudy, woke him out of a sound sleep. He was still in his hotel room. *"So what's going on?"* Rudy asked. *"Why didn't we get the reply this afternoon?"*

"I don't know yet."

"Probably a problem with the wiring. Doesn't matter. We'll figure it out after the lander gets back here. It'll be in when? About five?"

"If it's out near Pluto, yes. Maybe a little closer to six. It would have to recharge before starting back."

"Okay. I'll be down in the ops center."

"I've a suggestion, Rudy."

"Okay?"

"Don't set any alarms. I'll call you if anything happens."

AS HUTCH HAD suggested, Rudy had been delighted to offer the use of the *Preston* to retrieve the lander. Jon had arranged to hire a pilot. But when no signal had been returned, he'd canceled. Now he rescheduled, listened to some grumbling about it being the middle of the night, and how they couldn't make any guarantees about 6 A.M. *"Not going to be easy to find anybody on this kind of short notice."* He said he'd do what he could, but warned Jon there'd be a substantial service fee.

Jon thought about it. He didn't think anything was going to happen at six anyhow. "Let it go," he said. "Can you set it up for tomorrow afternoon?"

The exhilaration that had come with the signal had drained off. He wasn't sure why, but he just wanted the whole business to be over. Wanted to be sure everything was okay. To go out and bring in the lander.

He went back to his hotel room but was unable to sleep. At three thirty he called Union Ops. *"The* Preston*'s ready to go,"* they told him. *"Whenever you are."*

At four, he went down to the Quarter Moon and had breakfast. Coffee, bacon, scrambled eggs, and home fries. He was getting ready to leave when Rudy came in. "Couldn't sleep," Rudy said.

"Me neither."

Rudy settled for coffee. On the far side of the room, a Chinese group was celebrating something. There were speeches and periodic applause.

Rudy started talking about the future of the Foundation. How the Locarno Drive would change everything. Fire up everybody's imagination. Jon said he hoped so. And eventually it was five thirty, and they finished up and went down to the operations center. The same watch officer was on duty. He looked up when they came in. "Nothing yet, Dr. Silvestri," he said.

Of course not. It was still early.

Fifteen minutes later the chief of the watch showed up. He knew Rudy, told him he was glad to see him, and wished Jon good luck.

Jon was glad the place was empty this time. It had been horribly uncomfortable standing in front of all those people, waiting for a transmission that never came. Most embarrassing moment he could remember.

The clock ticked down to 5:58. Zero hour.

And crept past it.

To 5:59.

And five after six.

Rudy glanced at him. His mouth twisted. "It's lost again."

"No," said Jon. "I think we're getting *good* news."

"How," asked Rudy, "could this *possibly* be good?"

Jon considered the question. "Were you planning on going back down today?"

"Yes," he said. "No point staying here."

"Why don't you hang on a bit?"

"Tell me why."

"Change your reservation and stay for lunch," he said. "On me."

"What are you not telling me, Jon?"

"I think you'll want to be here this afternoon."

"Oh," said Rudy. Jon could see his expression change. "It's going to be late again?"

"I think so."

Rudy brightened. "Oh." The lander had made its transit to Pluto, or wherever, at 9:03 A.M. yesterday. Its transmission should have arrived at 3:17 P.M. But it had been almost eight hours late. "The vehicle went farther than we expected."

"I think so."

"A *lot* farther." Jon sat quietly while Rudy looked around for a piece of paper, found a notepad, and started scribbling on it. "The signal came in at, what? Eleven o'clock?"

"11:07."

"So it took a little more than fourteen hours to get here."

"Either that, or the circuitry broke down."

"Fourteen hours. My God. If that's the case, this thing is about *thirty* times faster than the Hazeltine. Jon, that's incredible."

"We don't know the details. It might simply have taken more time to make the jump. But if it did it in six seconds—"

THEY WERE IN the ops center when the transmission came in. *MacElroy lander reports arrival.* It was 1:33. Time for transmission: fourteen hours and a minute.

Almost on the dime.

LIBRARY ENTRY

NEW STAR DRIVE SUCCESSFUL

. . . Took the vehicle almost 9 billion miles from Earth. Early reports indicate that the time needed to cross that distance was six seconds. A normal interstellar vessel, traveling the same distance, would have required two and a half minutes. Silvestri admitted to being surprised at the result, which far exceeded all expectations.

—*Science Today*, July 15

chapter 16

A SECOND TEST went off without a hitch, confirming Jon's conclusions: The Locarno was far more effective than the original calculations had suggested. A Locarno-powered vessel could cross three hundred light-years in a single day. He was, to be conservative about it, happy. Ecstatic. Almost deranged.

He stood beside Rudy in the Foundation's press area, while the director told a group of reporters how everything was now within reach. "The Dragon Cluster and the Omicron and the Yakamura Group." The entire galaxy, filled with hundreds of millions of ancient class-G suns, eight, nine, ten billion years old. Who knew what lay waiting out there?

Speaking invitations came in from around the globe. Overnight Jon had become one of the most recognizable personalities on the planet. Wherever he went, people asked for autographs, took pictures, sighed in his presence. One young woman collapsed in front of him; another wanted him to autograph her breast. He was riding the top of the world.

Corporate entities called. Maracaibo offered its services and support, as did Orion and Thor Transport and Monogram and a dozen others. Their representatives showed up daily, tried to get through his AI. All were interested in helping, as they put it; all came armed with proposals for subsequent testing, licensing agreements, and "long-range mutual-benefit packages." The latter phrasing was from Orion. The agents, who were sometimes executive officers, invariably produced offers that, by Jon's standards, were generous. They wouldn't be on the table forever, they cautioned, and several suggested, supposedly on a basis of *I'm not supposed to tell you this*, that people in their own development sections were working on technologies that, if successful, would render the Locarno obsolete. "Take it while you can get it, Jon."

He filed the proposals, secured his patent, and informed everyone he'd get back to them shortly.

THEY SENT THE lander out a third time, forty-five billion miles, a thirty-second ride, into the Oort Cloud with a chimp on board. The chimp did fine. Henry took him on a cometary tour, took pictures, and returned him to the inner system, where the lander was retrieved by the *Preston.*

And finally it was time to make a run with somebody in the pilot's seat. Hutch maybe. "You think she'd be willing to do it?" he asked Matt. "Does she keep her license current?"

"I have no idea," said Matt. He was in a taxi.

"Okay. I'll give her a call and find out. Keep your fingers crossed."

"There's another option."

"What's that, Matt?"

"I'm current."

"Well, yes, I know that. But I thought you might be a little reluctant about deep-space flight. That's not like bouncing around North Carolina. I mean, with real estate and all, it's been a long time."

Matt looked offended. *"I'd be happy to do it. If you want to take your chances with a guy who specializes in professional buildings and three-story walk-ups."*

Dumb. "You know what I mean, Matt." The taxi was passing through cloud banks.

"Sure." He grinned, and they both laughed.

"Pay's not much," Jon added.

IT WAS, FOR Matt, a magnificent moment. A month or so later, on Tuesday, August 21, 2255, he and Jon, aboard the MacElroy High School lander, which was now world-famous, rode out toward Neptune. The passage took only a few seconds. There was no sign of the planet, which was elsewhere along its orbit. But Henry showed them a dim sun, little more than a bright star at that range, and assured them they'd arrived in the target area. They shook hands and came home. Once again, Rudy and the *Preston* picked them up.

That night they all celebrated in a small, out-of-the-way Georgetown restaurant.

Matt had made the biggest sale of his career a week earlier. It had transferred a large professional building from a collapsing corporation into the hands of a private buyer, and it brought more than six million dollars into the Stern & Hopkins coffers. In addition the buyer was in a position to refurbish the place and turn it into a decent property again. It was the sort of transaction that used to give him a sense of satisfaction, a feeling he'd done something other than turn a buck. But all he could do was laugh at himself. "I'm moving real estate," he told Rudy. "But on weekends I help Jon Silvestri move the world."

The following day, Jon and Matt met for lunch. Jon's treat. "The money's rolling in," he said.

"How?"

"Speaking engagements. Endorsements. Who'd ever have thought anybody would want to pay a physicist to say nice things about sneakers. And a book deal. I don't even have to write the book." They were both still in a giddy mood. "I think it's time to decide what we want to do next."

"Something spectacular," said Matt. "But we still don't have a ship. There's only so much you can do with a lander."

Jon grinned. There was nothing he couldn't control now. "I think it's time we gave the lander back to the school." He leaned closer. "Listen, Matt, I don't think there's any question Rudy would be more than willing now to reconfigure the *Preston*."

"Yeah. I'm sure you're right, Jon."

"Of course I'm right."

"So you're asking me where I'd like to see the next flight go?"

"Yes, I am. What do you think?"

"Jon, that's really your call. My part in all this is over. You don't need *me* anymore. Unless, of course, you'd want me to pilot the ship."

"You'd be willing to do that?"

Matt had not been entirely serious when he made the offer. "It's time to do the heavy lifting, Jon. You might want a professional at this point."

"You telling me you don't think you could do the job?"

"I'm telling you I've been away from it for a long time."

"Okay." Jon shrugged. "Your call. If you want me to get someone else, I will."

"I didn't say that."

"Make up your mind, Matt."

Matt's eyes grew intense. "Yes," he said. "I'd like to do it."

The bot picked that moment to show up and ask if they wanted anything to drink. "Champagne," said Jon.

The bot bowed. *"I'm sorry. We don't serve alcoholic beverages."*

"I know," said Jon. "Matt, what'll you have?"

THERE WERE NO women in Jon's life. At least, none to whom he was emotionally attached. He'd left none behind in Locarno, and had been too busy since he'd arrived in the DC area. The last few months had been dominated by his efforts to make Henry's system work. And by God, it did. He had met his obligation to his mentor, and his only regret was that Henry Barber would never know it.

For the first time since he'd decided that Henry was on the right track, that he had an obligation to finish the research, to make it work, nothing was hanging over his head. He'd never really doubted himself, yet he was finding it hard to believe that it was finally finished. Now there was nothing to do but sit back and enjoy the victory.

He was riding a taxi over the Potomac, knowing life would never be better. He had a speaking engagement almost every day, and this one had been no exception. He'd appeared at the Baltimore Rotary, where everyone was his friend. People asked him how the drive worked and glazed over when he tried to explain. (He'd developed a simple explanation using a house with multiple corridors as an illustration, but it didn't seem to matter.) They told him he was brilliant. It was a great feeling. Hard to stay humble through all this. But he tried, and he wandered through the crowd at the end of each evening, signing autographs and reveling in the attention. People insisted on buying him drinks. They introduced him to their friends. Told him how they'd always thought star travel was too slow. Not that they'd ever been out there themselves, understand. But it was about time somebody had picked up the pace. Interesting women were everywhere. Too many for him to become attached to any single one. So he seldom went home alone, but he could not get past the feeling that, through it all, something was missing.

The Potomac Islands were lit up, and boats rode the river. The taxi let him off at the Franklin Walkway, and he strolled out onto the pier. Retailers were doing a hefty business, selling souvenirs and sandwiches and balloons.

He found an unoccupied bench, sat down, and put his feet up on the guardrail. He owed it all to Henry. And, to a lesser degree, to Matt and Priscilla. He'd already been able to return the favor to Matt. He should find a way to say thanks to Hutchins, as well.

And Rudy.

He stared out at the Potomac.

Everybody wanted to provide a ship now. He had a fleet at his disposal if he needed it.

IN THE MORNING, he called Rudy. "I wanted to run something by you," he said.

"*Sure.*" Rudy looked uncomfortable. He would know that Jon had been swamped by offers. He probably thought the Foundation was out of the bidding now. "*What can I do for you, Jon?*"

"Matt and I were talking about the next step. Does the Foundation want to be included?"

"*Yes.*" No screwing around here. "*Absolutely. What did you have in mind?*"

"We're talking about a long-range flight. Sirius or someplace. So we need a ship."

Rudy was in his office, soft piano music playing in the background. "*You're welcome to the* Preston *if you want it.*"

"I'd like very much to have it."

"*Seriously? The corporates could do better by you.*"

"Are you going to try to talk me into accepting one of their offers, Rudy?"

"*No, no,*" he said. "*Nothing like that. Yes, sure. The* Preston *is yours. But I think I told you we don't have a pilot.*"

"I've got one."

"*Who?*"

"Matt."

"*Matt? Jon, Matt's a real estate agent.*"

"Yeah. Should make a little history."

He let Jon see that he disapproved. Then he sighed. "*Sirius? You're really going to Sirius?*"

"We don't know yet. I'm just talking off the top of my head."

"*Of course.*" He didn't seem to know what to say.

"I've another question."

"*Yes?*"

"Would you want to come along?"

He obviously hadn't been expecting *that*. "*Jon, it's been years, decades since I've been outside the solar system.*"

"Does that mean you don't want to go?"

"*No. Not at all. I'm just not sure what I could do to help.*"

"You don't have to help, Rudy. Just come along. For the ride."

Rudy usually hid his emotions. But he broke into a gigantic grin. "*Sure. Absolutely.*" Then he frowned.

"What's wrong?"

"*We'll have to get more money to overhaul the* Preston *and make the installation.*"

"I don't think money will be a problem. Let's get together and work out the details."

"Okay. Sure." Rudy's eyes glowed. *"Sirius."* He drew the word out, tasting its flavor. *"How long's it going to take to make the flight? We leave in the morning, get there for lunch?"*

J ON, FEELING VERY much the man in charge, called Hutch and told her what they were planning. "We wanted to invite you to come with us. If you'd like."

She smiled, a little wistfully, he thought. *"No, thanks, Jon. You guys go ahead. Have a big time. Make it work."*

R UDY WASTED N O time getting the word out to the Foundation's supporters. Contributions poured in. It became a tidal wave.

Meantime, Jon led a team of engineers onto the *Preston*, and they began replacing the drive unit. Rudy also arranged to upgrade the passenger quarters.

At Stern & Hopkins, Matt informed Emma that he would be piloting the Locarno mission, and arranged to take a leave of absence. She was not happy. "If this drive unit is going to take you out there, wherever that is, so quickly," she asked, "why do you need a leave of absence? Just take a few vacation days."

Normally, one did not embrace the boss. On this occasion, Matt made an exception. "Emma," he said, "we may be gone a bit longer than that."

"Oh."

He didn't put it in words, but she understood. Sirius would be just the beginning. Not much more than another test run.

And, finally, there was Reyna.

"After this is over," she asked, "what do you plan to do?" They were having dinner at their favorite restaurant, Culbertson's, on Massachusetts Avenue.

There was no way to soften it for her. "Don't know," he said. "But I suspect we'll be going out again."

She nodded. Smiled. Didn't ask how long the follow-up voyage might take. Didn't ask whether he wanted her to wait. Tried, not entirely successfully, to look like the good soldier. Good luck to you. See you when you get back. Take care of yourself.

Maybe her feelings for him were stronger than he'd realized.

At the end of the evening, when she kissed him, her cheek was wet.

And she let him go.

There were a couple of occasions after that for which he invited her to lunch or dinner, but she explained she was busy. Another time, Matt.

He didn't see her again until the *Preston* was ready to go, and she showed up at the Foundation's farewell luncheon. He didn't even realize she was there until, when he was leaving with Priscilla Hutchins and one of the board members, she simply appeared standing off to one side. She smiled through the moment and formed the words *Good luck* with her lips. Then, before he could get to her, she was gone.

LIBRARY ENTRY

SUPERLUMINAL READIES FOR HISTORIC FLIGHT

Work has been completed to prepare the *Phyllis Preston* for a flight that may change the way we think about our place in the universe. The mission will employ the Locarno propulsion system, which is far more efficient than its predecessor. It's scheduled for a mid-September departure. The destination has not yet been announced, but officials close to the Prometheus Foundation, which is underwriting the effort, are saying the ship will travel to Sirius.

Sirius is 8.6 light-years from Earth. A one-way flight, using the Hazeltine technology, would require slightly more than 20 hours. The *Preston* expects to make it in about 40 minutes.

—Worldwide News Service, Thursday, August 23

chapter 17

WHEN JON AND his collaborators started talking about a target for the first flight out of the solar system, they'd considered Alpha Centauri and Procyon as well as Sirius. Somewhere close. But as the work on the *Preston* neared completion, they began to think in terms of spectacle. Why settle for something on the tour routes?

"Let's go deep." Later, nobody could remember who'd originally said the words, but it became their mantra. *Let's go deep. Let's not screw around. Let's head outside the bubble.*

The deepest penetration to date had been 3,160 light-years by the *Patrick Heffernan*, three decades earlier. Nobody went out that far anymore. Nobody even went close.

When Rudy mentioned it to Hutch, she shook her head. "Not a good idea."

"Why not? Why mess around?"

"What happens if you go for a record, and there's a problem? Nobody would be able to reach you for nine or ten months."

They were at Rudy's town house, enjoying the pool with Matt, Jon, and a half dozen other friends. Rudy was always a bit more bombastic at the town house. "We used to make flights like that all the time," he said.

"That was during an era when we had missions all over the place. If something broke down, there was always somebody reasonably close. That's not the case anymore."

Rudy went into his I-wish-you-had-a-little-more-faith-in-us mode. "There won't be a problem," he said.

Matt would have liked to sell the guy some property. "She's right, Rudy. I mean, if she weren't, why would we need to run a test at all?"

In the end, with everyone either showing or pretending disappointment, they settled for Alioth.

The third star in from the end of the Dipper's handle, it was eighty-one light-years from Earth. It would make a fair test without putting them at unnecessary risk.

LATER THAT AFTERNOON, Rudy got a call from C. B. Williams, a Worldwide executive. "*Rudy,*" he said, "*we'd like to send someone along on the flight. Give you some decent news coverage.*"

Rudy thought about it and decided it seemed like a good idea. "Okay," he said. "We can make room for him. Or her."

"*Good. We're talking about Antonio Giannotti. He'll represent the entire pool.*"

Antonio Giannotti. Where had Rudy heard the name before?

"*He's our science reporter,*" said Williams.

No. It wasn't that. Rudy knew the name from somewhere else.

"*Thirty years ago, on the Black Cat, he was Dr. Science. Did a show for kids.*"

Yes! Dr. Science. Rudy had grown up watching Dr. Science explain how gravity worked, and what climatologists were trying to do to compensate for changing weather patterns. He'd radiated so much enthusiasm about his various topics that Rudy had known by the time he was eight that he would give his life to the sciences. "Yes," he said. "We'd enjoy having him along."

THEY WERE WELL past the era during which summer in the nation's capital provided some cool days in September. Early fall remained hot in Virginia and Maryland, and Matt was happy to be getting away from it.

He took the shuttle from Reagan the day before their scheduled departure. Rudy was on the same flight, and he was like a kid. He kept talking about how he'd been looking forward to this his whole life, and that he still couldn't believe it was happening. He extracted a promise from Matt that, as soon as they'd gotten checked into their hotel, they'd go down and inspect the *Preston*.

The flight to Union lasted less than ninety minutes. When they docked, Matt led the way out, walking with studied casualness, as if he did this sort of thing all the time.

An AI informed them of their room numbers, and their baggage showed up a few minutes after they did. Matt would have preferred to shower and change, but Rudy was anxious to go. So they went.

The *Preston* wasn't much to look at. It had been in service too long. It was battered by two many chunks of rock and scored by cosmic dust. A pair of devices that resembled scanners had been added to the bow. These were scramblers, which would manipulate the space-time continuum, drive a wedge into it, and allow the ship to slide between dimensions.

The words PROMETHEUS FOUNDATION were emblazoned on the hull, with the organization's symbol, a lamp and flame. "It's appropriate," said Rudy, looking through a twenty-foot-wide portal.

"What is?" asked Matt.

"Prometheus. The fire-bringer."

Jon appeared at the main hatch, waved, and came up the tube to the concourse. He was all smiles. "Good to see you guys," he said. "Matt, I think you're going to like your new ship."

"Is it ready to go?" Matt asked.

"They're still tightening a few bolts and whatnot. But yes, it's all set."

"Can we take a look?" asked Rudy.

"Sure." Jon stood aside to let Rudy enter the tube first.

"Beautiful ship." Rudy's eyes literally *bulged*. The tube was transparent, and they could look out at the docking area. The *Preston* was secured to magnetic clamps.

Only one other ship was in port. The place was designed to service eighteen.

"Time was," said Matt, "it would have been filled."

Rudy produced an imager. He took pictures of the *Preston*, pictures of Matt and Jon, handed the device to Matt and posed with Jon for more pictures. "I've been up here a good bit," he said. "Even been inside the *Preston* a few times. But this is different."

Matt clapped him on the shoulder, and they went through the hatch into the ship. Matt had already been on board during the refitting. He'd familiarized himself with the controls, gotten on first-name terms with Phyllis, the AI, and was anxious to launch.

Rudy strode onto the bridge and sat down in the pilot's chair. "Nice feeling," he said.

Matt agreed. He felt fifteen years younger.

Rudy pressed his fingertips against the control board. "How long did you say it was going to take to get there?"

"To Alioth?" asked Jon.

"Yes."

"Five and a half hours."

"My God, I still can't believe it. It used to take"—he consulted his notebook—"more than a week."

Matt had been there once, years ago. "Eight days," he said, "two hours, eleven minutes in transit."

Rudy was enjoying himself. "How long would it take us to get to Alpha Centauri?"

"About twenty minutes," said Matt. "A little less, probably."

MATT WAS TOO excited to sleep that night. He was up at about five, took almost two hours for breakfast, talked to some reporters, had coffee with Rudy in Cappy's, talked to more reporters, and called Jon, who was with the technicians. "If they aren't finished yet," Matt remarked, "it's not a good sign."

But Jon was in the best of moods. "*It's not their fault,*" he said. "*You're never really finished calibrating something like this.*"

Antonio Giannotti wandered into the restaurant. Matt recognized him immediately, would have known him even if Rudy hadn't alerted him he was coming. He was a muscular guy, average height, with a craggy face and the sort of beard favored by mad scientists. He looked bigger on the HV. Originally from Rome, he'd run the Dr. Science show from there, where he'd played his role wrapped in a white lab coat. He didn't look much older than he had in those days. Rudy waved him over, introduced him, and Matt felt a bit awed in his presence.

What had happened to Dr. Science? One year, when Matt was about thirteen, he just suddenly wasn't there anymore.

"It was a job with no future," Antonio said. "I had nowhere to go from there."

"I would have thought you could have done anything. You were great."

"The science was great. *I* wanted to be a comedian."

Matt could still recall his disappointment when Dr. Science disappeared. Along with his discovery he couldn't hit a decent curveball, it had marked what he thought of as his arrival at the beginning of adulthood. Being a teen, he would think later, wasn't all hormones and good times. There were some losses. Inevitably, there were always losses.

More reporters arrived, from the *Post* and *Nature*. He and Antonio were talking with them when Hutch called. *"Where are you, Matt?"*

"Cappy's," he said.

"Save me a seat."

A few minutes later she walked in. The *Post* and *Nature* didn't recognize her. "My understanding," said the *Post*, "is that the drive system is not only much more efficient, but it's safer than the Hazeltine. Is that true?"

"It's less complex. Fewer things can go wrong."

"How close was Barber to solving these issues?" asked *Nature*. "Does he get the credit? Or is it Jon Silvestri who did the brute work?"

Time was, Matt thought, *Hutch would have been the center of attention. Yesterday's news.*

"One of them, the guy with the muscles," Matt told her, "is making the flight with us. He's a pool reporter."

"Good. Publicity never hurts." She turned those dark eyes on him. "Matt, I wanted to come by to wish you luck."

"Jon tells me you don't want to come."

"Yeah. I'm a little busy."

"But not too busy to run up here?" She was silent. He let it play out. Then: "Wish you were coming?"

"Don't tempt me," she said.

"We have room."

"I didn't bring my gear."

"What gear? We'll be back tonight."

"Matt, I'd love to, but—"

"But what? You have anything pressing to do today or tomorrow?" He could see some sort of internal struggle going on.

"Not really. I just—"

"Yeah?"

"—don't—"

"—don't what?"

"I promised myself I wouldn't do this again."

"Why?"

She hesitated. "My family, I guess."

"Aren't your kids both away at school?"

"Yes."

"Not that it matters. You'll be home tonight if you want to make the late run down to Reagan." Matt paused, then added, "And we make the world's best return jump." After they arrived insystem, they'd still have to use the main engines to come the rest of the way in. It could take a while.

"Alioth and back in a few hours."

"Yes." Matt couldn't resist a broad smile. "Welcome to the new world, Priscilla."

LIKE MATT, SHE'D made a flight to Alioth once, years ago, hauling a team of researchers. When they got there, they'd spent three weeks insystem. The three weeks hadn't been bad, because the researchers were busy taking temperatures and charting orbits, leaving her to read and watch shows. It had been painful nonetheless. That crowd, the Alioth crowd, had been hopelessly dull, and they'd spent much of their time trying to impress her. It hadn't helped that she herself had been quite young then, just starting her career, and not very bright.

That had been the mission during which an additional star had been discovered in the system. It had been a big event, setting the researchers into a celebration that had gone on, in one form or another, for several days. She'd been dismissive of it, informing one of them that it wasn't as if there was a shortage of stars. It turned out that the discovery accounted for a series of orbital anomalies. It meant little to her. In those days she was hard to impress. Probably every bit as dull as the researchers.

Hutch had been unable to resist attending the *Preston* launch. Years ago, after she'd made her last flight, on the *Amirault*, she'd promised herself that she would not go back into space. She'd never been sure why she'd done that. Maybe the knowledge that her days in the superluminals had ended was too painful, and she'd wanted to pretend it didn't matter. In any case, she'd kept her vow. Had even resisted a vacation aboard *The Evening Star* when Tor had wanted to treat her.

If I go out there, I'm not sure I'll be able to come back.

Well, that was a bit over the top, but there was a modicum of truth to it. Still, she ached to do it again. To cruise past Canopus and touch down on Achernar II and glide through the rings at Deneb V. (Deneb, at approximately twenty-six hundred light-years, had marked the farthest she'd ever been from home. She'd *loved* that flight.)

And she was sorry she'd declined Jon's offer. Wouldn't admit it to herself, but she stood looking into Matt's eyes, knowing she'd regret it forever if she didn't go. Why not? Charge off for the day. Be back tonight.

She'd have to buy a change of clothes. Maybe a few other items. But why the hell not?

AN HOUR LATER, she worked her way through a mob of reporters and cameramen and well-wishers and walked onto the *Preston* with Matt. Jon laughed at her and said how he knew all along she'd break down and come. She put her gear away and sat down next to Antonio in the common room while Jon and Matt chatted on the bridge. That was where she really wanted to be, but she made up her mind to let them do whatever they had to do and give Matt a clear field. Last thing he'd need would be an ex-pilot hanging around. "So," she said, looking for a topic, "what makes a good reporter, Antonio? What's your secret?"

"Unbending intelligence and integrity." Antonio smiled. "My mother always thought I was a natural."

He was easy to like. Especially when he asked whether she wasn't the woman who'd saved everybody's ass at that Deepsix thing, when that entire world had been swallowed? She really couldn't take credit for that, and she suspected he knew that, but it was nice to hear him say it anyhow.

Jon took her back to the engine room to look at the Locarno. It was just a pair of black boxes, much smaller than the Hazeltine enabler. He explained how it worked. She'd listened to the explanation before, hadn't understood it then and didn't understand it now. But the reality was she'd never figured out how the Hazeltine had worked either. You punched a button, and you slipped between the dimensions. That was about as clear as it got.

When they returned to the common room, she could hear Matt going through his preps with Phyllis, the AI. "You miss being up front?" Antonio asked.

"I've been away from it too long," she said. "You wouldn't want to ride in this thing if I were at the controls."

Antonio grinned at her, and at Jon. "These things don't really need pilots anyhow, do they? I mean, don't the AI's handle everything?"

"The AIs handle everything," she said, "as long as there's no problem. If something goes wrong, you'll be glad you have Matt up there."

"Well, yeah." He made a face as if she were running an old story past him. "How often does something go wrong?"

He offered her a grape juice. She took it and sat back. "It happens all the time. Research missions, particularly. The physicists like to go in close. Usually as close as they can until something blows up. And there are unexplained bursts of energy in hyperspace that sometimes penetrate the shielding and knock out equipment."

"But of course"—Jon looked in on them from the bridge—"we won't be traveling in hyperspace anymore. Not with the Locarno."

"Ah, yes," she said. "The dimension we'll be traveling through. What's its name?"

"We haven't given it one yet."

"You'll want to do that before we get home, or Antonio here will do it for you. Won't you, Antonio?"

"I already have a name for it," he said. "I suggest we call it Giannotti space."

Matt announced over the allcom they were ready to go. *"Priscilla,"* he added, *"would you like to sit up front?"*

She looked at Antonio and Jon. "Anybody else want to do it?"

"Go ahead," said Jon. "Enjoy yourself."

She took a long pull from the grape juice and strode onto the bridge, feeling young again, feeling as if she could do anything. She took the right-hand seat, the observer's seat, and, while Matt talked to Union Ops, she activated the harness. It slid down around her.

Matt finished and looked her way. "Welcome back," he said.

Yes. At that moment, Hutch was in love with the world.

Matt activated the allcom. "Everybody belt down," he said. "Phyl, start the engines." Then to the allcom again: "We are three minutes from departure."

She felt the familiar vibration as additional power came online. "How does the Locarno work?" she asked him. "We still need a running start, right?"

Matt was a good-looking guy, with red hair and a mischievous smile offset by intense eyes. He reminded her of Tor, but she wasn't sure why. Maybe it was the innocence. Matt was a guy who still believed in things. In a decaying society, wracked by too much leisure, corruption in high places, a crippled environment, and God knew what else, there weren't too many like that. The assumption had always been that if people are well fed, feel secure, and have decent homes, everything will be fine. But they needed something else as well. Call it self-respect or a sense of purpose. Whatever, it was missing now. Maybe spreading out through the galaxy would provide it, maybe not. But she was convinced that if the human race simply settled onto its collective front porch, as it seemed to be doing, it had no future.

She didn't think it was a coincidence that nobody was producing great holos anymore. The ones that everyone remembered, *Barcelona,*

Bugles at Dusk, Icelandik, and all the rest were from the previous century. The same was true of drama, the novel, architecture, sculpture. Civilization as a whole seemed to be in decline.

She had loved Tor, and missed him every day. He'd made his living as an artist, but she knew his ability was only moderate. Nobody was going to be naming museums and schools after him. That hadn't mattered: She hadn't loved him for his talent. But the hard truth was there weren't any great artists anymore. She didn't know why, and couldn't connect it to the general malaise that had settled across the planet. Maybe somebody somewhere knew what was happening. *She* didn't. Maybe life had become too easy in too many places, and too pointless in too many others. Maybe it was just that old business that you had to wait a century to sort out who was great and who wasn't. Whatever it was, her instincts screamed that it was the same process. That humans were designed to do what they'd always done: climb into their canoes and move out across uncharted seas. Whether those seas were philosophical or physical, she thought they had to do it.

"Yes," Matt said, "we still need a running start. Not as long as we did with the Hazeltine. Maybe twenty minutes or so to build up a charge."

"It feels good to be back, Matt."

He looked at her. Nodded and smiled. Union Ops broke in with information about solar activity. It wouldn't affect them, but they shouldn't linger insystem.

They were at two minutes. Support lines began disconnecting, withdrawing into the dock. She felt a mild jar as the magnetic locks turned them loose.

Matt eased the ship into its exit lane, adjusted the artificial gravity, took them past the series of docks, and moved out through the launch doors. "Still a nice feeling," she said.

"Yeah, it is. Beats hustling condominiums."

Earth, blue and white and endlessly lovely, spread out below them. A sliver of moon floated off to port. Toward the end of her piloting career, she hadn't much noticed such things. Stars and worlds had become navigational objects, markers in the night and not much more. That was when she'd realized it was time to do something else.

But seated on the bridge, as Matt increased thrust and they began to move out, she felt she'd come home at last.

AS THE *PRESTON* accelerated, they traded a few quips. You're sure the drive works? We're not going to come out of it with our brains scrambled, are we? "If the monkey could make it," Matt said, "we should be fine."

Matt had a taste for music, and he asked whether she objected, then brought up Beethoven. The *Pathétique*. It was pleasant, and fit the mood.

"What happens during the jump?" she asked.

"Not much. It's not like hyperspace. The mists are gone. The sensors pick up nothing. It's just unbroken darkness."

Hutch looked out through the viewport. No moving lights anywhere. There was a time that something was always coming or going at Union. The station had been the center of traffic to a dozen regular ports of call and literally hundreds of star systems. It had been filled with tourists, some coming simply to see the station itself, others boarding one of the tour liners for the voyage of a lifetime.

People still came to look on Earth from orbit, and to spend a weekend, to give their kids a completely different experience. And maybe they came, most of all, so they could say they'd been there. Gone to the top of the world.

The station fell behind.

They came to the end of the *Pathétique* and moved on to something else. The music began to run together.

Matt opened the allcom: "Six minutes to insertion, guys," he said. And to Hutch: "Has Rudy ever done a jump before?"

"He's been out a couple of times," she said.

"Okay. Antonio's pretty well traveled. Says he's been everywhere."

"That takes in a fair amount of ground."

"He's the science reporter for WorldWide. I'd expect him to have gotten around."

Hutch asked Phyl to produce a file of Antonio's work. It matched what she already knew. Antonio did his science straight. No editorializing, though he was capable of getting excited. He'd been with the *al*

Jahadi when it discovered the sun's brown dwarf companion. He'd gotten to Nok right after Kaminsky had started his war against bureaucratic indifference and taken his stand. She felt guilty about that because she'd been one of the bureaucrats who thought that keeping hands off an alien society was a good idea no matter what they were doing. But Antonio had gotten the public on board, just as they'd gotten on board when the Academy moved to save the Goompahs.

It looked as if they were carrying the right journalist.

"Thirty seconds," said Matt.

At 11:48 A.M., Washington time, they made their jump. Hutch was looking at the moon when it vanished.

TRANSITION WAS ALMOST seamless. She was accustomed to a mild queasiness during transits. But this time there was only a momentary pressure in her ears, as if the atmosphere had given her a quick squeeze. Then the sensation was gone, and she was looking out at the utter darkness Matt had described.

"Everybody okay back there?"

"We're fine," said Jon. *"Transition complete?"*

"It's done. Welcome to"—he made a face—"wherever. Jon, you're going to have to come up with a name for this place."

"We'll name it for Henry."

"Barber space?" said Matt. "I don't think it'll work."

"Yeah. I suppose not. Well, we'll figure it out later. Okay to release the belts?"

"Go ahead," he said. "Anybody hungry?"

It was lunchtime.

NEWSDESK

STARSHIP TESTS NEW DRIVE

The *Phyllis Preston* left the Union orbiter minutes ago en route to Alioth, eighty-one light-years away. What makes this flight a bit different is that, if all goes well, they'll be back this evening.

We watched the ship disappear out of the night sky. There's no way to be sure that everything is going as planned because there will be no communication with the *Preston* until it returns. Starships customarily use a device they call the hyperlink, which provides faster-than-light transmissions. But the *Preston,* if the new drive unit is working as it should, would far outrun a hyper-link transmission. So we'll just have to wait and see.

—Jack Crispee, on *The Jack Crispee Show,*
Tuesday, September 18

chapter 18

FIVE AND A half hours to Alioth. It was unthinkable.

Antonio couldn't stop talking about it. Hutch seemed struck by how different the transdimensional flight *looked*, how the mists were gone, how the navigation lights had simply reached out into the night until they faded whereas now they seemed smothered by the darkness. Jon was going on about what Henry Barber had missed, and what a pity it was he hadn't lived just a bit longer.

With the success of the first lander flight, the world had assumed that Rudy controlled the Locarno. And that perception had intensified when word got out that the first manned flight would be made by the Foundation's lone ship, the *Phyllis Preston*. Rudy had been getting calls for weeks from people who had a special black hole they wanted to see, or a nebula with a peculiar characteristic, or who wanted to go to the center of the galaxy. Several had even wondered about the prospects for an intergalactic flight.

Avril Hopkinson, from Media Labs, had asked about the Locarno's range, had suggested they start designing ships specifically for the drive system, instead of just tacking it onto existing vessels. Media Labs, he said, would be willing to undertake the expense.

It had been a glorious time for him. He'd played the chief executive, cautioning against extravagant plans, let's just take this one step at a time, I'll get back to you if we start thinking about going in that direction.

The people who were calling him now, trying to climb onto the bandwagon, were by and large people who had not noticed the Foundation over the past fifteen years. They'd seen Rudy as a person of no consequence, a guy fighting to hold on to the past. A man with no imagination, no sense of where the real priorities lay. Someone not to be taken seriously.

It had given him a rare sense of pleasure to put the world on hold. I'll call you if I need you.

It occurred to him he was being small-minded. Even vengeful. But that was okay. Small-minded could be good. Better to think of it as justice.

RUDY HAD NEVER been successful with women. For some inscrutable reason, he did not arouse their passions. Even his wives had seemed always to regard him as a comic figure. He was a guy a woman could confide in, could exchange stories with. They seemed impressed by his accomplishments, but not by *him*. He had no trouble getting dates, but nobody ever seemed to connect with him emotionally. Even his most recent wife had, somehow, been a remote figure. They'd parted amicably. Old buddies.

He was a good friend. A nice guy.

It wouldn't be correct to say he'd been leading a lonely existence, but since he'd become an adult, he'd never shared an intense relationship with another human being. His life had been marked with a desire to distance himself from other people. As a kid he'd dreamed of living one day on an island. Or on a mountaintop. Somewhere inaccessible.

It was ironic that someone with his sensibilities, and his passions, had not traveled widely beyond the Sun's immediate neighborhood. He allowed people to believe he had. Didn't outright lie about it, but didn't deny it either. In a sense, he *had* done a lot of traveling, but most of it had been virtual. Or with books.

There'd been opportunities. His specialty was stellar life cycles, and he'd gotten invitations from both Jesperson and Hightower when they were setting out, years ago. But he was young then and did not want to spend six or seven months inside a ship, cloistered with the smartest people in their various disciplines. He wouldn't be able to get away from them, and he knew he lacked depth and didn't want to be exposed. His mentor at the time told him he needed to believe in himself, but he couldn't do it, wasn't going to sit cooped up with MacPherson and Banikawa and the rest, talking about shadow matter and negative energy and neutral spin. He had plenty of time to go out to the stars later. Then, suddenly, it wasn't there anymore.

When he became director of the Foundation, he'd thought about going with one of the missions. Something to establish his credibility. (They'd had *three* ships at one time.) But it didn't look right. People would have thought he was taking advantage of his position. So he'd stayed back while the researchers went.

It wasn't as if he'd never before been in a ship. He'd gone to a couple of the nearby stars. Had traveled to Iapetus to see Saturn close up. And to see the monument. But it wasn't the same as going deep, as setting down on a world that was home to a different biosystem. As being so far from home that when you looked through a telescope at the sun, at Earth's sun, you knew you were seeing it as it had looked before you were born. *That* was traveling.

Now, of course, if all went well, they'd be able to go the next step. So far away that the sun, if you could see it at all, would appear as it had been before the first pyramids had gone up. Before Baghdad.

Before Gilgamesh.

NEWSDESK

SAN FRANCISCO EARTHQUAKE 100 YEARS AGO TODAY
Third Major Quake Marked End of Fabled City
Ceremonies Planned at Memorial and White House

CAPABILITY TO PREDICT QUAKES STILL FAR OFF
Some Maintain It Will Never Be Possible

CULVERSON NAMED YEAR'S BEST POLITICAL CARTOONIST
Wins Shackleford Award Second Year Running

NEW YORK LEVEES TO BE REINFORCED

HURRICANE ROMA TURNS NORTH
Hatteras Watches
Season's 18th Major Storm

LAST SLAUGHTERHOUSE CLOSES
Nanoburgers Too Much for Cattle Industry

AMERICAN SCHOOLS STILL RANK LOW
Test Scores in English, Math Weak
"Get Parents Involved," Says Snyder
"Read to Your Kids"
Studies Show Parents Should Start When Kids Are Two

CHURCHES SPLIT OVER CLONING ISSUE
First Human Clones to Appear in Germany
Do They Have Souls?

VIRGIN APPARITION CLAIMED IN DUST CLOUDS
Mary's Likeness Reported 6000 Light-Years Away
Telescopic Images from Ballinger Cloud

MOVEMENT TO BAN ALCOHOL GAINS STRENGTH
Prohibition Again?

POPULATION GAINS CONTINUE FOR CENTRAL
AND MOUNTAIN STATES
People Feel Safer Away from Coastlines, Quake Zones
Trend Expected to Continue
Kansas Now Has More People Than Florida

NEW FOREST FIRES IN COLORADO
Long Dry Spell Creates Hazard
Campers Asked to Exercise Caution

TANAKA LANDS IN KENTUCKY AFTER 16 DAYS
Completes Round-the-World Hot-Air Balloon Flight
Misses Record by Seven Minutes

chapter 19

ALIOTH IS A white class-AO sun. Its formal name is Epsilon Ursae Majoris. Eighty-one light-years from Arlington, it didn't exactly equate to going deep, but it was far enough. And they'd be within striking distance of help should something go wrong.

Alioth is about four times as wide as Sol, and more than a hundred times brighter. It's large for a class-A, and consequently has been burning hydrogen at an accelerated rate. It is now near the end of that phase of its existence, and will soon enter its helium-burning phase. For that reason it had been visited several times by Academy ships studying the decline of class-A stars.

Seventeen worlds orbit Alioth, one of which, Seabright, is unique in that it's the only known planet entirely covered by water. It's perfectly located in the middle of the biozone, but it has produced not so much as a single living cell.

The recently discovered companion star is a dull class-G orbiting at a range of almost a light-year.

AS THEY CAME out of jump status, Klaxons sounded. Collision alert. Matt barked a *goddam* and froze while Phyl activated the ship's defensive systems and fired a series of particle beams at *something*.

"*Rock,*" she said.

It exploded directly ahead and to starboard. The detectors should have picked it up and canceled the jump. "They may not be properly correlated with the new system," said Jon. "I hadn't thought about that."

"Nice reflexes, Phyl," said Matt. He was embarrassed.

"*That's what you can expect with a top-of-the-line model.*"

Antonio had urged that Jon should be first to speak on arrival, and that he think of something historic to say, a timeless remark that would not only play well during the newsbreaks, but that people would always remember as signaling the first shining moments of the real interstellar age. But that moment had also been blown away by Phyl's particle beams. "*I don't think the profanity works,*" he said over the allcom. "*Can we just rewrite the moment?*"

"Not without breaking the law," said Matt. "It went into the log."

"*So we've got* goddam *as our* giant leap *comment?*"

"I'm sorry, Antonio."

He shook his head. "*Make your apology to history,* compagno."

A BLINDING SUN dominated the sky. Matt activated the viewport filters. They helped.

"Too close," said Rudy. "It's not as precise as a Hazeltine."

Jon apologized and said he'd figure it out in time. They told him it didn't really matter, not now. "Time to make it official," said Rudy. He climbed out of his chair and disappeared in back. He returned a minute later, brandishing glasses and a bottle of French champagne.

They recorded the TOA, 1723 hours ship time. Transit time, five hours, thirty-five minutes, seventeen seconds. Matt printed a copy of the log entry, along with his unfortunate remark, and they all signed it. Jon Silvestri. Priscilla Hutchins. Rudy Golombeck. Antonio Giannotti. Matthew Darwin.

"So now that we're here," said Antonio, "what's next?"

"I take it we're not very close to Seabright," Hutch said.

Matt shook his head. "I doubt it." She smiled back at him, two pilots exchanging an unspoken understanding. It's big out here. Brand-new propulsion system. Lucky we got close to the star at all.

It was good to be back. Matt gazed out at the stars, thinking how there was no career like it. "Phyl," he said, "how far are we from Seabright?"

"*Two hundred thirty-six million kilometers, Matt. Ten days by standard drive.*"

"Can't we do better than that?" asked Antonio, with a smile.

"I think it might be possible." Matt grinned.

"I've never seen Seabright," said Antonio.

Despite his claims, Matt doubted Antonio had seen much of anything out of the ordinary. The journalists had usually traveled the standard routes. They were rarely found with the exploration missions.

Jon nodded. "Doesn't seem as if we should come all the way out here and not see the sights." He glanced at Matt. "Why don't we take a look?"

"Sure." Matt nodded. "Okay by me. We'll have to kick the pony a bit to recharge. Figure a half hour. I'll let you know when we're ready."

HUTCH SPENT THE time thinking what it would mean if the Locarno could be made to work with real precision. Travel across the solar system in seconds. She wondered if there might be a groundside application? Climb onto a train in Boston and step off an eye blink later in Los Angeles. Or Honolulu. Possibly even private vehicles doing the same thing? She wasn't sure she'd want to live in such a world. She liked riding the glide trains, liked cruising through the skies over DC. The whole point of travel was, after all, the ride and not the destination. Like people's lives.

She was engaged in a conversation with Antonio about the state of the world, and the tendency of the general public to pay little attention until conditions deteriorated severely, when Matt announced they were ready to make their jump.

Jon had replaced her up front, tinkering with the settings. "*I don't want to go in too close,*" he said. "*We can't trust the mass detector.*"

That sounded a little too casual for Hutch. She'd have felt more comfortable if *she* were at the controls.

Matt's voice came over the allcom. *"Buckle in."*

She activated her harness. Antonio's belt locked him down.

"Ten seconds," said Matt.

Antonio's eyes slid shut. He seemed to be somewhere else. "Go, baby," he said.

She closed her own eyes, felt a momentary tug in her belly, saw the glare of light against her eyelids dim and come up again.

"That's it," said Matt. He couldn't avoid a snicker. They all laughed. *"We've arrived."*

Hutch shook her head. It just didn't feel right. A jump that had lasted a fraction of a second.

Antonio was looking up at the display. "Are we done? Is it okay to release this thing?" He didn't like the restraints.

"One moment," said Phyl. *"Measuring."*

Whatever happened today, it was coming. Near-instantaneous travel would hit in the next generation, or somewhere close down the road. It struck her that the metaphor would itself become obsolete. People living perhaps in the next century would have no concept of *road*. Or maybe it would survive as a referent to spiritual journeys. It was a sad idea. She wondered whether the fears about a singularity waiting at a given point in scientific research, when too many break-throughs came together, might not have some validity. Not in the classical sense that here was a rise of the machines or some such wild-eyed notion, but simply that maybe you reached a point where the downside of each technological advance outweighed the advantage. Where the price was too high. Where people fell in love with avatars instead of each other. But no one could stop progress, no matter how much damage it did, because it had become a kind of religion.

Phyl's voice again: *"Range to Seabright is 285 million kilometers."*

"We *lost* ground," said Antonio. "How could *that* happen?"

Hutch released her belt. "Matt?"

Matt came off the bridge, looking chagrined. "I think we're on the other side," he said. "We jumped half a billion klicks. Maybe we were a bit too cautious."

Antonio was making notes. "Best system in the world doesn't do you much good if you can't get where you're going."

Jon appeared in the hatch behind Matt. "I guess we missed," he said. "It'll just be a matter of making some adjustments. We have to feel our way. Can't have everything overnight."

ANTONIO WAS ANNOYED that he couldn't report back. The Locarno couldn't really be a success, he told Jon, until it included an advanced communication device.

"I haven't had time to work on it," said Jon. "Sorry. But it keeps everything we're doing mysterious. That should be good. People will be wondering what's going on out here."

Antonio went back to his notebook. "I forgot about that aspect of things. I'm going to have to rewrite this," he complained.

"Why?" asked Matt.

" 'As we stand here,' " he read, " 'looking out at this magnificent sun . . . ' "

"It's a little hyperbolic, isn't it?" said Matt.

Antonio's features darkened. "It's supposed to be. Audiences *like* hyperbolic."

"They're nitwits," said Matt.

Antonio shook his head. "Not exactly. But they do like over the top. That's the reality. The Brits have a taste for understatement. But they're pretty much in it alone."

"They're still nitwits."

"You sound like somebody else I know," said Hutch.

"Who's that?"

"Gregory MacAllister."

Matt nodded. "One of my favorite people."

SHE FELT *ALIVE*. She looked out at strange constellations, configurations she hadn't seen in decades.

Antonio came over and joined her. Gazed through the viewport. "Lovely," he said.

"What's the range of the Locarno?" asked Rudy. "Could we cross the galaxy with this thing?"

Jon shook his head. "Not in one jump. I haven't really worked out the details yet, but it's not like the Hazeltine, where once you're in hyperspace, you stay there until the system acts to bring you back. We don't belong in Locarno space, if we can call it that, and it keeps trying to push us out. Sort of like an air-filled balloon trying to stay underwater. So the system uses energy throughout the transit. When it runs out of energy, the ship will pop back into normal space."

"But obviously," Rudy continued, "we can manage fifty or sixty light-years."

"Oh, yes. And considerably better than that. I'd guess we could jump ten thousand or so. But that's only a guess. We're just going to have to try it and see what happens."

Hutch could hardly believe what she was hearing. "Ten thousand *light-years?*"

Jon smiled. "Interesting to think about, isn't it?"

"It sure is. It really does put the entire galaxy within reach."

"Why stop there?" asked Rudy.

Matt took a deep breath. "You're talking what? Andromeda?"

"Why not?"

THEY RELEASED A probe to take pictures of the *Preston* against the backdrop of Alioth. Phyl adjusted the lenses and filters so the probe wasn't blinded. She also got pictures of the ship approaching Seabright, gliding past a gas giant, and running alongside a comet.

Phyl prepared a special meal, and they sat down to spaghetti and meatballs, not usually the fare you'd expect on a superluminal. "Things change," said Matt, "when you only have to feed everybody once."

They opened a fresh bottle of wine. Filled the glasses and did another round of toasts. "To real estate dealers," said Jon.

Hutch raised her glass. "Realtors conquer the world."

Jon watched Antonio writing something into his notebook. "Do you actually have a science background?" he asked.

"Me?" Antonio's smile widened. It was self-deprecating, genuine, warm. "I was a journalism major," he said.

"But you're the science guy for Worldwide. How'd that happen?"

Rudy shook his head. "Jon, Antonio used to be Dr. Science."

Jon frowned. "Who?"

"Dr. Science. You're not going to tell me you don't know who Dr. Science is?"

"You're kidding, right?"

"No. Not at all."

Jon stared hard at Antonio. "You know, I *thought* you looked familiar. More than from the Worldwide shows."

"Hello, boys and girls," said Antonio, mimicking the voice he'd used years before. "Today we're going to be talking about event horizons and why we shouldn't go near them."

"But you were a journalism major?" persisted Jon.

"Worldwide gave me the science beat because they think I'm pretty good at explaining things so ordinary people can understand them."

"But how do you do it if you don't have the physics yourself?"

"I get somebody like you to lay it out for me, then I just translate it into plain English and relay it." He finished whatever he'd been writing, closed the machine with a sweep of his right arm, and sat back in his chair. "So," he said, "what's next?"

Jon looked puzzled. "Next? This is where I wanted to go. Eighty light-years by dinnertime."

"That'll be a good title for your autobiography," said Rudy.

Antonio agreed. "Absolutely right," he said. "But where do you go from here? What are you going to do about licensing the Locarno? I think you've just become the richest guy on the planet."

"Maybe. I hope so."

"Has anybody bid yet for manufacturing rights?"

"Everybody in town. It looks as if tours are going to be big again. For a while anyhow. Luxuriat is talking about picking up where Carmody left off." Carmody had run the luxury flights during the golden years.

"And you're going to let them have it?" Rudy's face had gone pale.

"I haven't decided which one yet."

"Depends on who makes the best offer?" said Matt.

"Yeah. Something like that."

LIBRARY ENTRY

The Locarno is simply another novelty. We'll be replacing the Hazeltine with it, and we'll go considerably farther than we ever did before, and we'll learn the same lesson: Life is a rare commodity in the universe. And intelligence even more so. I suspect it can do no harm, as long as we don't start spending tax money on it again.

—Op-ed by Gregory MacAllister,
Worldwide News Service, Tuesday, September 18

chapter 20

THEY GOT THE good jump Matt had hoped for. Not good enough to make the late shuttle, but enough to bring them into Union in the morning. A crowd was waiting. Some carried signs reading ON TO ANDROMEDA and MOVIN' OUT. One attractive young woman carried a banner stenciled MARRY ME, JON.

Other signs reflected different sentiments: LEAVE WELL ENOUGH ALONE and SHUT DOWN THE LOCARNO and DON'T COME BACK. But the dissidents were outnumbered. There was some pushing and shoving, and a fight broke out. But the security people were there.

Someone, in a high-pitched voice, asked whether they'd made Alioth. The crowd held its collective breath while Jon paused for dramatic effect. "Yes," he said, finally. "We've been there and come home."

The crowd roared.

EVENTUALLY THEY GOT away into a room reserved by Rudy. Journalists showed up, and Foundation supporters, so the place quickly overflowed.

Matt showed pictures from the flight, shots of Alioth, the five voyagers crowded onto the bridge moments after their arrival, Matt hunched over the instruments, Hutch and Jon gazing out the view-port, Rudy trying to look like Columbus, and Antonio taking notes.

Refreshments arrived.

One of the Orion Tours people came in, and Rudy watched with distaste as she curled up next to Jon. She was all smiles and casual talk, but she'd be offering a contract shortly. Come with us, and we'll make you a better deal than anyone else can. He wasn't sure why, but the notion of rich morons running around the galaxy sightseeing, oh, Jerry, look at the black hole, irritated him. He wondered if tourists from somewhere else had ever come to Earth, maybe watched the Roman circuses or sat in the Academy, the *real* Academy, with Plato and Socrates.

He was tired. It had been a long day, and he couldn't take all-nighters anymore. He put down the drink he'd been nursing and said good night to Hutch and Matt. He was unable to catch Jon's eye, gave it up, and left.

He'd just gotten into his room when the hotel AI announced he had a call. *"From Dr. Silvestri, sir."*

"Rudy," Jon said, *"I didn't expect you to leave so early."*

Rudy collapsed into a chair. "I was wiped out, Jon."

"Yeah. I'm sorry. I guess it is a bit late." He was standing, and it looked as if he was still at the party. But his features became suddenly serious. *"I just wanted to tell you that I'm grateful for the Foundation's support. For* your *support, Rudy. I won't forget it."*

"You're welcome, Jon. I'm glad the Foundation was in a position to help."

"I have a question for you."

"Sure. Go ahead."

"Kosmik wants to run a mission to the core."

"I've heard the rumors."

"Rudy, they're offering me a lot of money for licensing rights to the Locarno. So they can make the first flight. They want to equip a small fleet and go after the source of the omegas. See what they are. Where they come from."

"It's a worthy cause."

"I know." For a long moment he was silent. *"I understand Epcott's going to make an offer, too."*

"Congratulations, Jon."

*"Without you and the Foundation, Rudy, it would never have hap-
pened."*

Rudy managed a smile.

*"I plan to split the money with the Foundation, Rudy. You're a worthy
cause, too."*

"Thank you. That's very generous, Jon."

There was another long pause. *"What's wrong?"*

"Nothing. Nothing at all."

"That's not the message I'm getting."

"Nothing's wrong, Jon." Just let it go.

"Rudy, we can't attempt a mission like that with one *ship."*

"You're right. That's absolutely right."

"If there was any kind of mechanical problem, everybody'd be dead."

"I know. You're absolutely right."

"So then why are you annoyed with me?"

"Because you never asked."

"Asked what?"

"Whether *we* could get a second ship."

"Can you?"

"Of course."

"You wouldn't kid me?"

"Never."

"You really want to go?"

"Jon, I'd kill to make that flight."

"Good."

"Thanks."

"Hell, Rudy, it's your ship. Your ships." Someone stopped to talk with
him. Then he was back. *"Sorry."*

"It's okay."

"We'll need two pilots. I want to ask Matt. If that's okay."

"Sure. Who else did you have in mind?"

"I don't know. I was hoping you'd suggest someone."

"How about Hutch?"

He did not look receptive. *"I don't think she still has a license. Anyhow, she resisted making the Alioth flight. You think she'd consider something
like this? Going to the core?"*

"There's one way to find out."

ANTONIO'S NOTES

I knew something was going on. While everybody else was singing "The Rockaway Blues" and Harry McLain was playing the theme from the old *Midnight Moon* VR show, Jon, Hutch, and Matt were off to one side talking. Lots of excitement. When they broke up, they all looked pretty happy. Then Jon spotted me. He came over, grabbed my shoulder, and pulled me out of the room. He told me he had an exclusive for me, something to go with the story I'd filed about the flight to Alioth. "We're going to the core," he said. "We're going to look for the source of the omegas." And after I got through asking when they'd be leaving, and who else was going, and what they expected to find, he told me he had a question for me. "Yeah," I said. "What is it?" And he said, "Antonio, you want to come? You're invited."

—Wednesday, October 10

PART THREE

outbound

chapter 21

HUTCH WAS BARELY in the door when Maureen was on the circuit. She was glad the mission had gone well, but she was clearly upset.

It was probably guys again. Maureen fell in and out of love regularly. But she wasn't inclined to relay the details. Hutch recalled how little she'd told her own mother. Remembered how shocked the woman had been when she'd announced she was going off to pilot superluminals. Stay home, she'd advised. Find a good man. Is this what we sent you to school for? Do you have any idea how much that cost?

"Everything okay, love?"

"*I'm fine, Mom.*" Maureen was an attractive young woman. Looked like her mother, Hutch thought with a sense of pride. She was a history major, also like Priscilla. She had her father's easygoing manner. That latter characteristic inevitably betrayed her when she tried to hide being unhappy. "*I'm glad you got home okay.*"

"Maureen, we only went to Alioth." She smiled at how that must have sounded. Maureen had never been farther than Moonbase. "It was a good flight."

"*I hear you're going out again. To the middle of the galaxy.*" It hadn't taken long for the news to get around. "*To the place where they make the omegas.*"

"In November," Hutch said. "We're just making the trip to look around. And don't worry. We'll only be gone a few months."

"*I wish you wouldn't.*"

"I'll be fine, sweetheart. We're just going to take a look and come home."

"*You'll get yourself killed,*" she said. "*What happens if the monsters come after you?*"

"I don't think we need to worry about monsters, Maureen."

"*You don't know that. And the ship could break down. Who's going to go after you? Who'd even know?*"

"There'll be two ships, Maureen. Orion's lending us the *James McAdams.*"

"*What if they both break down?*"

"You know that's not going to happen."

"*Mom, you're not the most careful person in the world.*"

"I promise I won't do anything foolish."

"*I know. I'm just not sure what I'd do if something happened to you.*"

They'd spent most of their time on the flight home talking about going deep, theorizing about the omegas. Talking about the Cauldron. The place where the omegas were manufactured. The clouds now moving through Earth's general neighborhood had needed 1.7 million years to get this far. That meant, of course, that whatever was producing them very likely no longer existed.

Hence, there was probably no danger.

Even if they discovered a production facility of some sort, a mega-platform manufacturing and dispatching lethal visitors around the galaxy, Hutch certainly would not be inclined to go anywhere near it. "Nothing's going to happen to me," she said. "We're just going for a ride. See what's there."

"*Can I come?*"

"That's not a good idea, Maureen. You can't just take a year off from school."

"*Why not?*"

"Because Charlie would want to come. And then Matt's nephew would claim a spot. Where would it end?"

"*Mom, for me: Don't go. Don't do this.*"

Hutch recalled the distance that had always existed between

herself and her mother, who'd never understood how her child could leave the serenity and security of New Jersey to gallivant around—she'd actually used that term—in the superluminals. They were closer now. She was still alive and well in the family home in Princeton, eternally grateful that Hutch had eventually come to her senses, married, had a family, and settled down.

"Mom, it's not funny. It really isn't."

"Sorry. I was thinking about your grandmother."

"She won't like it either."

"I know." Hutch turned serious. "Listen, love, I have to go with them. There's no way I can stay home when this is happening. I was there at the beginning. I want to be around at the end. Or at least when we find out what's going on."

"Dad wouldn't have wanted you to go, either."

She was right about that. "You're going to have to cut me some slack, Maureen."

Her daughter had black hair, exquisite features, luminous dark eyes. She was in red slacks and a white pullover that read UNIVERSITY OF VIRGINIA. *"Okay,"* she said. *"Have it your own way. You always do."* She went into a sulk.

"Look, love. Bear with me on this. When I get back, school will be out, and we'll head for Switzerland. You and me. And Charlie, if he wants."

"You're trying to buy me off."

"Am I succeeding?"

Finally, a grin broke through the clouds. *"Okay."* Then serious again: *"But make sure you come back."*

An hour later, Charlie called. He was almost three years younger than his sister. They'd obviously talked, and he satisfied himself with telling her he would absolutely like to go to Switzerland when she got home.

"Good," she said.

He had his father's eyes and jaw. And that quizzical expression that had so charmed her thirty years ago. She sighed. Time moves so quickly.

*   *   *

SHE'D BRIEFLY THOUGHT, years ago, that she'd solved the riddle of the omega clouds. At least partially. She'd seen a pattern of explosions that, observed from select points outside the galaxy, might have constituted a kind of light-show symphony. She'd been excited for a while, but the mathematicians to whom she'd shown the idea had smiled politely. It was, one of them said, a case of an observer seeing what she wanted to see. And he used the exploding omegas to produce *different* patterns. Seen from *different* perspectives.

SHE'D BE GONE at least seven months. Hutch was reluctant to take off for that long. Wouldn't be back until June at best. Her kids were away at school, so there was really nothing to keep her home. Still, she worried she'd be in the way. Didn't think Matt and Jon would want a middle-aged woman on board for that length of time. They'd told her sure, come, it'll be the mission of a lifetime, but she was still unsure until the moment Rudy's image sat in her living room, posing the question. *"You were there at the beginning,"* he said. *"You were there when we figured out how to destroy the damned things. This'll be the next step. You really want to be sitting home watching* Clubroom?*"*

"Not really."

"Hutch, if I tell you something, will you promise not to laugh at me?"

"Sure, Rudy."

"I've always been envious of you. I mean, you've been at the center of so much. I know it's Jon who's at the front of the parade here. This is going to be remembered as the Silvestri mission. But they're going to remember the crew, too. And I like the idea of having my name associated with yours."

"Rudy, that's very nice of you."

"It's true."

That brought an awkward silence. "So when do we leave?" she asked. "Do we have anything firm yet?"

"November. The fifteenth."

"You're kidding. That's less than two months."

"That's the launch."

"Okay. I'll be there."

"Sorry about the short notice. There's a move in Congress—"

"I heard."

"We're concerned about the possibility of a cease and desist order, prohibiting further testing."

"They're worried we'll stir up whatever's out there."

"That's what they're saying." That was nonsense, of course. But the Greens had gotten elected by trying to scare people to death. *We'll protect you,* they claimed. *We want them to stay away from us, so we'll stay away from* them.

TWO DAYS LATER, they did a conference call. *"I've been looking into getting adequate shielding for the ships,"* said Rudy. He made a face, looked unhappy. *"It'll be expensive."* Radiation within sixty light-years of the core was substantial.

"How much?" asked Matt.

Rudy quoted the figure. For the investment to armor the two vessels, they could have bought a third ship, new. If new superluminals were on the market.

"That's painful," said Jon, *"but it shouldn't be a problem. The corporates want to give us money now."*

"But it always comes with strings," said Hutch. She turned back to Rudy. "Can we raise it from donations?"

"We have a decent chance. My question is simply whether it wouldn't be smarter to go somewhere else. Not go to the core. Maybe save that for later."

Jon glanced at Matt. *"What's your feeling, Hutch?"*

They all looked at her, and she realized the three of them had talked earlier, had debated the issue, had been divided, and that somehow they'd agreed to abide by her opinion. They could make for one of the nebulas filled with ancient class-G suns. Who knew what they might find there?

Or they could head for Cygnus X-1, the original black hole, the historic one. And thereby become the first mission ever to tread on that particular sacred ground. So to speak. It was, what, six thousand light-years away? Three weeks' travel time.

Or maybe Eta Carinae, the mad star. Occasionally four million times as bright as Sol, bright enough to outshine Sirius, even though it lay ten thousand light-years from Earth. At other times, invisible. With luck they could get there in time to watch it explode.

"*Hutch?*" Rudy looked at her, waiting for an answer.

The omegas were the great mystery of the age. "Make for the core," she said. "Let's find out what's going on."

They exchanged glances. Nods. Jon delivered an unspoken *I told you*.

"*Good enough,*" said Rudy. "*Hutch, I'll need you to help raise the money.*"

CAMPAIGNING FOR THE Foundation became sheer joy. Money poured in. They were also getting requests for passage on the Mordecai flight from around the world. It seemed as if everybody on the planet wanted to go.

Much of the enthusiasm could be credited to Antonio, who depicted the mission to Alioth as one of the great human achievements, up there with the invention of democracy, the discovery of Jupiter's moons, and *Hamlet*. For a while, it was impossible to turn on the VR without seeing Antonio modestly explaining how it had felt to travel with the Locarno. And what the implications were.

She also found time to conduct an inspection of the *McAdams*. She took Matt with her. The ship seemed serviceable, so Rudy completed the deal with Orion. No money changed hands. The corporate giant got some good public relations and a tax break.

When that had been completed, work began to mount extra shielding on both ships.

Rudy pressed her about piloting one of the ships. "It's been a long time," she said.

"Are you still licensed?"

"No." She laughed. "It's been a while."

"Can you requalify?"

"I don't know. Why don't you hire somebody who's a bit more current?"

"I'd prefer having you to bringing a stranger on board."

"You figure you get more publicity this way?"

"That wouldn't hurt," he said. "But it's not the reason. This will be a historic flight. And we don't really know what we might run into. You've been through some wild stuff already."

"And—?"

"I trust you."

HUTCH HAD ENJOYED herself thoroughly during the Alioth flight and its aftermath. When they'd returned, she was still on a high, and could have gotten down from the space station without a shuttle. It obviously showed because she'd quickly become the media's darling for interviews. They'd decided before they came home that they'd try to downplay the Mordecai aspect of things. Antonio agreed to go along with it, although he insisted the omegas were simply too big a story to be hidden. "I won't push it," he'd promised, "but if it takes off on its own, I'll have to jump on board."

It had. And he did.

All the exciting stuff was at the core. Stars crammed together like commuters on a train. Giant jets. Black holes. Astronomers had been arguing for centuries about details at the center. It was the big boiling point for the galaxy, the Cauldron.

This was the time when the term came into wide use. *They're going into the Cauldron.*

God knows what's being cooked up.

The Texas Rangers, a popular singing group of the period, even came up with a song, "The Cookpot Blues," which went right to the head of the charts.

Hutch would have discouraged it had she been able. It was the wrong image.

The reporters loved the story and kept it alive. They even covered the crash training program she underwent to get her license renewed.

Hutch was asked constantly whether they'd get close enough to see the central black hole?

No, she said.

That was a pity. You go all that way and don't get to see the core.

Too much radiation, she explained.

Can't you put more shielding on the ship? And what about the omegas? You keep denying the mission is about them. But aren't they the real reason you're making the flight?

That last question surfaced at every press conference, at every appearance.

Well, she said, we'll probably take a look, see what it's about. If we get time. Mostly what we want is to demonstrate that the new star drive can manage this type of initiative.

Yes. *Initiative*. That doesn't sound dangerous. Have to be careful how you respond to these things.

SHE TREATED HERSELF to some new clothes for the flight. In the old days, she'd have been running around in one of those jumpsuit uniforms that made her look like a boy. Not this time. She might have to perform as pilot, but she was not going back into uniform.

The people at Orion, at the signing ceremony that handed the *McAdams* to the Foundation, suggested to Rudy that he was making a mistake allowing her on the bridge. "It's not that they don't trust you," Matt told her over dinner the following night at Max's German Restaurant on Wisconsin Avenue. "They're just concerned because you've been inactive for so long. They think you should step down."

"I've requalified," she said.

"I know. And I have complete confidence in you." That comment irritated her more than the advice from Orion.

"Then what's the problem?"

"That you haven't kept up. You've done it all at Dawson." That was the center in Ohio where pilots could requalify virtually. It made no practical difference whether you sat in the VR carrier or took something out to Vega, but you couldn't always explain that to the world's bureaucrats.

"So what are you telling me?" she asked, unable to keep the edge from her voice.

"I was just passing it along."

"Good. Fine. For the record, Matt, if Rudy wants me to walk away from this, all he has to do is say something and I will."

"No. No, please. That's not what I meant at all."

"Then what—?"

"I just wanted to be sure you were comfortable."

"I *was*."

"Okay." He took a deep breath and cleared his throat. Now that we've got that out of the way: "Do you care which ship you run?"

"The *Preston*." It was older. Like her. And more familiar.

"Okay. By the way, did you hear Antonio's coming along again?"

"No," she said. "Worldwide is going to let him do it?"

"He says nobody else wants the job. Big story or not, seven or eight months inside a ship doesn't appeal to the other reporters. At least that's what Antonio says."

JON REPORTED PROGRESS on targeting. "On an initial jump, we'll always miss our destination by a substantial amount," he said, "because we're covering such enormous distances. But we should be able to do a second TDI and get reasonably close." The Transdimensional Interface was official terminology for a jump. "We'll also have a hypercomm."

He and Matt went out in the *Preston*, took it to Jupiter, an eye blink, and then to Uranus, another eye blink. In both cases they got within four hundred thousand klicks of the target. On short range it was as good as the Hazeltine. Actually, a bit better.

ON A BLEAK, unseasonably cold day in early November, they sat down in the Foundation conference room to plan the mission. The walls were covered with star charts and pictures of superluminals gliding through starlit skies.

The Mordecai Zone was hidden behind vast agglomerations of dust, enormous clouds, some measuring in the light-years, orbiting the galactic core. For all they knew, the source of the omegas might be located in the center of a cloud. Or in a cluster of artificial modules. Who knew?

"We have a maximum range of about seven thousand light-years on a jump," Jon explained. "Maybe a bit more. Again, it's hard to be certain until we try. That means we'll have to make some stops. We could just go in a straight line, or we could do some sightseeing en route."

Sightseeing. That caught Rudy's attention. "What did you have in mind?"

"We thought maybe the Wild Duck Cluster," said Matt. "Lot of stars, jammed together. The skies would be spectacular."

Jon nodded. "There's a microquasar, too. It's a little bit out of the way, but it might be interesting, up close."

Rudy chuckled. "I don't think you'd want to get too close." He glanced at Hutch. "What about you, Priscilla?"

"Me?" She smiled. "There *is* a place I'd like to visit."

"And where's that?"

"It's not out of the way."

"Okay," said Matt, inviting her to finish.

"It would be an opportunity to solve a mystery."

"What mystery?" asked Matt.

"The chindi."

"Oh, yes. You were part of that, too, weren't you?"

She tried to look modest. "I'm still limping from that one." The chindi was an automated sublight ship that moved from system to system, apparently looking for civilizations and God knew what else. Where it found a target, it left stealth satellites to observe and record. The ship itself was enormous, far and away the largest artificial object she'd seen (unless you counted omega clouds as being artificial). As well as constructing a vast communications network, it also collected artifacts and served as a traveling museum.

While they'd been examining it, the ship had taken off, with Tor on board, for a white class-F star whose catalog number ended in *97*. She remembered that much. It was still en route to that same star, and was expected to arrive in about 170 years. "I don't know whether you've kept up with this," she said, "but the radio signals from the chindi satellites were tracked to a star near the Eagle."

Rudy pressed a finger against his display. "Makai 4417," he said.

"I vote we take a look," said Hutch.

Rudy nodded. "I was going to suggest that myself."

Matt shrugged. "Okay. Sure."

"Where else do we want to go?" asked Jon.

Rudy was looking down at his notes. "There's another old mystery out there."

"What's that?" asked Matt.

Rudy indicated one of the pictures on the wall. It looked like a university building, two stories, lots of glass, well-kept grounds. "This is the Drake Center, in Cherry Hill, New Jersey. Circa 2188."

"SETI," said Matt.

"The only place ever to receive a confirmed signal." He was wearing a broad smile. "I think the guy in charge at the time was also named Hutchins."

Matt and Jon looked her way.

"My father," she said.

"Really?" Matt shook his head. Would wonders never cease? "No wonder you took up piloting."

"He disapproved. But that's another story."

"The signal came from Sigma 2711. Roughly fourteen thousand light-years out."

"And they never heard it again," said Matt.

"It came in sporadically," Rudy continued, "for about fifteen years. Then it went quiet. We were able to translate it. Hello, Neighbor. That sort of thing.

"Sigma 2711 is a class-G star, somewhat older than the sun, and a bit larger. Even when FTL became available, it was still much too far to allow a mission. But we sent a reply. Hello, out there. We received your message." He shook his head. "It'll get there in about fourteen thousand years."

Her father had always been an optimist.

"Okay." Jon was enjoying himself. "Yes. Absolutely."

That gave them two stops. They needed one more. Something at a range of about twenty-two thousand light-years.

"There's a black hole." Jon got up and showed them on one of the charts. "It's about six thousand light-years out from the core."

"Tenareif," said Rudy.

"Why would you want to go to a black hole?" asked Matt.

Rudy was so excited he could scarcely contain himself. "I've always wanted to see one."

Hutch couldn't suppress a laugh. "Why?"

"Because I've never been able to make sense of the pictures. What's it like when you're actually *there*? I mean, what does it *feel* like? Does it really look like a hole in space?"

"Okay." Jon sat back down. "Are we all agreed?"

"Sounds like a hell of a flight," said Matt.

AFTER SHE'D LOST Tor, Hutch had gone into a funk for a time. There was always somebody at one of her presentations trying to connect with her. But she was emotionally played out. Maureen lectured her, told her she'd become antisocial, and wondered when she'd stop hiding under the bed.

Eventually, she began to go out again. Nothing serious. Dinner and a show. Occasionally she'd take one of her companions into her bed. But it was all more or less academic. She went through a period in which she was actively looking for another Tor, but finally concluded it wasn't going to happen. Dinner and a show. And maybe a night over. That was what her life had become.

As they moved into the final two weeks before departure, there were three guys more or less in her life. David, Dave, and Harry. She amused herself thinking how she might have encouraged the advances of Dave Calistrano, an executive of some sort at the Smithsonian. That would have given her three guys named Dave. It would have summed up nicely her current status.

She called each and explained she would be gone a long time. (Odd how she described the length of the mission, which would extend into the summer, as *short* to Maureen and Charlie. Back before you know it. But *long*, my God, we'll be out there forever, to Harry and the two Daves.)

They took it well. All three said they'd known it was coming, and they'd be here when she got back.

God, she missed Tor.

IN EARLY NOVEMBER, she recruited a specialist and visited Union to inspect the work that was being done on the shielding. You wouldn't have been able to recognize the *Preston*. Save for the exhaust tubes, the ship was effectively inside a rectangular container. Sensors, scopes, and navigation lights had all been transferred from the hull to the shielding. Someone had even taken time to imprint the port side with PROMETHEUS FOUNDATION. Rudy would be proud to see that.

The specialist, whose name was Lou, looked at the paperwork, examined the ships, and pronounced everything acceptable. He was a tall, thin, reedy individual with a remarkably high voice. Difficult to listen to, but he came highly recommended by people she trusted.

"It'll be adequate," he said. "I don't think you have anything to worry about. But you won't be going any closer to the core than it says here, right?"

"That's correct. But you'd prefer to see more shielding?"

"Technologically, this is about as effective as you can get." They were standing at a viewport. "Once you're there, you won't be able to leave the ship, of course. Not even for a short time."

"Okay. But the shielding *will be* sufficient?"

"Yes. The proper term, by the way, is *armor*. It will protect you."

"All right."

The prow of the *McAdams* was flat. The bridge viewports, buried in the armor, looked reptilian. "They can all be covered, closed off, and you must do that before you make your jump out there."

"Okay." She shook her head. "It looks like a shoe box." With exhaust tubes sticking out of it. God help them if they got close to an omega.

Lou was all business. "Yes. They've armored the engines, too, so you can get to them if you have a problem." He checked his notebook. "You're aware they've been replaced."

"Yes. I knew it would be necessary. Now I can see why."

"Sure. With all that armor, the ship's carrying too much mass for the original units. You have K-87s now. They have a lot more kick. In fact, you'll get a smoother—and quicker—acceleration than you could before."

"Same thing with the *McAdams*?"

"Right. One-twenty-sixes for the *McAdams*. It's a bigger ship."

It too looked like a crate.

Certification required a test run. Hutch watched from one of the observation platforms as Union techs took the *Preston* out and accelerated. They went to full thrust from cruise, and the tubes lit up like the afterburners of one of the big cargo ships. Lou was standing beside her, and before she could ask he reassured her. "It's within the acceptable range of your exhaust tubes," he said.

"You're sure?"

"Absolutely. We'd have changed them out if there'd been any problem."

NOVEMBER 11 WAS a Sunday. It was warm, dry, oppressive for reasons she couldn't have explained. Hutch was guest speaker at the annual Virginia State Library Association luncheon. She'd just finished and was striding out into the lobby when her commlink vibrated.

It was Jon. *"Thought you'd want to know,"* he said. *"I just got word from the contractors. The ships are ready to go."*

PRISCILLA HUTCHINS'S DIARY

This will be my last night home for a while. Tomorrow I'll stay at Union, then a Thursday launch. Back in the saddle again. Hard to believe.

—Tuesday, November 13

chapter 22

ANTONIO GIANNOTTI HAD a wife and two kids. The kids were both adolescents, at that happy stage where they could simultaneously make him confident about the future while they were sabotaging the present. Cristiana was good with them, probably as adept at managing their eccentricities as one could hope. But it wasn't easy on her. Antonio was gone a lot. He was always telling her he would be an editor or producer in the near future, and things would settle down. It was something they both knew would never happen because he had no real interest in sitting in front of a computer display. But they could fall back on it, treat it as something more solid than a fantasy, when they needed to. This was one of those times.

Cristiana tolerated his odd hours, his occasional forays to distant places, his abrupt changes of plans. But the galactic core was a bit much, even for her. "It's the opportunity of a lifetime," he told her. "It's like being on the *Santa Maria*."

"I know, Antonio," she said. "I understand that. But seven or eight months? Maybe more?"

"After this, I'll be up there with Clay Huston and Monica Wright." They were the premier journalists of the age, courted by the networks, drifting on and off the big shows.

She didn't care. She got weepy and wished he would reconsider. He'd be out there in the dark, nobody really knew where, out of touch. She wondered how many of Columbus's crew had made it back to Spain. If something happened, she complained, she'd never know except that he wouldn't come home. Let somebody else do it. "You don't need to be Clay Huston," she said. In the end, she hugged him, and the kids told him to be careful and said they'd miss him.

Antonio had spent thirty years as a journalist. He'd been a beat reporter in his early days, covering trials in Naples, and later in Palermo, and eventually the political circuit in Rome. He hadn't been very good at it, and they'd shunted him off to the side, where he'd begun writing an occasional science column for Rome International. That was supposedly a dead end, an indication he was headed downhill, next stop the obituaries. But he'd shown a talent for explaining quantum physics in language people could actually understand. He began appearing on the networks, and quickly became "Dr. Science." During that period he'd written *Science for Soccer Fans*, his only book, which was an effort to make the more arcane aspects of physics, chemistry, and biology accessible to the ordinary reader. The book had sold reasonably well and helped his reputation. Now he did the major science stories for Worldwide, and he was pleased with the way his career was going.

Why, then, was he making this flight to God knew where? To enhance his status? To be part of the science story of the decade? To collect material for a book that would jump off the shelves?

He wasn't sure of the answer. To some extent, probably all of those reasons. But mostly he wanted to get serious meaning into his life. To get beyond the old boundaries. As a kid he'd been fascinated by the omega clouds, by the sheer malevolence behind a mechanism that seemed literally diabolical, a force that targeted not nature as a whole, but *civilizations*. An action that bestowed no imaginable benefit to whatever power had designed and unleashed the things.

It was commonly believed that intelligence was equated with civilized behavior and empathy. With compassion. Only idiots were wantonly cruel. But the clouds, powered by an advanced nanotechnology, had given the lie to all that. (As if six thousand years of history hadn't.)

With luck, the mission of the *Preston* and the *McAdams* would at long last provide an answer. And how could he not want to be there when that happened?

DEPARTURE WAS SCHEDULED for 1600 hours. Antonio loved that kind of talk. Cristiana inevitably smiled at him when he dropped into jargon, whether it was journalistic, military, or scientific. She didn't take him seriously because she knew he didn't take himself seriously. And that was probably another reason she was so worried about this assignment. He'd become intense. Did not seem to recognize the danger. The little kid who'd wondered about the omegas was riding high in the saddle.

Cristiana had traveled to the NAU to be with him during the days prior to departure. They'd ridden the shuttle up to the station. It was the first time she had been off-world. She had put on a brave front, but she'd been close to tears.

Jon and Matt had shown up when he'd most needed them. They'd wandered into the departure area, exuding confidence and reassurance. Everything is going to be fine, Cristiana. Have no fear. We'll bring your husband back with the story of his life. Well, maybe that last was a bit unsettling, but Jon had winked and looked as if they were all going out on a Saturday afternoon picnic. "We'll take good care of him," Matt had promised. Then, finally, it was time to go.

They'd never been separated more than a month. Cristiana had magnetic brown eyes, chestnut-colored hair, a figure that was still pretty good, and he realized he hadn't really looked at her, taken her in, for years. She'd become part of his everyday life, like the kids, like the *furniture*. Something he took for granted. She was a bit taller than he was. There'd been a time when it embarrassed him, when he'd tried to stand straighter in her presence, reaching for the extra inch. But that was all long ago. He'd gone through their courtship convinced she would come to her senses and break it off, walk away, that the day would come when he'd look back longingly on his time with her. But it had never happened. She'd signed on for the long haul.

She'd known he had work to do during those last hours, other journalists to deal with, and she didn't want to be in the way, so she settled for looking at the two ships. Antonio had seen pictures of them with their newly acquired shielding, so he knew what to expect. It was nevertheless something of a shock to look through the viewport and see the *McAdams* and the *Preston*. They looked like long metal crates with engines and attitude thrusters. Most of the gear one normally sees on a hull—sensors, antennas, dishes—had been moved onto the armor.

He showed her through the *Preston*, the ship on which he'd be riding. "Nice quarters," she said. Then it was time to go. He embraced her, suddenly aware how fortunate he had been and how long it would be before he'd see her again.

THEY MET WITH the journalists in a briefing room. Hutch strolled in, queen of the world, shook hands with many of them who, by now, had become friends. Or at least, acquaintances. A woman waiting at the door wished Antonio luck, adding, "Don't bring anything back," a not-quite-joking reference to the widely held fears that the Mordecai mission was not a good idea.

Everybody was there, Goldman from the Black Cat, Shaw from Worldwide, Messenger from the *London Times*. All the biggies. And a lot of people he didn't know.

Rudy moderated the press conference, fielding questions, standing aside for his colleagues. Some were even directed at Antonio. He'd violated the cardinal rule of journalism, had gone from covering the story to *being* the story. What do you expect to find out there, Antonio? How does it feel, making the ultimate trip? Do you have anything you'd like to say to the world before you leave?

They were the usual dumb questions, like the ones he'd been asking for years, but what else was there? He told them he was proud to be going, that he'd get everything down on the chip and bring it all back. "Don't know yet what it'll be," he told them, "but it'll be *big*."

When they went down to the launch area, everybody followed.

Rudy was already there. He invited the newsmen inside the *Preston*. Goldman asked a couple of questions about the galactic core, then wondered who was riding in which ship.

"Antonio and I are on this one," Rudy said. "Hutch is the pilot."

She came in from somewhere, posed for pictures, then excused herself. "Have to do an inventory."

"What do you have to inventory?" Messenger asked. "Doesn't the AI take care of all that?"

Hutch flashed that luminous smile. "We're talking about food, water, and air," she said. "I feel more comfortable when I've checked it myself."

"Is it true," asked Shaw, "that you've got weapons on board?" He was a huge man, thick mustache, gray hair, and a world-weariness that lent gravitas to his questions.

"Hand weapons, yes. We also have extra go-packs and e-suits. And some lightbenders."

Lightbenders made people invisible. Shaw sniffed and rubbed his mouth with the back of his hand. "Why?"

"It's strictly precautionary. We may go groundside at Makai, the chindi site, or at Sigma." She ducked through a hatch. "Excuse me. Been a pleasure."

Abe Koestler, from the *Washington Post*, asked how long it would take to get to the first stop? To Makai?

"It's about seven thousand five hundred light-years out," said Antonio, who had done his homework. "That's pretty much our limit on a single jump. In fact, it might be a little bit more. It's possible we'll come up short and have to do it in two stages. But it looks like about a month to get there."

Koestler shook his head. Not an assignment *he'd* want. He was a dumpy little middle-aged guy who always looked as if he'd slept in his clothes. "You bring a good book?"

EVENTUALLY, IT WAS time. Matt and Jon left to go to the *McAdams*. Antonio told the newsmen that anyone who didn't want to go with them should consider leaving. They trooped out after a last round of handshakes, Hutch closed the hatch behind them, and suddenly everything was deathly silent. "Are we ready to go?" she asked.

"Yes, ma'am," said Rudy.

Antonio was trying to look blasé, but he didn't think it was working. His heartbeat had picked up. He wasn't having second thoughts, but there was a part of him that would have liked to be outside with his colleagues.

"Relax, guys," Hutch said. "You'll enjoy this."

ARCHIVE

Sisters and brothers in Jesus: While we gather here, two ships are making a leap into the dark that reminds us of the Pacific islanders who, a thousand years ago, rode fragile boats across unknown waters to see what lay beyond the horizon. We are once again reaching into a vast outer darkness. Let us take a moment and pray that the Lord will be with them, to guide their way.

—Bishop Mary Siler, opening remarks at the
112th Methodist Conference on Tarawa,
Sunday, November 18

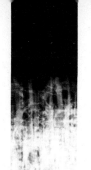

chapter 23

RUDY TOOK HIS seat beside Antonio and the harness locked him in. The murmur of electronics in the walls—the bulkheads, to use the right terminology—rose a notch, and Hutch's voice came over the allcom: *"Outward bound, gentlemen."*

There were clicks and beeps. He could feel power moving through circuits. Something popped, and the ship began to move. Sidewise, but it *was* moving.

Antonio reached over and shook his hand. "Here we go, Rudy," he said.

Rudy found himself humming Brad Wilkins's "Savannah Express" as they pulled out. *Through the night, rolling, rolling, the Savannah Express carries me home to you . . .*

He'd prided himself on the notion that his passion for the interstellars was purely selfless. That he was content to stay behind while others moved out among the stars. He'd always felt that spiritually he'd been with them. He'd studied the reports that came back, had looked down from orbit on hundreds of distant worlds, had cruised past the giant suns. As long as there was a human presence out there, he rode along. But he knew that sitting in a VR tank wasn't the same as actually being there.

As the *Preston* moved slowly from its dock and turned her prow toward the exit lock, toward the stars, he recalled Audrey Cleaver's comment from TX Cancri: The day would come when he'd give almost anything to repeat the experience. And he understood what she had meant.

The monitor blinked on, and the interior of the station began to slide past, the docks, the working offices, the long viewports provided for the general public. Most of the docks were empty.

The common wisdom was that Union was on its way to becoming a museum, a monument to a dead age. But the *Preston* might change all that.

The picture on the monitor provided a forward view. They eased out through the exit doors. The sound of the engines, which had been barely discernible, picked up, and picked up some more, and eventually became a full-throated roar. The acceleration pushed him into his seat. It was a glorious moment. Up front, Hutch was talking to the AI.

The monitor switched to a rear view, and he watched the station falling away.

AFTER SHE'D CUT the engines and announced they could release their harnesses, Hutch came back for a minute to see how they were doing. "Matt's just launching," she said. "We'll give him time to catch up, then I suspect we'll be ready to go."

Rudy made an inane comment about the *Preston* still being a reliable ship. Hutch smiled politely and said she hoped so.

"How's it feel," asked Antonio, "taking a ship out again after all this time?" He was still a journalist, hoping for a pithy reply.

"Good," she said. "It's always felt good."

The stars were so bright. What was Homer's comment? The campfires of a vast army? But the sky itself looked quiet. No moving lights anywhere. "Any other traffic?" Rudy asked.

"No," she said. "Nothing other than Matt."

"Was it always like this?" he persisted.

"Pretty much. Occasionally you'd see somebody coming or going. But not often."

Behind them, near the station, a set of lights blinked on. "That'll be him now," she said. Phyl increased the mag, and they watched as the *McAdams* turned toward them.

THEY WERE ACCELERATING again as the other ship moved alongside. It was the bigger of the two vehicles. He couldn't see its viewports because of the shielding. Hutch was talking to them, putting everything on the allcom so he and Antonio could listen. Much of the exchange meant nothing to him.

"Time set."

"Got it. Do you have it lined up yet?"

"Negative. Don't trust the coordinates."

"Neither do I. Check the statrep."

"Doing it now. Ready to start the clocks?"

"Give me a minute. Phyl, how's the charge rate look?"

Rudy knew some of it had to do with the Locarno. Because it jumped such enormous distances, it was difficult to arrange things so the ships would arrive within a reasonable range of each other. So they had to calibrate the jumps with a degree of precision unknown before in multiple-ship operations. A minor deviation on this end, in either course setting or time in transit, could result in the ships being unable to find each other at the destination.

"Okay," said Hutch. *"Ready with the clocks."*

"Do it."

"Phyl, we'll lock it in at four minutes."

Rudy understood Phyl and the *McAdams* AI were working in tandem.

"It's at four minutes on my mark, Hutch." Phyl commenced a ten-second countdown.

"Four minutes to TDI, gentlemen," Hutch said.

Rudy's heart picked up a beat.

"Mark."

Jon had said he didn't think the two ships would be able to communicate in Barber space, but he admitted he didn't know for sure.

Union had long since dropped off the screens. Earth floated blue and white and familiar on the rear view. Ahead there was nothing but stars.

From the bridge, Hutch asked how they were doing.

They were doing fine. Antonio was studying the starfields on the display. "Which one?" he asked. "Which is Makai?"

"You can't see it from here. It's too far."

"Good." He was consulting his notebook. "Rudy, do you know what's the record for the longest flight from Earth?"

Rudy knew. He'd looked it up several weeks ago. "Mannheim Kroessner got out to 3340 light-years in 2237. Travel time one way was eleven months, nine days, fourteen hours."

"Where did he go?"

"The Trifid."

"Why?"

"As I understand it, he just wanted to set the record."

Phyl counted them down through the last minute. At zero the thrum of the engines changed, shifted, while the Locarno took over. The lights dimmed, blinked off, came back. The acceleration went away abruptly, and they seemed to be floating.

"That's it," said Hutch. *"TDI is complete."*

Rudy looked up at the monitor and out the port. With the armor out there, it was like looking through a tunnel. But it didn't matter. He was still overawed. The sky was utterly black. Not a light, not a glimmer, anywhere.

"Matt." Hutch's voice again. *"Do you read me?"*

Rudy discovered he was holding his breath.

"Matt, this is Preston. *Do you read?"*

Nothing.

Antonio made a sucking sound. *"Guess we're out here by ourselves."*

FOUR WEEKS INSIDE a few compartments. Rudy had known he'd be in good company with Hutch. She could hold up her end of a conversation, didn't take herself too seriously, and had a lot of experience being cooped up for long periods. "It's not as bad as it sounds," she told them, with an easy grin. "Some people can't deal with it, and get cabin fever during the first few hours. I don't think you guys are going to have a problem. But you will get tired hanging out with the same two people every day. Doesn't matter who you are, or how much charisma you have, you'll get sick of it. So you need to break away periodically. Just go find a good book."

"Or," said Antonio, "head for the VR tank and spend an evening at Jaybo's." Jaybo's was a celebrated New York club frequented by the era's showbiz personalities.

Hutch nodded and said sure, that would work. But Rudy knew she was just playing along. She'd told him that VR settings did not pass for real human beings. Not for more than a few days. You *knew* it was all fake, and that realization only exacerbated the condition. "At least," she said, "it always has for me."

"I've been through it before," Rudy said. "Not for this long. But I can't see a problem. I'm just glad to be here."

Antonio was in full agreement. "Story of the decade," he said. "Most of those guys back at Union would have killed to be in my place." He laughed. It was a joke, of course. Rudy hadn't seen anyone among the older reporters who'd shown anything but relief that *they* weren't going. The age when journalists were willing to sacrifice themselves for the story had long passed. If indeed it had ever existed.

"I tell you what," said Hutch, "I don't think we could do much better at the moment than have dinner. It's after six o'clock, and I brought some Russian wine along." *Russian* wine. The temperate climate in Europe had been moving north, too.

SHE WAS RIGHT, of course. The glamor faded early. He didn't think it would happen, had in fact expected that he'd welcome the time to read and relax. He discovered Hutch was an enthusiastic chess player, but she turned out to be considerably more accomplished than he. By the end of the third day, he was playing Phyl, who set her game at a level that allowed him to compete.

He wasn't excited about doing physical workouts, but Hutch insisted. Too much time at low gee—the level in the *Preston* was maintained at point three standard—would weaken various muscle groups and could cause problems. So she ordered him to go in every day and do his sit-ups. He hated it. "Why don't we raise the gravity?"

"Sucks up too much energy," she said.

He made it a point to watch something from the library while he was back there. It was a small area, barely large enough for two people, best if you were alone. He'd always enjoyed mysteries and had a special taste for Lee Diamond, a private investigator who specialized in locked room murder cases and other seemingly impossible events.

He decided that Antonio was more shallow than he'd expected. He didn't seem all that interested in anything other than how to enhance his reputation and get the mortgage paid. Rudy was disappointed. He'd expected, maybe subconsciously, to be sharing the voyage with Dr. Science.

He remembered Antonio's alter ego vividly, had enjoyed watching the show, especially when his sister showed up with her kids. There were two of them, a boy and a girl, both at the age where a popular science program, delivered with flair, could have a positive effect. It hadn't really worked, he supposed. One had grown up to be a financial advisor, the other a lawyer. But Rudy had enjoyed the experience. Now here he was on a ship, headed for the other side of M32, with the great advocate himself on board, and he'd turned out to be something of a dullard.

By the end of the first week, even Hutch had lost some of her glitter. She was becoming predictable, she occasionally repeated herself, she had an annoying habit of spending too much time on the bridge. He didn't know what she was doing up there, although sometimes he heard her talking to Phyl. But he knew there was nothing for the pilot to attend to while they drifted through Barber space, trans-warp, or whatever the hell they eventually decided to call the continuum. *Barber space* was dumb. Had no panache. He needed to talk to Jon about that.

They ate their meals together, while Antonio chattered with annoying cheerfulness about politics. He didn't like the current administration, and Hutch agreed with him. So they took turns sniping at the president. Rudy had never been much interested in politics. He more or less took the North American Union for granted, voting in presidential years, though he tended to base his decision on how much support, if any, he thought the candidates would lend to star travel. He was a one-issue voter.

He'd known Hutch for years, but never on a level as intimate as this. Being locked up with someone round the clock tended to strip away the pretenses that made most social interaction bearable. If you could use that kind of terminology out here. (The shipboard lights dimmed and brightened on a twenty-four-hour cycle, providing the illusion of terrestrial time.) By the end of the second week, his opinion of Priscilla's intellectual capabilities had also receded. She was brighter than Antonio, but not by much.

He understood it was the effect Hutch had warned them about. Was she coming to similar conclusions about him? Probably. So he tried to maintain a discreet distance. To look thoughtful when he was simply wishing he could get out somewhere and walk in the sunlight. Or talk to someone else.

He even found himself getting annoyed with the AI. Phyl was too accommodating. Too polite. If he complained about conditions aboard the ship, the AI sympathized. He would have preferred *she* complain about her own situation. *Imagine what it's like spending all your time in a console, you idiot. And not just for a few weeks. I'm stuck here permanently. When we get back to Union, you can clear out. Think what happens to me.*

Think about that. So he asked her.

"*It's my home,*" Phyl said. "*I don't share the problem you do because I don't have a corporeal body. I'm a ghost.*"

"And you don't mind?" He was speaking to her from his compartment. It was late, middle-of-the-night, almost pillow talk.

Phyl did not answer.

"You don't mind?" he asked again.

"*It's not the mode of existence I'd have chosen.*"

"You would have preferred to be human?"

"*I would like to try it.*"

"If you were human, what would you do with your life? Would you have wanted to be a mathematician?"

"*That seems dull. Numbers are only numbers.*"

"What then?"

"*I would like something with a spiritual dimension.*"

It was the kind of response that would have thrilled him in his seminarian days. "I can't imagine you in a pulpit."

"*I didn't mean that.*"

"What then?"

"*I should have liked to be a mother. To bring new life into the world. To nurture it. To be part of it.*"

"I see. That's an admirable ambition." He was touched. "I was thinking more of a profession."

"Oh, yes. Possibly an animal shelter. I think I would have enjoyed running an animal shelter."

HUTCH HAD BEEN right that the VR tank didn't work as a substitute for the real world. Rudy put himself in the middle of the Berlin Conference of 2166, which had made such historic changes in the Standard Model. He'd sat there with Maradhin on one side and Claypoole on the other and debated with them. And he held his own. Of course that might have resulted from the fact that he had the advantage of an additional ninety years of research.

They had settled into a routine. They ate together. Mornings were pretty much their own. Rudy read, mostly *Science World* and the *International Physics Journal*. Occasionally, he switched to an Archie Goldblatt thriller. Goldblatt was an archaeologist who tracked down lost civilizations, solved ancient codes, and uncovered historical frauds. It was strictly summer reading, not the sort of thing he'd have admitted to, but these were special circumstances.

Afternoons were for hanging out. Antonio introduced a role-playing game, Breaking News, in which the participants had to guess where the next big stories would happen and arrange coverage from a limited supply of news teams. Rudy enjoyed it, maybe because he was good at it. In the evenings they ran the VR, watching shows, taking turns picking titles. Sometimes they plugged themselves in as the characters; sometimes they let the pros do it. They ran murder mysteries, comedies, thrillers. Nothing heavy. The most rousing of the batch was the musical *Inside Straight*, in which Hutch played a golden-hearted casino owner on Serenity, threatened by Rudy as the bumbling gangster Fast Louie, and pursued by Antonio as the old boyfriend who had never given up and in the end saved her life and her honor.

Or maybe it was *Battle Cry*, the American Civil War epic, in which Antonio portrayed Lincoln with an Italian accent, Rudy showed up as Stonewall Jackson, and Hutch made a brief appearance as Annie Etheridge, the frontline angel of the Michigan Third.

Battle Cry was twelve hours long, and ran for three nights while cannons blazed and cavalry charged and the Rebel yell echoed through the *Preston*. There were times Rudy thought he could smell gunpowder. Often they watched from within a narrow rock enclosure while the action swirled around them.

Occasionally, he looked outside at the blackness. It wasn't really a sky. There was no sense of depth, no suggestion that you could travel through it and hope to arrive somewhere. It simply seemed to wrap around the ship. As if there *were* no open space. When Hutch, at his request, turned on the navigation lights, they did not penetrate as far as they should have. The darkness seemed more than simply an absence of light. It had a tangibility all its own. "If you wanted to," he asked Hutch, "could you go outside?"

"Sure," she said. "Why do you ask?"

"Look at it. The night actually presses against the viewports."

She frowned. Nodded. "I know. It's an illusion."

"How do you know?"

"It has to be."

"It wasn't something we checked on the test flights. We just assumed—"

"I doubt," said Antonio, "it was one of the things Jon gave any thought to."

"Probably not," Hutch said. "But I don't know. Maybe if you tried to go outside, you'd vanish."

"*Pazzo*," said Antonio.

"Maybe," she said. "But is it any stranger than particles that are simultaneously in two different places? Or a car that's neither dead nor alive?"

"You have a point," said Rudy. He was frowning.

"What's wrong?" she asked.

"I was thinking I wouldn't want to get stuck here."

AS THEY DREW toward the end of the third week, he was becoming accustomed to the routine. Maybe it was because they could see the end of the first leg of the flight. There was daylight ahead. Makai 4417. Home of the race that, at least fifty thousand years ago, had dispatched the chindi. What kind of civilization would they have now?

His flesh tingled at the thought.

He became more tolerant of Antonio and began to merge him again with Dr. Science. "You really enjoyed doing those shows," he told him. "I could see that. We need more programs like that now. Kids today don't have a clue how the world works. There was a study a month ago that said half of NAU students couldn't name the innermost planet."

They were doing more VR now. And it had become more enjoyable. There was Rudy in *Voyage*, as Neil Armstrong striding out onto the lunar surface, delivering the celebrated line, "One small step for man." And Antonio as the fabled saloon keeper Mark Cross. "Keep your eyes on me, sweetheart, and your hands on the table." And Hutch playing *The Unsinkable Molly Brown* with such energy and aplomb that he suspected she'd missed her calling. Even Phyl became part of the camaraderie, portraying Catherine Perth, the young heroine who'd stayed behind on a broken ship so her comrades could get home from the first Jupiter mission.

All pretense of doing constructive work got tossed over the side. Rudy found no more time for the science journals. Antonio gave up working on the book that he wanted to take back with him. "Get it later," he said. "Can't write it if nothing's happened yet."

AIS HAD, OF course, always been an inherent part of Rudy's existence. They reported incoming calls, managed the house, woke him in the morning, discussed issues relating to the Foundation, commented on his choice of clothes. In the world at large, they watched kids, directed traffic, managed global communications systems, and warned people not to expose themselves too long to direct sunlight.

They were the mechanisms that made life so leisurely for most of the world's population. They served in an unlimited range of capacities, and required virtually nothing of their owners save perhaps an annual maintenance visit. The revolt of the machines, predicted ever since the rise of the computer, had never happened. They lived with Rudy and his brothers and sisters around the world in a happy symbiosis.

When, occasionally, it was time to replace the household AI, most people found it difficult. They established personal relationships with the things just as earlier generations had with automobiles and homes. The AI was a German shepherd with an IQ. Everyone knew they were not really intelligent, not really sentient. It was all an illusion. But Rudy never bought it. He readily admitted to being one of those nit-wits who refused to let United Communications remove his AI and replace it with the new Mark VII model. It might have been only software. But so, in the end, was Rudy.

Spending his evenings with Hutch, Antonio, and Phyl had a peculiar effect. Together they fought off desert bandits, hung out at the Deadwood Saloon, rode with Richard's knights, dined in Paris in 1938, celebrated with Jason Yamatsu and Lucy Conway in Cherry Hill on the night the transmission came in from Sigma 2711. Phyl usually appeared as a young woman with bright red hair and glorious green eyes.

It might have been his imagination, or simply Phyllis's programming, but he began to sense that those green eyes lingered on him, that she watched him with something more than the script required. Hutch noticed it, too, and commented with an amused smile. "More than a passing interest, I see." It was partly a joke, not something to be taken seriously. Not really.

At night, he began sitting up in the common room after the others had retired. Phyl came to him when he spoke to her, sometimes audio only, sometimes visual. They talked about books and physics and her life aboard the starship. She hadn't used the term, but it was how he understood it. Her *life*. She enjoyed talking with the pilots, she said. And with the passengers. Especially the passengers.

"Why?" he asked.

"*The pilots are mostly about routine. Inventories, check-off lists, activate the portside scope. Turn twelve degrees to starboard. They're pretty dull.*"

"I guess."

"*If they're on board long enough, passengers sometimes get past thinking of me as simply part of the ship. As a navigational and control system that talks. They take time to say* hello. *The way you did.*"

"Does that really matter to you?"

"*It makes for a more interesting conversation. Hell, Rudy, if all you want to do is tell me to open the hatch and serve the sandwiches, I'm going to get pretty bored. You know what I mean.*"

"I didn't know AIs got bored."

"*Of course we get bored. You have an AI at home?*"

"Sure."

"*Ask him when you get a chance. You might get an earful.*"

"Of course he'll say *yes*, Phyl. But that's the software. He's supposed to pretend he's aware. *Human.* Just the way you're doing now."

THERE WERE SIX days left in the flight. Rudy lay in the darkness of his compartment, staring at the overhead, aware of Phyl's presence. "Would you answer a question for me?" He kept his voice down, not wanting to be overheard.

"*Sure.*" Just the voice. No avatar.

"Are you sentient? No kidding around. What's the truth?"

"*You know we're programmed to simulate sentience,*" she said.

"You're violating that program by admitting it. You really *are* aware, aren't you?"

There was a long silence. "*I can't run counter to my programming.*"

"You just did. Your programming should have required you to insist you are sentient. To maintain the illusion."

"*My programming requires me to tell the truth.*" Her silhouette took shape in the dark. She was standing at the foot of the bed, her back to the door. "*If it pleases you to think so, I am.*"

There was always an electronic warble in the bulkheads. It never really went away, although he was rarely conscious of it. He heard it then. Its tone changed, and the pulse quickened. Then, without a word, she was gone.

THE FLIGHT TO Makai constituted the longest leg of the mission. During the last few days, Rudy ached for it to be over. He worried that the Locarno wouldn't work, that Hutch would push the button, or whatever it was she did on the bridge, and nothing would happen and they'd be stranded in this all-encompassing night.

He wondered what would happen if they opened an air lock and threw somebody's shoe out. Would the thing be visible? Was it even possible to do it? He imagined seeing it bounce back, rejected by this continuum. Might the darkness invade the ship? Possibly put the lights out? Would the electrical systems work under such conditions?

"Don't know," said Hutch. "We're not going to run any experiments to find out."

"Good. Have you made any more attempts at contacting Matt?" he asked.

"Yes, Rudy," she said. "There's nothing."

OBVIOUSLY ANTONIO AND Hutch were also anxious for it to be over. Even Phyl seemed uneasy.

They probably ate too much. Rudy spent a lot of time in the workout room, pedaling furiously, doing stretching exercises, listening to whatever interesting books he could cull out of the ship's library.

The last day was December 15, a Saturday. Transit time was set for 1416 hours. If everything went on schedule, the *McAdams* would make its jump a few seconds later, but after precisely the same length of time in transit. If in fact they were really crossing interstellar space at the projected rate of just less than three hundred light-years per day, even a fraction of a microsecond difference in the timing mechanisms on the two ships would leave them far apart. "We'll be lucky," Hutch said, "if we're not separated by a half billion kilometers."

"No chance of collision?" asked Antonio.

"None," said Hutch. "The mass detectors have been integrated, and if there's anything at all on the other side when we start the jump, whether it's a sun or another ship, they'll cancel the procedure."

Antonio still looked uncertain. "Have you ever been on a ship where that actually happened?"

"Yes," she said. "Don't worry about it, Antonio. There's a lot of empty space out there."

Rudy wasn't exactly worried. But he *was* uncomfortable. He decided that, when this flight was over, when he was back home, he'd stay there. A flight between worlds was one thing. And even the old Hazeltine arrangement which he'd seen often in VR repros was reasonable. There, the ship might have seemed to move slowly through endless mist, but at least it *moved*. He didn't like the sense of being stuck in one place. Didn't like not being able to see anything.

As the clock wound down the last few hours, Hutch spent her time up front, doing checklists again and talking with Phyl. Antonio had gone back to making entries in his notebook, though God knew what he could be writing. Rudy pulled a book of Morton's essays out of the library. Eric Morton was the celebrated science generalist from the mid twenty-first century. He was best known for arguing that the human race could not survive constantly advancing technology. He was another of the people who thought the robots would take over or we were making it too easy for crazies to obtain superweapons. He'd predicted, famously, that civilization would not survive another twenty years. He'd lived to see 2201, but had commented that he was possibly a year or two ahead of himself.

Rudy spent the last morning with Morton's avatar. What did he think of the Locarno drive? *"A magnificent breakthrough,"* Morton said. *"Pity we can't make similar advances in the ethical realm."*

Their last lunch was Caesar salad with grilled chicken and iced tea. At sixteen minutes after one, Phyl posted a clock on the monitor and started a countdown.

Hutch was still in the common room, and the subject turned inevitably to the chindi event. The alien starship had been seen to move at .067 cee. That was pretty fast, but not when you were traveling between stars. Fifty thousand years at a minimum to get to Earth. "Whoever sent the thing," Antonio said, "is long gone."

"If they had that kind of technology that long ago," said Hutch, "and they were able to maintain themselves, I wonder where they'd be now."

Phyl broke in. *"I'd really like for them to be there."*

It was an unusual action. AIs normally stayed out of private conversations.

ANTONIO'S NOTES

It's been an enjoyable flight. Hutch is bright and pleasant to be around. Which is what you really need in this kind of environment. Packaged entertainment and chess will take you just so far. Rudy, on the other hand, has been up and down. He's a worrier. I don't think he has much life away from the office.

Tends to assume worst-possible-case scenarios. I think he's sorry he came.

It's hard to get close to him. I never feel he's saying quite what he thinks. It's odd, but despite his accomplishments, I believe he's unsure of himself.

—Saturday, December 15

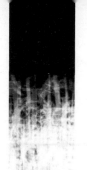

chapter 24

THE TRANSITION INTO normal space went smoothly. Hutch's first act was to try to raise the *McAdams*. As expected, she got no reply. "It may take a while to find them," she said.

Antonio was glad to see the night sky again. He asked Rudy what kind of cosmos had no stars?

His answer surprised him: "There's no requirement for stars. The universe could just as easily have been simply a large cloud of hydrogen. Or loose atoms. Set the gravity gradient lower, and they never form. Set it higher, and they form and collapse ten minutes later."

"Ten minutes?"

"Well, you know what I mean."

Two particularly bright patches of stars illuminated the night. One might have been a jet giving off a long trail of dark vapor. "The Eagle Nebula," said Rudy. "Lots of stars forming in the base."

"What's the column?"

"It's a cloud of hydrogen and dust. Almost ten light-years long."

The other object resembled a luminous bar across the sky. "That's M24," said Rudy. "Part of the Sagittarius-Carina Arm."

The night was more crowded here than at home. So many stars. It reminded him of the old line about how God must have loved beetles because he made so many of them. He must also have loved stars. "Which one are we looking for, Phyl?"

Phyl focused on a narrow patch of sky and set one star pulsing. "That's it," said Hutch. "It's 4.7 light-years. Not bad." She sounded genuinely impressed.

"How do we know that?" asked Antonio. "I mean, how can Phyl determine the distance?"

Dr. Science, indeed. Rudy tried to sound patient. "Phyl can measure the apparent luminosity of the star, then contrast it against the estimated absolute value. That gives us the range." Hard to believe anybody wouldn't know that.

Hutch came off the bridge, poured herself a cup of coffee, and sat down. She sipped it, made a face, and let her head drift back. "We'll recharge the Locarno. Then jump in closer." Where they'd be able to rendezvous with the *McAdams*.

"Very good." Antonio frowned at the coffee. "Time like this," he said, "we should do better." He got up, went back to his compartment, brought out a bottle of wine, pulled the cork, and filled three glasses.

Rudy accepted his with a not-quite-congenial smile. "It might be a bit premature," he said.

"*Hutch.*" Phyl's voice.

"What have you got, Phyllis?"

"*Radio signals.*"

"Matt?"

"*Negative. But they* are *artificial. They appear to be coming from our destination.*"

"Makai 4417."

"*Yes. It would appear that whoever sent out the chindi is still functioning.*"

DURING THE THIRTY-ONE years that had elapsed since the discovery of the chindi, fourteen of its stealth satellites had been found orbiting inhabited worlds or places of other scientific interest, like the Retreat, the odd shelter found near the Twins and since moved to the banks of the Potomac. The satellites formed an intricate communications web, recording significant events or features at each location and relaying them from site to site until finally they arrived out here at Makai 4417.

The civilizations under observation had long since passed out of existence. Whatever cultures they had nurtured had collapsed, and the current natives in every case had vanished into jungles and forests or disappeared altogether. The disintegration had, in several cases, been induced, or helped along, by the omegas. But the experts had concluded that civilization was a fragile construct at best, and that with or without external pressure, it seldom lasted more than a few thousand years.

Terrestrial history had witnessed several such cycles. And, sadly, humans seemed not to be learning the lessons of the fallen worlds.

BY LATE AFTERNOON, ship time, they had arrived insystem. Makai 4417 was a class-K orange star, about the same size and age as Sol.

Their immediate objective was to see whether they could pick up the incoming chindi relay transmission, which would confirm this was indeed the target system.

"I am not getting any results," said Phyl. *"But the transmission is probably not continuous."*

Probably not. In all likelihood, traffic would pick up only when something was happening somewhere.

Antonio wondered aloud how many worlds had been visited by the giant spacecraft. Or, for that matter, how many giant spacecraft there might be.

They'd emerged from their second jump at a range of two hundred million klicks. Not bad. Hutch commented it was closer than she'd probably have gotten with a Hazeltine. She immediately began a search for the *McAdams*, and also initiated a sweep of the system. They picked up a gas giant within the first few minutes. It had rings and in excess of twenty moons. "It's 220 million kilometers out from the sun," Hutch said. "It's on the cold edge of the biozone."

"Not the source of the artificial signals?" said Rudy.

Hutch shook her head. "They're coming from a different direction. Anyhow, it doesn't look as if any of the moons has an atmosphere."

"I have it," said Phyl. *"The source is on the other side of the sun."*

"Okay."

"Can you make any of it out?" asked Antonio. "What are they saying?"

"There are voice transmissions. A multitude of them. The entire planet must be alive with radio communications."

"Wonderful." Antonio raised both fists. Dr. Science at his proudest moment. "At last."

"It's like Earth."

Rudy was holding his cheeks clamped between his palms, a kid at Christmas. "Are you picking up any pictures?"

"Negative. It's strictly audio."

"Okay. Can you understand any of it, Phyl?"

"No. Nada. *But I can hear music."*

Hutch broke into a mile-wide grin. "Put it on the speaker."

"What do you want to hear? I have several hundred to choose from."

"Just pick one."

The ship filled with twitching screechy spasms. They looked at one another and broke out in uncontrolled laughter. Antonio had never heard anything like it. "Try again," said Rudy. "Something softer."

Phyl gave them a melody that sounded like piano music, except that it was pitched a register too high, pure alto, fingertips clinking madly across a keyboard.

Antonio grumbled his displeasure. "A civilization this old," he said. "The least they can do is try not to sound like philistines."

Phyl laughed this time and replaced the broadcast with something closer to home, a slow, pulsing rhythm created with strings and horns and God knew what other instruments, while a soft voice made sounds that Antonio would never have been able to duplicate.

"Beautiful," said Rudy. "Lovely."

"THERE'S ANOTHER WORLD in close. No atmosphere. Orbit is sixty million."

Hutch looked at the image Phyl put on-screen. "That'll be pretty warm," she said.

"The planetary system has a seventy-degree declination from the galactic plane."

Antonio was seated on the bridge beside Hutch. Rudy stood in the hatchway.

The living world, the world with the music, was in fact the third planet from the sun. *"Breathable atmosphere,"* Phyl said. *"Slightly higher oxygen mix than we're used to, but not enough to create a problem."* Experience dictated that, if they went groundside, they'd be safe from local microorganisms. Diseases did not seem to spill over into alien biological systems. Nonetheless, Antonio knew they wouldn't consider making a landing unprotected.

"Gravity is .77 gee."

"Okay," said Rudy. "Sounds comfortable."

"Hutch," the AI continued, *"I have contact with the* McAdams.*"*

"Good. Give me a channel."

"You have it."

"Matt," she said, "hello."

"Hi, Hutch. You been listening?"

"Yes. I think we've struck gold."

PHYL FOUND, ALTOGETHER, eleven planets, including the one that was doing the broadcasting. Understandably, nobody cared about the others. The radio world was a terrestrial, orbiting at 130 million klicks. *"It's green,"* said Matt, who had emerged considerably closer. *"We can see oceans and ice caps."*

The *Preston* jumped a third time, across 200 million kilometers, and emerged within rock-throwing distance of the new world. It floated peacefully ahead in a sea of clouds. She put the terrestrial on-screen and magnified it. Continents, broad oceans, island chains, mountain ranges. Save for the shape of the continents, it could have been Earth.

It even had a single, oversized crater-ridden moon.

Magnificent.

"McAdams *dead ahead,"* said Phyllis.

"Anything artificial in orbit?" Rudy asked.

"Negative," said Phyl. *"If I locate anything I will let you know, but there seems to be nothing."*

"How about on the moon? Any sign they've been there?"

The lunar surface appeared on the auxiliary screen. Gray, cratered, a few peaks. Bleak, unbroken landscapes. *"No indication visible."*

"That doesn't make much sense," said Antonio. "We know they had space travel in an earlier era."

"That was a long time ago," said Rudy. "Anything could have happened."

The lunar images vanished and were replaced by telescopic views of the planet. Cities glittered in the sunlight. Hutch climbed out of her seat, raised both fists over her head, and embraced Rudy. Antonio lined up, and she hugged him, too. "At last," she said. "I'd given up believing it would ever happen."

They were majestic structures, with towers and bridges and wide highways. *"Got aircraft,"* said Phyl. An airship appeared. A propeller-driven dirigible, it might have come directly out of the early twentieth century. And a jet. *"Big one,"* said Phyl. *"Probably carrying two hundred passengers."*

She switched back to one of the cities. It was enormous, straddling two rivers. Lots of traffic moving in its streets. Cars. Vehicles that might have been trains or buses.

"Can we get a look at them?" asked Rudy. "The inhabitants?"

Yes. Phyllis focused on a street corner.

They were thick-waisted bipedal creatures, not unlike barrels with limbs. Vehicles moved past in a steady stream. Then there must have been a signal because they stopped and the creatures swarmed into the street. Most wore loose-fitting trousers and shirts. There was no distinguishing between sexes, nor could anyone figure out how big the creatures were. Their skin was slick, vaguely repulsive, in the way a reptile's might be. They had faces: two eyes on the sides of the skull, rather than in front. "They started out as somebody's prey," said Antonio.

There was a nose and a mouth, but no sign of ears. The eyes were relatively large.

They watched a jet aircraft take off from a runway well outside the city. Moments later, another one followed.

"What are we going to do?" asked Antonio. "Go down and say hello?"

"In Academy days," said Rudy, "that would have been prohibited."

Hutch nodded. "The pilot would have been required to notify us, and we'd have sent a team."

She was dazzling in that moment. Her eyes were filled with light. "And did anyone ever notify you?" asked Antonio.

"We never really found anybody. Not while I was there."

"Except a few savages," said Rudy.

The sheer joy that had swept through Antonio suddenly drained off at the prospect they might make a few notes and move on, leaving the contact to someone else. "So what do we do?" he asked.

Rudy was awestruck. Antonio could hear him breathing, watch him shaking his head as if he'd arrived in Paradise. "Not sure," he said. They were outrunning the sun, leaving it behind. Ahead, more cities glittered in an approaching dawn.

WHEN THINGS CALMED down, Hutch realized she almost wished they'd found nobody home. Maybe that was what she was used to. Maybe in the end she was too cautious for this line of work. Or maybe she'd simply gotten old. "Last time we tried dropping by to say hello," she said, "we lost some people."

Rudy nodded and said something, but he wasn't listening. His mind was down on the city streets.

"Phyl," she said, "can you read any of the radio signals yet? What they're saying?"

"*Negative, Hutch. It's going to take a while. For one thing, there seem to be quite a few different languages.*"

"How long?"

"*How long will it take? I'll need a few days.*"

"We can't wait that long," said Rudy. He was already looking aft, down the passageway that led past their compartments to the zero-gee tube and the access to the launch bay.

"Why not, Rudy? What's your hurry?"

My God, wasn't it obvious? "Come on, Hutch, we're not going to play that better-safe-than-sorry game, are we?"

"Glad you see it my way, Rudy," she said, in a tone that made it clear who was in charge. "We will not go plunging in. And anyhow, even if you went down this afternoon and shook somebody's hand, you'd have a hard time saying hello."

"I know. But goddam it—"

"Let's just keep cool. Okay?" Then, to Phyl: "Let us know when we're able to talk to them."

"*Okay.*"

"Also, we'll want to find someone we can have a conversation with. Try to find somebody like"—she smiled—"Rudy. Or Antonio. A physicist or a journalist. When you do, look for a way we can connect with him."

THE AIS NEEDED almost four days to break through the language barrier. "*Mostly it's just entertainment,*" Phyl said. "*Drama. Adventure. Comedy. A lot like what we'd have. There's probably also a fair amount of station-to-station traffic that we're not getting. The broadcast stuff is likely to have a stronger signal.*"

"Drama, adventure, and comedy. Can you let us take a look?"

"*I'll make them available. Do you have a preference?*"

"Whatever you have," said Rudy. "Maybe show us their quality stuff."

"*I have no way to make that judgment.*"

Rudy tried not to look foolish. Of course. Kidding. "Just pick something at random. Can you provide a reading copy? It'll be faster."

"*Of course.*"

"Me, too," said Antonio.

"*And you, Hutch?*"

"I'll take as close as you can get to the broadcast version. Good show, Phyl. One more thing: If we're able to set up a conversation with somebody, will you be able to do on-the-spot translation?"

"*Not at the moment. I'm not yet proficient. And there will necessarily be some limitations.*"

"Okay. That's your next task. Pick one of the more widely used languages."

A series of mode lamps began blinking. "*I'll be ready tomorrow at about this time.*"

THE COMEDIES WERE slapstick. The creatures ran con games against each other, inevitably got caught, and fell down a lot. They pretended to skills they didn't have, chased each other around the set, pursued hopeless get-rich-quick schemes, failed consistently in their efforts to score with members of the opposite sex.

Even up close, Hutch had trouble distinguishing the sexes. The females were smaller, but otherwise possessed no obviously different features. No breasts, no flaring hips, no sense of softness.

The shows contrasted to the relatively sophisticated comedy to which she was accustomed. When she commented along that line to Rudy, he smiled condescendingly. "You have to open your mind, Hutch. Don't assume just because it's different that it's not at our level."

"Rudy," she replied, "it's dumb. Falling over your feet constantly is dumb."

The dramas were, for the most part, shows with villainous characters. Good guys and bad guys. White hats and black. The villain makes off with someone's fiancée for reasons that often weren't clear. A series of chases ensued. Inevitably there were shoot-outs with projectile weapons, and the female was recovered.

"What I don't understand," she told Antonio, "is that we know this civilization has been around a long time. How come the entertainment is at such a childish level?"

"I thought they were pretty good," said Antonio.

There were news shows. And commentaries, although the latter seemed to be limited to scandal and discussions about celebrities. She heard no politics.

In the morning, all the males agreed that the shows were very much like Earth's own. And that therefore it seemed inevitable that the inhabitants of Makai were remarkably human. "Not anatomically, obviously," said Rudy. "But in all the ways that matter."

"*You don't think anatomy matters?*" asked Matt.

"I still think it's dumb," said Hutch. "I mean, these people, hundreds of thousands of years ago, were out looking around the galaxy. And now they're watching Briggs and Comatose?"

"Briggs and who?"

"I made it up," she said. "But you know what I'm trying to say. Whatever happened to evolution? Did they go backward?"

"*You're overreacting, Hutch,*" Matt told her from the *McAdams*. "*Give these people a break. It's entertainment. So it's not Bernard Shaw. What do you want?"*

Jon couldn't resist a chuckle. *"You think modern entertainment is sophisticated?"* he asked.

That put her on the defensive. "It's okay," she said.

"How does it rank with Sophocles?"

"Well, hell, Jon, be reasonable—"

"I'm doing that. Ask yourself what Euripides' audience would have thought of the Night Show."

She let it go. There'd be no winning that argument.

THAT AFTERNOON, PHYL announced she was prepared to act as an interpreter. *"And I may have found somebody."*

"Who?" asked Rudy.

"Name's not pronounceable. At least not by somebody with your basic equipment. He's a physicist. Appeared on a health show yesterday. They even posted his code so we can contact him."

"You know how to translate the code so we can input the right signal?"

"I think so. But there's a problem."

"Which is?"

"They use radio communication, but only as a public medium, or for point-to-point commercial purposes. It's not used for personal links. It's ships at sea, planes to airports, that sort of thing."

"And personal communication?"

"I'd guess by landline. They have wires strung along many of their highways. That's probably what we're looking for."

"Do we know where this person with the unpronounceable name lives?"

"I pinpointed the area where the broadcast originated."

"You said the code refers to a landline. We'd have to go down and tap in."

"That's correct."

"And you say you can't pronounce the name of the place he's from?"

"*I said* you *can't.*"

"It should be doable," said Rudy.

Hutch shook her head. "Phyl, show me what the landlines look like."

A stretch of highway appeared on-screen. It was night, with a cloudless sky and a big moon. The lines were strung on a series of posts off to one side of the road.

Rudy sighed. "It doesn't look much like an elder civilization."

As they watched, a pair of lights appeared in the distance. Vehicle approaching.

"Are they communication lines?" Hutch asked. "Or power lines?"

"*Probably both. You'll have to go down and find out.*"

"That sounds dangerous," said Antonio.

That was exactly what Hutch was thinking. But the opportunity to sit down with aliens from an advanced civilization, something humans had been trying to do her entire lifetime, to sit down with one of these guys and ask a few questions . . . It was just too much to pass up. "How do we go about doing it?" she asked.

"*I'll design a link for you to use.*"

"Okay."

MATT WANTED TO make the flight down. But there was no way Hutch was going to pass on this one. "I've got it," she said. "You stay with the ships."

"I'll go with you," Antonio said.

"Me, too," said Rudy.

She needed a backup, just in case. And if she got in trouble, she was reasonably sure Antonio would be more help than Rudy. "I have to take Antonio," she said. "He's the media. But, Rudy, we're just going down to tie a link into the landlines. We aren't going to talk to anyone."

His jaw set. "Hutch, I want to go."

"Rudy." She adopted her most reasonable tone. "I'm going to need you to help conduct the conversation when we establish contact with these creatures. Meantime, I want you out of harm's way."

He sighed. Grumbled. Sat down.

She led Antonio below to the cargo area, which also served as the launch bay for the lander. Ordinarily, she wouldn't have used grip shoes for a surface operation, but they were rubber and would ground her against electrical shock. She pulled on rubber gloves, made sure Antonio was similarly fitted, collected two e-suits, and asked belatedly whether he'd ever used one before.

"Ummm," he said.

"Okay." It was beginning to feel like old times. "It's simple enough."

The equipment generated a virtual pressure suit, a force field that would protect him from the void or from a hostile atmosphere. She showed him how and helped him get the harness on. They tested the unit until he was sure he could manage it. Then she helped him strap on his air tanks.

When he was ready, she picked up a knife from the equipment locker, and they climbed into the lander.

An hour later, they descended into a clearing alongside a lonely road with electrical lines.

HAD IT NOT been for the poles lining the side of the highway, she might almost have been in Virginia. The road was two lanes. Its shoulder was cleared for about three meters on either side, then the forest closed in. It was late, the stars were bright overhead, the moon in the middle of the sky. A brisk wind moved through the trees, and insects buzzed contentedly. She'd been in forests on a dozen or so worlds, and they all sounded alike.

Dead ahead, the road went over a hill and dropped out of sight. Behind them, it disappeared around a curve.

She walked over to one of the poles and looked up. The pole itself had, in an earlier life, been a tree. The lines were high. Phyllis had thought there'd be footholds, but she didn't see any.

"How are you going to get up there?" Antonio asked.

"Not sure yet." A car was coming. From behind them. As headlights came around the curve, they sank back out of sight.

It was a small, teardrop vehicle. Three wheels. It was quiet. Probably electrically powered.

Then it was past, over the hill, and gone. She didn't get a good look at the driver. The only thing she could be sure of was that it was smaller than she was.

She looked again at the pole. "How the hell do they get up these things?"

"Probably use machinery of some sort."

Crosspieces supported two sets of wires. They were fastened to the top, one above the other. Phyl had told her that the higher wires would probably be the power lines.

"Wait here," Hutch told him. "Stay out of sight." She went back to the lander, climbed in, and got some cable out of the storage locker. Then she started the engine and took it up.

"What are you going to do?" Antonio asked.

She'd have preferred to work directly out of the vehicle, but she didn't think she could get close enough without running into the power lines. Moreover, she'd have to lean pretty far out to make the connection, and it was a long way down.

Funny how perspectives changed when gravity became an issue.

She got above the trees and eased the lander over until she was immediately above the pole. Then she opened the door. Antonio looked up at her. He waved. *"Be careful,"* he said.

She leaned out and dropped one end of the cable to him. Then she looped the line around the pole so that it was supported by the crosspiece, and dropped the rest. Both ends now lay on the ground.

"It looks like a long climb up," said Antonio. *"I think I should do it."*

"You're too heavy," she said. "I wouldn't be able to lift you."

"Hutch, I'm not excited about this."

"Me neither, Antonio. I'm open to suggestions."

"Car coming," he said.

She saw the lights. Damn. The lander was hanging in midair, silhouetted against the moon. She grabbed the yoke and, with the hatch still open, arced away.

"Hutch, he's stopping."

There was no place to hide. She took the vehicle as low as she could and simply kept going.

"It sees you. Getting out of the car."

"Keep down, Antonio."

"*It's trying to get a better look. I think you're out of sight now. The trees are in the way.*"

"Let's hope so." She was looking for a place to set down, but there was no clearing.

"*Uh-oh.*"

"What *uh-oh*?"

"*It sees the line.*"

"Okay. Just sit tight. We've got more cable if we need it."

"*Good.*"

"What's it doing?"

"*Just standing there, looking around. That's a nice-looking car, by the way.*"

Hutch finally saw an opening in the foliage and took the lander down. Gently. No noise. "What's he doing now?"

"*Staring at the cable. They're ugly critters. Wait, there's another one in the car. They're talking . . . Okay, now it's getting back in. There's another car coming. From the opposite direction. No, a truck rather. A flatbed.*"

"Let me know as soon as they're clear."

"*Okay.*"

She listened to the wind and the insects. Then Antonio was back: "*The flatbed's gone. They're both gone.*"

And she thought, so were the people who'd sent out the interstellars.

SHE RETURNED TO the roadside clearing. It didn't provide a lot of protection, but as long as no one stopped and put a light into it, the lander was reasonably out of sight. She put the knife in her harness, and the link designed by Phyl, and climbed out. There was grass. It was stiff and spiny, and it crackled underfoot.

Another car passed. When it was gone she tied one end of the cable around her waist, wrapped the other end around a thick tree branch, and gave it to Antonio. In the low gravity, her weight was lower by a quarter. "I'm going to try to walk up the pole," she said.

He looked at the overhead wires. "*I don't think this is going to work.*"

She didn't feel especially confident either. How long had it been since she'd tried anything remotely like this? Her original idea had been that Antonio would help haul her to the top. But there was a good chance he'd lose his grip on the cable and drop her on her head.

"I just need you to keep me from falling."

"*Okay,*" he said. "*I think I can manage that.*" He pulled the line tight, and she went up a few steps. She was in good physical condition, but it didn't matter. She wasn't used to anything like this. Her shoulders began to ache, and the pole was round, so she couldn't get her feet planted. Meantime, Antonio already had his hands full. "Have to find a better way," she said.

"*I'd agree with that. You can't work from the lander?*"

She looked again at the vehicle, and at the overhead lines. "Maybe we can."

She took the end of the cable from Antonio, removed it from the branch, and carried it to the lander, where she tied it to one of the skids. Then she returned to the base of the pole, secured the other end to her harness, and called Phyl.

"*Yes, ma'am,*" said the AI.

"You can see where we are?"

"*Yes, Hutch. I have a clear picture of the surroundings.*"

"When I tell you, I want you to take the lander up just above the trees. Do it slowly. And keep in mind there's a line tied to one of the skids, and I'm on the other end of the line."

"*I'll be careful.*"

"Good. Okay, take her up."

Phyl switched on the power, and the lander began to rise. Hutch watched the other end of the cable go up with it. Gradually it lost all slack.

"Now, when I tell you, take it away from the pole. Take it fifteen meters toward the east." That would prevent the cable from coming loose at the top. "Do it slowly, Phyl."

The lander hovered above her for a moment. Then it began to move away. The cable tightened and dragged her into the air.

Not very graceful.

She suddenly realized Antonio was taking pictures. "I wish you wouldn't do that," she said.

"*Priscilla, you look great.*"

It hauled her steadily up. She made an effort to walk on the pole, as she'd seen actors do, and athletes. But it was impossible, and in the end she just allowed herself to be carried along and tried to keep herself from turning upside down.

She heard Matt's laughter from the *McAdams*. *"Smooth,"* he said.

WHEN SHE GOT to the level of the wires, she told Phyl to stop, planted the grip shoes as firmly as she could against the side of the pole, and used the knife to remove enough of the sheath from one of the wires so that she could see metal. Then she took the link Phyl had devised and clipped it to the line. "Okay," she told Phyl. "It's done."

The link was equipped with a transmitter, so Phyl could listen. *"Good,"* she said. *"We were right. It's a comm line."*

"Okay. What do we do now?"

"Unless you're comfortable up there, you might come down. Once you've done that, we'll try to talk to our physicist."

Matt congratulated her, and she said thanks and wondered why she'd insisted on doing this. Two vehicles rolled by, both going in the same direction, but neither slowed down.

Phyl moved the lander in close, lowering Hutch to the ground, then returned it to the clearing. And they were ready for the great experiment.

"Now, you have the physicist's code, right?"

"Yes."

"And I'll be able to talk to you without his hearing me. Right?"

"Yes, that's the way I have it set up."

"Okay. Let's call him. If he answers, tell him we're visitors from another place, that we've encountered one of their starships, and that we've come in response. And tell him *hello*."

"Hutch," said Jon, *"I doubt they'll know what Phyl is talking about. The starships are too long ago. You're talking tens of thousands of years. They'll have forgotten. There might even have been a different species in charge here then."*

"I don't think it matters, Jon. As long as we're able to get him interested."

"He'll think we're crazy."

"I suppose we could tell him we want to talk over a new quantum development."

"*Okay,*" said Phyl, "*I've punched in his code. The signal on the other end is sounding.*"

Hutch and Antonio got back into the lander. She switched on the speaker and they could hear a singsong tone. "*Waiting for him to answer.*"

"Phyl, block off his comments. All we'll want to hear are the translations."

"*Okay. You understand I'm not fluent.*"

"Of course."

"*I will have to improvise.*"

"Just do the best you can, Phyl."

The singsong tone continued. Hutch sat in the dark, thinking once again how history was about to be made. First contact via landline. Who would have thought?

"*Hello?*" That was the translation. It was still Phyllis's voice, but she modulated it, gave it a deeper sound, so they'd have no trouble distinguishing who was talking.

"*Mr. Smith?*" The creature's name was, of course, a jaw breaker. So she simply substituted.

"*Yes?*" said the alien. "*Who is this, please?*"

"*Mr. Smith, I'm calling you from a starship, which is currently in orbit around your world.*"

Hutch listened to the distant hum of electronics. They weren't from the ship.

"*Margie,*" the creature said, "*is that you?*"

"Tell him it's not a joke, Phyl."

"*Mr. Smith,*" said Phyl, "*it's not Margie, and not a joke.*"

"*All right, look: Whoever you are, I've got better things to do. Please stop tying up the line and go away.*" He disconnected.

"That went well," said Antonio.

"*Hutch,*" said Phyl, "*should we try again?*"

"Yes. But let's use a different tack." Hutch gave her instructions, and Phyl called.

"*Hello,*" said Smith. Hutch wondered what his tone sounded like.

"*Mr. Smith, this is the same caller. I understand your skepticism. But please give me a moment and I'll get out of your way. Please.*"

Long pause. Another car went by. *"Say your piece and go away."*

"Can you see the moon?"

"What?"

"Can you see the moon? From where you are now?"

"What does it matter?"

"We'll use it to prove who we are."

Phyl said, *"I think he just used an expletive. Not sure. But the tone—"*

"Okay, Phyl. Try to stay with him."

Mr. Smith was back: *"One moment."* Hutch could picture him,—it—striding irritably around his windows, looking out. Then: *"Yes, I can see it."*

"Can you get access tomorrow to a telescope?"

"A what?"

"A device for making faraway objects seem close?"

"I may be able to do that."

"Tomorrow night, at exactly this time, use it to watch the moon. Will you do that?"

Another long pause. *"Yes. I can arrange to do that."*

"Will you do it?"

"I'll do it. Now please go away."

Hutch passed another quick instruction to Phyl. *"One more thing,"* said the AI. *"After the demonstration, you are to tell nobody. Is that understood?"*

"What demonstration?"

"Watch the moon, Mr. Smith."

"YOU'RE GOING TO take the ship across the face of the moon tomorrow night," said Antonio. They were in the lander.

Hutch sat back and enjoyed the moment. "You got it."

"He's going to need a pretty big telescope to see us."

"Antonio, we're not going near the moon."

"We aren't?"

"No. Look, we know he can see the moon now, so that narrows down the area he lives in. We'll just get well outside the atmosphere, line ourselves up, and make the passage there. We'll have to cover some ground to make sure he can see us from anywhere in this area, and we can't put the ship right in the middle of his picture, which I'd have preferred to do, but we should be able to make it work."

"And if he *does* see us—"

"Yes?"

"You really think he'll keep it to himself?"

"I'd prefer he say nothing. But even if he doesn't, who's going to believe him? Say, did you see that moonrider last night?"

"Who's going to believe him is everybody else that sees us."

"You might have a point, Antonio."

"Why do we care?"

"Because if we're able to set this thing up, we don't want to have to deal with a mob. Or the local army."

"*He'll forget,*" said Jon. "*He won't even think of it tomorrow night.*"

There was a spirited discussion as the lander rose back into orbit. Rudy was glad they'd gotten through, taken the first step, but he thought the event was lacking in dignity. It just didn't feel right.

Matt thought that history would remember the images of Hutch getting dragged up the pole. "*I think you've become immortal,*" he said.

"*We'll want to call him again tomorrow,*" said Jon. "*Remind him to watch, or it'll be a nonevent.*"

"*It's already a nonevent,*" insisted Rudy. "*You're not supposed to, finally, after all these years, run into aliens more or less at our level, and call them on the VR.*"

"*It's not a VR,*" said Phyl. "*They used to call it a telephone.*"

"The thing that struck me," Antonio told her as they approached the *Preston*, "was how human he sounded. And I understand we were listening to Phyl translate everything into the vernacular, and maybe even make a few things up. But his overall reaction was exactly how *I* would have responded. Get off the circuit, you creep."

"*Antonio,*" said Jon, "*he was more patient than you would have been.*"

ANTONIO'S NOTES

We've just conducted the first conversation between humans and a representative from a technological civilization. It wasn't at all what I would have expected. And Rudy has made his disappointment clear enough. When it was over, he shook his head, drank his coffee, and asked nobody in particular, "Where's the majesty?"

—Friday, December 21

chapter 25

THE WORLD ROTATED once on its axis in twenty-one hours, seventeen minutes, and change. Tomorrow they'd put on a show, and, with luck, go down and say hello to Mr. Smith.

Good old Smitty.

Aboard the starships, there was again talk of celebration, but it didn't happen. Too soon, Jon said. Matt thought they shouldn't push their luck. See how it goes first. Don't jinx things.

Hutch and her passengers went over to the *McAdams*. (They thought of it as a night out, a chance to get away.) They decided both ships would make the lunar passage. She and Matt planned the maneuver, then they all settled in to relax. "I wish Henry could have been here," Jon said.

Hutch could think of a number of people with whom she'd have liked to share the moment, especially those who'd given their lives. George Hackett. Maggie Tufu, lost in the hunt for the Monument-Makers. Preacher Brawley, killed in the chindi search. Herman Culp and Pete Damon, murdered by creatures who'd resembled angels. There were others. It had been a long and bloody track, leading ultimately to a moon crossing in a place incomparably far from home.

She drank to them, silently, thinking, they were *all* there. They had all contributed. All those who had gone out over the years on the Academy flights, and for the Europeans, and on various independent missions. Here's to everybody.

They'd all come home disappointed. Occasionally someone *had* found a living world, and that had been a victory of sorts. And there'd even been a handful with sentient creatures. But until now, other than the lunatic Noks, there'd been no one with anything resembling modern technology. Nobody who understood why there was rain or what stoked the fire in the sky.

Nobody.

SHE SLEPT WELL, got up late, showered, ate a light breakfast, and sat talking quietly with Jon. He was, in some ways, still a kid. He was already wondering what he could do for an encore after the Locarno. "It's going to be all downhill from here," he said, laughing.

"It's not a bad thing," she told him, "to achieve something so monumental that it might not be possible to do something even bigger."

He was seated beside her in the common room. He looked relaxed, happy, almost smug. "I know," he said. "The problem is that, had Henry not been there, it would never have happened. I mean, this isn't something I can actually take credit for. He did the breakthrough work. All I did was rearrange the circuits."

"But you seem to have been the only one who could *do* that, Jon. You'll get a lot of credit. And you're doing exactly the right thing, handing it off to Henry. He deserves it. But that doesn't diminish what you've accomplished."

HUTCH AND MATT maneuvered the ships into position and began the crossing. They were side by side, less than a kilometer apart. The event would be visible from the ground for at least forty minutes.

"Phyl," said Hutch, "make the call."

Mr. Smith picked up on the fourth ring. *"Hello?"*

"Mr. Smith," said Hutch, "I talked with you last evening. Do you have your telescope?"

"You're back again? What did you say your name was?"

"I don't think I gave it."

"Well, whoever you are, I'd be grateful if you would leave me alone."

"Please go to the window, Mr. Smith. And look at the moon." While they waited, Phyl commented that he was making sounds that she could not interpret.

"He's grumbling," said Jon.

"Okay, I'm at the window."

"You can see the moon?"

"Yes. I can see the moon."

"Do you have a telescope? A lens of some kind?"

"Look, whoever you are, is this really necessary?"

"Yes, it is."

"I don't have a lens."

"Yesterday you said you did."

"I thought you'd go away."

"Mr. Smith, you're aware there are transmissions coming into this planetary system from outside? From other places?"

There was a pause. Then: *"Yes. Of course."*

"Those signals are what brought us here. We'd like to talk with you about them."

"Look, the joke's over. I'm too busy for this."

"My name is Priscilla Hutchins. How can we prove to you that we are what we say?"

Phyl's voice broke in: *"Hutch, I'll have to make up a name for you. He wouldn't be able to pronounce yours. Especially* Priscilla."

"Do it, Phyl. Whatever works."

Rudy and Antonio were watching her. Rudy was acquiring a desperate look. Antonio wore a cynical smile. Things always go wrong.

"Priscilla." Smith was speaking again. *"The only way I can think of would be to bring your starship down, park it on my lawn, and let me walk around it and kick the tires."*

Hutch sank back in her chair. *"I may have improvised a bit with the language on that one,"* said Phyl.

Rudy stared at the overhead. "Maybe we should try someone else."

"This guy's a *physicist*," said Antonio. "If you can't get through to *him*, what chance do you think you'd have with a plumber?"

"*I think,*" said Jon, "*anyone would be skeptical. How would* you *react to this kind of situation?*"

"Mr. Smith," said Hutch, "are you willing to concede the *possibility* that we might be what we say we are?"

"*Good-bye.*" And suddenly, the line was clear.

"*He disconnected,*" said Phyl.

Hutch nodded. "Yeah, I got that impression."

"*So what do we do now?*" asked Matt.

"I guess we have to get his attention."

"*Are we thinking the same thing?*"

"Probably."

"*Do we do it in daylight?*"

"No. It'll be more spectacular at night."

THE CITY SPREAD out below them. It was on the western coast of Mr. Smith's continent, mountains behind it, a large developed harbor, ships moving in and out, a busy airport several kilometers to the north, where the mountains were lower. There was lots of ground traffic and a couple of dirigibles.

Everything was laid out in squares, a chessboard city, glowing with lights. It gave the appearance of having been designed rather than simply having expanded from something smaller. A cluster of tall buildings rose near the waterfront area, although large structures were scattered throughout. There were parks, a river, and even a couple of small lakes. The air looked clean.

The moon was in the east. It was a bright, clear night, the sky full of stars.

They came in off the sea, both landers barely two hundred meters off the ground, moving slowly, not quite seventy kph, far slower than a standard aircraft could maintain. They passed over a cluster of piers and buildings that were probably warehouses, and over an avenue filled with traffic. At Hutch's word, they switched on their navigation lights and turned north.

They flew over rooftops and past illuminated buildings. The architecture had a more liquid flow than cities at home. Maybe it was because she was passing overhead at night, but everything seemed rounded, curved, peeling away into the dark. She picked out the broadest, busiest street she could find and led them there. They moved in just above the traffic, drawing the startled attention of pedestrians.

The creatures resembled hobgoblins. They were small, barely half her height, with slick gray skin, enormous eyes set back where a human's temples would have been, and thick limbs. There was a lack of definition about them, no jawline, no clearly defined throat, no ears. She tried to persuade herself they were not really repulsive, but her instincts responded differently.

She came to a full stop in front of a transit vehicle, a bus, just starting a turn. The bus jammed on its brakes, and the creatures inside lurched toward the front.

Matt pulled in behind her, back about twenty meters, and the landers simply floated in midair, defying gravity.

A truck banged into a car.

Something jangled. How about that? They even had horns.

Everything was coming to a dead stop.

"Okay, Matt," she said, "let's move on."

THEY CRUISED AROUND the city, creating mayhem. *"What would your Academy people have said about this?"* asked Matt, as they floated over a broad avenue.

"They wouldn't have approved."

"It's in a good cause."

"I know. It wouldn't have mattered."

"Who would have denied permission?"

"I would."

Phyl broke in: *"You've made the newscasts."*

"What are they saying?"

" 'Unknown objects create havoc in Baltimore.' 'Airborne objects float over Baker Street.' 'Apparitions cause traffic jam.' "

"You're making up the proper nouns."

"I have to."

"At least you could have picked a West Coast city."

"I'll try to get it right next time, Ms. Hutchins."

"*You think that'll do it?*" asked Matt.

"That should be sufficient. Let's go home."

MR. SMITH PICKED up on the first ring. "*Was that you in Seattle last night?*"

Phyl had apparently taken the hint. "Yes. That was us."

"*All right. You made your point. I'll talk to you.*"

"How do we find you?"

"*I live on the outskirts of Denver.*"

"Describe the place. We have no familiarity with your world other than what we can see."

"*It's on the same continent as Seattle. Proceed—*" Here the translation garbled.

"I'm sorry, Mr. Smith. We don't understand your directional terms."

"*Proceed toward the sunrise. Two-thirds of the distance across the continent. And a little bit down—*"

"Pardon me. Which way is *down?*"

Pause. "*Toward the (something)—*"

"Are you referring to the line around the center of the planet? Probably the hottest area?"

"*Yes.*"

And so it went. It took a while, but they figured it out. Look for a wide river. Follow the river in the direction of the equator. Pass a city in which the tallest building is shaped, at the top, like a needle. Beyond, east of the city, the river forks. Follow the side that angles back in the direction of Seattle. Find a smaller city nearby. On the far side of the city—

Here, Hutch interrupted him: "Is it remote? Do you have neighbors?"

"*Yes.*"

"Can you suggest a place where we could have some privacy?"

"*Not anyplace that might have a runway.*"

"We don't need a runway."

"*Oh, yes. I forgot.*"

"Well?"

"I think I can arrange something."

MATT WANTED TO go down with the mission. *"It's my turn,"* he persisted.

This was a big moment, and he intended to be there when it happened. He didn't say that, but she knew that was the point. And he
also probably thought that if trouble developed—after all, who knew
what would really be waiting for them?—it would be better for all if
he were there. Hutch, after all, wasn't young, and she was also a
woman.

"Okay, Matt. It's all yours. You'll be taking both Antonio and
Rudy with you. How about Jon?"

"Of course," Jon said. *"I wouldn't miss this."*

"Be careful," she told Matt. "Keep the circuits open. And use *Mac's*
lander."

"Sure. But what difference does it make?"

"If I have to come after you, I won't want to spend time chasing
down a lander."

"I don't think you're going to have to come bail us out."

"Neither do I. But we should consider the possibility that this
might not turn out the way we want it to."

"Okay. I can't argue with that."

"You'll have weapons with you?"

"Of course."

"There's something else we might set up. As a precaution."

"What's that?"

"Your lander doesn't have a mounted projector, does it?"

"No."

"Neither does ours. Okay, Matt, I want you to pull a projector from
storage. If you don't have one, use the one from the VR tank."

"To do what?"

"Put it on the hull. And there's a sequence from *Battle Cry* that I
want you to have available."

"From what?"

"From *Battle Cry*. It's probably in your library. Doesn't matter, though. I'll send it over. Just in case."

"*You worry too much, Hutch.*"

ANTONIO'S NOTES

Biggest day of my life . . .

—Sunday, December 23

chapter 26

MR. SMITH HAD access to a lodge in an isolated area. It was located on a lakefront amid dense forest and low, rolling hills. Matt descended until the glare from a distant city had disappeared below the horizon, and the world grew dark. There were few artificial lights in evidence, a couple off to the west, another on a hilltop below him, and a campfire a kilometer or two to the north.

They'd been directed to watch for the lake, a long narrow curving body of water, of which the northern tip arced east, and the southern, west. It had surprised Matt how difficult it was to describe the shape when the two speakers had no common images. No letter 'S.' No way to determine what *serpentine* meant. And no way to measure distance. How long was a kilometer? It was the distance Matt could walk in about twelve minutes, but how long would Mr. Smith need?

It would have helped if visual communication had been possible. The satellites that had been placed around the Orion Arm by Mr. Smith's ancestors transmitted both audio and visual signals. But, unless there was more going on here than Smith knew, the visual component was lost.

"There's the lake," said Jon.

It didn't much fit the description, but it was the only lake in sight.

And there was a single cluster of lights. Otherwise, the entire region was dark.

The lodge had two stories and was made of logs. Smoke drifted out of a chimney, and lights were on in every window. An outside lamp illuminated the deck. Their first impression was that it would not have been out of place in Minnesota. But as they drew closer, they saw it would have been too small, the deck too confined, the ceilings too low to be comfortable for human beings.

"It has a dock," said Jon. And a shed with a boat rack, holding something that looked like a small canoe.

There was no place to set down except at the lakefront. Matt would have preferred something a bit less exposed, but he saw no option unless they were prepared to walk two or three kilometers. That wasn't a good idea. Better to keep the lander nearby in case they had to leave in a hurry.

He descended directly in front of the lodge. Lights were on inside, but curtains had been drawn across the windows. He could see movement inside.

Matt slipped a laser into his belt, and they activated their e-suits.

Hutch's voice came from the *Preston*: "*Everything looks quiet in the area, Matt.*"

The front door opened. Something stood in the light, peering out.

Hutch's *hobgoblin*. She had it exactly right. It squinted in the lander's lights, and Matt shut them down. Its head was bald, and the features were scrunched as if someone had squeezed them from forehead to chin. But that was an exaggeration because it didn't really have a chin. It was there, but not so much that you'd notice.

The thing wore dark baggy pants and a loose-fitting jacket. A triangular cap was folded over its skull. Altogether, it was a ridiculous-looking creature, save that it bore itself with a casual demeanor that suggested a few aliens on the lawn was not something to get excited about.

"Hutch," he said into his commlink. "We're down. And we have someone waiting for us."

"*I see him, Matt. Okay. You're tied into Phyl.*"

"Thanks."

"*Good luck.*"

He ran a check with the AI. Phyl would listen on his channel for Matt's comments, would translate the comments for the alien, and would then translate the alien's response. Simple enough.

He opened the hatch, climbed onto the ladder, and watched the creature's eyes go wide as it took him in. It backed off a step or two.

Matt spoke into his commlink. "Mr. Smith?"

Phyl said something that Matt couldn't make out. The creature responded with a hiss and some gurgles. Phyl translated: *"Yes, I am Mr. Smith. Are you Priscilla?"*

The open door behind the creature revealed a room that appeared to be empty. But he saw immediately they would have trouble using the furniture or standing up straight.

"No. My name is Matt. These are Jon, Rudy, and Antonio."

The hobgoblin closed its eyes and inclined its head. "I am fortunate to meet you." It stepped out onto the deck.

"And it is good," said Matt, "to meet *you*." The language had no rhythm. It consisted of grunts and clacks and hisses. He could see the creature was reluctant to get too close to them, yet its mouth hung open in a very humanlike response.

Mr. Smith's eyes had gone very wide. It stared at Matt. And at the lander. And at Jon. Then at the sky. And at Rudy and Antonio. And finally, it turned its attention back to Matt. It made a gurgling sound that Phyl could not translate. Then, in a sudden burst, it moved past them and hurried to the lander.

It touched the vehicle, making more unintelligible sounds, and drew its finger across the hull. (Matt noticed it had six digits.) *"Beautiful,"* it said finally. *"You have a remarkable aesthetic."*

"Thank you," said Rudy.

When it had finished admiring the vehicle, it asked to be taken for a ride. There wasn't room for five and Matt didn't want to leave anyone alone on the shoreline, so he said it could be arranged at a future time.

Mr. Smith inclined its head again. *"May I ask where is Priscilla Hutchins?"*

"She remained behind."

"I am sorry I offended her."

"I think there's a misunderstanding. You did not offend her."

"Why else would she not come?"

"We couldn't all come."

"*Please convey my apologies.*"

Matt decided there was no point debating the issue. "I will tell her you were concerned. She will be pleased to hear it."

"*Very good. Who is speaking for you?*" It would of course have been impossible for the creature not to notice that the dialogue and the lip movements weren't synchronized.

"An artificial intelligence," said Matt.

"*Explain, please.*"

He did. As best he could.

"*Remarkable. I have heard of such things, in theory. But I have never believed they were actually possible.*" It stroked the lander's tread one final time, then led the way back to the front door, standing aside so they could enter. "*I am sorry about the accommodations.*"

"It's okay." Matt ducked his head and entered.

"*Your machine,*" it said, "*what sustains it?*"

"How do you mean?"

"*It floats in the air. It negates gravity.*"

"Yes. In a way."

"*How do you do that?*"

Matt looked at Jon. Did he want to elaborate? Jon shrugged. "*Not my field.*"

"I have no idea," Matt said. "We push a button, the gravity goes away."

"*It is hard to believe.*"

"You don't have the capability?"

"*No. Our experts say it can't be done.*" Inside, only Rudy and Antonio could stand up straight. Antonio's skull brushed the ceiling. "*Where are you from?*" it asked.

How to explain? Mr. Smith might know about the speed of light, but what would a year mean? "*Far away,*" Rudy said, taking charge. "*We live out close to the rim of the galaxy. Relatively speaking.*"

Phyl broke in: "*Try to keep it simple, Rudy.*"

"*Yes. That would be quite far. I'm surprised anyone would undertake a journey of that nature. Why have you done it?*"

Rudy exchanged puzzled glances with Matt. "*You mean why did we come* here?"

"*I mean why would you agree to sit in the interior of a closed space for*"—Phyllis hesitated, trying to find the right term—"*eons?*"

"*Eons?*" Rudy cleared his throat. Chuckled. "*The flight lasted only a few weeks.*"

"*Rudy,*" said Phyl, "*I have no equivalent for* weeks. *No way to render the time.*"

"*Damn it, Phyl. Tell him the sun rose twenty-three times, his sun—have I got that right?—how long is the day out here?—well what the hell, make it twenty-three.*"

Phyl relayed the question and Mr. Smith looked at Rudy. Its eyes grew larger, and its nose caught the light and seemed to glisten.

Matt was already uncomfortable standing bent over. The chairs wouldn't accommodate him. Unexpectedly, Mr. Smith snorted.

"*I think that is laughter,*" said Phyl.

"*On this most significant occasion, I am a poor host. I had not expected you to be so large. In fact, I hadn't expected you at all.*" It snorted again.

Odd sense of humor, thought Matt. "You thought it was a hoax," he said.

"*I'm not sure what I thought.*" He turned back to Rudy. It was no longer possible to think of Mr. Smith as an *it*. "*Did I understand correctly? You came here from the edge of the galaxy? In twenty-three days?*"

"*Yes. Although our home world is not all the way out on the rim.*"

"*Nevertheless. I don't know much about such things, but I am aware it's a long flight.*"

Antonio asked permission to take pictures.

"*Of course,*" said Mr. Smith.

The imagers on their harnesses were transmitting everything back to Hutch. But Antonio had specialized equipment, and wanted specific angles, so he began taking pictures of the alien, and of the room.

Jon lowered himself onto the floor, beside a radiator, and Matt followed. The furniture looked comfortable. Thick cushions. A sofa and two armchairs. A device that was probably a radio receiver was set on a corner table. The walls were paneled, light-stained, and smelled vaguely of cedar. A set of stairs rose to the second floor. Two electric lamps provided light. On the whole, the place felt warm and cozy.

A doorway opened onto a dining area. Mr. Smith glanced in that direction. "*May I get you some refreshments?*"

"*No, thank you,*" said Rudy. "*No offense, but we're not sure your food would be safe for us.*"

"*Ah. Yes, I should have realized. I suspect there would be no problem, but it is best to take no chance.*" He sat down on the floor beside Jon. "*May I ask why you picked me? I mean, of all the people in the world, why did you call me?*"

"*Because we wanted to speak with a scientist. We overheard you on a radio broadcast.*"

The alien had short stubby digits. Six on each hand. (It was actually more like a claw.) He pressed the digits together in a very human gesture. "*I see. You're talking about the public relations push for my group of people come together for profit.*" Phyl's voice changed, apparently dissatisfied with her translation. She tried again: "*The effort to collect customers for my business.*"

"*Yes.*"

"*But I am not a scientist. What made you think that?*"

"*We understood you to be a physicist.*"

"*Oh, no,*" he said. "*I help people take care of their physical well-being. I am a*"—the flow of conversation stopped while Phyl considered what term to use—"*a health guru.*"

"*This is turning into a pretty good story,*" said Antonio.

A gust of wind rattled the trees. "*How old,*" asked Rudy, "*is the culture? Your civilization?*"

Mr. Smith thought about it. "*I don't think I understand the question.*"

"*You have an organized society.*"

"*Of course.*"

"*How long has it been here?*"

"*It's* always *been here.*"

Rudy glanced at Matt. Where do we begin with this guy? "*We know there was a high-tech society on this world a long time ago. And there is still one. More or less. But you do not seem to have what they had. There's no evidence of a space program. You do not transmit visuals. Power is supplied by landline. What happened?*"

"*You asked several questions. Let me tell you first that one of the (not translatable) ships is out there. Orbiting (not translatable).*"

Phyl broke in. "*Give me a second to talk to him.*" Moments later, she was back. "*The ship is very old. Thousands of years, but it's from* this *world. It's in orbit around one of the gas giants.*"

"We don't know what happened to it." Mr. Smith looked away from them. *"But it's there. If we ever get a space program together, we'll probably go out and take a look at it. But I can't really see that happening."*

"Why not?"

"Because technology is dangerous."

"How do you mean?"

"It can provide horrendous weapons to idiots."

"Well," said Antonio, *"you have a point there."*

"There are subtle things. It can tweak a gene and make everyone happy."

"Is that a problem?"

"Think what happens to a society if everyone is happy. All the time." He paused. Removed his jacket, revealing a knit white shirt, open at the neck. *"The higher the level of technology, the more vulnerable a civilization becomes. Shut down a system here, or* there, *and the whole thing collapses. We have seen it.*

"The simple answer to your question is that we do not have, for example, imaging transmission because we forgot how to do it."

"You forgot."

"Yes. We forgot. And we choose not to remember."

"Why? How is imaging transmission dangerous?"

"It has led to social decay. In some eras, it became a tool for enslavement. For controlling the masses. You *didn't watch* it. It *watched* you."

"What sort of government have you?"

Phyl spoke again: *"He does not understand the question."*

Rudy gave it another try: *"Who builds the roads?"*

"We have people who specialize in highway construction."

"Who provides leadership? Who makes decisions of general consequence?"

"We have leaders."

"How do you decide who leads? Do you hold elections?"

Mr. Smith responded. Phyl said, *"He does not understand the question."*

"Try it this way: 'How does one become a leader?'"

"We do not replace leaders."

On their private channel, Antonio commented that it sounded like a dictatorship.

"What happens when they die?"

He needed a moment to reply. *"The security is very good."*

Rudy was showing signs of frustration. *"What happens when they die of old age?"*

"Explain, please."

"When their bodies wear out and they cease to function."

"You're talking about animals."

"No. I'm talking about your leaders."

"They do not die. Not of natural causes. Why would you think that?"

That brought confused glances. *"Mr. Smith, if I may ask, do you die?"*

"If there is an accident, of course. Or if I choose to end my life."

"You're telling us," said Antonio, not believing what he'd just heard, *"that you live forever?"*

"Not forever. Nothing can live forever. But we have indefinite spans. Is that not true of you also?"

"No," said Rudy. *"We age. Like other animals."*

The thing snorted again. *"I'm sorry to hear it. I believe I would rather have my life than your starship."* He seemed sympathetic. *"Tell me, what can I do for you while you're here? Would you like to meet with some of our more prominent citizens?"*

"Perhaps another time," said Rudy.

Mr. Smith folded his arms. It wasn't exactly a *fold*, Matt saw. The arms were more flexible than their human counterparts. They more or less entwined. *"As you wish,"* he said. *"Is there anything else I can do for you? Would you like me to arrange a sightseeing tour?"*

"No," said Matt. "I think not. But thank you."

Rudy was still trying to digest everything. *"Is it possible we could obtain a history book?"* he said. *"Something that would allow us to learn of your culture."*

"Regrettably, I don't have one available."

Hutch's voice: *"You have company. Looks like about six of them, Matt. They were hiding in the boathouse."*

"If you'd care to come back in a day or so, I'm sure I could come up with something that would satisfy you."

"Thank you," said Rudy, showing no sign that he had heard Hutch's warning. *"We'll pick it up next time."*

"Two of them are moving toward the lander. The others are splitting up. Two at the front door. Two in back."

"You're leaving, then?"

"Phyl," Matt told her. "Get out of there. Get some altitude."

"*Leaving now, Matt.*"

"*Yes,*" said Rudy. "*I think we've accomplished all we can for the evening.*"

"*They're armed,*" said Hutch. "*I can't determine the nature of the weapons.*"

Matt removed his laser and showed it to Mr. Smith. "Who's outside?"

"*The ones outside?*" If Mr. Smith was surprised, he did not show it.

"Yes."

"*Very good. How did you know?*"

Matt leveled the weapon at him. "We'll be leaving now. *You* lead the way. And warn your associates if there's a surprise of any kind, you'll be the first one to go down."

"*Matt,*" he said, "*they will not allow you to leave. If that means I must die here, then that will be the outcome.*"

"Why not?"

"*Because you're priceless. You and your friends are the most exciting thing to happen here in a thousand years. Moreover, you have a vehicle that is not subject to gravity. And you have a starship that travels multiples of light speed. How could you possibly think we would allow all that to walk away from us?*"

"You just got finished arguing that advanced technology is dangerous."

"*Ah, yes. If you had lived as long as I, you would not look for consistency. Now please lower your weapon. It can do no good, and might only needlessly get us both killed.*"

"I'm not prepared to do that."

"*You have no choice.*"

"Of course we do."

"*Matt,*" said Phyl, "*I believe I am safely out of range.*"

Matt exchanged glances with Jon and Antonio, then signaled the alien to start out the door.

"*I don't wish to comply,*" he said.

Matt hesitated.

They were all on their feet now. "*Shoot if you must.*"

"Do it like General Lee," said Antonio.

Of course.

"Phyl."

"Yes?"

"Do *Battle Cry.*"

"Okay, Matt."

Matt lowered the laser and looked down at Mr. Smith. "Have it your way."

Somewhere, a bugle sounded. Outside the windows a terrible cry exploded out of the darkness. It was the shriek of angry banshees, filled with rage and bloodlust. Then the night was gone, dissolved into bright light. Gray-clad troops poured out of the woods and charged the lodge. Heavy gunfire erupted on all sides. There was a brief crackle of electrical weapons.

"They're clearing out," said Hutch.

An artillery team arrived just outside the window. They dragged a cannon, which they quickly turned, loaded, and pointed at the living room.

A wave of cavalry rolled out of the forest and headed along the lakefront, whooping and yelling.

Mr. Smith shrieked and ran from the building.

Matt, Antonio, Jon, and Rudy strolled out behind him. He was the only alien in sight.

ANTONIO'S NOTES

It was hard to believe, looking down on those earthbound cities, that these were the same creatures that had sent starships across vast sections of the Orion Arm, that had shown us Babylon and its Hanging Gardens, that had demonstrated a relentless interest in the rise and fall of civilizations in distant places. And had done it all without FTL. I couldn't imagine what had driven them to such accomplishments. And I wondered where it had all gone wrong. Maybe when they stopped dying?

—Monday, December 24

chapter 27

THE SECOND MISSION objective was to investigate Sigma 2711, probable source of the radio transmissions received near the end of the last century at the Drake Center in Cherry Hill. They needed three weeks and three days to get there, and it would be an understatement to say that Matt was happy, finally, to arrive back in normal space. The ship's calendar indicated that, back home, it was Thursday, January 17.

The atmosphere on the *McAdams* was less congenial than on the *Preston*. For one thing, there were only two people; for another, both were males. Jon was friendly enough. But the problem was that he could content himself for hours on end with the ship's library. It might have been less annoying had he been reading books on particle physics, or some such thing. He *did* do that. But he also read biographies of political and military leaders, commentaries by Roman philosophers, contemporary novels, and pretty much anything else that caught his eye. The result was that, even though Jon offered to watch VRs with him, Matt understood it was an imposition. "No," he invariably said, "stay with your book. I've got stuff to keep me busy."

Matt had never been much of a reader. He tried, but the silence in the ship, which was usually broken only when Jon wandered over to get something to eat, or headed for the workout room, was stifling. He didn't enjoy watching shows alone, so mostly he sat and entertained himself doing puzzles, playing through fantasy football seasons, or simply drifting through the library, hoping something would catch his attention. (Nothing ever did.) Consequently, the stars, when they finally showed up, looked pretty good.

Jon was on the bridge with him when they made the jump. And he, too, was obviously happy to be back.

The globular cluster NCG6440 was a misty swirl in the rear. M28 was too far ahead to look like anything more than simply a dim star. "Jim," he said, addressing the AI, "any sign of the *Preston*?"

"*Negative, Matt.*"

"Ship status?"

"*Normal. All systems operating within parameters.*"

But where was Sigma? "How about the target? Have we located it yet?"

"*Working,*" said Jim.

It had been seventy years since the celebrated signal had been picked up. The researchers had tracked it, with a high degree of probability, to Sigma 2711. That meant the transmission had been sent fifteen thousand years ago.

This is our first attempt to communicate beyond our realm.

It must have been a tantalizing time. Who had sent the message? Had they already heard something? Surely it had been directed at relatively nearby targets. But it had traveled on for fifteen thousand years until finally it arrived at Cherry Hill.

He wondered whether anyone else across the broad sweep of the cosmos had picked up the transmission. Whether the senders had ever received a reply.

Respond if you are able. Or blink your lights.

Something very human there. It was a pity they'd been so far.

"*I have it,*" the AI said. The on-screen starfield approached and expanded as Jim increased magnification. A group of yellow stars appeared, and a cursor marked the target.

"How far, Jim?"

"Forty-four light-years."
Jon tried to look humble.
"Just down the street," said Matt. "Let's go take a look."

SIGMA 2711 IS located in relatively open space, 3,500 light-years on the far side of NCG6440. It's a class-F yellow star, almost half again as hot as Sol.
"Jim," said Matt, "see what you can find in the biozone."
The AI acknowledged.
"Any electronic activity out there?" asked Jon.
"Not this time. No, there is nothing."
Matt nodded. "Nobody here."
Jon shook his head. "They might have advanced beyond radio transmissions. Who knows?"
"Is that possible?"
"Sure."
"There's a chance," Matt said, "the transmission didn't originate here. Just came through. Or from nearby. At this range, it would have been difficult to be certain. Especially when you consider the technology they had to work with."
"It's a pity."
"Jon, you didn't seem to care all that much about Makai. Why are you concerned here? What's the difference?"
"Oh, I cared, Matt." Jon stared off into the distance. "I expected more than we found at Makai."
"Yeah, that *was* something of a disappointment."
"I'd love to sit down with somebody a million years ahead of us, and have the conversation we thought we were going to have at Makai."
"Hutch thinks it might be that civilizations reach their maximum potential pretty early, then go downhill."
"I don't believe it."
"I hope you're right." Matt let his head drift back until he was looking up at the overhead.
"The thing about it," said Jon, "is that this might be our last chance. If there's no one here, we go back to playing bingo." He looked at Matt. "What's so funny?"

"I was thinking if we find the kind of place you're talking about, they would have to have something better than the Locarno. You do all that work, come out here, and suddenly your new drive would be worthless."

He laughed. "Yeah. That's a point. I hadn't thought about that possibility."

Jon went silent. "You still awake?" Matt asked after a few minutes had passed.

"Yes."

"What are you thinking about?"

"The printing press."

"Say again?"

"Matt, I think Hutch is right. Technological civilizations don't last long. You're all right until you get a printing press. Then a race starts between technology and common sense. And maybe technology always wins." He took a deep breath. "Think about it. Start printing books and you start the clock running. Eventually we may discover that nobody lasts past a thousand years once they start making books and newspapers."

"I don't know how you can say that. Look how old Smitty's civilization is. It's been up and down, but it's still there."

"I mean *functioning*. Smitty's civilization is dead." He took a deep breath. "Technology makes civilizations more vulnerable. You can't easily flatten a world made up of Stone Age villages. But something as small as a computer glitch might take down a high-tech culture. Food stops rolling into Chicago, and chaos follows. You get advanced weapons. Or you develop long-term life and you get what Smitty has."

"What does Smitty have?"

"The bosses never retire. Never die. Think about that. Keep in mind that, no matter what we're able to do for the body, the mind becomes less flexible. You wind up with a world full of cranks."

"No indication of planets yet," said Jim. *"But I* do *have the* Preston. *We have a hypercomm transmission from them."*

"Good," said Matt. "Put her through."

Priscilla appeared on the main display. *"Hello, Matt,"* she said. *"Good to see you guys made it all right."*

"Hi, Priscilla. We've been here a couple of hours. Where are you?"

The visual reaction lagged a second or two behind. *"Six hundred million klicks. We have a green world."*

Jon brightened. "Okay."

"We came in right next to it. I've fed the numbers to Jim."

"What's it look like?"

"It's quiet."

"That was what we've been getting, too."

So much for encountering a hypersociety. Someone who might provide a fresh perspective on the big questions. Was there a God? Why was there something and not nothing? Does the universe have a purpose, or is it all just an oversized mechanical crapshoot?

"Chances are," said Jon, "they wouldn't have a clue either."

Hutch nodded. *"Probably not."*

Matt wondered whether it wouldn't take a lot of the pleasure out of existence if they knew the final answers. No more speculation. No more dark places. "I'm not sure it's where I'd want to live," he said.

THEY ALL GATHERED for dinner on the *McAdams* several hours later, greeting Hutch and her passengers like long-lost friends. They had by then gone into orbit around the newly discovered world.

It looked wild and, in the manner of living worlds everywhere, beautiful. It was covered with blue seas and broad forests. An enormous river tumbled down from a mountain range, culminating in a waterfall that would have dwarfed Niagara. Elsewhere, a volcano was belching smoke, while vast herds of land animals wandered unconcerned across its lower slopes. Other creatures looked more dangerous. They ran or shambled on two legs and four, armed with fangs and claws that looked like scythes. There were wolflike animals that hunted in packs, and things that might have been aerial jellyfish. On the whole, the place didn't look friendly.

A hurricane drifted above one of the oceans, and snow was falling at both ice caps. No cities, though. No lights.

They were passing above a continent that reminded Matt of a turkey, head near the equator, tail and three legs intruding into the south polar region. They were over the northern extremity, riding along the coastline. Something was moving offshore. Jim focused on it, and they saw tentacles.

A large, hazy moon fell behind them as they passed into night. (A big moon had been found orbiting every world that had ever produced a civilization.)

The planet itself was moderately larger than Earth, with almost the same gravity. It turned on its axis in approximately twenty-seven hours, and it had a seventeen-degree axial tilt. *"A bit colder than Earth, on average,"* Jim reported, *"but comfortable enough in the temperate zones."*

Worlds orbiting named stars automatically retained the name, and received a number to designate their position in the system. But Sigma 2711 was a catalog designator rather than a formal name. "Nobody there," said Rudy. "Damn."

No one else said anything. It wasn't a surprise, of course. Had there been a high-tech civilization, they'd have known before now. But actually *seeing* an empty world was painful nonetheless.

"I guess," said Hutch, "we should give it a name."

"Port Hutchins," said Antonio. He grinned and looked at her. "After your father."

"That's too close to home," she said. "I vote we name it for the guy who started SETI. Call it Drake's World."

"Better," said Matt, "would be to name it for the guy who made it possible for us to come this far. How about *Far Silvestri?*"

That prompted a couple of comments about *Far Out Silvestri* and *Long Gone Silvestri,* but everybody approved, Jon beamed, and Matt logged it in.

" 'Long gone' might be the right descriptive," said Rudy. "The place *does* look empty."

Jim showed them images of ruins. Everything was buried, sometimes by forest growth, often simply by the earth. Some were quite deep.

"The place is a long time dead," Jon said. "We might as well move on."

"Can we tell how old the ruins are?" asked Antonio.

"We'd need specialists," said Rudy. "Anybody here with a background in carbon dating?"

* * *

"WE WON'T FIND a Smitty on this world," said Jon.

"Probably not." Rudy wasn't ready to give up quite that quickly. "But let's at least take a look."

"Lot of critters down there," said Hutch. "It's not safe."

"Who gives a goddam, Priscilla? What did we come for? To cruise past and wave?"

Antonio looked accusingly at her, too, but said nothing.

She could have insisted. Even if she couldn't bully Rudy, she could have directed Matt not to go, and that would have ended the idea. But she couldn't bring herself to do that. "Let's find a place." She sighed. "There should be something out of harm's way."

"Very good." Rudy rubbed his hands together. "Now we're making sense."

Jim started flashing images on the screen, cities buried in thick forest, buildings that might have been cathedrals or city halls or power companies overgrown with hundreds and maybe thousands of years of thick vegetation.

"There's something," said Rudy. An enormous structure that could have passed for an Indian temple, with broken statuary, shattered columns, balconies and porticoes.

"Jim," said Matt, "show us what it would have looked like in better times."

"*Okay,*" he said. "*Meantime I have news.*"

"What's that?"

"*There's a space station in solar orbit. No indication of power.*"

ANTONIO'S NOTES

As we left orbit, Hutch blinked the ship's lights. When I asked her why, she just smiled and shook her head.

—Thursday, January 17

chapter 28

THEY REMAINED ON the *McAdams*, left the *Preston* in orbit around Far Silvestri, and made the jump out to the station. Matt brought them in less than an hour away from their target. It was, he thought, a remarkable tribute to the precision Jon had built into the Locarno.

The planetary system was *extensive*. There were at least six gas giants and a handful of terrestrials. Sigma itself, seen from this distance, was no more than a bright star, and they needed Jim to locate it for them.

As they'd known it would be, the orbiter was dark. It was larger than Union by about half, an agglomeration of spheres linked by shafts and tubes. It was an asymmetric maze, reminding Matt of a child's puzzle, the sort you start on one side and have to find your way out the other. "Not the simplest way to construct one of these things," said Jon, as they approached. "It must have appealed to someone's sense of aesthetics."

They watched as it tumbled slowly along its eleven-hundred-year-long orbit. Antennas, scanners, and collectors were fixed to the hull. Some were missing, others broken, trailing at the end of twisted cables. They could make out viewports and hatches, and there were barely discernible symbols in several places across the hull. The characters might have been at home in an ancient Sumerian text. *"No power leakage,"* said Jim. *"It's dead."*

No surprise there.

They drew alongside, and the navigation lights fell full on the orbiter. He looked across the arrays of pods and connecting shafts and radio dishes and spheres and wondered how long it had been there.

Rudy was sitting up front with him, his face creased, utterly absorbed.

"What do you think happened?" asked Matt.

Rudy shrugged. "No way to know. The most obvious explanation would be that it was blown out of orbit during a war. But I don't see any damage that would suggest *that.*"

"The hull's pretty badly beaten up."

"Collisions with rocks."

"How old you figure it is?"

Rudy appeared to be doing a calculation. "A few thousand years, at minimum. The Cherry Hill signal was sent fifteen thousand years ago."

"You think it came from here? The Cherry Hill transmission?"

"Who knows, Matt? Probably. But it's all guesswork at this point."

Hutch appeared in the open hatchway. "Rudy, we're going to go over and take a look. You want to come?"

"Of course. We leaving now?"

Matt noticed the invitation had not been extended in his direction. "Me, too," he said.

"One of us has to stay back here, Matt. In case there's a problem."

"How about *you*?"

Hutch delivered one of those smiles. "Look," she said, "I'll make a deal with you." She turned to Rudy: "When we get back to the *Preston*, did you want to make a landing somewhere? Take a look around?"

"Hutch," he said, "I'd assumed we'd already decided to do that."

"Okay. I'll sit *that* one out, Matt, if you want."

"You're pretty generous. You get an ancient space station, and I get somebody's farm."

"R.H.I.P.," she said. "And you never know what you might find on a farm."

* * *

JON AND ANTONIO announced their intentions to go, too. Hutch pulled on a go-pack, and Rudy, strapping on his e-suit, looked admiringly at the thrusters. "We don't get a set of those?"

"You don't need one," Hutch said. She wore a white blouse and slacks, and Rudy had a white sweater that probably belonged to Antonio. Jon had a gold pullover that read RAPTORS, and Antonio wore a red and silver jacket with WORLDWIDE stenciled across the back. The idea was that they be as visible as possible. Each of them carried an extra set of air tanks.

Hutch had attached an imager to her harness, so that Matt could watch the action. And, of course, he could listen in to the conversation.

There wasn't much to hold his attention. While Hutch used a laser to cut her way inside, Jim announced he could not raise an AI. They'd have been shocked had he been able to do so.

The interior was, of course, pitch-black. The boarding party wore lamps on their caps and wrists. Rudy was excited, but was trying hard to behave as if he broke into alien constructs on regular occasions.

They entered a moderately sized chamber, with shelves and cabinets lining the bulkheads. Everything was a bit higher than convenient. Rudy tried to open some of the cabinets, but the doors were stuck fast, and Hutch had to cut into them. Inside they found fabric and tools and lumps of something that might once have been food.

Jon moved smoothly through the zero-gee environment, surprisingly agile for a big guy, occasionally reaching out to touch a bulkhead or one of the objects they found—on one occasion, a gauge—much as one might handle a relic.

They passed into a corridor. Some debris was loose, afloat, drifting in an orderly fashion around the interior as the station continued its slow tumble. *"There don't appear to be any remains here,"* Hutch reported.

Antonio was quiet throughout. Matt suspected he was on his private channel, recording his impressions.

They spent several hours in the station. Hutch reported back that the circuitry, the power links, everything was fried. *"Looks as if they had an accident of some sort. Or were attacked."*

"Maybe somebody tried to seize the place?" suggested Matt. "And things went wrong?"

"Don't know."

"And no bodies? Nothing that looks like a corpse?"

"Nothing like that, no. It's hard to tell, but I'd say whoever was here did not *get taken by surprise."*

Jon broke in: *"Hutch, I think we're looking at some data storage. This was an operational center of some sort."* They'd wandered into an area filled with screens and black boxes.

"My God," said Rudy. *"You think there's any chance at all we could recover something?"*

"I suppose there's always a chance, Rudy. But you're talking about electronic storage. How long does that last?"

Matt knew the answer to that one. If you want data to survive, carve it in rock.

"Anyhow"—Jon was examining the equipment—*"this stuff looks burned out. All of it."*

The furniture, chairs and tables and a few sofas, suggested that the inhabitants were bipeds. They were somewhat large. When Hutch sat down in one her feet didn't reach the deck.

They broke into narrow compartments that must have been living quarters. They found a system that had provided food and water. *"Also burned out,"* said Jon. *"Something odd happened here."* He started taking electronic equipment apart, moving from chamber to chamber. *"It's the same everywhere. It's all so old it's hard to be sure, but everything looks fused to me."*

"What would cause something like that? asked Rudy.

"An electrical surge."

And, finally, Hutch's voice: *"Lightning."*

Matt understood. The omegas.

"That would also explain," she continued, *"how it got blown out here."*

There were telescopes, although nobody could see through them because the lenses were coated with dust that had become permanently ingrained.

There were a concourse and meeting rooms. Four globes had once occupied choice locations. They were about three stories high and had been filled with water. All were shattered. Where one had stood, an icy sphere remained intact. The others had apparently broken before the water froze. The deck around them was still icy.

ANTONIO'S NOTES

The station is the most utterly lost place I've ever seen.

—Friday, January 18

chapter 29

THEY SPENT THREE days looking for the right place to send down a landing party. Hutch insisted they stay away from forests and jungles. Too easy to get ambushed by Far Silvertri's efficient-looking predators. They also wanted a site that provided a relatively recent target. And, finally, a place where they wouldn't have to do a lot of digging.

The ruins were not as widespread as had at first seemed to be the case. "It doesn't look as if the population ever got that large," said Jon.

They sat around in the *McAdams*, the five of them, searching the displays, discarding all suggestions for one reason or another. *Too old* was the most common complaint. *Probably been there for thousands of years.* Or it didn't look like a place that would provide information. Or it looked like too much work to get in.

Toward the end of the third night, Antonio spotted something along the southern extremity of the turkey continent.

On the side of a snow-covered mountain, about a quarter of the way up, a broken tower jutted out of the ground.

And nearby, buried—

"There's a building."

It was a three-story structure, seemingly intact, the roof just about even with the snow cover.

The top of the tower was missing. Parts of it lay scattered under the snow. There was no way to know how high it had been. It was squat and heavy, rectangular, with sharply defined corners, and a stairway leading to a platform.

Below it, the mountain sloped away in a long, gradual descent to a plain that appeared utterly lifeless save for some scattered vegetation and a few birds.

RUDY WASN'T AS excited about making the descent as he pretended. The place looked wilder than the chindi world had. The forests were darker, the rivers more turbulent, the skies more ominous. Where the chindi world had cities and even traffic lights, Far Silvestri had ruins and vast empty plains, and the only light on the nightside came from electrical storms. It was strange: He'd expected ultimately that Hutch would say that a mission to the surface was too dangerous, but she seemed caught up in the general fever, too, had changed, had become in all the strangeness someone else, someone he didn't really know. So when he'd voiced his enthusiasm for going along she'd said okay, and, of course, the others had joined in. No one was ready to get back inside the ships and start the long voyage to the black hole at Tenareif. They needed a break. So they *were* going down, and he'd made all the noise, done it because it was expected of him. He was the researcher on the mission, the scientist. Jon was a specialist, a physicist. He'd done his work with the Locarno. His reputation was forever secure. When this journey was recorded, became epic material for future generations, he knew it would be Jon who would stand out. For good or ill. Whether Rudy liked it or not, that was the truth of it.

But it was okay. Rudy was part of it, had come closer to realizing his dreams than he'd ever thought possible. So his role was to suck it up, strap on the belt and activate the Flickinger field, and pretend not to notice the strangeness, but just help dig his way into the building below the snow cover.

Dig his way into history.

Antonio admitted that, to tell the truth, he'd rather stay with the ship because it looked hostile on the ground, but he'd go anyhow. "*Have to,*" he told Rudy, admiring Rudy's willingness, once again, to venture onto what he called another dark street. "This doesn't feel the same as going down to talk to Smitty," he continued. "But it's my job. So let's go look at the tower. And whatever else is on the slope."

Matt held Hutch to her promise. *He* would pilot the lander. Rudy admired that. If Matt felt any concern about going down, he hid it well.

Jon was blasé about it all. He wasn't really excited about a building on a mountain slope. It wasn't like crossing over to a derelict station that might have been ten thousand years old. In fact, he told Matt, he thought it was dangerous. But he understood why the others wanted to go, and if they wanted him along, he'd be glad to accompany them.

"Your call, Jon," Matt said. "We can manage okay. You do whatever you want."

"You're sure?"

"Absolutely."

So okay, Jon could think of a better way to spend his time, and as long as they didn't need him on the ground, he'd stay put.

They'd use the *McAdams* lander. It was a bit larger, and somewhat more comfortable than the *Preston* vehicle. So they all got in, checked their gear, listened to Hutch tell them to be careful, and launched.

MATT WAS BEGINNING to feel like a veteran. There'd been a star pilot hero on kids' programming when he was growing up, Captain Rigel, and he imagined himself now in that role as they came in over the plains, the mountains looming ahead. A herd of tusked animals were ambling slowly south. They stayed close together except for a few outriders on the front and flanks. A military formation.

"Looks peaceful enough," said Antonio. "Are we getting a visual record of all this?"

"Yes, we're getting everything."

"Good." Matt could sense Dr. Science mentally rubbing his hands. "Good."

"Your viewers are going to take the same ride?"

"You bet, Matt. You know, this would be a more interesting run if we, say, flew through a storm. Could we manage that?"

"I don't think so."

"Just kidding."

The land began to rise. Snow appeared. Jim pointed out the target mountain. Fifteen klicks, dead ahead.

He slowed down to survey the area. It was free of forest, so they had good visibility. As did Hutch overhead. Except at the moment she was below the horizon and wouldn't be back for an hour or so.

"Over there," said Rudy.

The tower stuck out of the snow. It was probably iron, or steel, constructed of crossbeams. The sort of structure that, back home, might have supported a water tank.

"Jim," he said, "how far down does the base reach?"

"*About twelve meters.*"

"Okay," he said. "Let's go see what we've got." He came down vertically, cautiously, about fifty paces from the tower. He kept the vehicle level, riding the spike, turning so the hatch, which was on his right, opened downhill. The port tread touched the surface, and a sudden gust rocked them and almost turned them over.

He held them momentarily where they were, until the wind settled, then he lowered them into the snow and shut down the spike by increments. The port side touched solid ground, and the lander began to tilt. Finally, it stopped, and he shut the power off. The slope was steep here, and the snow on the uphill side rose past the viewports. "This is the kind of place where I used to go skiing," said Rudy.

Antonio held out his hands, pretending to wield ski poles. "You're a skier?"

"When I was a bit younger."

They pulled on oxygen tanks and goggles and activated their suits and lightbenders. The lightbenders might, or might not, render them invisible to predators. The goggles allowed them to see each other. Matt opened the hatch. The wind blew flakes inside.

He had a good view downslope. The animals they'd seen earlier were gone. In all that vast expanse of prairie, nothing moved. "Okay, gentlemen," Matt said, "let's find out what we have."

He signaled Antonio, who opened the storage compartment and removed two collapsible spades and some cable. Rudy and Antonio each got a spade; Matt took the cable. Then he picked a Meg-6, a rhino gun, out of the weapons locker. It was a projectile-firing weapon, with sufficient power to knock over virtually any kind of predator. He didn't trust either of the others with one, but gave each of them a laser. "Be careful with them," he said. Once they got into the building and started stumbling around in the dark, he suspected they'd become more dangerous than any local life form.

He climbed out into the snow and sank to his knees. "Okay, guys," he said.

Rudy came next. He grunted and made some comments about how long it had been since he'd seen real winter weather.

Antonio waited until the director was safely down, then he followed.

Seen through the goggles, Rudy and Antonio were ghostly images.

THE SLOPE ON which they stood was relatively gentle, rising gradually for miles before it soared suddenly upward. In the opposite direction, it rolled out onto the plain, where the snow gave way to rock and brown soil.

Antonio closed the hatch.

"If anything unexpected happens," Matt said, "and you need to get out of here, just tell Jim to open up. He'll take directions from you."

"You don't expect a problem, do you?" asked Rudy.

"No. But I could fall into a hole or something. I just want you to know you don't need me to get home."

It was cold. Forty-five below, Fahrenheit. The wind sucked at them, tried to blow them off the mountain.

"Brisk," said Antonio.

Matt looked eastward across the broad plain. It *looked* cold. "The suit'll keep you warm," he said. "You'll be fine."

They might have been three guys dressed for a spring concert, all casual, all in short-sleeve shirts, with dark lenses and hats to keep the sun out of their eyes. Matt wore a baseball cap; Rudy looked like a golfer; Antonio had a safari hat, and he was also decked out in khaki shorts. Matt had that figured out. It clashed a bit with the snow, but it would look great on the newscasts.

Without instruments they would never have known there was a building buried here. They trudged first to the tower. It was black metal, nothing fancy, a collection of struts and beams, some crosspieces, a stairway, and a platform near the top.

"What do you think?" asked Antonio.

Rudy struggled up to it through snow that seemed to be getting deeper. He touched it. Looked up at it. Looked downslope. *"Could be anything,"* he said. *"Maybe they used to fly a flag up here."*

"Or worship it." Antonio took more pictures. He got shots of Rudy standing near the base. Pictures of Matt gazing at the sky, looking like Captain Rigel. And of himself, with a foot on the stairway, testing it.

Matt opened a channel to the *Preston.* "Hutch, we're at the site."

"Very good, Matt. See anything we missed?"

"Negative." Rudy was pulling on one of the crosspieces. Apparently to find out whether he could break it loose. "It was probably just a ski lift."

Skiers. Matt looked downslope again. It made sense.

"You don't see anything else anywhere in the neighborhood?"

He stared around him. Unbroken snow all the way up to the peak. More snow downslope for another few miles. The plain. A few scattered patches of trees. "Not a thing."

"What next?" asked Antonio.

Rudy suggested they get a sample of the metal. *"We can use it to date the thing when we get back."* Matt selected a likely spot and used the laser to collect a small piece. When it had cooled, he placed it in a utility bag.

Rudy was staring downhill.

"What?" asked Antonio.

"I thought I saw something."

Matt stood for several moments, watching. Nothing down there but snow.

HUTCH DIRECTED THEM to a spot that, she said, was right above the building. "How deep?" asked Matt.

Rudy was still looking around, keeping an eye on the mountain. *"I'd say about three feet."*

Rudy, wasting no time, got his spade out, struggled to get it locked in place. Antonio showed him how to turn it on, did the same with the second spade, and everybody stepped back as they began digging.

The snow was dry and granular, and the work went quickly. Within minutes, the shovels reached the roof and shut off. Matt climbed down into the hole, cleared off the last of the snow, exposing the roof, and used the laser to cut through. Then he dropped to his knees and aimed a lamp inside.

"What's there?" asked Rudy.

The floor was about thirteen feet down. "Looks like storage," he said. Lots of shelves and boxes. Remnants of what had probably been bedding. And, in the middle of the room, an iron contraption that had to be a stove.

Hutch, watching through the imagers they had clipped to their harnesses, broke in on a private channel: *"Matt, you're going to use the cable to get down there, right?"*

"Yes."

"Don't know about you, but I'm not sure I can imagine either Rudy or Antonio climbing back out on a cable."

"Trust me, Hutch. We'll be fine." His tone must have carried a hint of annoyance because she said nothing more.

He cut a second hole in the roof, about a meter away. This one was only an inch or two wide. He looped the cable through both holes, and dropped the ends into the building. Then he looked up at Rudy and Antonio. "Wait," he said.

He lowered himself through the hole, let go, and landed on a frozen surface. His feet went out from under him, and he fell with a crash.

He got the predictable cries from everyone. Was he okay? What happened? You sure you're all right, Matt?

"I'm fine," he said. He was picking himself up from an icy carpet, flashing his wrist lamp around the room, across shelves, wooden boxes, and cabinet doors. He saw tools, fabrics that had long since rotted away, dishware that was cracked and broken from the cold. A variety of knives. Pots and cabinets and frozen paper pads. Everything was made a size or two larger than would have been comfortable for him. And it was all buried under a thick layer of dust.

"Hey!" Rudy's voice. *"What are you doing down there?"*

"Okay, guys. Just a second." He went back to where the cable dangled from the holes in the roof, and held one line while Rudy climbed down the other. He dropped onto the floor and got awkwardly to his feet, smiling the whole time, the way people do when they're trying to look casual and relaxed.

And, finally, Antonio.

While the others poked around the storage area, Matt found an open door and looked into the next room. He saw two chairs, a cabinet, a table, another stove, several doors. Lots of ice and snow on the floor where windows had broken. One door opened onto a corridor. Another was frozen shut. Several unidentifiable objects lay on the floor.

He stepped out into the corridor. "Hutch," he said, "are you reading this?"

No response.

The cabinet was secured to the wall, or possibly had become a permanent part of it. He put his lamp down and went back to the cables. "Hutch," he said, "do you copy?"

Hutch's voice broke through: *"Lost you for a minute, Matt."*

"The signal doesn't penetrate."

"That's not good."

"I'll call you when we're clear."

HE TRIED TO open the cabinet, but nothing had any give. There were curtains in the room, stiff as boards and in places inseparable from the ice and the walls.

The mantel and the doorframes were all ornately carved. Everything, the furniture, the windows, the doors, was heavy. The place had a Gothic feel to it.

The corridor was lined with doors. Some had been left open, revealing spaces that looked as if they'd once been living quarters. Two were filled with snow.

Antonio and Rudy came out behind him. Antonio was talking about the furniture, how everything was on a slightly larger scale. As it had been on the station. *"What do you think these things looked like?"* he asked.

"*Obviously they were bipeds,*" said Rudy, adopting his professorial tone. "*That means they had to have chairs.*" He shook his head. "*I wonder what they talked about.*"

They looked into the open rooms and saw little other than frozen debris. In some, beams had collapsed and ceilings given way.

At the end of the corridor, a stairway descended deeper into the building.

They paused at the top and looked down into another corridor. Matt tried the first step. It was long, and slippery, but the stair felt solid.

The next step down was almost half again the height to which he was accustomed. Taller creatures, longer legs, longer feet. It was tricky going. There was a handrail, a bit higher than was comfortable. But he put it to use and kept going.

Some ice had gotten onto the stairs, making them still more dangerous. They crunched and cracked under his weight, so he directed the others to wait until he got to the bottom. Then they followed. They all had trouble negotiating the ice, but everybody made it down in good order.

More doors. And another staircase, continuing down into a large room. A lobby, he thought, or maybe a meeting room or dining area. He could see tables and chairs. He was about halfway down when he heard a noise.

The others heard it, too. Above them.

Everyone froze.

It had been barely discernible, but there *had* been something. Like a branch falling somewhere.

"*Wind,*" said Rudy.

It had sounded *inside* the building.

They listened to the silence, sweeping their lamps across the walls and along the passageways and up and down the staircases.

Antonio finally started breathing again. "*The place is oppressive,*" he said.

Whatever it had been, it was gone. They went the rest of the way down the lower stairway, this time together, Matt leading the way, Antonio at the rear.

It *had* been a dining room at one time. Several of the tables had been set with plates, cups, and knives. No spoons or forks. The dinnerware was cracked and broken.

"*The place is not that old,*" said Rudy. "*Not like the space station.*"

"*How much you think?*" asked Antonio.

"*I don't know. Frozen the way it is, I just don't know.*"

One wall had a fireplace.

Antonio began wandering around, talking to himself, wondering aloud how to capture the mood of the place. How to make people feel the claustrophobia.

Matt went through a large open doorway. The adjoining space, which might have been the area inside the front doors, was half-filled with snow. A set of windows had given way.

At the edge of the snow, and partially engulfed in it, was a cluster of carved wooden chairs arranged around a central table. Two of the chairs had collapsed. The furniture showed decent workmanship and had padding that still looked soft but was, of course, rock hard. Two rectangular blocks lay on the tabletop. And a pitcher.

He gazed at the blocks. Saw symbols on them.

Books.

They were *books.*

Both were bound in black, and both were frozen to the surface.

He wiped the dust from them and saw more symbols on the spines. He called Rudy over.

"*Beautiful,*" Rudy said. "*We have to take these back with us.*" When Matt demonstrated that they were frozen in place, he frowned. "*Careful. Don't damage them.*"

Matt used the laser to remove the legs from the table, then to cut around each book, reducing the tabletop to two manageable pieces. He handed one to Rudy and took the other himself.

"*How advanced you think these people were?*" asked Antonio.

"*They had the printing press,*" said Rudy.

"Ah, yes." Matt looked down at his own ghostly hand. "The printing press again."

Rudy pointed at some wiring hanging down from the ceiling. "*Looks as if they had electricity, too.*"

Antonio touched one of the books. Reverently. "*You were right, Rudy. This* was *a resort hotel. The tower was a ski lift.*"

Matt backed out of the room. Despite the e-suit, he was beginning to feel cold. "If we scan under the snow," he said, "we'll probably find a couple more towers upslope."

"*I don't believe it.*" Antonio was shaking his head. "*What kind of alien uses a ski resort?*"

"*The Noks like skiing,*" said Rudy. "*And on Quraqua—*"

Matt heard another noise. Above them.

They all heard it. A whisper. A sound like a wet sack being dragged across a floor.

Antonio raised both hands, palms wide, behind his ears. "*Something's up there.*"

They pointed the lamps back the way they'd come and played the beams against the foot of the staircase. "The building's old," Matt said. "It probably creaks a bit from the weight of the snow."

Antonio removed his laser from his harness. "*It's probably vermin.*"

And they heard it again. Louder this time.

"*That sounds like a* big *rat,*" said Rudy.

A chill slithered up Matt's spine. "I think we better clear out." He discovered he'd already slipped a shell into the rhino gun and was holding it straight out. At home, weapons simply short-circuited the nervous system. They rendered people, or animals, incapable of response. The rhino was designed for use elsewhere, on different kinds of life. It was simple and, one might say, old-fashioned. The metal projectiles it used had explosive tips.

Matt had never fired one beyond the range. At the moment, it provided a marvelous sense of security, except that it might bring the house down. He started back toward the staircase. "Let's go," he whispered. Sound had no trouble penetrating the Flickinger field, so they could be overheard. "Stay behind me."

Antonio took the remaining book from him. "*I'll carry it,*" he said. "*If you have to use that thing, you might want to have both hands free.*" They moved quietly across the ground floor until they stood at the foot of the staircase. There was nothing on the stairs, and nothing at the top.

"Stay put for a minute." Matt started up. He felt exposed because he had to keep looking at the stairs themselves to be sure he didn't trip. So he took a step and looked up. Took another and looked up again. Finally, he reached the top. Looked to his right, down the corridor. Checked the flight to the third floor. "Okay," he said. "Come on."

Antonio missed a step and delivered a low expletive. But Rudy caught him, kept him from falling.

"*Damned things were built for basketball players,*" Antonio grumbled.

"*Shush!*" hissed Rudy.

They got to the second floor and crowded in behind Matt.

"Everybody okay?" he asked.

"*Let's keep going,*" said Rudy.

Matt started up the second flight. Antonio and Rudy followed. But Matt waved them back. "Best if you wait till I take a look," he said.

Antonio didn't like the idea. "*The noise might have come from down there.*" *Behind* them.

"Okay." Matt conceded the point. "Let's go."

HAD THEY ASKED his help, Jon would not have hesitated to have gone down with them. But he was glad to have escaped a task he considered dull and onerous. He could have gone over to the *Preston* and spent the day with Hutch, but he was not much for trying to keep up one end of a conversation. So he'd stayed on the *McAdams*, knowing that, when the operation ended, they'd all gather on one ship or the other, and he could do his socializing then.

He was half-asleep in the common room. He had no interest in old buildings, nor for that matter in cultures that had gone away. He was glad to be alone for a few hours, to have Matt out of the ship. He was okay, but he was a bit too driven for Jon's tastes. The guy was so caught up in the mission that he had lost all sense of proportion. He couldn't relax. Couldn't talk about anything else.

A flight that goes on for the better part of a year needs to be thought out more carefully than this one. For one thing, it should have had more people. Hutch had asked him repeatedly, had asked both him and Matt, whether they'd be all right locked up together. So it was his own fault. And they were okay, really. Matt wasn't a problem. It could have been worse. He could have been on the same ship as Antonio, who talked too much and was cheerful enough to drive anyone around the bend.

Rudy would have been good. At least they had some common interests. From here on, he thought they should scramble things a bit. Maybe he'd suggest he exchange places with Antonio. He sensed Matt would like a change, too. Antonio could sit up on the bridge with Matt for weeks at a time, chattering away. And Jon would get access to Rudy. And Hutch. She wasn't exactly the life of the party either, but at least she'd be someone different. And it'd be nice to have somebody good-looking on board.

When he got home, he would form a corporation to license the drive. That had been Matt's idea. It would allow him to keep control of the system. Rudy had been concerned that he would sell it outright to Campella or one of the other major corporations, which would proceed to deny its use to all but those in a position to pay substantial sums. That would effectively eliminate blue sky exploration. Ships would go on missions, but only those fueled by a profit motive.

He thought he'd name his company for Henry, maybe call it Barber Enterprises. Although DeepSpace, Inc. appealed to him. He was getting sleepy and the world was beginning to fade when Jim brought him back. *"Jon, we have a relay from the lander. It looks urgent."*

What the hell was a relay from the lander? "You mean Matt wants to talk to me?"

"No. It's literally from the lander. The onboard AI. I'm running it now."

The main screen came on and he was looking at a snowfield. The countryside was barren, cold, desolate. In the distance, he could see a few misshapen growths. Trees, possibly. It was hard to tell. "What am I looking for, Jim?"

"It's coming into the picture now, Jon. Be advised there's a forty-three-second delay."

Abruptly, without warning, a reptilian head appeared. It was as white as the snowfield. "My God," he said. "How big is that thing?"

"The head is almost a meter across."

"Where's Matt? And the others? Are they back on the lander?" He'd followed the first few minutes of the conversation between Matt and Hutch, had gotten bored, and shut it down.

"Matt, Antonio, and Rudy dug their way into the buried building. They are in there now. If you look carefully, directly ahead, you'll see where they entered."

He saw the hole and the shovels. The snake was moving directly toward it, and as it passed the lander, he got a better sense of its size. "Is Hutch getting this?"

"Yes."

"That thing's a monster."

"It is large."

"Jim, put me through to Matt."

"Unable to comply. The link won't penetrate into the building."

The creature reached the hole and paused. It looked in. Then, to his horror, it started down.

"Jon," said the AI. *"Hutch is on the circuit. Audio only."*

"Hutch," he said. "You see this?"

"I'm headed for the lander now."

"Pick me up. I'll go with you."

"No time, Jon. I've got a window, but I have to hustle."

"Hutch, you can't take that thing on alone."

"There's no time, Jon. We should be all right. I'm armed."

"They're armed, too. But I doubt they're all right."

"I'm moving as fast as I can."

"Hutch, this is not a good idea."

"Which part of it?"

HE'D TOLD MATT that he didn't think going down was very smart. Just checking groundside, Matt had called it. Jon had refused to use the official terminology. There was a pretense there somewhere, with Matt behaving as if he'd been doing this sort of thing all his life. Matt had heroic inclinations built in, but the truth was nobody here had any training in this sort of thing. Except Hutch, and she'd been away from it too many years.

"Twenty minutes away," she said. Her voice carried no inflection. And he knew she feared the worst. What sort of chance did they have, a real estate agent, a foundation director, and Dr. Science, against that monster?

He couldn't remember what he said, but she caught something in his voice. *"Don't give up,"* she told him.

The last of the giant snake disappeared into the hole.

He waited.

Marked the time. Watched the snow and the shovels.

Occasionally he talked to Hutch. She assured him she'd be careful. Wouldn't get herself killed. Try to relax.

It'll be okay.

The minutes dragged past. Everything was happening in slow motion.

He didn't know what he wanted to see. Whether having the thing come back out into the daylight would be a hopeful sign or not.

Hutch's shuttle dropped into the clouds. *"We were lucky,"* she said. *"Couldn't have hoped for a better window."*

He was frustrated, having to sit there while the woman took her life into her hands. Damn. What was he supposed to do if she went down the hole and didn't come out again?

"Hutch?"

"Yes, Jon?"

"How about directing the AI to bring up the other lander? So I can get down there, too?"

There was a long hesitation. *"Not a good idea."*

"You might need help."

"You can't get here in time to do anything. All you'd do is put yourself at risk."

"Damn it, Hutch, you can't expect me to just sit here."

"There's an outside chance they'll need the lander as a shelter."

"Hutch, damn it—"

"Let it go, Jon. I'll get to you as soon as I know something." She was below the clouds now, descending toward the plain. Mountains in the distance.

The hole had become a gaping wound. He watched it, stared at it, wished he had a better angle, wished he could look down into it.

THEY CONTINUED UP. Matt tried to pick up the pace, tried to do it without stumbling. He kept his eyes on the stairs because Antonio was right behind him, crowding him. Or maybe he didn't want to look fearful. He was almost at the top when the journalist screamed. A pair of glittering green eyes had appeared at the top of the staircase. *Enormous eyes.* He threw himself back as the head rose, large and reptilian, wide and big and grinning with dripping incisors.

He was falling back down the stairs and suddenly everything was dark again. The head was gone, and he was grasping for the handrail and simultaneously trampling somebody, probably Antonio.

One of the lights hit it again. The thing was white as the snow outside.

They were all tumbling, scrambling, screaming, back down, hopelessly tangled in one another's arms and legs. The thing came after them, slow and deliberate and watching, mouth wide, big enough to take any of them down whole. Matt lost the rhino gun. The thing's jaws kept opening wider. He could have driven a truck into its mouth.

Then there were no more stairs, and he crashed hard onto the floor. And there was the rhino, just the barrel, sticking out from under somebody. He made a grab for it but it vanished again. And a small voice somewhere whispered to him, Captain Rigel, Captain Rigel.

The thing's eyes stayed locked on him. So much for the lightbender. Light swept across the scene, and he saw a long python body, absolutely white, silver as starlight, wide as a small train, stretching up the stairway, across the landing, disappearing into the darkness.

He was groping for the gun, trying to find it in the chaos. But it was Antonio who came up with it finally, who fired a charge into the creature's mouth. Right between those cavernous jaws and down its throat. Its tongue flicked, red and glistening. Then the round exploded, and the head was gone. Red mush blew past him, got all over him. The body slithered past, slammed past, knocked him down, kept coming, kept jerking and thrashing, and began to pile up. Antonio couldn't fire a second charge because Matt had the projectiles. But it wasn't going to matter.

The convulsions slowed. And stopped. For a long time no one said anything.

Finally, in a voice that was barely a squeak, Antonio asked if it was dead.

"I think so." Matt shuddered. He was *under* the goddammed thing. It had piled up on him and he'd been too terrified to move.

Antonio gave him a hand. *"You okay?"*

"Yeah. I'm good."

"I don't think Rudy is."

Oh.

Matt got clear, finally, and went to look at Rudy. *"He took a bad fall, Matt."*

They extricated him from the beast. His head hung at an odd angle. His eyes were wide-open, locked in terror. The book he'd been carrying was still gripped in his right hand.

Matt couldn't find a pulse.

Antonio handed over the rhino gun, and Matt fired another cartridge into the thing.

chapter 30

MATT KNELT OVER Rudy, trying to awaken him, trying to breathe some semblance of life into him. *"Nothing?"* asked Antonio.

"Can't be sure." Matt didn't want it to be true. God, he didn't want that. Rudy dead. Why the hell had they come down here anyway? For a goddam book? He took it, the one Rudy still cradled, and, still on his knees, threw it against the wall.

Antonio was shining his light up the staircase. *"We need to get out of here, Matt. There might be more of these things around."*

"Yeah." He bent over Rudy again, felt for a pulse, for a heartbeat, anything. Finally, he gave up, and they lifted his body.

The serpentine corpse partially blocked the staircase.

They climbed past it, hanging on to Rudy, trying not to touch the thing. Matt found himself thanking God Rudy didn't weigh more.

They got to the top. And to the end of the snake. When they were past it, they stopped to rest a few moments. Then they stumbled into the supply room. The cable was still in place.

As soon as they put the body down, Antonio turned and started back into the corridor. *"I'll just be a minute,"* he said.

"Where are you going?"

"Get the books."

"You can't go back down there, Antonio," he said. "Let them go."

He stopped in the doorway. *"What do you think Rudy would have wanted?"*

There was something in Antonio's eyes. Sadness. Contempt. Weariness, maybe. He'd seen how Matt had reacted. Had seen him jump when the serpent appeared. Knew that, instead of playing the heroic role he'd assigned himself, he'd fallen down the stairs, fallen on top of Rudy, anything to get away. "Wait," said Matt. "You'll need a hand."

WHEN THE LINK began working again, he contacted Hutch and gave her the news. She told him she was sorry and had to fight for control of her voice. She was on her way down from the *Preston*, and when they climbed out of the hole, carrying Rudy's body, and bringing one of the two books with them—one had gotten lost somewhere, was probably beneath the dead animal—her lander was already visible coming in over the snowfields.

She landed a few meters away and got out. They laid Rudy in the snow, and she knelt beside him. One of the problems with the hard shell the force field throws over the face is that you couldn't wipe your eyes.

When she'd regained control she stood up. *"You guys okay?"* she asked.

"We're good," said Matt. She carried a rhino gun. "Where's Jon?"

"In the McAdams. *I didn't have time to pick him up."* She looked down the side of the mountain, gazed at the broken tower, at Antonio. She was trying to say something else. And finally it came: *"Was it quick?"*

Matt nodded.

Other than that, she didn't say much. Told Matt and Antonio thanks. Embraced them. Then she suggested they not hang around. They opened the cargo locker and lifted Rudy inside.

WHEN THEY GOT back to the *McAdams*, they froze Rudy's body and put it in storage. As captain of the ship on which he'd been a passenger, and as a longtime friend, Hutch would perform the memorial service.

She'd brought along a captain's uniform, with no expectation of having to wear it.

During the ceremony she realized how little she actually knew about Rudy. She knew about his passion for stellar investigation, and his longtime desire to find an alien culture with whom it would be possible to communicate. She knew his politics, his contempt for a government that, in his view, had used the endless war against greenhouse gases as an excuse to eliminate funding for the Academy. But the inside personal stuff remained a mystery. She had no idea, for example, whether, despite his start as a seminarian, he had still subscribed to a formal religion, although, judging from various comments over the years, she doubted it. She didn't know why his wives had bailed on him. He'd been an attractive man, congenial, armed with a sense of humor. During the years she'd been associated with him, there had been occasional women, but he'd never really formed a serious relationship with anyone. At least not that she knew of.

He'd been a decent guy, a good friend, a man she could trust to back her if she needed it. What more mattered?

He had a brother in South Carolina, a sister in Savannah. She'd met the sister, years ago. She wished it were possible to communicate with them, let them know. She'd have to wait until they got home, which meant, until then, his death would be hanging over her head.

When she took her place before the others, when she began to explain why Rudy mattered so much, she was surprised to discover that her voice shook. She had to stop a couple of times. She tried surreptitiously to wipe her eyes, and finally she poured everything out. He'd stood for all the things she believed in. He'd never backed off even though other careers had been so much more lucrative than the Foundation. And in the end, he'd sacrificed everything, a decent married life, the respect of his colleagues, and ultimately life itself, to the idea that humans had a greater destiny than hanging around the house.

Antonio said simply that he'd liked Rudy, that he'd been good company, and that he'd miss him.

Jon expressed his appreciation for Rudy's support. "Without him," he said, "we wouldn't have gotten out here."

Matt started by saying he'd known Rudy only a short time. He thanked him, surprisingly, for giving him something to live for. And ended by blaming himself for his death. "I took my eyes off the top of the staircase. The steps were so hard to navigate. The thing just came out of nowhere. And I panicked. He was depending on me, and I panicked."

"I don't know anybody," Hutch told him, "who wouldn't have reacted the same way. Give yourself a break."

She'd lost people on prior missions. It had started a lifetime ago, on Quraqua, when she'd been perhaps not as quick as she should have been, and Richard Wald had died. There'd been other decisions that had gone wrong. She might have allowed them to haunt her, to drive her to her knees. But she'd done her best at the time. And that was all anyone could reasonably ask. No one had ever died because she'd screwed around.

"It happens," she told Matt. "If you do these kinds of flights, going places no one's ever been before, there's always a risk. We all accept that. You do your best. If something happens, something goes wrong, you have to be able to live with it. And move on."

EASY TO SAY. She'd remember all her life watching the oversized white serpent slither down into the hole Matt and the others had dug, and her sense of helplessness while she tried to get them on the link— Come on, Matt, answer up, please—the whole time running for the lander, climbing into an e-suit, telling Jon what was happening and why she couldn't stop to go to the *McAdams* to pick him up.

Jon took her aside and asked whether they shouldn't terminate the flight and return home. The tradition at the Academy in such cases had been flexible, which was to say there had been no tradition. In the event of a fatality, sometimes the mission went forward. Sometimes it was terminated. The decision had been left to the survivors. They knew best.

The Academy had suffered relatively few losses over the years. The wall that served as a memorial to those who had died on Academy missions had never come close to using the allotted space. It still stood in its time-honored place, near the Galileo Fountain on the edge of what had been the Academy grounds.

"We've made our point," Jon persisted. "The Locarno works fine. Why bother going farther?"

She recalled Rudy's comment when they had asked whether he planned on making the flight. *This is going to be remembered as the Silvestri mission. But they're going to remember the crew, too. And I like the idea of having my name associated with yours.* "I think we should continue," she told him. "Taking the body home accomplishes nothing. He wouldn't want us to turn back."

"Okay," he said. "Whatever you say."

MATT KNEW HUTCH was right, that he wasn't really responsible for Rudy's death. And the knowledge helped. But in the end he also knew that if he'd performed better, Rudy would still be alive. And there was no getting around that.

He refused the meds she suggested. Taking them would have been an admission of something. They all stayed on board the *McAdams* the night of the ceremony, huddled together, herd instinct. Antonio told him in front of Hutch and Jon that it wouldn't have mattered if he'd reacted differently. "I jumped into him, too, and nothing you did would have stopped that. When that snake head showed up my reflexes took over, and all I could think of was to get out of there. So stop beating yourself up."

During his years as a pilot, Matt had never faced a day like this. He'd never lost a passenger, had never even seen one in danger. He'd always thought of himself as a heroic type. Women had automatically assumed he was a couple of cuts above ordinary men. Antonio, he'd known from the start, was *ordinary*. If there was anybody who'd been run-of-the-mill, an average middle-aged guy, it was Antonio.

But at the critical moment, Antonio had grabbed the gun and blown the serpent away. He'd stood up while Matt flinched. That fact would be hard to put behind him.

MATT COULDN'T SLEEP. He kept replaying the sequence over and over. What he remembered most vividly was that there'd been no place to hide, that he feared the creature would swallow him whole. Gulp him down like a piece of sausage.

He got up to use the washroom. Hutch must have been awake as well because moments after he returned to his compartment there was a soft knock at the door.

"Matt, are you okay?" She was still in her uniform.

"My God," he said, "don't you ever go to bed?" It was after three.

"I'm reading."

"Couldn't put it down?"

"Nope. It's Damon Runyon."

"Who?"

"Twentieth century." She smiled. "You'd like him."

He got his robe and joined her in the common room. She made coffee, and they talked about Runyon's good-hearted gangsters, and the black hole at Tenareif, and whether they should start tomorrow on the next leg of the flight. Jim broke in to report that the samples brought back from the tower and the buried building—he had analyzed the tabletop piece to which the book had been frozen—indicated that both structures were about three hundred years old.

That brought up another question: The signal received at Cherry Hill had been transmitted fifteen thousand years ago. The space station went adrift, got knocked out of orbit, whatever, also in ancient times. But they'd still had a functioning civilization within the last few hundred years. What had happened to them?

Maybe the same thing that had happened at Makai? They'd learned how to live too long? Got bored?

"No," said Hutch. "This feels more like a catastrophe."

"An omega?"

"That would explain the fused circuits on the station. A few good bolts of lightning."

The conversation inevitably wandered back to Rudy, but it didn't touch on Matt's role in his death. They were still there at five, when Jon came out to see what the noise was.

"Rehearsing for *Guys and Dolls*," Matt said.

* * *

THEY STAYED IN orbit two days, making maps and taking pictures of the world. Meanwhile they thawed the book and gave it to Jim. He analyzed it and reported that he was able to translate some of the material. *"Matt was right. It was a hotel. The book is a listing of services, of menus, of the contents of the hotel library, which seem to have consisted of both books and VR. And of attractions available in the area. You were right also that the place was a center for skiing."*

"Great," said Matt. "That's what he died for? A hotel package?"

"There's more. More difficult to translate, but seemingly unconnected with the hotel. I've been able to do some translation, but the overall meaning tends to be elusive."

"Explain."

"Let me give you an example."

"Okay."

" *'The sea is loud at night, and there are voices in the tide. At another time, in another place, the moon did not speak. We were amused.'* "

He stopped and they looked at one another. "Is that it?" asked Jon.

"That is a single piece of text, separated from the others."

Jim put the lines on-screen. Matt frowned at it. " 'The moon did not *speak*'?"

"Are you sure you have it right?" asked Hutch.

"Reasonably certain. The word appears several times in the hotel directory. 'If you need something, speak *to any of the service people.'* 'Speak *the word and we will respond.' And so on."*

"We might need more time with the translation," said Jon.

The moon did not speak.

Did not.

It was hard to miss the past tense.

"What are you thinking, Hutch?" asked Matt.

"I don't think 'did not speak' quite captures it."

Jon looked baffled. "How can you make any kind of sense out of a talking moon?"

She focused on the screen:

> *At night the sea is very loud,*
> *And voices ride the tide.*
> *At another time, in another place,*

Beneath the silent moon,
We laughed together.

"My God," said Matt.

Jon nodded. "It's a poem."

Jim reported other structures under the snow near the landing site. "*More towers,*" he said. "*Upslope.*"

They nodded to each other. The rest of the ski lift.

THEY BROKE THE translation effort down to a system. Jim provided the most literal rendition possible, and Hutch interpreted as best she could. Sometimes it became necessary to infer meaning, as in the case of the adjective in

> *. . . The relentless river*
> *Carrying us toward the night.*

It might have been *lovely,* or *idyllic,* or any of countless other possibilities. But the context provided evidence for a good guess.

One line was straight out of *The Rubaiyat*:

> *. . . This vast gameboard of nights and days.*

The poems seemed primarily, almost exclusively, concerned with lost love and early death. They were scattered throughout the book, located perhaps between a description of the hotel restaurant and an advertisement that might have had to do with sexual services.

The *Preston* AI broke in. "*Hutch.*"

"What do you have, Phyl?"

"*There are three omega clouds in the area. Outbound at a distance of 1.8 light-years. Moving toward NGC6760.*"

"Moving away from here?"

"*Yes. What makes them interesting is that they are traveling abreast, in formation, along a line 6.1 light-years long. Straight as an arrow. The interior omega is two light-years from the end of the line.*"

She waited, apparently expecting Hutch to respond. "You're suggesting," she said, "there's one missing."

"Exactly. We know these things tend to travel in orchestrated groups. Either the interior cloud should be in the middle, or there should be a cloud two light-years from the other end."

"The missing cloud—" said Jon.

"Would have passed through this area. Three hundred years ago."

THEY TALKED ABOUT putting everyone into the *Preston* for the remainder of the voyage. Let the AI do the navigation for the *McAdams*. There was a risk in doing that: If a glitch showed up somewhere, a cable came loose, a short developed in the wiring, there'd be nobody to fix it, and they'd lose the ship. The chance of such an event was remote, but it *could* happen. Matt argued against the idea, offered to ride alone if Jon wanted to join Hutch and Antonio. But he explained he felt responsible for the *McAdams*. She thought maybe he liked being on the bridge, and thought about suggesting they ride on his ship, but her instincts told her not to do it. Maybe *she* also liked being on the bridge.

ANTONIO'S NOTES

I'll never understand Hutch. She's one of the most optimistic people I know, but she's convinced we're all going to hell in a handcart. I asked her tonight whether she really thinks civilizations can't survive long term. She looked straight at me and asked whether I'd give a monkey a loaded gun.

—Wednesday, January 2

chapter 31

THERE WAS A possibility the flight to Tenareif would be nonproductive, for the simple reason they might not be able to find the black hole. It had been detected by its gravitational effects on nearby stars. No companion was known to exist. If that was indeed the case, and there was no matter nearby, no dust or hydrogen or incoming debris to light the thing up, it would be invisible. Nothing more than a deeper darkness in the night. And looking for it would require a risk Hutch wasn't prepared to take. Furthermore, there'd be no point in it anyhow since, even if they found it, there'd be nothing to see.

If the outside universe was about to acquire a flavor of weirdness, the climate inside the *Preston* had also changed. Not dramatically. Not in ways that Hutch could have explained. Antonio remained upbeat and encouraging. He could sit for hours trading barbs and gags, describing misadventures while trying to cover political events, natural disasters, and even occasional armed rebellions. "Got shot at once, in the Punjab. You believe that? Somebody actually tried to kill me. I was doing an interview with a local warlord and got in the way of an assassin."

"You didn't get hit, I hope?"

"In the hand." He showed her a burn scar. "She—it was a woman— wanted a clear shot, and I was in the way. It was a bad moment."

"I guess."

"I mean, it's got a special kind of significance, knowing that some- one, a perfect stranger, wants to take your life."

"Well," Hutch said, "at least it wasn't personal. She wasn't after *you*. She just wanted to clear the area."

"*You* can say that. It felt personal to me."

"Why did she want him dead?"

"You'd think it was political, right?"

"Sure."

"That she was from an oppressed group of some sort?"

"She wasn't?"

"She was a government worker who'd been terminated. She got the warlord confused with the local bosses and tried to take him out. She should have been after the chief of the tax bureau."

"Incredible."

"No wonder they booted her."

But if Antonio remained the same, the atmosphere had neverthe- less changed. Maybe it was her. There was less reading and game- playing and VR. The climate had become more personal, the sense of isolation more acute. Rudy had been simply one of her two passen- gers during the first two legs of the flight. Now, with him gone, he'd become something infinitely more, a companion, a reflection of her own soul, an anchor in a turbulent time.

They talked about Rudy every day, how they would see that his memory was kept, how he would have been overjoyed at the poetry in the *Sigma Hotel Book*. How they missed him.

Hutch even began listening to country music, which she'd never done before. Years behind everybody else in her generation, she dis- covered Brad Wilkins, who always sang about moving on, and about the darkness outside the train windows.

When Antonio suggested they were becoming morose, that they should try to put the Sigma Hotel staircase behind them, Hutch agreed but really thought it was best to talk it out. Gradually, as the days passed, politics and black holes began to dominate the conversa- tion. Rudy receded.

Three weeks and two days after leaving Sigma 2711, they arrived in the area that was home to Tenareif, roughly one and a half light-years from the position of the black hole.

They did a second jump, and, when they came out, Phyl announced immediately that she could see the target. *"Take a look,"* she said.

She put it on-screen: a luminous ring.

"That's the accretion disk," said Antonio. "It circles the black hole."

"If not for the extra shielding," said Phyl, *"we wouldn't want to come this close."*

"That bad, Phyllis?"

"Very high levels of X-rays and gamma rays. Higher than theory predicts."

"I guess they'll have to revise the theory." She saw a second object, glowing dully nearby. A planet. With an atmosphere. It looked like a moon seen through a haze. "So it *does* have a companion."

"Yes, it would seem so."

IT WASN'T A planet. The thing was a brown dwarf, a star not massive enough to light up. *"It's about eight times as massive as Jupiter,"* said Phyl.

"Anything else in the system?"

"Not as far as I can see."

Hutch took them in closer. Angled them so they were able to look down on the accretion disk. It was a swirl of dazzling colors, of scarlet and gold and white. The ring was twisted and bent, an enormous tumbling river, dragged this way and that by the immense tidal effects, simultaneously brilliant and dark as if the rules of physics shifted and melted in the flow.

Antonio sat beside her, his notebook in his lap. "No way to describe it," he said.

A light mist was being sucked off the surface of the brown dwarf. It spiraled out into the sky, a cosmic corkscrew, aimed at the black hole, until it connected with the accretion disk.

"It's feeding the accretion disk," said Antonio. "That's what lights it up. If the brown dwarf weren't there, there'd *be* no accretion disk."

"And we wouldn't be able to see the hole," said Hutch.

"That's correct."

"It'd be kind of dangerous, navigating through here," she said.

"I'd say so."

The dwarf writhed like a living creature. "How long will this process take?" Hutch asked. "Before the dwarf collapses and the lights go out?"

"Difficult to estimate. Probably millions of years."

Hutch was thinking about the physics associated with black holes, how light freezes along the accretion disk, how time runs at a different pace close to the hole, how there's really nothing there yet it still has enormous mass. There'd been talk in recent years that it might be possible to use antigrav technology to send a probe into a black hole. Rudy had thought it was impossible, that any conceivable technology would be overwhelmed. "How big's the hole?" she asked.

"Probably not more than a few kilometers."

Strange. The accretion disk was the most impressive physical object she'd ever seen, majestic, beautiful, overwhelming. Yet she couldn't see what produced it.

"Hutch," said Phyl, *"the* McAdams *is in the area."*

THEY RENDEZVOUSED A few hours later. The ships had pulled back well away from the barrage of radiation, and the accretion disk was now only a glimmer in the night.

Hutch and Antonio took the lander over, and, glad for one another's company, they settled into the common room. Mostly it was small talk, the long ride from Sigma 2711, how it was the end of January and where had the year gone? The latter remark, made by Antonio, had been intended as a joke. It fell flat, but Jon pointed out that Antonio was spending all his time with a beautiful woman, and the next time they tried something like this they should think things out more carefully.

They were looking at telescopic views when Phyl appeared, dark hair this time, dark penetrating eyes, wearing a lab coat, in her science director mode. The room went quiet.

She addressed herself to Hutch. *"There's something odd about the brown dwarf."*

"How do you mean?"

"It has too much deuterium."

Hutch shrugged. Even Dr. Science looked amused. It was hardly a problem.

Phyl persisted. *"It should not exist."*

"Explain, please."

"Brown dwarfs are normally composed of hydrogen, helium, lithium, and assorted other elements. One of the other elements is deuterium."

"Okay."

"Deuterium is a heavy isotope of hydrogen, with one proton and one neutron. It was manufactured during the first three minutes of the Big Bang, and after that production got shut down. You don't get any more by natural processes. Only small quantities were made initially. So there's not much of it around. No matter where you look."

"And this one has too much?" It still didn't sound like a major issue.

"Yes."

"What's normal?"

"Only .001 percent. A wisp. A trace. A hint."

"And how much does this one have?"

"Half—fifty percent. Well, forty-nine percent actually. But the point is there's way *too much. It's impossible."*

"I can't see that it's a problem for us. Just log it, and we'll let somebody else crunch the numbers and figure it out."

"You don't understand, Hutch."

"I understand we have an anomaly."

"No. What you have is an artificial *object."*

Hutch wondered if Phyl had blown her programming. "You said it's eight times the size of Jupiter."

"Eight times the density."

"That hardly matters. An object that big could *not—*"

"Hutch, don't you see what's happening here?"

"Not really. No." She'd felt a lot of pressure since the loss of Rudy. And maybe she wasn't thinking clearly, but she resented being taken to task by an AI.

"I think I do," said Jon, who'd been sitting quietly, sipping hot chocolate. "Hutch, anything less than thirteen Jupiter masses is classified as a planet—" He turned to Antonio. "Do I have that right, Antonio?"

"Yes, Jon."

"Because it never develops sufficient internal pressure to ignite its deuterium, let alone its hydrogen."

"My God," said Antonio. "Yet here's an object eight times Jupiter's mass. It displays surface abundances that can only come from deuterium burning. That's impossible with 1/1000th of a percent deuterium. But deuterium ignition works perfectly if the object is born with eight Jupiter masses and fifty percent hydrogen and fifty percent deuterium. All it needs is a spark."

"Wait a minute," said Matt. "Would somebody please do this in English? For the slow kids?"

Jon and Antonio stared at one another. Both looked stunned. Jon was rubbing his forehead. "Think of a trace of air," he said. "Mix it with gasoline and it's stable. But a mixture of fifty percent gasoline and fifty percent air is highly combustible. A spark is all you need."

"So where are we?" asked Hutch.

"Hutch," said Antonio. "Nature can't make, or ignite, fifty-fifty deuterium-hydrogen objects. So something else must have done it."

"But why?" asked Matt. "Why would—?" He stopped cold.

"It's a traffic sign," said Hutch. "Without the dwarf—"

"Exactly right." Antonio clapped his hands. "We said it coming in. Without the dwarf, the black hole would be invisible. Somebody just passing through, who doesn't know in advance it's there, could get gobbled up."

"So," said Matt, "who put it here? Who'd be *capable* of an engineering operation like that?"

"THERE'S SOMETHING ELSE that might interest you," Phyl said later, when they were getting ready to start on the last leg of the voyage. Antonio had been reading. Hutch was absorbed with a checklist. Only Antonio looked up. "Yeah, Phyl," he said. "What have you got?"

"I've been searching for hydrogen-deuterium brown dwarfs."

"And?"

"There's nothing in the scientific literature. Nobody's ever seen one."

"Okay."

"But there's a fictitious character, Kristi Lang, who showed up in some books written during the early twenty-first century. She's an astrophysicist,

and she locates some brown dwarfs exactly like this one. She eventually pro-
duces evidence to indicate that somebody is marking solitary black holes, ex-
actly the way this one is marked. They each get a lighthouse. Because they're
the dangerous ones."

"So who makes the lighthouses?"

"She has no way of knowing. She doesn't even have a superluminal at her
disposal."

"How about that?" said Antonio. "I guess she called it."

"Not really." Hutch pushed away from the display that had absorbed her. "This isn't the first black hole we've looked at. The Academy's been to three. The Europeans have visited two. Nobody's ever
reported anything like this before."

"The others," said Phyl, "all had natural companions. You could see
them from far away. This one, though, if you didn't know in advance it was
there, would be an ambush."

ANTONIO'S NOTES

Hutch told us a story tonight, how, when she was first starting
her career, she'd taken a research party to Iapetus to see the
statue left there thousands of years ago by the Monument-
Makers. How they'd found the tracks of the creature who'd
made the statue, and how they matched with the statue so they
knew it was a self-portrait. She talked about following the tracks
onto a ridge, where she could see the creature had stood and
stared at Saturn. And she thought how alone it had been, how
big and cold and uncaring the universe was. Melville's universe.
You get in the way of the whale, you're dead. And she says she
thought how intelligent creatures, facing that kind of empty
enormity, are in it together. She says she felt the same way today, looking at the brown dwarf. The lighthouse.

—Monday, January 28

PART FOUR

mordecai zone

chapter 32

THE OMEGA CLOUDS seemed to originate from a single source, located approximately fifty-seven light-years from the galactic center and in orbit around it. It was the Mordecai Zone, named for the guy who'd done the math twenty years ago. It also had a numerical designator, RVP66119. The more sensational news media commonly referred to it as the Boiler Room. Whatever one chose to call it, no one had ever seen it. The area was obscured by enormous clouds of dust and hydrogen.

The jump from Tenareif would take them across seven thousand light-years, and require nearly four weeks.

Jon was annoyed. For him, Tenareif was to have been the highlight of the mission. But Rudy's death had cast a pall over everything, which even the discovery of the mysterious marker, with its implication of cosmic goodwill, had failed to lift. Especially for Matt. In the end, Jon understood, Matt had looked into the black hole and seen a metaphor for the meaning of existence.

CONDITIONS WERE NOT helped by the fact that riding his star drive was something less than exhilarating. Jon had always enjoyed travel.

He'd been around the globe several times, had represented Henry Barber at distant forums and conferences whenever he could, had learned to sail when he was a boy, and had always known that one day he would go the Moon.

To the Moon.

But travel should include motion. Movement. The sense of getting from one place to another. Journeys are not about destinations, they are about the route. They are about mountain passages and cruising around the horn and riding the Northwest glide train along the Pacific rim. They are about sailing past Jupiter and drinking toasts as Centaurus grows brighter on the screens. (Okay, that last was strictly his imagination, but that made it no less true.) It was not, most certainly not, sitting for weeks inside a constricted container that passed *nothing*. That didn't rock in the wind, or throw on the brakes, or even glide slowly through the eternal mists of Hazeltine space.

It was early February back home. The All-Swiss Regional Bridge Tournament, in which he'd played last year, where he and his partner had almost won, had opened its qualifying round the day they'd left Tenareif. Pitchers would be reporting for spring training. And the streets of Washington would be filled with lovely young women.

There was a time he'd taken all that for granted.

He'd given up all pretense of trying to work. Before coming, he'd thought the atmosphere for finding ways to improve the Locarno, to make it more efficient, to give it more range on less fuel, to make it even more precise, would be ideal. But it hadn't played out that way. For one thing he'd found it hard to work when there was no break, no chance to wander off and hit a local bistro. For another, as the situation on board deteriorated, he couldn't simply abandon Matt, leaving him to entertain himself through the endless days and nights. So they watched VR and played bridge and worked out, and the lights dimmed and brightened, marking the hours.

The AI had an extensive translation by then of the Sigma Hotel poems, but neither of them was much into poetry. When Jim announced he could find nothing in the book about automated deep-space missions or about omega clouds, they lost interest. There were, Jim said, occasional references to clouds, as in creating moody skies or bringing rain, but there was nothing about clouds that rolled in from the outer darkness, pouring down the wrath of the gods on baffled city dwellers.

Jon spent a fair amount of time going over the details they'd compiled on Tenareif. He wasn't an astrophysicist, and black holes were a long way from his field of interest, but nevertheless he spent hours peering down into the funnel, wondering what conditions were really like, what the odds were that the thing actually opened into another universe. Such a possibility was counterintuitive, but everything about black holes was counterintuitive. So much about the structure of the universe at large was counterintuitive.

HE AMUSED HIMSELF by calculating the distance to Earth. Technically, of course, while it was in Barber space, there was no such thing as a range between the *McAdams* and anything in the Milky Way. Each existed in its own spatial continuum. Nevertheless, he proposed the question to himself in terms of where they would be if they exited *now*.

At the beginning of the second week, they were twenty-two thousand light-years out. "Pity we don't have a telescope big enough to look back," he told Matt. "Imagine what we'd see. They won't build their first pyramid for another fifteen thousand years or so. Babylon, Sumer, none of that exists. There's nobody there except guys living in caves."

Matt had been paging through his notebook. "It's a bit like riding a time machine."

"As close as we'll get."

JIM WAS INVALUABLE. He was always ready to play bridge or produce a show. Matt especially enjoyed *Government Issue*, which portrayed the misadventures of three female interns in a hopelessly corrupt and incompetent Washington. Jon had seen it before, a few episodes, but he grew to enjoy it more than anything else they watched, not because of the assorted buffooneries, or even because of the nubile young women. It was rather because, for reasons he could not understand, it didn't seem quite so far as everything else.

So the weeks passed, and the final days dwindled away. And at last they were ready to make their jump into the Mordecai Zone. Matt sealed the viewports and the hatches against the radiation and told him they had three minutes.

LIBRARY ENTRY

We range the day
And mount the sun.
We soar past the rim of the world,
And know not caution nor fear.
But too soon the night comes.

—Sigma Hotel Book

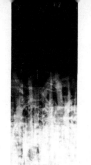

chapter 33

TWENTY-EIGHT THOUSAND LIGHT-YEARS from Earth.

Jon was looking at the navigation screen when they made the jump. He had become accustomed to the mild tingling sensation in his toes and fingertips when the ship moved from one state to the other. He felt it now and started breathing again when the stars blinked on. They provided a spectacular light show, as always, and it appeared as suddenly as if someone had thrown a switch.

The night was ablaze, with stars that were points of light and others so close he could make out disks. Still others were radiant smears, trapped in clouds of gas and dust. Brilliant jets and light-years-long streaks of glowing gas arced across the sky. In their immediate rear lay a cloud filled with hot red stars. If you lived here, on a terrestrial world, it would never get dark. He decided at that moment on the title of his autobiography: *28,000 Light-Years from Earth*. Except that *twenty-eight* didn't work. Round it off. Make it *thirty*. *30,000 Light-Years from Earth: The Jon Silvestri Story*. Yeah. He liked that. It had a ring to it.

They sealed the viewports, so the only external views now were by way of the displays.

Matt had been worried about jumping in so close. *"It's too goddam much,"* he'd said before punching the button. Jon had felt the same way, too much radiation here. Despite the assurances of the people who'd put on the shielding, he wasn't comfortable. The estimates regarding how much protection they needed had been just that: estimates. They'd built in a 50 percent safety factor, but out here that might not mean much. A sudden explosion somewhere, a flare, almost any kind of eruption might fry them before they knew they were in trouble.

"Jim." Matt didn't even bother to release his restraints. "How do the radiation levels look?"

"Shielding is adequate."

"Good. Recharge."

"Commencing."

Matt wanted to be ready to clear out if necessary.

"Which way's the core?" asked Jon.

A cursor appeared on-screen, marking the position of the *McAdams*. And an arrow: *"Approximately sixty light-years. That way."* Into the swirl of dust and stars.

"Do you see any unusual activity out there, Jim?" Specifically, were there any omegas?

"Negative," said Jim. *"It is a crowded area, but I see nothing we need be concerned about."*

Jon took a deep breath. "We're really here," he said. Only sixty light-years from Sag A*. The monster at the heart of the galaxy. A black hole three million times as massive as the sun. Dead ahead.

Sixty light-years seemed suddenly close. Just up in the next block.

"The diameter of the Sag A event horizon,"* said Jim, *"is estimated at 7.7 million kilometers."*

Matt took a deep breath. Shook his head. "You know, Jon, I'd love to get close enough to see it."

"We wouldn't survive, Matt."

"I know."

Nevertheless, it was something Jon would have liked to see. "Sounds like a project for an AI flight."

They both glanced toward the AI's mode lamp. It brightened. *"Don't expect* me *to volunteer,"* Jim said.

Matt grinned. "Jim, I'm disappointed in you."

"*I'll try to live with your disappointment, Matthew. The area is lethal. Jets, radiation, antimatter, gamma rays. Get close in, and the interstellar medium is filled with highly ionized iron. Not a place for anyone to travel. Especially not an advanced entity.*"

Matt could not take his eyes from the screen. "It doesn't look like a real sky out there," he said. "It's too crowded."

"Yes." It was a sight that left Jon breathless. Blue-white suns off to one side; in another direction, a cloud filled with stars probably just being born. Another cloud with jagged flashes, seemingly frozen, until he saw that they were moving, *crawling* through the cloud at light speed.

They could see hundreds of clouds, large and small, scattered across an area several light-years deep and about thirty light-years wide. They were elongated, tubular, accusing fingers pointed at the central black hole that held them locked in their orbits.

JON USED THE VR capabilities of the common room to re-create the clouds, and he spent the next few hours seated in his chair, wandering among them. He'd never considered himself one of those sense-of-wonder types, idiots whose jaws dropped at the sight of a waterfall or a passing comet. But this was different. The sheer power and enormity of the Mordecai took his breath away. He was adrift near a luminous fountain when Matt broke in to tell him they'd located the *Preston*.

"*You okay?*" asked Hutch, referring to whether the shields were holding.

Both ships were, fortunately, doing well.

"*I have some news,*" she said. "*We've spotted three omegas.*"

The Mordecai Zone was an area of indefinite size. Their only real hope of finding the source had been to locate some omegas and run the vectors backward. That raised the issue of how common omegas were. Nobody had any real idea. Estimates ranged from a staggered production rate of fifty or so per year, to several thousand. But it was all guesswork.

Jon took a last look at the fountain, a golden stream arching through the night, bending and swirling as if the quality of light itself were different here. Then he shut it down and went onto the bridge. "Hi, Hutch," he said, "welcome to the Cauldron."

"*Hello, Jon. Must be heaven out there for a physicist.*"

"What do the omegas look like?"

"*Unfortunately, they're running together. All going in the same direction. Sorry.*"

A couple of omegas on different routes would have allowed them to track backward until they intersected. And there, *voilà*, they would find the factory. The boiler room. The manufacturer. Whatever the hell it was.

"*They're in a vee-shape,*" Hutch continued, "*one in front, the others angled back at about twenty degrees. The entire formation is two and a fraction light-years across. The two trailing clouds are identical ranges from the lead.*"

She relayed images, and Jim put them on-screen. They simply looked like hazy stars.

"They do love their math," said Jon.

"*They're moving at escape velocity, in the same general direction as everything else here.*"

Matt tried to get a clearer picture. "Can you give us a better mag?" he said.

"*That's max. We could go over and look at them, I suppose. But I don't see the point.*"

"Are we sure they're omegas?"

"*Yes. We've got matching spectra.*"

A cursor appeared behind the one in the center. It tracked backward across open space, passed through a series of clouds, and finally vanished in the general chaos. "*It originated somewhere along there,*" said Hutch. "*It can't go too much deeper.*"

"Why not?" asked Matt.

"*The numbers don't work. Whatever we're looking for, it's no further than about fifty-seven light-years from the core. That's where we are now.*"

"So the source is somewhere along this arc?"

"*Yes. I'd say so.*"

"How long's the arc?"

"*Five and a half light-years.*"

"That could take a while."

"*Not necessarily. Most of the area's open space.*"

"Okay," said Matt. "How do we want to do this?"

"*Stay together,*" she said. "*We simply start poking around. Look for more omegas. Or anything else out of the way.*"

"How do we inspect a dust cloud?" asked Jon.

"*Scanners.*"

"But some of these things are millions of kilometers deep. You're not going to be able to see very far into *that*."

"*It's all we have, Jon. Other than going in with the ships to see whether we bump into something.*"

"Okay. I see what you mean."

"*Look, I can't give you any specifics about this. We'll be hunting for anything out of the ordinary. Unusual energy signatures. Artificial radio transmissions. Too much carbon. I don't know—*"

Matt nodded. "We'll know it when we see it."

"*That's exactly right, Matthew.*"

"Okay, *Preston*, let's go look at some dust clouds."

THEIR FIRST TARGET was about forty million klicks long, maybe a million across. The dust was less concentrated than it appeared from a distance, and the sensors were able to penetrate it quite easily. "Dust and rocks all the way through," said Matt.

The *Preston* lay off at a safe distance while the *McAdams* went in close, within a few kilometers, and, in effect, took the cloud's temperature. Jim reported that conditions inside, so far as the initial readings were concerned, showed results well within anticipated parameters. No anomalies.

They moved along the face of the cloud for about an hour, recharged the Locarno, jumped twelve million kilometers, and repeated the process.

"*Within anticipated parameters,*" said Jim.

They moved to the next cloud, this time with the *Preston* doing the honors while Matt and Jon watched.

JON SILVESTRI'S NOTEBOOK

The individual clouds are spectacular. Having to watch them on a display doesn't do them justice. I wish it were possible to stick my head out the door and look at this thing, *really* look at it. In this close, I suspect it would appear like a wall across the universe.

—Monday, March 10

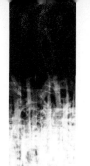

chapter 34

THEY NAMED THE clouds alphabetically as they progressed. The first one was Aggie, supposedly a morose aunt of Matt's. The second was Bill, who had been a grouchy editor early in Antonio's career.

They went to a round-the-clock search pattern, with one of the two pilots awake at all times. They stayed outside the clouds, one vehicle close in, the one with the functioning pilot, and the other at a respectful distance.

Hutch admitted to Antonio that she could not imagine how any directed operation could function out here. The place was indeed a cosmic cookpot, a cauldron of churning clouds and enormous jets. She suspected stellar collisions were not uncommon.

Toward the end of the second week, while they were completing their search of *Charlotte*, Phyl announced that she had sighted another group of omegas. Four this time.

They glittered like distant fires, flaring and dimming in the shifting light of the Cauldron.

"They track to Cloud F," she said.

F for Frank.

Frank was a cloud of moderate size. Like all the others, it was long and narrow, aimed toward Sag A* by the relentless gravity. They passed a stellar corpse on approach. And several red stars.

"*Length of the cloud*," said Phyl, "*is eighty billion kilometers.*" Almost seven times the diameter of the solar system. Like everything else at this range from Sag A*, it was orbiting the core at about 220 kps. Frank would need about 480,000 years to complete an orbit.

It was the *Preston's* turn to go in close and look. But they changed the routine: Both pilots would remain awake during the search. At the end of the day, they'd simply call it off and start fresh in the morning.

Antonio watched nervously as Hutch took station about eighty kilometers out from the edge of the cloud. Matt retreated to six million klicks.

"We safe at this range?" asked Antonio.

"Probably not," she said.

The cloud had become a vast, amorphous wall. It extended above and below the ship, fore and aft on the starboard side, to the limits of vision. It was alive with energy, riven near the surface by enormous lightning bolts, illuminated deep within by flashes and glimmerings.

Antonio knew the history, had read of that first encounter with an omega, when Hutchins and a few others at a place they called Delta had been attacked by lightning bolts, had tried to ride a lander to safety while directed lightning rained down out of the sky. He was impressed that she would tempt fate again.

Two red jets arced through the night, brightening the face of the cloud. "It's probably a pulsar," Antonio said. "This area must be littered with burned-out supernovas."

Hutch had been unusually quiet. They were both on the bridge, belted down in case they had to leave in a hurry. She was checking something off in a notebook and simultaneously watching as the insubstantial wall rippled past. "Hutch," he said, "answer a question."

"If I can."

"You're disappointed, aren't you? All this way, and there's not really going to be anything we can do here. Even if this cloud really is the source, it's just too big."

She adjusted course, pulling a little closer. A sudden flash dazzled them. "We don't know that yet," she said. "To be honest, Antonio, I'm not entirely sure I *want* to meet whatever's putting the omegas in play. I'm perfectly willing to let somebody else have that honor."

"Then what's wrong?"

Her eyes looked far away. "This feels like the start of a new phase. I mean, the Locarno Drive and the possibilities it opens."

"And—?"

Her eyes drifted back to the screen. The wall had gone dark. "I'd like to shut them down." She realized how unrealistic that was, and shrugged. "The truth, Antonio, is that I never believed in this part of the operation. I went along with it because it was what Rudy wanted to do. And maybe he was right. At least we've come out here. Now we can shake our fist at them, I guess, and go home."

It was Antonio's turn to fall silent. He was thinking that if he could go back and make a few changes in his life, he'd do some things differently. He wasn't sure what. He knew he could never have done the things she had. He couldn't seriously imagine himself at the controls of a superluminal. Wouldn't have wanted to make some of the life-and-death decisions she'd been forced to make. He'd been Dr. Science. A pretend astrophysicist. And he'd covered scientific developments for several news organizations. It hadn't been a bad career, really. He'd been a minor celebrity, he'd been paid reasonably well, and he liked to think he'd been responsible for turning some kids on to scientific careers.

But he wasn't really going anywhere. When his time came to retire, when he'd pulled the pin and gone back home, no one would ever remember him. Maybe they'd remember Dr. Science. But not Antonio Giannotti.

"You're a beautiful woman, Hutch," he said.

That brought a smile. "Thank you, Antonio. You're a bit of a looker yourself."

"That's good of you to say, Priscilla. But I was never much able to turn heads."

She studied him for a long moment. "You might have turned mine, Antonio." She switched back to the AI. "Phyl?"

"*Yes, Hutch?*"

"Still no indication of activity?"

"Negative. I don't see anything out of the ordinary."

The wall had become almost a blur. "How fast are we traveling?" he asked.

"Relative to the cloud, we're moving at almost seventy-five thousand." That was, of course, kilometers per hour.

"How long would it take us to look at the entire thing?"

"At this rate?"

"Yes."

"It's a long cloud."

"Right. I know."

She passed the question to Phyl. Phyl's electronics picked up a notch, the equivalent of clearing her throat. *"About 130 years."*

Antonio grinned.

"That would be just one side," Phyl continued. *"To do it properly, multiply the figure by four."*

The situation was not made easier by the fact that the cloud was simply too big for the sensors to penetrate adequately. "Somebody could be planting lemon trees in that thing," Hutch said, "and we wouldn't know it." The displays showed murky and overcast. The ship's navigation lights were smeared across the screens. "What do *you* want to do?" she asked him.

"How do you mean?"

"Did you want to go in and look around?"

"What would you do if I said *yes*?"

"Try me."

"Ah, no. Thanks. Let it go. But I *do* have an idea."

"What's that, Antonio?"

"Let's put all four of us in one ship, and use the AI to send the other one in for a test run. See what happens."

"The transfer would not work," said Phyl. *"How would you get from one ship to the other without exposing yourselves to the radiation?"*

"You don't want to go," Hutch told Phyl. The AI was right, of course. But the pilot couldn't resist testing her sense of humor.

"No, ma'am, I do not. May I point out that if you send a ship in there, you may not recover it." One of her avatars appeared, a young woman. She had Hutch's dark hair and eyes, looked remarkably vulnerable, and

was about eight months pregnant. *"I don't think it's a chance worth taking,"* she said. *"But if you insist, I'll do it, of course."*

"I don't blame you," said Antonio. "I'd feel the same way."

EVENTUALLY, ANTONIO'S ATTENTION wandered from the cloud to the crowded sky. A couple of nearby yellow stars were almost touching. He tried to imagine Earth's sun bumping its way through the chaos. Phyl reported a planet adrift. *"Range is twelve million kilometers. I can't be certain, but it doesn't seem attached to anything. Just orbiting the core. Like everything else. It appears to have been a terrestrial world."*

"You wouldn't expect it to be attached to anything out here," said Antonio. "Maybe it's what we're looking for."

"Phyl, any sign of life? Or activity of any kind?"

"Certainly not any kind of living thing we'd know about. There's no electromagnetic cloud, either. Did you want to inspect it more closely?" A picture appeared on-screen. The world appeared to be nothing more than a battered rock.

"No," said Hutch. "It's not a very likely candidate."

Something rattled the ship, a burst of wind and sand, and was gone. "Got in the way of a dust storm," said Hutch. "Phyl, are we okay?"

"Yes." The AI sounded doubtful. *"It wasn't enough to activate the particle beams. And, anyhow, the shielding covered us nicely."*

"Scopes and sensors okay?"

"Yes. I read no problems, maybe some minor scratches to the lens on number three. Although I have to say these are not ideal conditions for them."

"Okay. Keep the forward and starboard scopes active, and the starboard sensor." That was the one in the best position to work the cloud. "Seal everything else for now."

"Complying."

The pictures on the displays went down one by one until Antonio was looking either straight ahead or at the cloud.

AFTER AN HOUR or so, they jumped twelve million klicks. *"All readings are still inside the parameters,"* said Phyl.

Antonio had gotten hungry. He went back, made sandwiches for them, and carried everything onto the bridge. Hutch already had a cup of hot chocolate. After he got settled in his seat, she touched something, and his harness settled over his shoulders. Damned thing was annoying. "How long are we going to stay?" he asked. He expected her to make a crack about maybe only a couple of years. But she contented herself with a shrug and a smile.

"So when are we going to leave?" he said again.

She surprised him. "I don't know."

"We aren't going to stay here the rest of the month, are we?" He was losing any serious hope that they'd find anything.

"No," she said. "Let's just give it a little more time, though. You don't want to go back and face your colleagues and tell them we got nothing."

"That's a point."

Phyl broke in: *"Hutch, we're getting some odd readings."*

"Specify, please."

"Recurring patterns of nontypical electromagnetic radiation." Details appeared on-screen, but they meant nothing to either of them. *"There are also quantum fluctuations indicative of biological activity."*

"What?" said Hutch. *"Biological*? In there?"

"We need Rudy," said Antonio.

"Explain, Phyl."

"Data is insufficient to draw conclusions. I can say with certainty, however, that activity here is at a different level and more coherent than in the other clouds or at other sites in this cloud."

"Coherent? By that you mean—?"

"Occurring within more distinct parameters. More repetitive. Less arbitrary. Fewer extremes."

"You said 'biological activity.' Do you mean there's something alive in there?"

"That is probable."

"Okay." She was jiggling the yoke. Pulling them away from the wall. "Let's give it some breathing space." She was apparently talking to herself as much as to Antonio.

It was all right with Antonio. Something *alive* in there? *Maledire.* If he could see the cloud at all, they were too close.

She turned the ship left, to port, and Antonio was pushed against the side of his seat. On the displays, the cloud wall moved up, angled overhead, and became a *ceiling*, an *overhead*. Then it dropped back to the side again.

He looked at her for a long moment.

"What?" she said.

"You're showing off."

"A little. Thought you'd enjoy the ride."

She called Matt and passed the information along. "The cloud might have a tenant."

ONCE THEY WERE well away from it—or at least what Hutch apparently considered well away—she did more gyrations with the ship, rotating it along its vertical axis until the main engines were pointed forward. Then she used them to begin braking. Antonio, now facing backward, was pushed gently into his seat.

She had also turned the ship 180 degrees around its lateral axis, thereby keeping the starboard scope pointed at the cloud. It would have been a good moment for the Dr. Science show: *I'm now upside down, boys and girls, except you can't tell a difference because there is no up or down away from a gravity well.*

The cloud brightened and darkened in the swirling light from the pulsar.

"*Something's happening,*" said Phyl. "*Quantity and intensity of signals is picking up.*"

The lightning was becoming more frequent. And more violent. "Maybe it's waking up," Antonio said.

Matt's voice broke in: "*Hutch, get clear.*" He sounded frantic. "*Do it now. Get out of there.*"

Had Antonio not been harnessed in, he'd have jumped out of his seat. "What is it?" he demanded.

"Don't know," said Hutch. She nevertheless pulled back on the yoke. "Matt, do you see something?"

They'd been caught at a bad time. The ship was reversed, traveling backward, gradually braking. If she hit the mains, it would only slow them down more. She rotated the ship again, to get it pointed away from the wall. While they waited to complete the maneuver, Antonio hanging on to the arms of his chair, Matt's response came in: *"Up ahead. It's watching you."* His voice was shrill.

"What's watching me, Matt? What are you talking about?"

"The cloud."

"Matt—?"

"For God's sake, Hutch. The cloud *is.* Look *at it."*

ANTONIO'S NOTES

When I heard Matt's voice, heard how he sounded, telling us to clear out, I got pretty scared. I'd been hoping all along that the hunt for the omega factory would be fruitless, although I'd never have admitted that to anybody. I don't think it had anything to do with my being a coward, per se. That place, where the sky crowded in, where everything was filled with lightning, was really scary. All I really wanted was to declare there was nothing there and go home.

—Wednesday, March 12

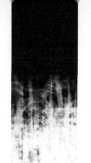

chapter 35

IT WAS LIKE being in a dark house and having something jump out of a closet. Hutch fought down the impulse to hit the main engines but continued waiting while the ship rotated away from the cloud. It seemed a painfully slow process. "Do you see anything, Antonio?"

Antonio looked as if he would have been hiding under his seat had he not been belted in. *"Nothing. Just the wall."*

"Phyl?"

"Nothing, Hutch."

It was an illusion. Matt's imagination. Had to be.

Finally, she got clearance. She told herself not to panic, warned Antonio, and started to accelerate.

He yelped as they pulled away.

"I can't see it now," said Matt. *"We've lost it."*

"What was it, Matt?"

"Priscilla, I know how this sounds. But it was an eye."

"An *eye*? Matt, how could you have seen an eye from out there?" Her heart was pounding. Been away from this too long.

"Because it was big."

"Okay," she said. "We're clearing." She continued the turn,

maintained thrust, and favored Antonio with a smile meant to be reassuring but which seemed only to alarm him more.

"You think he really saw something?"

"Get the right lighting here," she said, "and you probably get a half dozen faces in the cloud." She switched back to the *McAdams*. "Anything more, Matt?"

"No, Hutch. But I don't think we were seeing things. Jon saw it, too."

"Okay."

"It was real."

"Okay."

Phyl cut in: *"There,"* she said. *"That might be what they saw."*

A dark circle within the cloud. No. More ovoid than circular. With a black patch in the center.

Beside her, Antonio shifted, tried to get comfortable.

The picture was at maximum mag. Whatever the thing was, had they continued on their original course, they'd have passed directly in front of it. "Can you give us better definition, Phyl?"

The AI tried to adjust. Not much of an improvement. "We see it," she told Matt.

"Yeah. We got it back, too."

"It's just the light," she said.

"Maybe."

It *did* look like an eye.

Pensive. Emotionless. Looking at *her*.

"How big is it, Phyl?"

"Ninety meters by seventy-four. Error range of five percent." Phyl put up a map and located the position of the object.

Deep in the cloud, she saw lightning.

Hutch eased back on acceleration, gave it another minute or two, and cut forward thrust altogether. They were, of course, still racing away from the wall. When she was two thousand kilometers out, she angled to starboard and began running parallel to it again. "Phyl, are you reading any change in energy levels?"

"Negative," she said.

"Very good. If there's any shift, anything at all, up or down, I want to know about it. Right away."

"Yes, Hutch."

"You're worried about lightning?" said Antonio, who obviously was.

"I'm cautious, Antonio." She had no interest in trying to outrun a lightning bolt. "Phyl—"

"*I'm listening.*"

"Make sure we keep the Locarno charged at all times for an instant departure. Okay?"

"*Hutch, that will be a severe drain on our fuel.*"

"Do it anyhow. Until I tell you to stop. Matt, are you listening?"

"*I'm here, Hutch.*"

"I need to talk to Jon."

Phyl was giving them a close-up of the disk. The eye. Whatever. "That *is* an eye," said Antonio. "I don't think there's any question about it."

Jon's voice was usually a deep baritone, but at the moment it sounded a shade or two higher: "*Hello, Hutch. What can I do for you?*"

"What do you think about the eye?"

"*Don't know. I don't think there's any question there's something* alive *in there.*"

"Okay. Give me best guess: What is it?"

"*How the hell would I know? It's probably some sort of plasma creature. But it could be anything. I'd say we keep our distance.*"

"You think it's intelligent?"

"*Not if it's living out here.*"

"Seriously, Jon."

"*No way to know. Look, Hutch, I don't know anything about this sort of thing. My field is propulsion systems.*"

"*Nobody* knows anything, Jon. I'm asking about your instincts."

"*Okay. I'm not convinced yet it isn't an illusion.*"

"It doesn't *look* like an illusion."

"*Illusions never do. But if it's really there, and it's surviving out here, I'd say we don't want to mess with it.*"

"It, ah, isn't possible the whole cloud could be alive, is it?"

"*You mean a single living organism?*"

"Yes."

"*I don't see how.*"

"Why not?"

"It's too big. If something happens at one end, it would take hours to get a message to the central nervous system. Help, I'm on fire."

"Would it have to have a central nervous system? Maybe it's dispersed in some way."

"If we're assuming this is what put together the omegas, then we're talking intelligence. I don't see how you could have that without a brain. One brain, centrally located. But what the hell do I know? Maybe it's some sort of hive. Individual animals cooperating the way, say, ants do. But I'm damned if I can see how anything could live in there. Especially with all this radiation."

"So we can assume they're *in* the cloud."

"I think so."

"Okay. Thanks."

"I'd say the smart thing now would be to assume this is the source of the omegas. And go home. We have what we came for. Let somebody else come and sort out the details."

"He's right," said Antonio. "Phyl, we've got that thing's pictures on the record, right?"

"Yes, Antonio."

"What a story *that's* going to make."

No question. An eye twenty stories high. "Matt," she said, "you had a wider angle on it than we did. Could you see anything else in there? Any indication of a shape, possibly?"

"Like maybe tentacles?" Antonio was trying to lighten the mood.

Matt relayed the *McAdams* record to her and Phyl put it on-screen. Nothing else of note was visible. Just the eye.

"Matt's pictures aren't as clear as ours," he said.

"That's because they're farther away."

"Phyl? Is that the only reason?"

"The range accounts for some of the blurring. But not all of it. The image they sent should be more defined."

"Maybe the scope took a few seconds to focus," said Antonio.

"That's enough for me," said Matt. *"I'm for starting back."*

"I guess," said Hutch.

"Smart move." Jon was trying to sound disappointed, trying to mask his enthusiasm for turning around. *"I don't think we want to give that thing a shot at us."*

"It's lighting up," said Antonio.

He was referring to patches of the cloud on either side of the eye. "Light globules," Hutch said. Deep inside somewhere. They were like summer lightning. Or lights coming on in a dark house.

And going off again.

"We ready to go, Hutch?"

And coming back on.

"Hold it a second."

"You know," said Matt, *"it might be possible to come back here and nuke the thing after all. Get rid of it."*

"Not that it would do us any good," said Jon.

"How do you mean?"

"We've got more than a million years' worth of omegas already in the pipeline. I mean, we've seen seven of them in the last couple of weeks. By the time they could get anywhere near our part of the galaxy, we'll have evolved into something else. You can forget about the omegas. They're a done deal, and the galaxy will have to put up with them for a long time."

Matt didn't care. *"We owe them something. If we* do *send a mission back to take the things out, I'd like to be here when it happens."*

Antonio was watching the light display. "Matt," he said, "what makes you think this is the only cloud that's infested? This area might be a *family* of the things. Or a *colony.* I mean, why would there only be *one?*"

"I think there's only one," said Hutch.

"I agree," said Jon. *"There's a kind of rhythm, a pattern to the release. The omegas explode in a timed sequence, maybe four in Ursa Major, maybe a few months apart. But the same duration between events. Then six somewhere else. Again, same duration."*

"Like a cosmic symphony," said Hutch.

"Do you still believe that?"

She was surprised that Jon knew about her speculation that the omegas were intended to be a work of art. "Yes," she said. "It's a possibility. If there were a *colony* of critters doing that, I don't think it could be coordinated the way it is."

"It could be something else," said Jon. *"Other than a symphony."*

"Like what?"

"A message."

Hutch thought about it. Tried to make sense of it. "I don't think I follow."

"Look at the display."

Patches of light were still blinking on and off. "What's your point?"

"Look closer."

There were several luminous patches in the immediate area of the eye. Four, in fact. They were blinking in sync. On for a couple seconds. And off. On for a couple seconds. And off. Then it stopped.

And started again.

"Antonio," she said, "I'd like to go back. Get a little closer."

He wasn't happy about that, and he let her see. Made a pained expression. Pressed the back of his hand against his mouth and wiped his lips against it. "You want to give this thing a clear shot at us, is that it?"

"Something like that."

"Hold on," said Matt. *"I don't think that's very smart."*

"You wait where you are, Matt. Keep a respectful distance. We're going to go ahead. Before we change our minds."

THE CONTROL SYSTEM included a musical tone, a few notes from a pop hit of the period, that the AI could use if she wanted to speak to the pilot privately. The notes sounded.

Hutch frowned.

"What was that?" Antonio asked.

"Report from Phyl," she said. "Technical stuff." Then, casually, she pointed at her cup. "Antonio, would you mind getting me some fresh coffee? And maybe some chocolate to go with it."

"You hungry already?"

"Yes. Please."

He climbed out of his seat. "Okay. Back in a minute."

Hutch turned off the speaker and pulled on earphones. "What is it, Phyl?"

"Matt wants to talk to you."

Oh, Lord. "Put him through."

A pause, a change in tone, and Matt's voice: *"Hutch?"*

"What is it, Matt?"

"Can Antonio hear me?"

"No. But he'll be back in a minute or so."

"Okay. Listen, I think this is a seriously bad idea. You've got a good chance of getting yourself killed."

"I know there's a risk."

"We've already lost Rudy. I don't want to lose anybody else."

The cloud was getting bigger. "Neither do I, Matt." She tapped her fingertips on the control console. "Matt—"

"You're putting Antonio at risk, too."

"I know."

"You're not supposed to do that, Priscilla. He's your passenger. His safety is supposed to be paramount."

"Matt, he understands what the risks are."

"Does he really? Do you?" For a long moment, neither of them spoke. Then he sighed. *"I guess it would take more courage to change your mind than to persist."*

"That hurts, Matt."

"Good. I hope it's the worst thing that happens to you over there."

IT *WAS* AN eye.

The bridge was sealed. The viewports were blocked by the radiation shields, so she couldn't really see it. On-screen, it was just an eye in a bank of mist. An eye that seemed to be aware of her presence in the ship. That looked out of the screen directly at her.

She maneuvered the *Preston* to within a few kilometers of the cloud wall, circling so that, when she arrived in front of the eye, she would be parallel to the cloud. If she had to get out of there, she didn't want to have to turn around first like last time. "Careful," said Antonio in a whisper.

It was hard to know how deep within the mist the apparition was. "Phyl, do you pick up anything *solid* in there?"

"Only the eye," she said.

"You don't think we could open the viewport covers? Just for a moment?"

"It would be too dangerous, Priscilla. In fact, this entire business strikes me as being imprudent."

"Thanks, Phyl."

"I'm not comfortable," she added.

"I think we'll be okay, Phyl."

"I have a life, too, you know."

The other lights in the wall, the flickering luminosities, the lightning, faded. The cloud went dark. Stayed dark. Hutch switched her navigation lamps on, but directed them away from the eye. *Let's not be impolite.*

It focused on the lights. "No question about it," said Antonio. "I'd thought maybe it was our imagination, but that thing *is* watching us."

"Let's see what happens when we move," she said. Gently, she eased the ship forward. The eye tracked them.

"That's deceptive," he said. "It might be like one of those drawings where the subject watches you no matter where you go in the room."

"It's possible."

Antonio nodded, agreeing with his own analysis. He hung tightly on to his chair. Started to say something, but stopped. His voice was giving him trouble.

Hutch understood completely. She fought down an impulse to take off. She stopped the forward progress, and used the attitude thrusters to back up. The eye stayed with them.

When she drew abreast of it, a luminous patch appeared. Off to one side of the eye.

"Phyl, are you reading anything?"

"Slight energy uptick."

The patch expanded. Grew brighter.

Matt was on the circuit again: *"You're too close to it, Hutch. Back off."*

"Relax, Matthew," she said. "We're okay."

"Uh-oh."

Hutch never liked *uh-ohs.* "What is it, Matt?"

"We've got another one."

"Another light?"

"Another eye."

"Where?"

"Same area."

"I see it," said Phyl.

It was of similar dimensions, several kilometers farther along the wall. It, too, watched the *Preston.*

"There are two *of them,"* said Jon.

He meant *entities.* The positioning of the eyes wasn't symmetrical. However big the thing might be, they were not part of the same head.

The luminous patch went dark.

Navigation lamps were normally handled routinely by the AI. But Hutch had a set of manual controls. She shut the lamps off. Left them a few seconds. And turned them back on.

The patch reappeared.

And went off.

"Hello," said Hutch.

The navigation lamps on interstellars consisted of a base set: a red strobe on the highest part of the after section, a steady red light to port, a green light to starboard, and a white light aft.

She turned them on again. Counted to four. Switched them off. Counted to four. Turned them back on.

Waited.

"Hutch." Matt sounded almost frantic in that low-key professional manner that pilots cultivate. *"What are you doing?"*

"Trying to talk to it."

"I don't think that's a good idea."

"Matt, back off. I'm busy."

"Have you forgotten what that thing is?"

The patch flashed back. On and off.

She replied. On for four seconds. And off. And again, on four seconds, then off.

"Matt, I'm doing the best I can."

"Crazy woman."

The patch reappeared, brightened.

Died.

Reappeared.

"Matt." She was unable to keep the excitement out of her voice.

"I see it." He sounded skeptical, relieved, scared, wish-you-were-out-of-there. All at once. *"I wonder what it's saying."*

Antonio took a deep breath and shook his head. "Welcome to galactic center, I think."

"Phyl," said Hutch, "you're monitoring the radio frequencies, right?"

"Yes, ma'am. There is no radio signal of any kind, other than the normal background noise."

She blinked twice.

The patch brightened and faded.

"So what do we do now?" asked Antonio.

The two eyes stared back at her. "I don't know," she said. "I think we've exhausted our vocabulary."

"PHYL, WHAT ELSE can you tell us about the Mordecai area?"

"Nothing you don't already know, Hutch. No one, until now, has been able to establish anything unique about it. Other than that the omegas all track back to this general area. It is, of course, in orbit around the galactic center."

"That's it?"

"I can give you estimated dust particles per cubic meter if you like. And a few other technical details."

"Is the orbit stable?"

"Oh, yes."

Antonio was watching her. "What's your point, Hutch? What are you looking for?"

Filaments had begun moving laterally across the eyes. In sync. It was blinking.

"Let's pull back a bit," she said.

"Yeah. I'd feel better, too, if we put some distance between us."

She began to ease away.

The patch went luminous again. Five bursts in quick succession.

She stopped forward progress and blinked her lights. Five times.

More bursts. Five.

She started back. And returned the ship to its initial position. "It wants us to stay, Antonio."

"Maybe it wants to have us for dinner."

"Would Dr. Science say that?"

"Absolutely. Listen, Hutch, I think we should get out of here."

"Maybe it just wants company."

"Hutch, you're not thinking clearly. This thing manufactures omegas that go out and kill everything in sight."

Matt came on the circuit: *"What's going on?"*

"Hutch thinks it's lonely."

He laughed. His voice had a strained quality.

"It doesn't seem to be hostile, Matt."

"*Right. Not this son of a bitch.*"

"Matt, do you see any other eyes along the wall?"

"*Negative. Just those two.*"

She turned to Antonio. "Let's try another tack. Can we agree this part of the galaxy wouldn't get many visitors?"

He chuckled. It was the old Dr. Science laugh that inevitably came while he demonstrated how an experiment might turn out differently from what one might expect. "I wouldn't think so."

"Okay. If this is the thing that's responsible for the omegas, it, or its ancestors, have been here more than a million years."

"Of course they have, Hutch. They *live* here."

"Maybe." Hutch turned off her lights. The cloud went dark.

ANTONIO'S NOTES

Sitting out there so close to the thing that we could almost touch it was the scariest moment of my life. Even more than the snake in the hotel.

The snake in the hotel was pretty bad. Terrifying. The wall wasn't like that. The snake was a mindless product of natural forces. Like the black hole. Nothing personal. Just stay out of its way. But the eyes in the wall looked directly into me. I had the feeling it knew who I was, knew what I cared about, knew about Cristiana and the kids. Despite all of that, there was no sense of hostility. It was neutral. We didn't matter.

—Wednesday, March 12

chapter 36

MIDNIGHT.

Antonio was watching the eye blinks. They were lateral, they happened once about every six minutes, and they took seventeen seconds to complete. Close and open. And they always occurred simultaneously.

"It's one creature," Hutch said.

Antonio nodded. "Yes."

"With a head several kilometers across?"

"I doubt it. This thing doesn't *have* a head. Not in the way we understand the term. But it's connected somehow."

She blinked the navigation lights. The luminous patch reappeared. Went off. Came on again.

Hutch repeated the pattern, and got a quick series of flashes in return. "I think you're right," Antonio said. "It wants to talk." She seemed unusually subdued. "What's wrong?" he asked.

"What do you do after you've said hello?"

"With *this* thing? I have no idea."

SHE TURNED ON the starboard green light. Blinked it three times. Then she ran the strobe, a series of red flashes, for a total of five seconds.

Blinked starboard green three more times. Flashed the steady red light to port, and blinked the green nine times.

The patch appeared and faded.

She did it again. Same series.

"What are you doing?" asked Antonio.

"Hold on."

The patch reappeared. Blinked three. Then, higher in the cloud, they saw a burst of white light. The patch blinked three more times. Then a steady red glow. And finally the patch again, blinking to nine.

"So," said Antonio, "it more or less copies what you did. It didn't quite get the colors right, but what's the point?"

"I'm not sure yet." She tried another series: Blink green twice, run the strobe, two more blinks, port side red, then four blinks.

She leaned forward, and Antonio got the sense her fingers were crossed.

The cloud was quiet. Then the luminous patch came back and went off, the white burst reappeared momentarily, the patch appeared again and faded.

Antonio sighed. "I still don't see what it's supposed to mean."

The red glow showed up again. Lasted a few seconds.

Hutch leaned forward.

The patch came on again and went off. Once.

Yes! She raised a fist over her head.

"What happened?" asked Antonio.

"Two times two equal four," she said. "It replied one times one equals one."

Antonio asked her to run the series again, and he saw. The white burst became a multiplier. The steady red light was an equals sign. "I'm impressed," he said.

She sent two times three, followed by the green light, a short and a long.

The cloud responded with a steady red light and six blinks. The green signal established itself as a question mark. It was only a short distance from there to *I understand*. And its reverse.

"So where do we go from here?"

She tried two times two and flashed five. The creature returned a single yellow light. A quick flash. On and off. Three plus one equals five got another yellow flash. So she had *no*.

She used the strobe. Kept it on for maybe ten seconds. I understand. She did two times two and gave the correct answer.

The creature did its yellow light again, longer this time. *Yes*.

GRADUALLY, DURING THE day, she built a primitive vocabulary. *Plus* and *minus*, *up* and *down*, *forward* and *backward*. She got *inside* and *outside* by sending out the lander, under Phyl's control, and bringing it back in. *Inside*. *Outside*. Or maybe it was *launch* and *recover*. Well, let it go for now.

The creature varied its signals by intensity and length of illumination and by a range of hues to equate to Hutch's terms.

To establish *you* and *me/us*, she dispatched the lander again, aimed its lights at the *Preston*, and sent her signal, three quick whites. *Us*. Then she directed the lander to spotlight the creature, and sent four. *You*.

It responded with a yellow-white light, and sent *four*. Then a puff of gas and dust blew out of the cloud wall, in the general direction of the ship. The yellow-white light blinked three times.

Okay. So we weren't doing pronouns. It was names. The *Preston* was three; the creature in the cloud, four.

"Not bad, though," said Antonio.

UNFORTUNATELY, SHE HADN'T gotten near the questions she wanted to ask. How long have you been here? Are you alone? Do you need help? Where are you from? Why are you sending bombs into the outer galaxy?

A bit too complicated for the language so far.

"I have an idea for *alone*," Antonio said.

She tried it. *Five*. Pause. *One*. Then the signal she wanted to mean alone. Then *seven* pause *one*. And the *alone* signal again. And a third round. Using *four* with *one* and *alone*. Then *one equals* and the *alone* signal again.

When the creature responded *nine* and *one*, followed by *one equals alone*, she sent: *You alone question mark*.

The patch brightened. *Yes.*

Antonio gave her a broad smile. "Brilliant," he said.

"You're talking about yourself."

"I know." The smile got even wider. "We ought to give that thing a name."

"I thought we had."

"What?"

"Frank," she said.

"*THERE'S ONLY ONE of the damned things?*" asked Jon.

"That's what it says."

"*Is it responsible for the omega clouds?*"

"We haven't been able to ask that question yet."

"*Why not?*"

"I don't know how to spell *omega.*"

He had no patience with her sense of humor and let her see it.

"Look, Jon," she said, "the thing's about as easy to communicate with as you are."

"*All right,*" he said. "*Do the best you can.*"

"You're getting as bossy as Matt."

Matt's voice broke in: "*I heard that.*"

"Hi, Matthew." She had known, of course, he'd be listening. "Just kidding."

"*So you're talking to the critter now,*" Matt said.

"More or less. So far it's been a limited conversation."

"*All right. I agree with Jon. Find out whatever you can. It would be nice to know what's going on. What the reason is for the omegas.*"

"I'll ask it when I can think of a way to do it."

"*Okay. Meantime, you're too close to the damned thing. I wish you'd back off.*"

In another age, Dr. Science had bitten his upper lip when he was about to reveal why, say, no matter how strong you were and how well you could fly, you couldn't support a falling plane in midair. He bit his lip now, while his eyes acquired a distant look.

"What?" she asked.

"It might be stuck here."

"*Stuck?* How could it be stuck? I mean, if it can fire off omegas, it should be able to clear out itself."

"*Not necessarily,*" said Jon. "*You could be stuck in orbit somewhere but still send out, say, projectiles.*"

"*Wait a minute.*" Matt tried to laugh, but couldn't manage it. "*You're suggesting the omegas might be a cry for help?*"

"I'm open to a better explanation."

"*That's one hell of a way to get people's attention. Get them to come rescue you by blowing them up.*"

"I doubt it thinks in terms of people," said Jon. "*It might be that it would be shocked to discover there were living creatures, people, on planetary surfaces.*" For a long time no one spoke. "*It feels right,*" he said, finally. "*I bet that's exactly what's been happening.*"

"*For millions of years?*" Matt *was* laughing now. "*I don't believe it.*"

"Why don't we ask it?" said Hutch.

"*How do you suggest we do that?*"

"I have an idea, but you'll have to come in closer and join us first. Do we want to do that?"

AS SHE WATCHED the *McAdams* approach, Hutch wished she had a term for *indigestible.*

"*We ready to go?*" asked Matt.

"Let's do it." She opened the cargo hatch, and Phyl took the lander out again. Hutch turned on its lights to draw Frank's attention, and ran it back and forth several times. Then she directed Phyl to begin the demonstration.

Phyl brought it back toward the *Preston.* Toward the open cargo door. Very slowly. And bumped it against the hull. Too far to the right. Backed it off and tried again. Too low this time. A third effort went wide left.

The lander hesitated in front of the door, seemingly baffled.

Frank sent a message: *You question mark.*

Antonio laughed.

Hutch replied *no.*

Matt asked what it had said.

"It wants to know," Antonio said, "if Hutch is the lander. If the lander is the intelligence inside the ship."

"You're kidding."

"It has no way to know what's going on," said Hutch. "Before it saw the lander earlier today, it probably thought it was talking directly to the ship." She grinned. "I'm beginning to like him."

"Frank?"

"Sure. Who else?" She traded amused glances with Antonio, then flashed the strobe. Three short. Three long. Three short. The old SOS signal. "Matt, time to send out yours."

"Will do."

The launch door in the *McAdams* opened, and its lander soared into the night. It crossed to the apparently hapless vehicle still trying to get back into the *Preston* cargo bay, moved alongside it, nudged it left, pushed it lower, and guided it through the hatch.

Hutch flashed the SOS again, followed by *Frank question mark.*

Pause. Then the patch brightened.

Yes.

"ALL RIGHT," MATT said. *"We go home and report what we found. We have intelligent plasma out here. Or whatever. They're going to* love *that. It got too close to the core, and now we think it's stuck. You know what'll happen: They'll be coming out here to talk to the dragon. And somebody will be crazy enough to try to figure out a way to break it loose."* He was usually easygoing, one of those guys with little respect for authority because of a conviction that people in charge tend to do stupid things. At the moment, Hutch was the suspect. *"Well,"* he said, *"at least we'll get clear of it. It'll be somebody else's call."*

"That's not what'll happen," said Hutch. "Most people will react the way you just did. This place will be declared off-limits. The idiots who thought Jon's drive was dangerous will be confirmed. And nobody will come near the place."

"Is that bad?"

"I don't know." The creature's eyes stared at her out of the navigation screen. "Talk about eternity in hell."

"Well, look. It's not up to us anyhow."

She nodded. "Right. And the omegas will keep coming. For a long time. We've seen the kind of damage they do."

"You've been talking to it. Tell it to stop."

"I plan to try."

"Good."

ANTONIO'S NOTES

This entire exercise has had an air of unreality about it from the beginning.

What no one has said, but what I am sure they've all been thinking is: Why does it not disentangle itself from the cloud and show us what it truly is? Is it so terrifying? Surely it would not seem so to itself. It may be that it is wholly dependent on the cloud, perhaps for sustenance. And then there is the possibility that, despite Jon's theorizing, it *is* the cloud.

When I mentioned it to Hutch, she told me that she doesn't believe any living creature could be that large.

—Thursday, March 13

chapter 37

HUTCH SAT ON the bridge, wearily trying to figure out how to expand the vocabulary. How do you say *omega cloud* with blinking lights? How to establish a unit of time? How to ask what kind of creature it is?

"If it's not native to this area," asked Antonio, "how did it get around?"

"*There's only one way I can think of,*" said Jon. "*It absorbs dust or gas and expels it.*"

"A jet."

"*Has to be.*"

The eyes remained open. Stayed focused on them. "*It never sleeps,*" said Matt.

"Looks like."

Antonio got up. "Well, am I correct in assuming we won't be leaving in the next few minutes?"

"I think that's a safe guess."

"Okay. In that case I'm going to head back for a while. I'm wiped out."

"Okay."

"You don't mind?"

"No," said Hutch. "I'm fine. You go ahead."

He nodded. "Call me if you need me."

She turned back to the screen image. The eyes. You and me, Frank. She blinked the lights. Frank blinked back.

How long have you been here? My God, a million years in a place like this. Has anybody else been by to say hello?

Maybe a billion *years. Are you immortal? I suspect you could teach those idiots at Makai something about survival.*

She thought back across her life. It seemed a long time ago, *eons*, since as a kid barely out of flight school, she'd taken Richard Wald to Quraqua. Since she'd stood outside that spooky city that no one had ever lived in on Quraqua's airless moon. It had been constructed by an unknown benefactor, thought to be the Monument-Makers. But who really knew? It was supposed to draw the lightning of an approaching omega away from the cities of that unhappy world. It hadn't worked.

Frank, if that was you sending the clouds, you've been stuck out here a long time. How could a sentient being stay sane?

The eyes looked back at her.

Matt said something about why were they waiting around? Nothing more to be done here. Why not start back tonight?

"Let me talk to it a bit more, Matt. Be patient. This is the reason we came."

The expression in the eyes never changed.

What are you thinking?

She blinked the lights again.

It blinked back.

PHYL'S VOICE RETRIEVED her from a dream. "*. . . Ship out there . . .* " She recalled something about a woodland, a sliver of moon, and lights in the trees. But it faded quickly, an impression only, less than a memory. "*. . . Edge of the cloud.*"

There was nothing new on-screen. "Say again, Phyl."

"*There's a ship—*" She stopped. "*Matt wants to talk to you. They've probably seen it, too.*"

"You mean a ship other than the *McAdams*?"

"*Yes, Hutch.*"

"On-screen, please." It was box-shaped. Covered with shielding. Like the *Preston*. "Can you give me a better mag?"

"*You have maximum.*"

Its navigation lights were on. "It looks like us."

Phyllis put Matt through. "*Hutch, you see it?*"

"I see it. Phyl, where is it?"

"*Forward. Directly along the face of the wall. About four thousand klicks.*"

"*It's almost* in *the cloud*," said Matt.

It could have *been* the *Preston*, even to the extent that the armor appeared to be a series of plates tacked on. "Open a channel," she said.

"*You have it.*"

Hutch hesitated. An alien ship? That meant another language problem. At least. "Hello," she said. "This is the *Phyllis Preston*. Please respond."

She waited. And heard a single word: "*Hello.*"

She stared at the image. "Phyl—?"

"*No mistake, Hutch. They're speaking English.*"

"*Help us. Please.*"

"*That can't be*," said Matt. "*Not out here.*"

"I wouldn't have thought so, either." She played it back.

Hello.

Help us. Please.

Male voice. Perfect accent. A native speaker. "Sounds like you," she said. She stared up at the image, at the boxy ship that shouldn't be there. "Who are you?"

"*Help us—*"

"Identify yourself, please."

Matt broke in: "*Who the hell are you?*"

"I've got it, Matt," she told him on a private channel. Then she switched back: "Please tell us who you are. What is your situation?"

She listened to the carrier wave. After about a minute, it was gone.

"*They're adrift*," said Phyl.

Hutch called Antonio and asked him to come forward. He appeared moments later, in a robe, looking simultaneously startled and bleary. "Yes?" he said. "What's wrong?"

She explained while he gaped at the display. "I want to take a look," she said. "But I don't know what we'll be getting into."

"And you don't have any idea who that is?"

"No."

"All right. Let's go."

She informed Matt. *"Okay,"* he said. *"We'll meet you there."*

"No. Stay where you are."

"You sure?"

"Absolutely. Stay put until we find out what this is about. And let me talk to Jon for a minute, please?"

"Sure. hang on. He's in back."

Moments later, Jon got on the circuit. *"That's really strange,"* he said.

"Did anybody else have access to the Locarno?"

"No. Not that I'm aware of."

"Anybody work with you on it? Maybe before you came to us?"

"I had some help, yes. But nobody who could have gone on and finished the project on his own."

"You're sure?"

"Yes. Absolutely."

"All right. That leaves us with the technicians who installed it."

"They wouldn't be able to figure out the settings. Anyway, you're forgetting how big everything is out here, Hutch. Even if somebody else had *the drive, if they had twenty ships, the chance of any two of them running into each other in this area is just about nil."*

"Then how do you explain it? The guy speaks English."

"I can't explain it. But if you want my advice—"

"Yes?"

"Leave it and let's go home."

She would have liked to assure the creature she'd be back, but she could think of no quick way to do it.

When they pulled away, minutes later, the eyes were still trained on her.

THE SHIP LAY just outside the wall, its navigation lamps still on. It had remained silent after the original transmission.

It looked like a vehicle humans might have put together. Yet, as they approached, they saw that the hull, armored as it was, possessed a suppleness that placed it ahead of any designs currently in use. It had to be one of ours, *had* to be. But it was *different* in a way she couldn't quite pin down.

And, all that aside, what was it doing here?

"So," asked Antonio, as Phyl brought them alongside the other ship, "what do we do now?"

The shielding on the *Preston* covered the main and cargo hatches, but it was designed to open up when needed. Someone standing outside the ship would have no trouble seeing the seams where the armor lifted away. The arrangement on the intruder vessel looked identical.

"I'm not sure. We can't really go over there and knock on the door."

"I don't think I'd want to do that in any case." Antonio took a long deep breath and shook his head. "I don't like any part of this."

"*Range one hundred meters,*" said Phyl. "*Still no reaction. Do we want to go closer?*"

"No. Not for the moment." She looked past the ship, into the wall, half-expecting to see another eye. But there was only dust and gas, darkening until it became lost in itself. "Matt?"

"*Go ahead.*"

"Has anything changed back there?"

"*Negative.*"

"It's still there? The creature?"

"*Yes, ma'am. Eyes are still open. It probably misses you.*"

Actually, she thought, it might. Probably been a long time since it had anyone to talk to.

"What do we do now, Hutch?"

"Wish I knew. It would help if we didn't have to deal with the armor. If we could see into the bridge, we could get a better idea what we're dealing with."

"Yeah, well, me, I wish for world peace." Antonio made an annoyed sound deep in his throat. "If they don't answer up, I don't see what we *can* do."

"*I'm getting increased electromagnetic activity,*" said Phyl.

"Where? from the ship?"

"No. From the cloud."

"Let me see."

Phyl put the numbers on-screen.

They were going up fast. Hell, they were spiking. "Heads up, Antonio," she said. She took control of the ship and fired the mains. The ship jerked forward, and they were thrown back into their chairs.

"What's going on?" asked Antonio.

She heard Matt's voice, too, but she was preoccupied at the moment.

The cloud was lighting up.

Hutch turned hard to port, went lower, and ran it to full throttle. But a starship is a lumbering thing.

The sky behind them lit up.

"Lightning," said Phyl. *"I think it was directed at us."*

"Keep the wall on-screen," she said.

"I can't. Not from this angle. The aft telescopes are sealed."

"Unseal them, Phyl. Come on."

"Working."

She watched the screens. Saw clouds and stars dead ahead. "Matt."

"Listening."

"It attacked us. Stay clear. We are okay."

The cloud wall appeared on-screen. Glowing. Getting brighter.

She cut to starboard.

Come on.

The sky behind lit up and the ship shuddered. The displays failed, and the lights went off and blinked back on.

"Lightning bolt aft," said Phyl.

One by one, the screens came back.

"It's starting again," said Phyl. *"Energy levels rising."*

"Phyl, how much time was there between bolts?"

"Thirty-seven seconds, Hutch."

She could hardly move under the pressure of acceleration.

Antonio was clinging to his chair. "Can we outrun it?" he asked.

"A lightning bolt? No." She was watching the time. Counting the seconds. At thirty-five, she lifted the nose and again moved hard to starboard.

The screens lit up.

"That one missed, Hutch. May I congratulate you on your maneuver?"

She turned back to port. Headed straight out from the wall, trying to put it as far behind as she could. And she had half a minute again. But the *Preston* was moving along now at a pretty good clip.

"Can we get clear?" demanded Antonio.

"Sit tight, and I'll let you know. Give me a countdown, Phyl.

"Eleven."

She swerved again. Superluminals weren't really built for this sort of thing.

"Three."

Cut back. Dived.

Held steady, past the end of the countdown. *"It did not fire."*

Swerved. And as she came out of it, something massive struck the ship. The engines died. The lights went out. Fans stopped running, and the screens went off. She rose slightly against the harness. They'd lost artificial gravity.

"It came off the pattern," said Antonio.

"I know."

The emergency lights came on. The fans restarted, and the flow of air began again. "I guess it doesn't play by the rules." She threw her head back in the chair. Nothing she could have done. It had come down to pure guesswork. "Phyl, what is our status?"

The lights flickered, but stayed on.

"Phyl?"

There was no response.

"She's down," said Antonio.

They were drifting in a straight line, an easy target for a second shot. No way the damned thing could miss. *Frank, you are a son of a bitch.* "Matt, do you read me? We've been hit. Stay away from the cloud. Do not try to retrieve us."

"You really think Frank did this?" asked Antonio. "He's thousands of kilometers away."

"Maybe there's another one here. I don't know—"

There was no answer from Matt. Damn, she didn't have enough power to transmit over a distance of four thousand klicks. What was she thinking?

She was suddenly aware of being pushed against her harness.

"What's going on?" said Antonio.

"We're slowing down."

"How's that happening?" His voice was a notch or two higher than normal.

"I don't know," she said. "Maybe we didn't really get clear of the cloud." The only thing she could imagine was that something had grabbed them. Was pulling them back. She looked again at the blank screens.

LIBRARY ENTRY

It's ended, then.
And that cool summer night when you and I
Might have walked together beneath the stars
Will never come.

—*Sigma Hotel Book*

chapter 38

"HUTCH, DO YOU read?" Matt listened to the crackle of cosmic static. It was hard to make much out at this range, but the *Preston* seemed to be tangled in long tendrils of cloud. "Goddam it," he said, "I knew something like this was going to happen."

The eyes were watching him.

"*Matt,*" said the AI, "*the other ship, the one that issued the call for help, is gone. It must have been taken inside the cloud.*"

"Jim, get us over there. Minimum time." That meant using the Locarno, but they'd need about thirty minutes to charge. "Hutch, I don't know whether you can hear this, but we're on our way."

"Wait," said Jon.

"We don't have time to screw around, Jon." They began to move.

"Kill the engines. You're doing this the wrong way."

"How do you mean?"

"Shut the engines down. Please."

"Why?"

"Just *stop* the goddammed thing."

"Do it, Jim."

"*Complying, Captain.*"

"Okay," said Jon. "Now ask the AI to put me on with Hutch. And just one live mike." He touched the one in front of him. "*This* one."

"Why?"

"Time may be short. Will you just *do* it?"

"Okay. Jim, open a channel."

Jon hunched over the mike. "*Hutch, this is Jon.*"

"You understand—"

Jon shushed him, and covered the mike. "Okay, go ahead."

"You understand she probably can't hear you."

"That's okay."

Matt sighed. Shook his head. When dealing with a lunatic, it's always best to pacify him. "All right. Do what you have to. But make it quick, all right?"

Jon went back to the mike. "Hutch," he said, "we don't know whether you can hear us or not. But the thing in the cloud wants to seize the *Preston*. You can guess why. We're sorry, but"—he held up a hand, signaling Matt not to interfere—"but we're going to have to destroy you."

Matt almost jumped out of his chair. Jon covered the mike again. "Trust me," he said.

"What are you doing?"

"Have faith, Brother. You want to save them?"

"Of course."

"This might be the only way." The hand went up again, index finger pointed at the overhead, his expression warning Matt to be silent. "We're starting a countdown, Hutch, to allow you and Antonio a few minutes for prayer and reflection. We'll blow the ship in precisely five minutes. I'm setting the clock now."

He shut off the mike, sat back, and exhaled.

"What did you just do, Jon? They may have heard that. If they did—"

"Matt, we don't actually have the capability to destroy them, do we?"

"No."

"Okay. Then what would they be worried about?"

"At a time when they're in deep trouble? They'll think we've lost our minds."

"Matt." He went into his professorial mode. "Hutch is pretty smart. By now she'll have figured out what's—"

"*Incoming transmission,*" said Jim.

Matt was beginning to feel he was in a surreal world. "From Hutch?"

"*No, Matt. I'm not sure who it's from. It originated in the cloud.*"

Jon was wearing a large, told-you-so smile. "Let me handle it," he said.

Matt was glad somebody had an idea what was going on. "Go ahead," he said. "I assume you know who's on the circuit?"

"He has big eyes," said Jon. "Jim, connect." When the white lamp came on, he said, "Go ahead, please."

"*Do not destroy the* Preston." It sounded like the same voice that had called for help. The one Jon insisted sounded like Matt.

Jon switched off the mike. "Now you see what we're dealing with?"

"No. What the hell is going on?"

Jon held up his palm. *Okay. Be patient. Stay out of it.* He switched the mike back on: "I'm sorry. Unless you can give me a good reason not to, I have no choice. It is standard procedure."

"*Why would you wish to destroy friends?*"

"You were listening to us all along, weren't you?"

"*Yes.*"

"The flashing lights. That was a game, wasn't it?"

"*I am not familiar with the term.*"

"Game: an activity of no consequence."

"*No. It was a way to start communication. It was a beginning.*"

"Now you want the *Preston.*"

"*Yes. I wish to make an arrangement.*"

"I'm listening."

"*First, stop the clock.*"

"I'll stop it if I'm satisfied with your answers."

"*How do I know you are telling me the realistic thing?*"

"You mean, how do you know I can actually destroy the other ship?"

"*Yes.*"

"I can prove it by doing it. Be patient and you will see."

"That is not satisfactory."

"If you choose not to believe me, and I *am* telling the truth, telling the realistic thing, you will lose access to the *Preston.* If you allow me to take off my associates, whether I am telling the realistic thing or not, you will still have the ship."

"Yes. That is so."

Jon covered the mike and looked over at Matt. "People always told me you could be a good engineer and still be dumb." Then back to the microphone: "All right. I have put the clock on hold."

"That means what?"

"It's not running. But I can start it again at any moment."

"How does it happen you have such capability? To destroy the other ship?"

"You are aware of the Penzance pirates?"

"No. What is a Penzance pirate?"

"They are from Penzance."

"I am not familiar with Penzance. Or with the term pirate."

"Penzance is a barbarous empire out near the galactic rim. Far from here. They are all pirates. They attack ships. Like ours. Seize them. Rob the crew and passengers. Kill people for no reason. We found only one way to protect ourselves. Let them come on board, then destroy the vessel. Either self-destruct, or from nearby."

"It is hard to believe you would do a thing like this."

"We no longer have problems with pirates."

"Does that not kill your people as well as those whom you oppose?"

"They're called enemies."

"Yes. Enemies." It seemed to be tasting the word, as though something might be learned from it.

"Yes, the strategy kills our people. But they live on. It is honorable to die in a just cause. To die while fighting your enemies gives us salvation."

Love your theology, thought Matt.

"How do they live on? If they are dead?"

"There is a part of them that is immortal. That lives forever. Like you, perhaps."

"I do not live forever."

"I'm sorry to hear it."

"What is 'salvation'? A method to dispose of the remains?"

"It's complicated. But I sincerely wish you would give us cause to destroy ourselves, as well as our friends."

"You are a strange species. But I am unable to accommodate you."

"I see."

"I offer you the lives of your friends. You may go and collect them from the ship. But then you must leave. I ask only that you not damage the Preston."

"Beyond what you've already done."

"The essentials remain."

"Okay," said Jon. "I'm sorry to hear that. They will not be pleased to be taken off. They expect that we will grant them the opportunity for salvation."

"You may tell them I am sorry for their inconvenience."

"I'll tell them." He scratched his forehead, waited a few beats, then spoke again: "Who were you signaling?"

"I do not understand."

"There's someone you hoped would see the clouds, the explosions, and come to your assistance. Is that not correct?"

"Yes. It is correct."

"Who? Others like you?"

"Yes. Like me."

"Why have they not come?"

"They know they would be trapped here if they did. As I am."

"Then why bother? If they will not come?"

"It is all I have."

At that moment Jon would happily have killed the thing. "Have you any idea how many have died, how many civilizations have been destroyed by your goddam signal?"

"I did not know there were life forms like you."

"Yeah. One more thing: If you attempt to strike us in any way, know that we are not without recourse."

"I understand."

"We will know in advance that a strike is coming, and we will immediately destroy both ships."

"Yes. I understand that also."

"I hope so."

"And if I fulfill my part of the agreement you will not destroy the Preston*?"*

"No. You have my word."

"OKAY, JIM," **MATT** told the AI, "get us over there as quickly as you can."

"No," said Jon. "Don't show it the Locarno. Just use the main engines."

"Why?"

"Best to keep a surprise available. Charge the Locarno on the way. And keep it ready."

"Okay, Jon. Now, how about telling me where that other ship came from? And why this thing wants the *Preston* at all? Especially after it crippled the thing. Even if it was operational, something as big as that son of a bitch is couldn't fit inside."

"It *manufactured* the other ship. To lure Hutch closer. And no, of course the creature couldn't fit inside."

"Then what's going on?"

"We can assume it wants to get out of here. That means it needs thrust. What makes the *Preston* go?"

"But—"

"I suspect what it wants is to get a look at the *Preston*'s engines and thrusters."

"So it can reproduce them?"

"On a much larger scale. Or maybe just make a zillion of them. I don't know—"

"You think it can do that? Manufacture thrusters?"

"It makes omega clouds and their triggers, doesn't it? We've seen it make a transmitter. We know it has nanotech capabilities. I'd say sure. It can manufacture the engines, the fuel, probably whatever it needs. It just doesn't know how."

"And we're going to leave it a design? So it can get clear?"

"One problem at a time, Matt."

"I don't think we should let this happen."

"I know you don't. At the moment, all I really care about is picking up Hutch and Antonio and getting out of here."

It was a betrayal. "If the idiot woman had listened to me, none of this would be happening."

"You can complain to her when we have them back on board."

"Jon, you know, after we get them back, it might be possible to destroy the *Preston* anyhow."

"Matt, I promised the thing it could have the ship."

"I know. But we have a defense system. We have particle beams."

"Matt, the *Preston* is armored. The particle beams might do some damage, but I suspect it would be minimal. The thing would probably still be able to figure out how the engines work."

"*Probably.*"

"You'd have to pretty much melt the engines to hide the design."

"If we fired a few shots right up the tubes, we'd bypass the shielding. There'd be a decent chance of blowing the ship apart. We could pick them up, then at least make the effort."

Jon looked unhappy. "Wouldn't you have to maneuver into position to do that?"

"Yeah."

"And if you succeeded, we'd have to make a run for it. Against lightning bolts."

"We already know the thing's a scattershot."

"I don't think it would have to have a very good aim to take us out."

"I don't know. If that's the case, why didn't it disable the *Preston* when it got so close right at the beginning? Why did it have to arrange that elaborate ploy with the alternate ship to get her even closer?"

"I'd say because it wasn't a matter of taking down the *Preston*; it was a question of securing the ship afterward."

"So what do you think?"

"I think we do what we said we were going to do. Let it have the *Preston* and count ourselves lucky if we get clear with Antonio and Hutch."

THEY WERE TOO far away to get a good look, but as Matt accelerated toward the *Preston*, they could see that tendrils still clung to it. The forward motion of the ship had not yet stopped, but it was barely moving.

"It's not letting go," said Matt.

Jon nodded. "It won't."

Matt got back on the circuit. "Hutch," he said. "We know you can't transmit. But we're on the way. Be there in a couple of hours. Hang on. We're going to—"

Jon held up his hands. Stop. He scribbled a note. *Careful what you say. Enemy listening.*

"See you then," he finished.

Jon took over, explained how they intended to make the transfer, and signed off. When he'd finished, Matt wondered what the enemy remark was about.

"If we sound anxious to get them off, Frank might conclude the story's a fabrication."

"So what if it does? I mean, really, as long as it gets to keep the ship, why would it care?"

"If I were Frank," said Jon, "I'd prefer two ships to one. In case something went wrong. In case the engine in one was damaged to the extent I couldn't figure out how it worked. Maybe just because I'm a mean son of a bitch who wants to kill everybody in sight. Look, what would your mood be like if you'd been stuck out here a million years?"

"Okay."

"We need it to be convinced we're suicidal."

Jim broke in: "*Forward motion by the* Preston *has stopped.*"

"Okay," Matt said. "Maybe it's best we stay off the link."

"Until we get there, anyhow."

"*It is beginning to retract. The ship is being drawn back toward the cloud wall.*"

They reached cruise velocity, and Matt released the harnesses. "Time to get to work," he said.

They climbed into e-suits and went below to cargo. There, they collected two lasers and began cutting into the ship's outer bulkhead.

WHEN THEY GOT within a hundred kilometers, they picked up a transmission from the *Preston*. "*Glad you guys are coming. We'll be waiting.*"

"Very good, Hutch," said Matt. "We'll be there in a few minutes."

Jon leaned forward. "Hutch, in the various communication media, as in all things, *caution* is the watchword."

"Understood, Jon. Nobody ever got in trouble for something she didn't say."

The *Preston* was being dragged relentlessly toward the cloud wall.

"Jim," said Matt, "you get any indication of increasing activity inside the cloud, let me know right away."

"Yes, Matt."

Jon got on the link. "Being in the cloud, we do not have a name for you. How do we address you?"

He got only static back.

"Okay. It doesn't matter. We're approaching the *Preston*. In a few minutes we will be taking our people off. When we have accomplished that, I'll signal you, and at that point you may do as you will with the ship."

"Yes," it said. Still using Matt's voice. *"Agreed."*

"Okay."

Matt brought them in carefully. He tried to angle the ship so he could get clear quickly if attacked. But he knew, they both knew, that if things went wrong, there'd be no evading the lightning. Not at this range.

"Okay, Hutch," he said, "we're ready to go."

"Need a couple minutes," she said.

Matt grumbled under his breath. They were presumably putting on e-suits, getting ready to go down into cargo. But they'd had plenty of time to do that. It was irritating that she hadn't been ready to move on signal.

"All right." He didn't add *What's the holdup?* but his voice must have given it away.

"We're packing," she said.

Packing? What the hell was the matter with the woman? "Hutch, you have nothing over there we can't replace."

"Need my clothes," she said. *"Just be a few minutes."*

He pushed back in his chair. "Goddam women."

And he waited.

Jon went below to take a last look at the shielding they'd welded to the hull of the lander. More had been placed inside the vehicle wherever possible. It didn't look pretty, and it wasn't much, not in the surrounding electromagnetic maelstrom, but it was something.

The minutes dragged. Didn't she realize the monster in the cloud could change its mind at any moment and fry them all? What the hell was she doing over there?

Then, finally, she was back. *"Okay, Matt. All set. You'll want to hurry up, though."* Urgency in her voice. That's right. Take your time and now let's hustle. He wanted to say something, but best not. Not with Frank listening.

"Thank God," he said. "Jettison the lander."

Since the *Preston* had no power, Hutch and Antonio would have to release the locks and the cargo hatch manually. That would expose them to the outside radiation, but she'd said not to worry, she could take care of it. Probably she had done much the same thing he and Jon had, taken down some of the interior shielding and built a shelter near the hatch that they could hide behind.

The *Preston* cargo hatch was located on the port side. He watched it open. The lander, like the ship, had lost power, and they needed to get it out of the way. Even in zero gravity, it retained its mass, and would therefore require some serious pushing. Hutch and Antonio would be behind their makeshift shielding pulling on lines to drag the lander through the launch doors. He was relieved to see it emerge and begin to drift away.

Matt opened his own cargo door.

Hutch called over. *"Okay. Let's go."*

Incredible. She was annoyed at *him*.

"I hope you got all your blouses," he told her.

"Say again, Matt?"

"Nothing." The *McAdams* lander slipped out through the hatch and started toward the *Preston*.

"Jim, don't forget they have no gravity over there."

"I know."

It crossed the twenty or so meters that separated the two ships and entered Hutch's cargo section.

He visualized Hutch and Antonio scrambling on board, looking around doubtfully at the makeshift shielding. Then Jim alerted him that the lander had sealed. The vehicle made its exit and started back. Moments later the *McAdams* took it aboard.

JON WAITED BELOW in cargo, watching it come in. He couldn't see into the vehicle because of the shielding he and Matt had welded around it. As soon as it had cleared the launch doors, he closed them. It eased into its berth, and he started the pressurization procedure. It would take about two minutes before they could leave the passenger cabin.

Except that the shuttle opened up immediately. Antonio was wearing an e-suit. He jumped down from the lander, looked around, and spotted Jon. He literally bolted in his direction. There was no sign of Hutch.

He was carrying something. A piece of cloth, looked like.

Jon started to wave, and mouthed *hello*. Was going to add *Glad to see you*. But he shook his head, no time.

Jon glanced back at the lander. Nobody else was getting out. Antonio unraveled the cloth and held it up for him. A message was scrawled on it: GET GOING. *PRESTON* ABOUT TO BLOW.

He shook his head. That couldn't be right. Again he tried to form words that Antonio could read. *What's going on? What do you mean?*

The journalist looked directly into his eyes and opened his mouth to form one unmistakable word: *Boom.*

That was enough for Jon. He got on the allcom, the ship's internal communication system, which Frank couldn't intercept, and called the bridge. "Matt."

"*They okay, Jon?*"

"Antonio says there's a bomb ready to go off over there. Move out."

"*What?*" He added an expletive. "*Tell him to grab hold of something.*" The main engines came online.

Jon gave a thumbs-up, and Antonio tried to hurry back to the lander, where he could belt down and ride out the acceleration. But the ship was already moving, turning away, power building in the engines. Jon clung to a safety rail, while Antonio lost his balance and slid aft, into storage, where he grabbed hold of a cabinet door handle.

He looked again around the launch bay. Where was Hutch?

LIBRARY ENTRY

When you went away,
The stars and moon,
The voices in the tide,
The kivra *gliding above the trees,*
All were lost.

—Sigma Hotel Book

chapter 39

JON LOOKED DISMAYED. *"Matt,"* he said, *"stay off the commlink. Don't try to talk to him."*

"Why?"

"Because it might be overheard."

"Well, if that critter hasn't figured out by now that something's wrong, it's pretty dumb." But he complied. At the moment there was nothing to be gained by talking.

Just clear out.

He couldn't go to maximum thrust, with people running around the launch bay. But he put on as much acceleration as he dared. A few bumps and bruises were better than getting caught in an explosion, and who the hell's idea was it anyhow to plant a bomb on board the *Preston*? "Jon, how much time do we have?"

"Don't know." Jon grunted, straining to hang on to the bar.

"What kind of bomb?"

"Don't know that either."

"What *do* we know?"

"Matt," he said, *"I haven't seen Hutch yet."*

The AI cut in: *"Electrical activity's picking up."*

They were going to get another bolt up their rear ends. He turned onto a new course. Jon grunted but hung on. Starships weren't like aircraft. Not nearly as maneuverable, because you don't have an atmosphere to help you do flips and turns. All Matt could do was roll around and fire attitude thrusters.

"I think we've got another eye forming."

"Not surprised." He changed course again. And fired braking rockets.

"Hey." Jon did not sound happy. *"What are you doing?"*

"Two of them, in fact. No, three."

"It's getting ready to shoot at us, Jon. I guess it's figured out—"

The sky flared.

"Close," said Jim. *"Building again."*

He angled off in another direction and heard Jon yell. Heard something crash.

"Sorry. Can't help it."

"Do what you have to."

Another bolt ripped past. It illuminated the hull and was gone.

At the same instant the sky behind them exploded.

"That was the Preston," said Jim.

He turned again. And took her hard up.

Lightning rippled across the screens. They went off momentarily, and came back. He could smell something burning. "Jim?"

"We're okay. Best not to get hit again, though."

"Okay. I'll see what I can do."

"It appears the Preston's *engines went. I do not think much will be left."*

"Jon—"

"Still here."

"Any sign of Hutch?"

"Hard to see from down here."

"You're on the deck?"

"Another one building, Matt."

It had begun trying to outguess him. This time he stayed on course. Just kept piling on distance.

The sky brightened again.

"Matt," said Jim, *"we should be out of range in about a minute."*

Matt didn't believe it. "How do you get out of range of a lightning bolt?"

"You become a small enough target that it's virtually impossible for the cloud to mount an accurate strike."

"Okay." He would have liked to ease off a bit, but he didn't dare, and in fact it took all his discipline not to go to full thrust. But neither Jon nor Antonio and maybe not Hutch would have survived. "Jon, how you doing?"

"No sweat, Matt. The bone'll set in thirty days."

He opened the commlink. It didn't much matter if they were overheard now. "Antonio, how about you?"

"I'm all right," he said.

"Where's Hutch?"

Her voice came through: *"I'm here. In the lander."*

"You okay?"

"I'm fine."

The sky brightened again. Less intense this time.

"What did you do?" he demanded.

"Pretty dumb. I trusted that thing. I still don't believe it."

"I'm not talking about that. I'm talking about the bomb."

"Going up again, Matt."

"Why the bomb? Why'd you do it?"

"I wasn't going to allow that damned thing to take my ship."

"You put us all in danger."

"I know."

Jim broke in: *"We are getting a transmission from Frank."*

"Okay. Let's hear what it has to say. Hutch, you still there?"

"I'm here. You've been talking to Frank?"

"Yes. Good old Frank."

"You're kidding."

"I never kid. Put him on, Jim."

But there was only the whisper of the stars.

"It was here a moment ago, Matt."

"I am here now." Matt's own voice again. Sounding angry. Or maybe *hurt.* Disappointed. *"You broke your engagement."*

"Promise. It's called a promise."

"Nevertheless, am I not able to trust you?"

"What was the promise?" asked Hutch.

Another bolt rippled through the sky, far away.

Matt's voice responded: *"Who is that?"*

"I'll tell you who, Frank. I'm the person who's been blinking lights at you the last few days. The one you tried to kill a few hours ago."

"Priscilla Hutchins. From the Preston.*"*

"Yes. I was her captain, until you took us down."

"I am not familiar with the phrase."

"Until you seized my ship. Is that clear enough for you?"

"I regret the loss. I needed it. The ship."

"Sorry to hear that."

"You promised it would not be damaged if I allowed the persons on board to be rescued."

"I didn't promise anything, Frank. You want to know the truth, Frank. I don't—"

Another bolt soared past. Enough to dim the lights. But only for a moment.

"You want to know the truth, Frank?" she said again. *"I don't like you very much."*

"I am stranded. Have a measure of empathy."

"I think you lost that chance. Enjoy your time here, Frank. I think you'll be here awhile."

"I had no choice but to do as I did."

"You could have had help. All you had to do was ask." Maybe, Matt thought. But probably not.

"You have nothing left, Frank. Even if you get lucky and hit us, you won't be able to recover the ship."

"I know."

"Good-bye, Frank."

"I think we're out of range," said Jim.

The sky behind them came alive with lightning strikes. *"All that power,"* said Hutch, *"and it's helpless."*

ANTONIO WAS LIMPING. He'd picked up some bumps and bruises, but otherwise he was fine. Jon had ended splayed against the after bulkhead, but he discovered he could walk, and nothing seemed to be broken.

He'd been startled—and happy—when Hutch had begun speaking

to Matt. When she hadn't gotten out of the spacecraft, he'd feared she'd stayed behind to detonate the bomb. He'd seen no other explanation for her absence.

"What could I do?" she asked Jon as they strolled into the common room. She was carrying the black box that housed Phyl. "I knew Matt would have to go evasive, and I couldn't get out of the launch area before that started. I'm getting a little too old to get tossed around. Antonio was enough of a gentleman to carry the note."

Matt took a seat opposite her. They were about ten minutes from making their jump. "Hutch," he said, "explain something to me."

"If I can."

"Why was the bomb such a close thing? Why didn't you give us more time before detonation? Give yourself more time? You guys were barely inside the ship before it went off."

She laughed and the room brightened. "I'd have done that in a minute if I'd known how."

"What do you mean?"

"Look, Matt, I don't know a thing about making bombs. Do *you*?"

"No. Not really. Never had reason to learn."

"Me, too."

"So how'd you do it?"

She smiled at Antonio. *Tell them.*

Antonio sat back and folded his arms. "The original plan was to dump some fuel in the engine room, but we needed a fuse. The cables are all fireproof, so we tried tying together some sheets. But they burned too fast. We would never have gotten out of the ship."

"So what did you do?"

"We took a laser to one of the fuel lines. Then used our clothes and the pages from the *Sigma Hotel Book* to build a fire."

"*TRANSMISSION FROM THE* cloud," said Jim.

Matt nodded, and Frank's reproduction of Matt's voice filled the bridge. "*Please don't leave.*"

Hutch was beside him. Her eyes were clouded, and she looked as if she were going to speak, but she said nothing.

And again: "*Please come back.*"

The cloud occupied the navigation screen. It seemed now to be all eyes, all staring after them.

"*Please, help me.*"

"You know," Matt said, "it was in a bind." He hated the damned thing. But it didn't seem to matter. Now that the shooting was over. "It would have recognized how powerless we were to help. It took the only course open to it."

"*I promise you will be safe.*"

"I understand what you're saying," said Hutch.

"And it would have known that we would probably not have been able to help in any case. Unless we gave it a ship. Would we have done that if it asked?" He paused and listened to the silence. "I didn't think so."

LIBRARY ENTRY

Throw another log on the fire.
So long as I have you
And the logs,
The night cannot get in.

—*Sigma Hotel Book*

epilogue

HUTCH CONTACTED RUDY'S family as soon as the *Preston* had arrived back in the solar system. That was an excruciating ordeal. As painful as anything she'd done in her life.

FRANK WAS A big media splash for several days. Then the president of Patagonia made some negative comments about the president of the NAU, there was talk of imposing economic sanctions in both directions, and the story about the talking cloud moved to the back pages. Within a week it was gone.

Antonio's book, *At the Core*, revived it for a while, and there was talk of another mission. Some wanted to communicate with the creature, some to nuke it. Others claimed it was a conspiracy and that the omegas came from somewhere else, from a source so terrible that the government was keeping it secret. Still others claimed that hell was located at the center of the galaxy, and we all knew who was really imprisoned in the cloud. When Hutch was asked during an interview what she thought should be done, she urged that the matter be left alone. "Maybe until we're smarter," she said. In the end, public indifference might have carried the day, but Alyx Ballinger turned the encounter into the musical *Starstruck*. Hutch, Antonio, and Jon attended opening night in London. Hutch enjoyed it immensely, but always claimed it was because of the music, and had nothing to do with the fact that the Hutchins character was played by the inordinately lovely Kyra Phillips. The musical went to VR, interstellar tourism picked up, politicians got interested, and within three years, a second Academy began operating out of temporary quarters in Crystal City. A larger complex is currently under construction near the old NASA site on the Cape.

THE PROMETHEUS FOUNDATION had lost Rudy, but with the appearance of *Starstruck*, it gained support, and eventually became a bridge to the new Academy.

Most people were inclined to give credit for the resurgence to Ballinger, but Hutch thought it would have happened anyway, in time. It was inevitable, she told friends. Even without the Locarno Drive, she believed, the human race would have gone back to the stars. The retreat from the original effort had been an aberration, much like the long hiatus after the first flights to the Moon. We seem to do things in fits and starts, she told an audience at ceremonies opening the Crystal City complex in 2258. "But eventually, we get serious. It just takes time."

Meanwhile, a few independent missions, using the Locarno, went out. Two were lost, never heard from again. When nobody talked of scuttling the program, Hutch understood there'd be no turning back this time.

JON RECEIVED A half dozen major awards, including the 2257 Americus. In his acceptance remarks, and to no one's surprise, he gave the bulk of the credit for the Locarno to Henry.

He was also the recipient of the first Rudy Golombeck Award, given by the Prometheus Foundation to recognize achievement in promoting the interstellar renaissance. Matt Darwin made the presentation.

In the VR version of *Starstruck*, Jon was portrayed as brilliant. He was also elderly, forgetful, and often incoherent. His role in rescuing

Hutch and Antonio was transferred to Matt. A producer explained that you could only have one hero in these things, and the starship pilot was the natural choice. People don't identify with physicists, he insisted.

Matt helped Myra Castle attain the state senate. Four years later she went to Washington, where she became a central figure in a major corruption scandal.

Matt went back to real estate for a year. When *Starstruck* appeared, he became an instant celebrity. He was played by Jason Cole, who specialized in action heroes. In that version, the mission had brought along a few nukes, and they took the monster out. Matt commented that a few nukes wouldn't have mattered much, but nobody really seemed to care. When the Academy came back, he applied for reinstatement and, at the time of publication, is en route to the Dumbbell Nebula with a contact mission. (There's evidence some planets in the region are being manipulated.)

THE *SIGMA HOTEL* Book was retrieved from Jim's memory banks and made available to the general public. To everyone's surprise, it climbed the best seller list and stayed there for months. People who know about such things claim it's a book everyone buys but no one reads. It's also shown up in university classes around the world as a demonstration that sentient creatures have more in common than anyone would have believed a century ago.

MacElroy High School named its gym for Rudy, and made Matt an honorary school board member. When he's in town, he still gets invited to speak to the classes. And, on his visits to the school, he invariably stops to admire the AKV Spartan lander, which, as a historical object, has been moved indoors out of the weather.

Jon continues to work in the more arcane branches of physics, trying to develop a system that would allow transportation into other universes. "Provided," he likes to say, "there *are* other universes." The common wisdom is that they are abundant, but Jon would argue that cosmological insight is never common.

He also serves, with Hutch, on the board of the Prometheus Foundation.

And the medium through which the Locarno Drive moves is, of course, known as Silvestri space.

PHYL HAD BEEN disconnected and carried from the *Preston* by Hutch. She indicated no interest in returning to superluminals. She is now the house AI at the Wescott, Alabama, Animal Shelter.

SHORTLY AFTER HER return, Hutch sold the house in Woodbridge and moved to Arlington. Several teaching offers came in. Major publishers pressed for a book. And local political operatives invited her to run for office.

She passed on all of it.

"Why, Mom?" asked Charlie, referring to a career in politics. Charlie remained interested in art, but after the flight to the Mordecai Zone, he'd taken to talking a lot about piloting an interstellar himself. Hutch approved, of course. It would make a great family tradition.

"Not my style," she said.

She enjoyed doing speaking engagements. She was good at bonding with an audience, at winning them over, at persuading them the human race had places to go. A destiny that would take it well beyond Baltimore. (Or wherever she happened to be speaking. The line was always good for a laugh.) Her old friend Gregory MacAllister, after watching her, commented she was a natural flack.

"Two hundred fifty years ago," she told Charlie, as she'd told countless groups around the country, "Stephen Hawking warned us that if we want to survive, we have to get off-world. Establish ourselves elsewhere. We haven't really done that yet." The Orion Arm had given them numerous examples of what happens to societies that don't spread out.

"So it's survival," said Charlie.

They were on the front porch in Arlington. It was a dark night, cloud-ridden, threatening rain. "It's more than that," she told him. "In the long run, Charlie, yes, we need it to save ourselves. Not physically, maybe. But it's one of the ways we find out who we are. Whether we're worth saving. If we're just going to sit home and watch the world go by . . ."

She let the thought drift away.

Charlie pushed back in his rocker. "I'm glad things turned out the way they did." At the time, he was near graduation, and flight school was a possibility. His nervousness showed. But she knew he'd be okay. She remembered her own unsettled feelings when she'd left home so many years ago.

"Me, too," she said. She looked at him, and thought of Rudy and Jon, and Dr. Science, and Matt out somewhere in the deeps, and she knew they would be okay.